Dacia Wolf

& the Darkness Within

A dark and magical paranormal fantasy novel

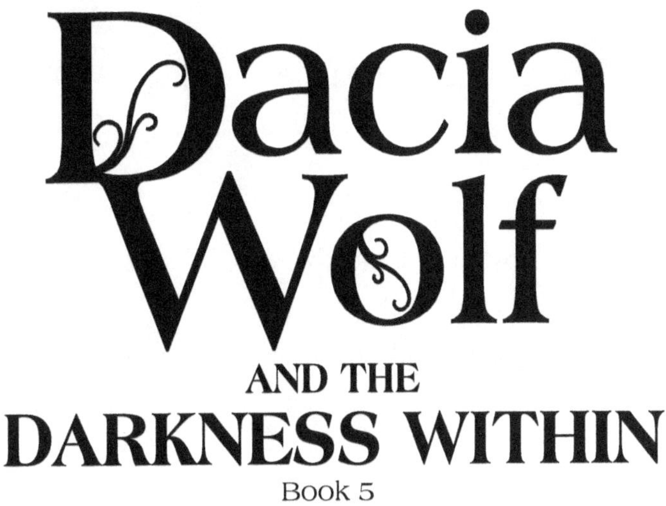

Book 5

Visit Mandi Oyster online at
www.MandiOyster.com

Facebook: https://www.facebook.com/MandiOysterAuthor
Instagram: https://www.instagram.com/MandiOyster/

This book is dedicated to all the First Responders who put their lives on the line to help others.

You are loved.

Chapter 1

Dragons watched me.

Night and day, they tracked every movement I made. They stared into my irises, making sure the black flecks hadn't spread.

They lifted their noses, scenting the air when my moods changed, confirming I was still me and not some monster.

They siphoned my power. It'd been two and a half weeks since Mavros boosted my magic with his to help me defeat Argentum. I'd commanded him to do it, but I'd had no idea what the consequences would be.

If he hadn't held back, he would've destroyed me. As it was, his energy mingled with mine, threatening to corrupt it.

The fairies had told me not to use my magic for a couple of days, but I had used it twice after that. Once to prevent the dragons and Nephilim from killing each other and once inadvertently to heal dream wounds.

Since that night, Malcolm held my dreams at bay. It was a relief to get uninterrupted sleep and not awaken to residual wounds, but it also meant I had no forewarning. I had no idea why Arion had dumped me in my dream. I didn't know if something else was hunting me or if I was getting a reprieve.

Every morning, as soon as I woke up, Malcolm left without saying a word to me. This morning he had looked at me with such profound sadness in his bronze eyes that I felt like I had lost someone close to me. I couldn't shake the melancholy that had settled over me.

"Why does he leave?" I asked Cash.

He lifted his shoulder toward his ear. "Holding your dreams is … taxing." He looked around my room. The loft beds were empty. I was curled in the corner of the couch wrapped up in a blanket. He sat in Cookie Monster with his legs stretched out in front of him. Dan and Cody were on their way to class, and Samantha was most likely still asleep in Dan's room. "This place is cramped. Maybe he just needs to spread his wings."

I couldn't help but notice his gaze darting away from mine. There was more to it, but whatever it was, the dragons didn't want me to know. "What aren't you telling me?"

Pinching his mouth shut, he shook his head. "Let it go."

"I can't." Anger coursed through my veins, burning in my chest. My powers flared in response.

Cash knelt in front of me on the lavender carpet and lifted his hand to me. "I know, but you really need to this time." Sympathy softened his amethyst eyes.

"Did somebody die?"

His head flinched back slightly, and his eyebrows pinched together. "No. Why?"

"You and Malcolm both looked at me with so much grief. Whatever it is, it has to be bad." I slipped my fingers into his, and my energy flowed into him. The relief was instantaneous. "Is it any better?"

"There's so much." Purple and blue shimmered along his skin. His pupils dilated. "I don't know if it's the demon's taint or you."

My heart seemed to slam to a stop. "What—" I had to swallow the lump in my throat before continuing "—what do you mean by that? Am I turning?"

He inhaled deeply, closing his eyes and savoring the scent of my emotions, then slowly released the breath through his mouth. "We've always known you'd be formidable. Mavros' energy may have fueled this surge in your magic."

"So, if you take me back to the fairies, will they be able to tell?" I tugged my hand through my tangled curls. "Is there any way to stop it?"

He strode to the window and opened it, breathing in the fresh mountain air.

"Sorry." I pulled my legs up onto the couch and wrapped my arms around them, resting my chin on my knees. "I don't mean to make this harder on you. I know you'd all like to get on with your lives and not have to babysit me."

Cash spun around. "No. I vowed to protect you. If need be, I'll do it until I die. Without you, I'd still be a captive, still serving that maniac."

"You're still trapped."

He sat down next to me. "I'd give my life for you, and that gives mine meaning."

I laid my head on his shoulder, needing comfort. It was hard to believe that he'd been the dragon that had terrified me more than any of the others. When I looked at him now, I saw one of my closest friends, an older brother, a protector.

"You're going to be okay." His words sounded less like a promise than a plea to whatever god the dragons believed in.

I squeezed his arm. "Don't lie."

Malcolm appeared between the couch and the TV. The black and bronze beads in his cornrows clinked together. The sadness was gone from his eyes.

"Where do you go?" I knew it was rude of me. It wasn't like he owed me any explanations. He didn't owe me anything. "Why do you leave as soon as I wake up? Did I do something?"

Cash growled so low that had my arm not been touching his. I wouldn't have known. He scooted over slightly, putting some space between the two of us.

Malcolm held his breath for a moment. "After keeping your dreams from you, I have to get away. They're intense ... overwhelming. I usually go hunting."

I chewed on my bottom lip, processing what he said. "Do you see my dreams then?"

"Yes." He sat down in Cookie Monster and dropped his head into his hands.

"Do I need to be worried about whatever monster or madman comes next?" I folded my arms around my stomach afraid of what he might say.

He looked at me through his fingers for a few minutes before saying anything. "Not right now. I keep seeing Argentum dying, the serpent that I assume is the manifestation of your powers, and Mavros."

"I'm sorry I wasn't strong enough to kill him." I wiped my hands down my face. "You shouldn't have had to do it."

His expression seemed to darken. "Dacia, I don't see his death because of guilt. I see his death because *you* are dreaming it."

I walked to the window, turning my back on him, not wanting to see his reaction. "What do I dream about Mavros?" The first time I had returned him to the Abyss, he'd deserved it, and I had still felt horrible about doing it. The next two times, I had sent him back even though he had helped me. The guilt I felt every time I thought about him tightened my chest and made me hate myself. What kind of a person exiles someone to save themselves?

"I'm not sure that you're dreaming about whim."

I spun around in time to see Malcolm's lips lift in a snarl. "What do you mean?"

"Even from the Abyss, he seems to be interjecting himself into your dreams."

"He did that before." I remembered waking up with his coat thrown over me, my room smelling like warm summer nights and sulfur. Plopping down next to Cash, I leaned my head against the back of the couch and stared up at the ceiling. "I wish I'd've known what would happen. I wish I'd've known not to ask him to lend me his power."

Chapter 2

About To Explode

Skipping class was not an option. Finals week was only a few days away, and it would already take a miracle for me to pass any of my classes. I'd gone from being somebody who fretted over grades to somebody who barely scraped by. The dragons offered their vast knowledge, but I didn't know if I would ever be desperate enough to cheat. The guilt would eat me alive.

I sat in Scientific Computing surrounded by my friends—five of who were also my guardians—trying to make sense of what Professor Granite said. His gray and black mustache wiggled over his lip when he talked, reminding me of a woolly worm.

After class, I shoved my things into my bag, and we all walked to Sedum Student Center. Dark clouds threatened to bring more snow. The wind whipped between the buildings, catching my hair and blowing it around my face. Red strands caught in my sunglasses. I tugged my hood up, hoping to nullify the breeze.

The dragons strolled along more relaxed than they had been for quite some time, so I assumed that whatever they weren't telling me wasn't in regard to my safety.

Diana and Olivia trailed behind us, talking and laughing with a group of friends they'd made while babysitting me for the Nephilim. Seeing them more at ease, I wondered how long they would stay here to watch me.

Russ held the door open for me. "Relax," he said as I walked past him.

The cafeteria smelled like burgers, fries, chicken, and pasta all mixed together, but none of those options sounded appealing to me. Students clustered together, and chatter filled the vast dining hall. I grabbed two tacos and Spanish rice.

As I strode across the room, some people waved at me. I smiled and nodded. Even though several rumors still floated around campus about why I needed bodyguards, many of the students seemed to have gotten over their concerns about me.

Cash and Malcolm had taken to sitting at the same table as my friends and me, but this time, they positioned themselves on either side of me with their legs pressed against mine.

Cody sauntered toward us. He looked from me to the dragons, then back again. "Everything okay?"

"She's overly emotional today." Malcolm squeezed my hand and power shot from me to him. "It's just precautionary."

Cody sat next to Cash. "What's goin' on?"

"I don't know." The words came out with a hard edge on them. "They're keeping something from me, finals are coming up, and I'm going to fail. I can't use my magic, and my eyes aren't mine anymore."

Cassandra plunked her tray down. "Maybe not, but they're really wicked."

"Wicked?" I slammed my fists against the table, and my tray shot up. When it landed, lettuce and cheese spewed across the surface. "That's the word you're using, and you don't see the problem?" I threw my arms up, and anger surged inside of me, flooding my body.

Malcolm and Cash both reached for my hands, snatching them out of the air. Shadows writhed under my skin, diminishing as the dragons extracted my magic.

"Did you see that?" Trying not to be obvious about it, I slid my sleeves down my arms and folded them over my chest.

Malcolm dipped his chin slightly, and Cash whispered, "Yes."

I rubbed my hand over my mouth. "Great." I'd been hoping it was just my imagination.

"See what?" Cody stared at my hands.

Malcolm threw his arm over the back of my chair, keeping in contact with me. "Her power."

"You can see her power?" Cassandra set her fork down. Her expression was stuck somewhere between horror and astonishment. She scooted closer to Bryce.

Samantha and Dan strolled toward us, looking at each other and laughing. As they neared our table, they took in the somberness and slowed. Dan tilted his head to the side, and his eyebrows pinched together.

Samantha's chin dropped to her chest. "What's going on?"

"The demon's magic—" Cash dragged his fingers along his forehead "—or maybe her own. I really don't know. It's growing rapidly. Dacia cannot contend with the influx of power."

Malcolm squeezed my shoulder. "The magnitude is overwhelming. Every change in her emotions pushes them closer to the surface where even the smallest catalyst may cause them to erupt."

I shoved my plate forward and laid my head down on my arms. "So, what do I do?"

"Learn how to contain it."

I lifted my head in time to see Bryce shove fries into his mouth. My eyes narrowed, and heat filled my stomach. Did he really think it was as easy as that? Did he think I wasn't trying that already? Rage burned inside of me. I slammed my chair back and strode to the door. My fists were clenched at my sides. I breathed deeply, trying to calm myself. There was no reason for the anger, but I couldn't hold it back.

Stepping outside, I lifted my face to the cold air. I felt the dragons behind me, but I didn't look at them. I needed to cool the fury inside of me. Pressing my eyes closed, I pictured the mountain lake I'd used to calm myself when I first learned to control my powers.

The serpent slithered across the rocky ground. Its pearlescent scales shimmered in the sunlight, flickering between the same blue color as my flames and lavender. Shadows slipped along its body, dissipating like vapor.

The snake had grown immeasurably since the last time I'd seen it. Its body was as big around as a dinner plate. Its tongue flicked out of its mouth, tasting the air. Its copper eyes gazed up at me, and the black flecks in them mirrored my own.

I knelt down and stretched my hand forward with the palm up, letting it see I meant it no harm. "You are mine." My voice was soft but firm.

It slithered closer. *And you are mine.*

"We need to work together." I slid my hand over its head and along its body. Its scales were smooth and glossy. "I can't contain all this power."

So, release it. It nuzzled against my fingers.

"I can't." I pinched the bridge of my nose and rocked back on my heels. "If I do, Mavros' power will corrupt us."

It will make us stronger. The serpent puffed its body up and lifted off the ground, making it appear gargantuan. *We will be invincible.*

Images of Draconian flashed through my mind. Was this what had happened to him? With nobody to help him, had the power overtaken him? I shook my head. "We cannot give in to it. We must fight it and not allow it to destroy us."

The serpent's head swayed as it rose higher into the air.

My heart raced. I knew this was a challenge, and I couldn't let it win.

A hand clasped my shoulder, tearing my focus from the snake.

Malcolm whispered, "Come back now."

The serpent lunged just as my eyes sprung open. "How'd you know?"

"I watched." He didn't look apologetic or ashamed. "We needed to make sure that you were going to be able to get your powers under control. If the serpent had its way, you wouldn't have."

I tugged my hand through my hair. "How do I fight myself and win?"

Sitting in Shakespeare surrounded by my guards, I felt at ease. It was the dragons' doing, but it was a relief. With their power calming me, I didn't need to worry about flying off the handle. All I needed to concern myself with was taking notes and trying to figure out how to pass this final when the time came.

The walk back to my room was the same. Someone bumped into me, knocking my shoulder back. Earlier, my powers would have threatened to explode, but with their magic soothing me, I took it in stride.

Tiny snowflakes drifted down from the sky. They collected in the curls of my hair and clung to my sweatshirt.

As soon as we stepped into the entryway of the dorms, they melted. My guards stayed with me when I walked into my room. I expected to see Cody and possibly Dan hanging out, but they weren't there. I turned to the dragons. "They're okay, right?"

Cash stared down at the floor while he toed the lilac carpet with his boot. "We thought it would be best for them to stay away until we get this figured out."

"How long?" Even with their magic consoling me, I felt my anger begin to rise.

Arianna brushed the water out of her hair and wrapped her arm around my shoulder. "We would like to take you to the fairies again. Aurelia thinks they are the best chance to help you."

"When?" The single word was filled with venom.

Val leaned close to me, lifted his nose, and breathed in deeply. "Now."

Chapter 3

Fairy Magic

The cavern was dark, but thousands of tiny pinpricks of light dotted the ceiling. They grew larger as they descended. Rayne landed on my outstretched hand. Her long, silver hair fluttered with every beat of her tiny, iridescent wings. She stared into my eyes for several moments. Her purple irises softened with concern. "Darkness must not prevail."

"I'm trying not to let it." The words squeezed past the lump in my throat. Tears burned my eyes. "But my powers … they want to merge with his. They long for his magic to join them, to make me invincible."

"You must do everything you can to keep that from happening." She strode to the end of my palm.

I swallowed, forcing the lump down. "I'm trying, but I'm just so angry."

She waved her hand, and the other fairies landed on me. Squeezing onto every space they could. When no more could stand on me, they hovered in the air around me. Their bodies glowed with silver light, and they chanted in their high-pitched voices in a language I couldn't understand.

Peace flowed into me. My anger, despair, and negativity were pushed aside, toppling like dominoes. I closed my eyes, and the stress in my shoulders released. Focusing on my magic, I pictured the serpent. Shadows drifted off its back, disappearing when they hit the fairies' light. The snake seemed to share my relief.

"The anger was not your own." Rayne's voice was soft. "It was contained in your powers. Follow the light. Do not allow the darkness to corrupt you." She hovered in front of my face staring into my eyes. "Do not use your powers in hatred or wrath. You may use them to heal yourself or to protect yourself or others."

My shoulders slumped with relief. "I can use them again?"

"As long as you stay true to yourself." She lowered herself onto my palm.

"How can I ever repay you?" Tears burned my eyes. I had half expected them to tell the Nephilim to take me to their sanctuary.

Smiling up at me, she said, "Stay true. Do not let darkness prevail."

Malcolm stepped forward and knelt in front of me. "Thank you for all you've done for Dacia."

"It has been our honor." The other fairies' shrill voices filled the cavern. They were too high for me to make out what they were saying, but Malcolm seemed to understand.

"She dreams of the demon." His voice turned to a growl, and I couldn't help but wonder what he'd been seeing.

Rayne flew off of my hand and landed on Malcolm's knee. It was the first time I'd seen one of the fairies go anywhere near the dragons. "How do you know?"

"I have been holding her dreams at bay to keep her from using her powers." Some emotion flickered across his face too quickly for me to identify it. "But, I don't … I'm not sure that he's a dream."

Rayne's wings stopped fluttering for a heartbeat. "The demon needed to be bound to a mortal to stay on Earth." She paced along his leg. "With his magic in her, maybe the curse has been broken."

The dragons growled, and their forms rippled.

"You can't blame him." I fisted my hands at my sides. "I'm the one who summoned him. I'm the one who commanded him to give me his power. I could have ordered him to kill Argentum, but I didn't. He could've killed me if he hadn't held back."

"Yes." Cash stepped toward me. A thin stream of smoke rolled out of his nostrils. "Did he know he would be bound to you? Would he have spared your life otherwise?"

Anger flared inside of me. The serpent reared its head. "How many times does he have to save me or protect me for you to realize there is some good in him?"

Rayne and several other fairies landed on me. "You must control your temper, Dacia."

"How?" I tugged my fingers through my hair.

She stretched her hand out, and I leaned closer. She placed it on the tip of my nose, and even though it was tiny, I felt warmth and power in it. "You must find a way."

"If I can use my powers to heal or protect, why are you still keeping my dreams from me?" I paced in front of the couch. The dragons still wouldn't let me see Cody or the others. They wanted to make sure I wasn't going to fly off the handle at the first sign of trouble.

Malcolm sat on the end of the couch with his legs stretched out in front of him. Cash sat in Cookie Monster. Neither of them planned on leaving me alone tonight.

Holding his head in his hands, Malcolm said, "I can barely handle your dreams." He looked up at me, and anguish showed on his face. "I would like to spare you from them at least until your magic calms down." He patted the couch next to him. "Sleep here. Let me hold your dreams at bay. Let me protect you for as long as I can."

"Why next to you?" The thought of lying down beside him without Cody here made me extremely uncomfortable.

Cash lifted his head and breathed in deeply. His eyes drifted shut, and he moaned softly.

Malcolm's face pinched as though he was in pain. "Put your feet on my lap if it will make you more comfortable."

I grabbed my pillow, a blanket, and Glacier, my teddy bear. Then I set my pillow on his lap and lay down. "Why?"

"If I touch you, I can pull out your excess energy and soothe you. Maybe I can make your dreams less vicious." He rubbed his hand over his mouth and nose. "This new emotion is difficult."

"I'm sorry." Heat crept up my neck and onto my face. "Why can't you just make me sleep without dreaming like you've done before?"

"Dreams help you cope with the difficulties of life." His arm lay over the top of mine, not intimately or possessively, but comforting. "I'm hoping your mind is still processing them even though you don't remember what they're about. I hope it will make things easier for you in the long run."

I fell asleep much quicker than I thought I would. Malcolm and Cash must've been sending soothing energy into me. I felt calm and at ease.

Chapter 4

Supervised Visitation

$\mathcal{S}$unlight poured in through the window. I peeled my eyes open and looked up into Malcolm's face. For a moment, I was confused, but then everything came back to me.

"Good morning." He looked more at ease than he had since Argentum died.

"Morning." I sat up and pulled my hands through my hair. "Was last night easier on you?"

He stood and stretched his arms above his head, then turned from side to side. "Yes. Your dreams were nowhere near as powerful as they had been."

I got up and stuffed my clothes into my bathroom bag. "Will you let me see my friends today?"

Cash walked over and rested his hand on my shoulder. "With supervision."

I couldn't help the sarcastic laugh that slipped out of me. "When was the last time I wasn't supervised?" I pushed his hand off my arm. "I can't even kiss Cody without one of your voices in my head. The Nephilim are constantly watching me. Who else? I'm sure there are others that I don't even know about yet."

"If anyone else is watching you"—Malcolm walked over to me—"we are also unaware of it." He leaned against the wall, scrutinizing me. "I am sorry about your lack of privacy. We need to keep you safe."

"I know." Pinching my eyes shut, I tried to fight the anger welling inside of me. "I need a shower."

Creative Writing was the one class I wasn't worried about failing. Our final was to write a 10-20,000-word story. Mine was about dragons, Nephilim, and a demon. I had over 15,000 words written already, but the end was nowhere in sight. The only problem I foresaw with the assignment was keeping it short enough not to get downgraded.

When class ended, my heart felt like it jumped into my throat. I laid my head on the desk and focused on my breathing, trying to fight the anxiety building up in me. I wanted to see Cody, more than anything, but I didn't know if he'd want to see me, and I didn't want to risk hurting any of my friends.

"Dacia." Malcolm's voice was a low rumble. "What's wrong?" He knelt on the floor in front of my desk.

My hand trembled as I tugged it through my hair. "What if I hurt them? What if they don't want to see me?"

Malcolm clasped my shoulder. "Cody wants to see you."

"How do you know?" There was a desperate edge to my voice.

"Because Arianna, Russ, and Val had to fight to keep him from coming to your room this morning." He wiped a tear off my cheek. "Because he loves you."

Cash laughed. "You forget we can smell more than just your emotions."

Without intending to, I cocked my head. I hadn't thought about that. I wondered what it must be like to see people's reactions, to hear them, and then to smell them. I wondered how often the three of them lined up. "Does he—" I chewed on my lip. Did I want to know the answer? I looked into Malcolm's eyes. They were laced with sympathy for me. "Does he fear me?"

Other students started coming into the room, getting ready for the next class. One guy stood at the end of the aisle I was in, looking at my desk, and tapping his foot. I slung my backpack over my shoulder and walked out with the dragons following behind me.

As soon as we were in the hall, Malcolm lifted his arm, and I pressed against his side. He draped his arm over my shoulders, comforting me. "He fears for you," he whispered. "He fears you'll be hurt or lost or broken beyond repair."

"I fear that, too." I squeezed his hand, then let mine drop back down to my side. "And so much more."

The dragons led me to Sedum Hall. I sat at a table in the back of the room, waiting for my friends to arrive. I drummed my fingers on the table, staring at the door. Malcolm and Cash sat to either side of me with their legs pressed against mine.

Cody strode in, barely stopping to show his ID to the attendant. He walked back to me and held my face in his hands. "You okay?"

"I am now." Tears slipped out of my eyes.

"Hungry?"

I shook my head.

He looked at the dragons. "You'll stay with her?"

"Of course," Malcolm said.

"Be right back." Cody brushed his lips over mine, a soft promise. "Don't leave."

Malcolm held onto my hand, and a sense of peacefulness washed over me like a wave caressing the sandy shore. I slumped back in my chair and closed my eyes.

"Hey." Cassandra's voice was delicate and uncertain.

"Sorry about yesterday," I said to both her and Bryce. I glanced at all the people walking by and tried to figure out the best way to word my apology. "Hopefully, I'm on the mend."

"That's good." Bryce smiled and sat directly across from me.

Cassandra glanced at Malcolm's hand on mine and said, "Are you sure?"

"Yeah."

Cody walked back over carrying two trays, and Cash stood. Looking at Malcolm, he asked, "Do you want me to get your food?"

Malcolm stared into my eyes, searching for something. *Do you want me to stay?*

Are they afraid?

His chin dipped slightly, and my heart plummeted. *Yes.*

Malcolm nodded at Cash. "That'd be nice. I've always wanted a servant."

Cash directed Cody to the chair he'd just vacated. "She needs you."

"It's mutual." Cody slid one of the trays in front of me. It had a plate of chocolate chip cookies, a glass of water, a glass of milk, and a glass of pop.

My eyebrows pinched together, and I looked up at him.

"Wasn't sure what you'd drink." He sat next to me, scooting his chair as close to mine as he could.

Samantha and Dan came to the table together. He looked at the plate of cookies in front of me and shot me a sympathetic smile. "Bad day?"

"Just a day." I broke a cookie and put a piece in my mouth. *What about them?*

No. Malcolm shook his head. *Just Bryce and Cassandra.*

I dipped a chunk of cookie into my milk and tried not to let it drip all over on its way to my mouth. While I was chewing, Justin stopped by our table. "Anyone up for a game this afternoon? I could use a break from studying."

Cody and Dan both looked at me as if gauging my reaction. I nodded. "We've got class until 3:30, but I have a lot of energy to burn off if you guys are up for it."

Malcolm nodded. "I'll be there."

"Count me in." Bryce lifted his fist, and Justin bumped his into it.

I sat in Mythology doodling in my notebook instead of taking notes. My attention span wasn't what it used to be. My pencil skidded across my paper when Dr. Cedar said, "Dragons." I looked up, and he was staring at my guardians. "Dragons are found in many legends from the past. Why would they have a place in so many cultures if they never existed?"

Somebody in the front of the room shouted out, "Because they're awesome."

"Don't let it go to your heads," I mumbled.

Arianna laughed. "But we are."

"Oh, I know."

Dr. Cedar looked at me. "Did you have something to add, Dacia?"

"No, sir." My cheeks heated. "I think they'd be pretty awesome and also scarier than hell."

Malcolm's laughter rumbled through the room. *You better believe it.*

Other students joined in his laughter, pulling Dr. Cedar's attention off of me.

Do you think he knows? I thought to Malcolm.

He lifted one shoulder toward his ear. *It would seem so.*

Aren't you concerned?

Through the years, many people have known about us. He watched Dr. Cedar pace in front of the class. *This human is not a threat.*

When class ended, I shoved my things into my backpack and walked to the door surrounded by my friends and guardians.

"Dacia," Dr. Cedar said as I neared his desk, "may I see you—just you—for a moment?"

I looked around, confused by the request, and shrugged. "Sure."

Everyone else stepped out into the hall.

"What's up?" I asked.

He smiled at me. "Are you okay?" He couldn't mask the worry in his light brown eyes as they darted toward the hallway.

"Yeah." I shoved my hands into my hoodie's pocket. "I'm fine."

"Are you in some sort of trouble?"

How was I supposed to answer him? He obviously knew about the dragons. He must've guessed there was more to me.

"Your watchers have been severely depleted." He tapped his pen on the desk. "I can't help but feel that's a good thing."

"It is." I hefted my backpack onto my shoulder. "My guards helped with that." I looked at the door. "I'm always in some sort of trouble, but I do my best. Dean Aspen usually knows what's going on."

"Good, good, good." He folded his hands over his stomach. "I mostly wondered if they'd let you out of their sight. I wanted to make sure you weren't a prisoner."

"No." I laughed. "Not now. They're actually my friends." I tipped my head toward my shoulder. "Believe it or not."

"You'll let me know if I can help with anything."

I nodded. "Thanks."

I stepped into the hall, and Malcolm slung his arm over my shoulders. "You should've told him you could make us your prisoners at any time."

Cash pulled his lips back in a snarl.

"That's not funny." I pulled away from him. "Why would I even joke about it?"

"We could back off a little," Arianna said. "We could be unseen in your classes and at lunch."

Cody slid his arm around my waist. "Why'd she want that?"

"It might stop some of the rumors." She dipped her head to the side.

Malcolm pushed the door open, and we stepped outside. The Snowfire Mountains were covered in a white blanket and stood out against the bright blue sky. The sun beat down, but it was no match for the brisk wind that whipped across campus.

"Today would be a good day to teleport." Cassandra pulled her hood up and stuffed her gloved hands into her pockets.

I thought about warm summer days. Heat radiated off of me, and the wind blew it over my companions. It had been nearly three weeks since I'd done anything with my powers besides let the dragons take them from me. I felt whole.

Samantha lifted her face to the warmth. "That's so nice. I'm ready for summer already."

"Keep waiting." Malcolm chuckled. "This is going to be a long, hard winter."

Dan looked over his shoulder at him. "What makes you say that?"

"Two thousand years of experience." He stared at the mountains, and a sense of foreboding swept over me. "We can feel it."

Justin stood on the far end of the court, shooting hoops. As soon as he noticed us come in, he dribbled toward us.

Arianna had planned on staying behind with Samantha and Cassandra to watch them while they studied, but we'd realized we'd be one player short.

Malcolm had rolled his neck. "They'll be fine. There has been nothing in Dacia's dreams to suggest otherwise." He looked at me, and sympathy softened his eyes. "Right now, the only one who needs our protection is Dacia."

Samantha's shoulders relaxed with that comment. I knew that constantly being threatened and under surveillance had to weigh heavily on my friends, and not for the first time, I couldn't help but wonder how long any of them would stick around.

Malcolm and Cash decided they were the team captains for today's game. Malcolm's first pick was me, and I wondered how long they'd had this planned. Cash chose Justin, and Malcolm took Val. *I don't want him guarding you.*

Cash rubbed his chin while surveying the remaining players. "You better take Arianna. That way we can be skins. Cody."

Bryce and Arianna ended up rounding out my team.

While the skins threw their shirts on the floor, I whispered, "Why'd you need me on your team?"

Malcolm cocked his head and looked at me like I was crazy. "So I can keep an eye on you," he said the words slowly like he was afraid I wouldn't understand them.

I smacked his arm. "Wouldn't that be easier if you were defending me?"

"That's what he's for." He glanced at Cash.

I should've known he'd have thought of everything. I ran out onto the court. Since we had nobody to toss the ball up for a jump, I said, "Malcolm chose first. You guys can have the ball."

Playing basketball was what I should've been doing every day for the last three weeks regardless of any other responsibilities. When I played, it was like a switch was flipped inside of me. I didn't worry about what the dragons were hiding from me. I didn't need to siphon off my powers. I didn't care that I was about to fail all of my classes. I cared about getting the ball from the other team and getting it to the right person on mine to put it through the hoop. I loved the sound of shots swishing through the net. I loved the competition, the team spirit, the strain on my muscles, and the release from my worries for even just a little bit.

The only problem was being the shortest player on both teams. Far too many of my shots were batted out of the air by Cash, and he took way too much pleasure out of doing it.

By the time we were finished, my muscles ached, and I was ready to collapse.

Justin slid his arms through his sleeves and held the neck of it open ready to pull it over his head. "Why do you need guards anyway?"

My mouth fell open, and I floundered for a moment. The question caught me totally unprepared. I hadn't expected anybody just to come out and ask me. "My life is complicated."

"Obviously." He tugged his shirt on and smoothed out his hair. "Thanks for the game."

I tried to smile, but I wasn't sure if it worked. "Anytime."

Cash's eyes transformed into his dragon's as he watched him walk away.

I rested my hand on his arm. "It's okay. I'm sure everyone wants to know."

"It probably took a lot of guts for him to ask it, too." Dan pulled his shirt on, then grabbed his sweatshirt off the floor.

"Why?" Arianna tipped her head.

"Have you seen yourselves?" Bryce laughed. "You're all a little intimidating. Even Dacia." He nodded at me. "There's something so intense about you. Something that warns of danger."

"Really?" My shoulders slumped forward.

"Yeah." He bounced the ball, switching hands as it crossed in front of him. "It's in your eyes."

I wiped my hands over them, wishing there was some way to get rid of the black flecks that had taken up residence in my irises.

"It's been there since sophomore year started. Cassi would've apologized sooner, but she was scared." He let the ball bounce up to his side and held it there. "We should've. We should've swallowed our pride and apologized. It was the right thing to do."

I pulled my hand away from my face. It was a relief to know it wasn't Mavros' magic that made me intimidating. "The right thing isn't always easy. I should've fixed your hand a long time ago."

"No worries." He spun the ball on his finger. "It's good now."

Chapter 5

Holding My Dreams At Bay

The dragons kept the others out of my room for the next few nights. Malcolm brought an ottoman in, sat down, stretched his legs out, and patted the couch next to him.

"Why can't Cody be here?" I dragged my hands down my face. I sounded like a whiny little toddler, but I didn't understand. I'd kept my powers under control. I hadn't had any mishaps since the fairies saw me last time. I'd even been doing a fairly good job of suppressing my anger.

Malcolm leaned his head against the back of the couch and stared up at the ceiling. "Please, Dacia. It's just easier this way." He turned his head toward me. "Cody wouldn't want to curl up with me anyway." He flashed his fangs at me in a pathetic attempt at a smile.

I threw my pillow at him, and he snatched it out of the air. "What makes you think I do?"

He shrugged and stood up. "Lie down with Cash then."

"Uh …" I looked at Cash, and heat blasted my face and ears.

The dragons both lifted their noses and breathed in deeply. "That emotion is my favorite." Cash's voice was husky.

"So, you'd rather it was me?" Malcolm repositioned himself on the couch.

I looked between the two of them. Malcolm was a two-thousand-year-old dragon with dark skin and long cornrows. He was attractive in his human form, but he looked closer to thirty. Way too old for me. Cash was at least five hundred years younger. Since he decided to befriend me instead of hating me, his features had softened. His black hair had purple streaks in it that matched his eyes. He looked to be in his lower twenties, much closer to my age than Malcolm. "I'd rather it was Cody."

"But Cody can't keep your dreams away." Malcolm patted the couch again, and I sat next to him.

I pulled the blanket over me and lay down. "He has many times. So, what are you guys hiding from me? Don't you think I have the right to know?"

Cash turned his gaze away from mine and nodded. "You have the right, but once you know, you'll wish you didn't."

"Give it a little longer, Dacia." Malcolm stretched his arm out along mine. "If I give you your dreams back, I'm afraid of how your powers will react."

I looked up into Malcolm's face. "Is there something after me?"

"I'm sure there is. I think there always will be"—he squeezed my arm—"but I haven't seen any evidence of it in your dreams … not yet anyway."

I clutched Glacier to my chest. "So how long?"

"I don't know." He pulled his other hand down his face while Cash walked over to the window and opened it. "You'd never forgive yourself if you hurt one of your friends."

Being in a small room with two dragons when my emotions were out of whack was dangerous. Luckily, they'd both vowed to protect me, and to them, nothing was more sacred than that.

I woke up with my arms wrapped around Malcolm's legs, holding onto him like he was Cody. I yanked my hands back and sat up. My face was hotter than a three-alarm fire.

Malcolm stretched like a cat, and Cash chuckled while opening the window.

I'm sorry, I thought to Malcolm. I didn't think I'd be able to talk over my embarrassment.

"It's all good, Dacia." He sat next to me and threw his arm over the back of the couch. "You were sleeping peacefully, and that's what we want."

I pinched my eyes shut. "Cody's never going to understand."

"He will." Cash kept his face turned toward the window. "Malcolm is helping you, not trying to win your heart like Mavros was." He glanced at me. "And, if you think it will hurt him, don't tell him. Problem solved."

"Is that how dragon relationships work?" My voice was harder than I meant it to be.

Cash shrugged and sat down in Cookie Monster. "Sometimes." He rocked back. "It's been a long time since either of us was in a relationship."

"Yeah." I pulled my hand through my hair and laid my head on Malcolm's shoulder. He draped his arm over me. "I'm sorry about that."

"Why are you sorry?" Malcolm's words rumbled through his chest, bouncing my head. "Without your help, we would've been Draconian's pets forever."

"Not a lotta room for romance there." Cash's words were snarled.

"I'm sorry you had to go through that. You deserved better." I walked to my closet. "And now you're trapped here with me."

"I thought I'd cured you of thinking that way." Cash strolled over and leaned against the wall. "You have given our lives meaning, a purpose. We don't think like humans. Yes, we can be selfish, greedy bastards, but we have honor."

I looked up at him, not sure what he was trying to say. "Humans can be honorable."

Malcolm came over. "When you freed us, most of us went to our lairs and curled up on our treasure hoards. When we were asked to protect you, it gave our lives a purpose, something we'd been missing for centuries." He knelt down and gazed into my eyes. "We do not feel trapped. We feel needed."

Malcolm and Cash walked me to the Scientific Computing classroom. I jogged up the steps and threw myself into Cody's waiting arms.

"Hey." He pushed me back and studied my face. "You okay?"

"Yeah." I nodded and pulled him closer. "They won't tell me how long they're going to keep you away from me. Malcolm doesn't want me to face my dreams."

His arms stiffened for just a moment. "You gotta trust 'em."

"Are you scared of me, Cody?"

He lifted my face so I could see the intensity in his eyes. "No, Dacia. Never." He brushed my hair back. "For you."

I nodded and sat down with him on one side of me and Malcolm on the other. Cody held my hand, rubbing his thumb along mine.

Cody, Malcolm, Cash, and I sat in my room. "Where's everyone else?" I asked.

"Arianna and Val went to see her son." Malcolm stretched his legs out in front of him. "Russ is with his whelp. Your friends are around."

I held onto Cody's hand. *Do you trust me?*

He nodded almost imperceptibly.

I teleported us to the cavern where we'd hidden from the Nephilim. Our bodies stretched out and squeezed in.

Malcolm shouted, "No!" and Cash roared. The sound was deafening.

As soon as I got my balance, I lit a fire in my palm, lighting up the room. Cushions were still strewn across the floor.

"What's going on?" Cody stepped away from me.

"They say there aren't any monsters after us, and I needed some time alone with you."

He stacked up some of the cushions and sat down. I settled myself on his lap, facing him, and wrapped my arms around his neck. He held my face in his hands. "Sure you're okay?"

Dacia, come back. Malcolm's voice blasted through my head.

I winced.

"Dacia?" Fear widened Cody's eyes.

"Malcolm's not happy." I played with the hair on the back of Cody's neck. *I will. Give me an hour alone with Cody, please.*

The clock starts now. His words were more dragon than human.

I brushed my lips over Cody's. "We have an hour."

"Then what?"

I shrugged. "Malcolm might kill me."

He wrapped his hands around my waist and pulled me against him. "Better get back then."

I traced the outline of his face with a feather-soft touch. His eyelids fluttered shut, and had he been a cat, I was sure he would have been purring.

"Are you sure you're not afraid of me?"

His hands tightened on my waist. "Never. Why?"

"I think everyone else is, but I'm trying to control it."

He kissed the tip of my nose. "I know." He held me against him with one arm and leaned back, laying us down. "Nobody's watching?"

"No dragons." I slipped my hands under his shirt, running my fingers along his ribs. "Fairies might be."

I brought my lips down on his and wrapped my arms around him. He flicked his tongue against my mouth, and I opened it up to him. With a moan, he rolled us over.

I kicked my shoes off and rubbed my foot along his leg. It had been far too long since we'd been alone. I'd almost forgotten how good he smelled. A cold winter's day. Fresh, brisk, and clean. I pushed his shirt up as high as I could get it with him on top of me. He pulled it off and threw it to the side, before bringing his mouth crashing down on mine again.

His fingers glided along my sides, up under my shirt. He tugged on it, and I lifted my arms.

"You sure?" His husky voice stirred something inside of me.

I nodded, and he slid it over my head. His eyes dilated as he looked down at me. He'd seen me in a bra before. He'd helped bandage my wounds, but this felt different. I pulled him on top of me, savoring the feel of his skin on mine.

"I love you, Dacia."

I planted a trail of kisses along his collar bone. "I love you, too."

He nudged my face, moving my lips back to his. Our kiss deepened, becoming more passionate. I clung to him, needing his strength and his love. My fingernails dug into his back. Our breathing accelerated, and our hearts raced. Time disappeared, nothing else mattered.

He pushed back, pulling his body off of mine, breaking my hold on him.

Hovering over me, his eyes were bright. His face was flushed. "Unless you're ready, we need to stop."

Part of me wanted to say yes, but this wasn't how my first time should happen. I didn't want to return to my room to the knowing glances of the dragons. "I'm sorry."

He rolled over, lying next to me.

I pinched my eyes shut. "Not yet." I snuggled against his side, trailing my fingers over his abs. His hand skimmed up and down my arm, and my eyes drifted closed.

Argentum kneels in front of Aurelia. His silver hair pools on the ground between them.

Malcolm warns me to stay vigilant. I heal his wounds, feeling unfathomable power pulsing inside of me, a bottomless sea of magic.

Argentum latches onto Aurelia, taking control of her. I call the dragons to me. Their power floods into me. "Chaódis Skotádi, I summon thee. Come forth, and stand before me."

Mavros kneels in front of me. "What do you command of me, my prothymós?"

"It means liege." Arianna's normally lyrical voice is filled with disgust.

I stare into his black eyes. "Lend me your strength."

"I can kill him for you." Mavros slips his hand into mine and stands. "I can save you the pain."

I realize now that I can't make him kill for me. The guilt would still belong to me.

His power slams into me. It is dark and dangerous, wrong. I prowl toward Argentum. Blue and black flames burn in my palms. "Let Aurelia go." My voice has a violent edge to it.

He lunges, and Mavros knocks me to the ground. Argentum clutches Mavros' body in his jaws.

The magic inside me pulses in response. Without my consent, it transforms me. Pain shoots through my body. Bones break and rearrange. Three long necks sprout from my shoulders. A tail whips the air behind me. My fingernails become long, sickle-like claws. Leathery wings tear through my back. My senses are overwhelmed.

Argentum drops Mavros to the ground as he takes in the latest threat.

This new body is vicious and bloodthirsty. I lunge for Argentum with one head while another one sneaks up from underneath. I sink my fangs into his neck and savor the power that runs down my throat.

His claws tear into my hide. Pain lances through me, but I don't let go.

Malcolm and Cash latch onto his neck, and we drag him down. His strength wanes, and my other heads sink their teeth into him. Ancient power flows into me.

Malcolm nudges me, but I growl at him, protecting my kill, ready to end them if they interfere. Flames explode all along my body.

Chapter 6

Drowning

*M*y eyes snapped open. I rolled onto my hands and knees and retched.

"Oh, God. Oh, God. Oh, God." Tears streamed down my face as the memories came surging back.

Cody reached for me, but I pulled away.

"Don't touch me!" Sobs tore from my chest. "Oh, God." I rocked back and forth, clutching my hair. "I'm a monster."

The overwhelming sadness in Cody's eyes reminded me of the way Malcolm had looked after holding my dreams at bay.

"You knew?"

He nodded.

"How … how can you—" a sob choked out my words "—look at me?" The fires dimmed and flickered out.

"Wasn't you." He scooted closer to me, and I backed away. "Was the demon magic."

"I ki-killed him, and I savored it. I … I wanted more." I bent over and heaved. "Somebody needs to kill me before I end up like Draconian."

Cody wrapped his arms around me from behind. Clutching me against his chest, even though I fought his hold. "Stop, Dacia." His words were soft. "Wasn't you. Was the demon magic. It took control. Doesn't mix well with human powers. You didn't know."

I quit thrashing against him, but I didn't believe a word of what he was saying. Even with Mavros' power burning inside of me brighter than a supernova, I should've been able to control myself. I shouldn't have relished in Argentum's death. I shouldn't have wanted every drop of his blood.

Cody murmured something that I didn't hear. I was too wrapped up in my thoughts to listen to him.

He let go of me, but I kept rocking, Holding my head, wishing the memories would go away. Wishing the dragons would have let Argentum kill me before I turned into the monster he knew I would be.

Cody came back and pulled my shirt over my head, then dragged each arm through its sleeve. When his hand brushed against my wound, he sighed. "Oh, Dacia."

I remembered being injured by Argentum's talons in my dream, but I was too numb to feel the pain.

He grabbed me under my legs and pressed me close to his body, standing in the middle of the cavern.

I felt the dragons before I saw them. Malcolm roughly grabbed hold of Cody and me, then teleported us back to my room. I pressed my eyes shut, holding the light back, not wanting to see their faces. I would never be able to look any of them in the eye again.

"The fairies told us." Cash's voice was an inhuman growl. I imagined dragon features were showing through his disguise. "She's bleeding."

Cody sat down, still cradling me while I clutched my stomach. "She is."

"What happened?" Malcolm snarled.

"She fell asleep." Cody sounded like he might shatter into a million pieces. "I didn't realize."

I opened my eyes and stared blankly, trying to get the images out of my head. "Take it away," I whispered.

Both dragons watched me. Their faces were covered in scales and rimmed by horns. Their eyes were wild. Fangs jutted from their mouths.

Cody gazed into my eyes with so much sorrow in his that it broke my already shattered heart.

"Please." My word was barely a breath. "Please take them away."

Malcolm held his hand over mine, and a calming flow of energy burst through my veins. My despair burned it away. He waved Cash over to add his power.

Russ, Arianna, Val, and Aurelia all teleported into the room. Val moaned as soon as he fully formed.

"Val"—Malcolm's voice was harsh—"if you can't control yourself, leave now."

He walked over and put his hand on top of my head. "She needs us."

The dragons pooled their powers, and soothing energy streamed into me, strong enough to suppress my anguish. My eyes drooped, and I fell into a deep, dreamless sleep.

The room smelled crisp and cool, like a winter's day. I opened my eyes expecting to see Cody. Instead, Malcolm held me against his side. It was still dark, but the streetlights shone in through the windows.

Malcolm smiled down at me. I twisted my head, searching for Cody. Cash sat in Cookie Monster. His elbows were on his knees, and he leaned forward, watching me for any sign of trouble. Nobody else was in the room.

Dropping my chin to my chest, I realized why I smelled Cody. I was wearing his blue t-shirt with my leggings. I remembered him dressing me in the dark cave and realized he hadn't been able to see, but he'd wanted to save my modesty anyway.

"What difference does it make?" I mumbled and lay back down, clutching my pillow, trying to keep my self-loathing and disgust from drowning me again.

Malcolm's power surged into me, sending me a false sense of calm.

"Why won't you take them away?" Tears pooled in my eyes and soaked into my pillow.

Cash dragged his hand through his hair, making it stand on end. "Oh, Dacia. We can't." He knelt in front of me, dropping his head. "I'm so sorry."

"You warned me." I remembered the day he'd told me not to press, that I didn't want to know what the dragons were hiding from me. "You knew I couldn't cope with it." I sat up and held my head in my hands. "I wanted to kill both of you. I would have. Why are you still here with me?"

Malcolm scooted right next to me and wrapped his arm around my shoulders. "It was the demon's taint, not you."

"How can you say that?" Anger flared inside of me. "I was still there. It was still me!"

Cash took my hand in his and siphoned my powers out. "Mavros took your memories before." His skin sparked blue and purple. "He didn't know how long it would hold. He just hoped it would be long enough for you to be able to cope with it."

"News flash." I jerked my hand away from him. "It wasn't."

"I knew it wouldn't be." Malcolm's voice was soft and soothing. "That's why I was still keeping your dreams from you. I wanted to give your psyche a chance to heal."

I didn't deserve their comfort. I pulled away from Malcolm's hold, walked to the window, and stared outside at the snow-covered trees. "I just wanted to spend some time alone with Cody. I felt like I was losing myself and him in the process." Turning, I looked at them. "I didn't mean to fall asleep.

I didn't mean for this to happen." I slid down the wall and wrapped my arms around my legs, hugging them against my chest. "How'm I ever going to cope with what I did? I'm a monster."

Malcolm and Cash came over, sitting on either side of me. Cash pulled me against him, and Malcolm held my hand.

Cash stroked my arm and whispered right into my ear, "You have to forgive yourself. You have to let it go. It wasn't you."

I shook my head and remembered savoring Argentum's blood. "I don't think I can."

The whole time they held me, they drew on my powers, draining me of them.

"Why?" I asked.

"We cannot risk you using them." The voice that answered surprised me. I looked up to see Aurelia in front of me. Like always, she looked perfectly put together, not a hair out of place, not a wrinkle on her blouse or slacks. "With all of these emotions running through you, it is too big of a risk."

"Can you fix me?" I hated the pathetic sound of my voice.

She knelt down in front of me. Her gold skin sparkled even in the dim lighting. "I can try to do what I did with your dreams of Draconian." She brushed the tears off my cheeks. "I have no idea if it will work, but we can try."

I chewed on my lip and nodded, not meeting her eyes, not wanting to see revulsion in them. "If it doesn't, I'll have to summon Mavros back."

All three dragons snapped their heads toward me. Their pupils were tiny slits.

"I can't handle what I did." I clutched my hair in my fists. "I'm a monster."

Aurelia pulled my hands down and held them in hers. "Malcolm, hold her while she sleeps. Keep the worst of her emotions tamped down. Cash, lend Malcolm your strength if he needs it." She stood, pulling me to my feet.

Malcolm sat on the couch. I grabbed my pillow off the floor and joined him, keeping my eyes downcast the whole time.

You can look at me, Dacia. His voice was filled with understanding. *I have done so much worse.*

I couldn't speak inside his mind without using my powers, so I kept my voice low. "You were under Draconian's control."

Not for all of it. I did bad things under his influence. I did worse on my own. His remorse flowed into me, showing me his guilt.

I glanced up into his eyes. "Thanks. It doesn't make things better, though."

I know.

Aurelia stood in front of us. "I am going to make you sleep, but you will be able to dream."

I squeezed my eyes shut and nodded. Even with Malcolm's help, I never wanted to see those images again. "Okay."

Chapter 7

Take Away My Pain

Argentum kneels on the ground. Aurelia reaches for him, and he latches onto her, transforming into a massive silver dragon with broken horns and rheumy eyes. His laugh fills the cave.

I call the other dragons to me and use their magic to summon Mavros. He stands in front of me tall, dark, and handsome as hell. His obsidian eyes sparkle. I command him to lend me his strength. He pauses, telling me he will kill Argentum so I don't have to, offering to save me from the pain.

I refuse and instead set ground rules for him. His power slams into me with the force of a hurricane. It's sinister, ominous, and seems to have a mind of its own.

Argentum strikes at me, and Mavros jumps between us. His blood drips from Argentum's fangs, and the magic reacts, transforming me into the demon version of Mavros.

I strike out at Argentum, making him drop Mavros. My fangs sink into his neck. His claws tear through my hide. Malcolm and Cash latch onto his neck, and the three of us bring him down. His last breath shudders through his body, and we step back.

I woke up, gasping. Deep claw marks ripped through my side. Aurelia held my hand while she sent healing energy into my body. I stared up into Malcolm's face. His eyes were completely bronze with a thin, slitted pupil slashing through them. Black scales covered his cheeks and neck. He gripped my arm harder than was necessary.

Cash opened the window to clear the smell from the room. Snowflakes blew in on the breeze.

The pain receded enough for me to catch my breath. "Are you okay, Malcolm?"

"I won't hurt you." His voice was feral.

"I knew that would happen. I should've warned you." The wound closed up, and Aurelia let go of my hand, rocking back on her heels.

Malcolm rubbed his hand over his face, and I wondered how much more he could handle. "I was there. I've relived it every night for weeks. I knew it would happen, too." He released his hold on my arm. "I was prepared for it this time."

"That's why you left every morning."

He nodded, and I realized his fangs were longer than normal. "Even in your nightmares, your emotions were overwhelming. I took out my aggression on the poor creatures who were unfortunate enough to be roaming in the woods after you woke up. It was easier once I started staying on the couch with you."

Sitting up, I said, "Well, I need to get this blood off of me." I grabbed my clothes and looked at the dragons. "Am I on my own, or is someone coming?"

Aurelia walked over and grabbed my hand. Turning both of us invisible, she teleported to the bathroom. "When you are done, I will need to burn your shirt."

While I got ready to shower, I wondered if she was manipulating my emotions. After remembering what I'd done to Argentum, I'd felt like I was drowning under a flood of guilt, grief, disgust, and self-loathing. I still regretted taking his life, but I didn't feel like a monster anymore.

Watching my blood run down the drain, I pondered whether or not this would ever end. Until I'd turned eighteen, my dreams had been like everyone else's. I hadn't woken from them broken and bleeding. I knew the dragons and Nephilim believed I would fight monsters for the rest of my life, but would my nightmares remain this way?

I tried to turn off my thoughts while I finished showering and got dressed. Then while I braided my hair, Aurelia burned Cody's shirt, washing the ashes down the drain.

By the time we got back to my room, Malcolm's appearance had returned to normal. The blanket I'd been covered up with was gone, most likely torched as soon as I was out of sight.

"How are you feeling?" Aurelia sat on the opposite side of the couch from Malcolm. Cash stood at the open window.

I set my bathroom bag down, walked over to Cookie Monster, and shrugged before plopping down. "Like someone's controlling my emotions."

The dragons looked from one to another. "We are not," Aurelia said.

"Well"—I rocked back in the chair—"I guess for now I'm doing all right then."

I woke up with my head on Malcolm's thigh, and my arms wrapped around it. I didn't feel as self-conscious about it this time. He was my friend and protector. I rolled over and looked up into his eyes. "Morning."

"Good morning." He lifted his arm off me and stretched. "How are you feeling?"

I sat up and pulled the braid out of my hair, then ran my hands through it. Red strands clung to my fingers. I rolled them into a ball, focusing on it instead of my guards. "Like I should be locked away in some deep, dark dungeon."

Cash growled, and chills raced up my spine. The sound was that of a cornered, wild beast.

Malcolm lifted my chin up, so I was looking into his eyes. "Why should you be imprisoned?"

"I'm a menace." I lowered my gaze. "I've killed twice. How many more will I murder?"

"First, it wasn't murder. It was self-defense." He wrapped his arm around my shoulders and pulled me against his side.

"Second, if there had been any other choice with either of them, you would have taken it, and you know it."

"You need to forgive yourself, Dacia." Cash's voice was gruff, and I realized my emotions were wreaking havoc on him. "They wouldn't have given up. Draconian wanted to control you, like he did us, and Argentum wanted to eat you."

I shook my head, and a dry chuckle escaped my lips. "So I ate him instead." I walked over to my closet and stared at the clothes. A lot of my favorite, most comfortable sweatshirts had been destroyed by demons, dragons, or dreams. "Turnabout's fair play, right?"

I spun around, and Malcolm was right there. My nose nearly bumped into his broad chest. "You didn't eat him. You had a demon's magic wreaking havoc inside of you, and you were transformed into a feral beast." He pointed at Cash and then at himself. "We are more in control in our human forms. Our senses can be overwhelming when we are in our natural state. Instincts guide us. You had never experienced something like that before, and yet, you stopped. You were able to control your bloodlust." He slowly lifted his hands and settled them on my shoulders. "I vowed to protect you. I care about you, but when Mavros attacked you, and your blood splattered on my face, I wanted to drain every drop of blood from your veins."

I remembered the look in his eyes, trying to talk him down, how he'd stood away from me, refusing to look at me for the rest of the night, trying to figure out a way to get him past his self-loathing when we were supposed to be training. "That was my fault. My—"

"No." The word was a low rumble. "It was my fault. My dragon wanted to tear you limb from limb. You—" the words seemed to catch in his throat "—you forgave me and made me forgive myself. Now, you must do the same."

I dropped my chin to my chest. "I'll try."

"And remember Argentum wanted you dead—" he tilted my face up "—but, you trusted me, and I nearly betrayed that trust."

I bobbed my head slightly. It wouldn't be an easy thing, but I would try to forgive myself. "Can I see him today?"

"Cody?" Cash chuckled. "If we tried to keep you two apart, he'd find a way to come anyway. He's driving Russ nuts."

"We had to make sure you were okay first." Malcolm backed up a few steps. "Please, stay with us today. We know you want privacy, but give it some time first."

"Yeah." I rubbed my hand along my arm, wishing I wouldn't have snuck away with Cody, wishing I could go back and change things. "You're not hiding anything else. Are you?"

Malcolm shook his head. "No."

"Guess I'll go get dressed then." I walked down to the bathroom, seemingly alone, but Malcolm and Cash were with me.

When we got back to my room, Cody was waiting inside for me. He started to walk toward me but stopped. "How're ya?"

I went through the motions of putting my pajamas and bathroom bag away, wondering why Cody was acting so hesitant, wondering if the dragons had warned him to be cautious around me, or if his fear was driving him. "Better … trying." I chewed on my lip, looking from Cody to the dragons. "Can we have pretend privacy?"

"Don't make us regret it," Malcolm said before the two of them disappeared.

Cody looked around the room. "They gone?"

"Gone or invisible and blocking me from sensing them." I tipped my head toward my shoulder. "Either way, it at least looks like we're alone."

"So whadda you wanna do?" He stepped toward me, but he was still too far away.

I stared at my feet. "I just want to know we're okay."

He closed the distance between us. The tips of his toes touched mine. "Why wouldn't we be?"

"You were over there, and I was over here, and it felt like there was a rift between us."

He brushed his finger under my chin and along my neck. I tilted my head back and closed my eyes. His lips swept over mine. "I'm scared, Dacia."

My body tensed, and I stared up at him. "Of me?"

"Did this already." He pressed his lips to my forehead. "For you."

I backed away from him and slid down the wall. "You should be scared of me. Why else would the dragons watch me so carefully?"

He sat next to me on the lilac carpet and took my hand in his. "You'll beat this, just like everything else. Of that, I've no doubt."

"What if I hurt one of you?"

He tossed his arm over my shoulders and said, "Movie, Althea, basketball, pool, kissing on the couch, eloping. Whadda you wanna do?"

"Eloping?" I couldn't resist smiling. "Really?"

His eyes sparkled. "If you want."

I turned and threw my legs over his. "I want to know what brought this on."

"Wanted to see you smile." He lifted his hand, gently cradling my cheek.

I bit my lip, trying to keep my expression serious. "So how do we go about it?"

His grip slackened a little. "Let's find out." He lifted my legs off his and stood, holding his hand out to me.

I shook my head. "Cody, I was just joking."

"I'm not." He opened and closed his fingers, and I stuck my hand in his, allowing him to pull me to my feet. "Go home end of next week, and don't wanna be away from you." He turned and walked a few steps. "Know I'm not a lotta help, but I hate not being there."

I moved behind him and wrapped my arms around his waist. "Is it really what you want?"

"Wanted to watch you walk down the aisle. See the love in your eyes." He turned in my arms. "Just don't want you alone."

"I don't think you'll have to worry about that." I tugged my hand through my hair. "I'm sure at least two dragons will be with me constantly."

His posture stiffened, but he showed no other signs that their constant presence bothered him. "Whadda you want?"

"A small wedding with a few friends and family." I slipped my hands under his shirt and brushed my fingers over his ribs. "To spend forever with you."

He rested his forehead on mine. "Eloping's out." Tracing along my jawline, he said, "So what's in?"

I leaned into his touch. "I need to study sometime this weekend. Probably won't help much, though." His fingers slid down my neck, melting me a little with their gentle touch. "How 'bout Althea? Just us."

"Sam's studying anyway." Pressing his thumbs against the bottom of my chin, he tilted my head back. His lips crashed down on mine. I tightened my grip on him, pulling him closer to me, and matched the hunger in his kiss. His hands slid down my arms, along my sides, and onto my thighs. Lifting me, he carried me to the couch. He knelt, slowly, carefully, never pulling his mouth from mine, and laid me down.

I wrapped my legs around his waist, drawing him closer to me. Shivers of pleasure shot through me. His mouth moved onto my chin and down my neck. "I love you." The words escaped me as a breathless whisper.

He lifted up and smiled down at me. "I love you, too, Dacia."

"So"—I slid my hands over his abs—"kissing, then Althea?"

"Yeah."

Cody drove my truck to Althea, looking more relaxed than I'd seen him in a long time. His hair was tousled. His eyes were bright. He held onto my hand, gently rubbing his thumb along mine.

I knew we were being watched, but even so, the drive felt closer to normal than any had since freshman year. Snow-covered trees and mountains whizzed by, and a feeling of contentment settled deep, down inside of me. This wouldn't last forever, but I would take a break while I could and deal with whatever came next when it happened.

We spent the day wandering through shops, holding hands, and just enjoying each other's company. For lunch, we went to Rocky's Bar and Grille. We walked in, and every step we took made a crunching noise. Peanut shells littered the floor. Country music made it impossible to overhear other people's conversations. The air smelled like steak and homemade bread. We sat on the same side in a booth, letting our legs touch. I couldn't help but wonder if Cash and Malcolm sat on the other side or if they were just watching from nearby. Either way, I was glad to spend some time seemingly alone with Cody for once.

On the way back to campus, I turned my focus inward. The serpent slithered toward me. Its scales were pearlescent. Shadows no longer darkened them. I let out a relieved breath and stepped toward it. "Is Mavros' magic gone?"

The snake lifted, stretching its head into the air until we stood eye to eye. *His power will always be here.*

"Always?" My heart plummeted.

It turned its head to the side, and I followed its gaze. A snake with midnight scales slithered toward us. My magic turned back to me. *It no longer fights us for control. It has become its own.*

Chapter 8

$\mathcal{M}$alcolm sat in Cookie Monster trying not to make it obvious he was watching me. The dragons had insisted that I try to sleep alone to make sure I could handle whatever horrors my nightmares might bring.

He was there to monitor my dreams and to heal me if I got injured. Cash was in Aurelia's room, keeping an eye on me from there. *This experiment won't work if you don't go to sleep.*

"I'm aware of that," I mumbled.

Why are you fighting?

I remembered what I'd done to Argentum, but that wasn't it. Whatever Aurelia had done was helping me cope with that for now.

No.

This was the ebony snake. It horrified me. How had Mavros' power broken apart from mine and survived inside of me? Would it be there forever, waiting for the right moment to strike? Would it eventually corrupt me?

Malcolm and Cash didn't know. I hadn't been able to bring myself to confide in them yet. How much would the dragons allow before sending me to the Nephilim's sanctuary? The alliance between the two species was already fragile. There were mistrust and prejudice on both sides.

Dacia?

"I'm scared all right." My words were sharp as knives. "I'm afraid of what I'll dream and what it'll do to me. I am breaking, and you guys aren't going to be able to glue my pieces back together forever." A heavy weight settled over me. I hadn't meant to say it, but every word was true.

Malcolm walked over and nudged my shoulder. "Lift up. I'll sit here with you until you fall asleep."

The wind howls through the trees. Snow blows up from the ground, swirling around me like a cyclone. The moon and stars are blocked by clouds. Mavros appears suddenly, strolling out of the darkness toward me. His hands are tucked in his pockets. He looks just like he did the last time I saw him. Tall, dark, and perfect. He smiles at me, and my heart clenches in response. His eyes rove over me, and something about the gesture reminds me of him when he's in his panther form. "I've missed you." His voice is as smooth as silk.

"Hello, Mavros." I don't know what to think or say. The last few times I've seen him, he's helped me, but the first time I'd seen him, he'd wanted to bind himself to me. "How are you here?"

He lifts his shoulders. "This. This is just a dream. I'm not really here." He reaches for my hands. I let him take them, hoping he won't try to control me. "I haven't been able to get past your dragons since you returned me to the Abyss. Are you okay?"

I shiver, and he slips his leather jacket off, handing it to me. "I'm coping." Shoving my arms into the sleeves, I savor his warmth. "I'm sorry I sent you back there." I stare down at my bare feet, ashamed that I took the easy path, not the right path. "I should've fought for your right to stay here."

He tilts my chin up so that I look into his face. "What happened to your eyes?"

"I used my magic, and yours—" I wave my hand in front of my face "—did this to me."

He pinches his eyes shut. "I'm sorry, Dacia. You freed me from my curse, and this is how I repay you."

"I did what?" I gasp and stagger back. "How?"

He chuckles, and the sound warms my heart. "All this time, I thought I had to have a physical bond to a mortal to remain on Earth, but you and I are bound. You took my magic as your own, and I didn't allow it to kill you."

"So—" I try to process what he just told me, but it doesn't make any sense "—why haven't you come back?"

The scene changes. We're standing on a white, sandy beach. It's nearly impossible to tell where the sky ends and the turquoise water begins. The sun beats down on me, and I pull Mavros' coat off. "This is where I get to spend this year. I told you it wasn't what I made it out to be."

"Then why?" I wiggle my toes until they're buried beneath the sand.

He stands beside me, looking out at the water. "I'm a demon." He shrugs. "I was angry with the dragons, and until you, nobody had ever given me a reason to do the right thing." He slides his hand into mine. "If I come back, the Nephilim will blame you. For now, I will only return if you need me."

He stares over my shoulder. "Dragon."

"Demon." Malcolm's voice is a low growl. "Don't hurt her."

Mavros lets go of my hand and turns to face Malcolm. "I don't want to hurt her. I just wanted to see her, to make sure she's okay."

"She's not." Malcolm strides toward me. "She remembers everything. Every time she uses her powers, your magic threatens to corrupt her."

Mavros reaches up and holds my cheeks, staring into my eyes. "How? I thought your power would cleanse it and make it right."

I explain to him how I see my power as a serpent and how the fairies were able to pull his magic from mine. Then I look at Malcolm and bite my lip. I really don't want to tell him about the ebony snake, but I don't have much choice.

Malcolm's face becomes stony. "Why didn't you tell me?"

"Because one of these days, you guys are going to decide I'm not worth it and give me to the Nephilim." Tears burn in my eyes.

He growls, deep and ominous. "We vowed to protect you."

"I know." I tug my hand through my hair. "I just found out tonight. I planned to tell you."

Mavros grabs my wrist, and a jolt of power zaps through me. The serpents writhe under my skin. My powers seem to settle down, but his stay where I can see them. He focuses on them and runs his finger along my arm. "I put them to sleep, but I don't know how long it will last."

"Thank you." I watch the obsidian serpent sink beneath my skin.

He lifts my hand to his mouth and presses a kiss to my knuckles. "If you need me, don't hesitate to ask."

My eyes shot open. Malcolm sat in Cookie Monster, staring at me. His hands clutched the arms of the chair. His muscles were tight. "Is it dormant?"

I closed my eyes and focused on my powers. They hadn't grown since the last time I visited the fairies and Mavros' power had separated from mine. The serpent slithered toward me. Its copper eyes had the same black flecks in them as my green ones did.

Mavros' power lay on the ground with its head buried inside its coils.

My magic wrapped around my leg, climbing, squeezing. *You are mine.*

And, you are mine. I thought to it.

I am free.

I looked at the sleeping snake. *I hope so.* I stroked my serpent's head before returning to Malcolm. "For now," I answered.

He glowered at me. "Why do you still not trust me?"

"I do, Malcolm." I got up and knelt in front of him. "When Cody and I were coming back from Althea, I saw Mavros' powers inside of me. It terrified me." I lowered my forehead, barely touching it to his knee, hoping he would forgive me. "I thought they would turn me into a monster, like Draconian, like the one I became when I killed Argentum. I wasn't ready to say anything about them. I didn't even tell Cody."

He put his hand on top of my head and brushed my hair back. His touch was gentle, unlike anything I had expected from a dragon. He was my friend, and I did trust him. "I can't help you if I don't know what's going on." *No matter what, I will stand by your side and protect you with my life. I will never let the Nephilim take you unless you wish for that fate.*

"I'm sorry, Malcolm." I rocked back on my heels. "I will try to do better." I lay back down on the couch and pulled my blanket up to my chin. "Goodnight."

"Sleep well, Dacia."

My jaws clamp onto Argentum's neck. His blood runs down my throat. The ancient power stokes my bloodlust.

Argentum lashes out, not wanting to die. His claws tear into my side. One of my other heads latches onto his foot. Malcolm and Cash join me in bringing him down. His dying breath shudders through his body.

I woke up before facing the rest of the nightmare. Malcolm knelt over me. His hands were pressed against my side. His energy flowed into me, soothing, relieving, healing. He held his breath, fighting his instincts.

"I'm okay." I pressed my hand to his cheek. "Let me get cleaned up."

Chapter 9

I'd Rather Fight Monsters Than Take Finals

The sun peeked in through the curtains. I opened my eyes to find Malcolm watching me. "Don't you ever sleep?" I asked as I sat up.

"Not lately."

"I'm sorry about that, too." I walked over to the sink and grabbed my toothbrush. My mouth tasted like blood. The thought made my stomach heave, so I tried not to focus on it, to think about something else. "Did you know Mavros was bound to me?"

His bronze gaze darted toward the door, and he lifted his fingers to his lips, tilting his head to the side. "There are ears everywhere."

"I thought you kept my room soundproofed."

He nodded. "They have ways around it. It should be safe now."

"So … did you know?"

"Not for sure." Malcolm's voice had something in it that I didn't recognize. Fear? Maybe, but it seemed so out of place in him. "We suspected."

I spit in the sink and waved my toothbrush toward the hall. "Do they know?"

"I don't know." He seemed deflated. "If he comes back, they will."

I rinsed my mouth and turned around. Malcolm held his head in his hands. "Is there something I should know?"

"No." He looked up and shook his head. "I need to stretch my wings today. Cash will be with you. I'll be back by night-fall."

My friends and I spent the day in the library seated around a table with our heads bent over our books and notes. Cash had his arm thrown over the back of my chair. Every so often he siphoned off my energy. The Nephilim sat nearby watching, and I wondered if they knew what Cash was doing and why.

The words blurred together on the pages within front of me. I couldn't focus on them at all. *Is there something going on that you guys aren't telling me?*

Cash didn't let on that I was talking to him. *What makes you think that?*

Malcolm. I set my pen down and rubbed my forehead. *This morning he seemed afraid. Then he left.*

He rubbed my neck, drawing my energy into him. *He went hunting and to his lair to rest. Like all of us, he is afraid for you, not of you. Mavros is powerful. Knowing he is free to come and go ...* He dropped his hand and stood up, pacing behind our table. *We'll worry about that when it happens. Right now, you should be studying.*

I'm just going to fail anyway. I shrugged.

He sat back down, picked up my notes, and quizzed me on them without saying a word out loud.

I lay in my bed wishing I would've told Cody he could stay here tonight. I'd wanted him to get sleep before his finals, but I missed his warmth and comfort. Cash was stretched out on the couch, and Malcolm looked up at me from Cookie Monster. It had been so long since I'd slept in my loft that I had a hard time getting comfortable. I was used to the separate cushions on the couch, not one solid mattress.

"What is it?" Cash's voice was gruff.

I knew him well enough now to know the harshness wasn't out of anger or hatred. It was because my emotions were wreaking havoc on him. "I don't know." I propped up on my elbow and looked down at the dragons. "I feel like I'm waiting for the other shoe to drop. It's been about four weeks since someone wanted me dead. It's weird."

"Be grateful for the reprieve," Malcolm said.

"I am." I plopped back on my pillow and stared at the ceiling. "I guess I just don't want to get used to it, then have it taken from me. I keep wondering what else is out there. Are there worse things than demons and dragons?"

Since starting college, I'd avoided capture by the Nephilim, I'd killed a crazed wizard, I'd fought demons and dragons, and I'd been injured countless times, but finals week had been its own special brand of horror.

Friday, I sat in the lunchroom surrounded by my friends. My brain was fried, but I was glad to have this semester finished. By the looks of it, everyone else felt the same.

Bryce spun his sports drink between his palms. He kept looking at me, then away. Finally, he said, "Are you gonna be okay by yourself?"

"By myself?" I huffed out a laugh and shook my head. "I won't be alone. Cash and Malcolm will be with me. I'm sure the others will be—" I waved my hand in the air, trying to decide what to say "—on call." I stared down at my grilled cheese. "I haven't had any new nightmares, so maybe it'll be a nice, relaxing break." I didn't want to jinx it, but I hoped I wouldn't bring any problems home. Even though Mom and Dad knew, I didn't want them to witness the craziness firsthand.

I lay on the couch in Cody's arms. The dragons couldn't keep him away, not tonight. Tomorrow, we were going home, and Cody wasn't willing to sleep in his own room. His breathing had evened out a long time ago, and his grip had gone slack, but I couldn't sleep.

Thoughts zipped through my head too quickly for me to corral them. Malcolm had stayed away, leaving just Cash to watch over me. I knew Malcolm could be here quicker than a sneeze if needed, but I wondered if he was hiding something from me. I didn't want to push to find out because if it was something like what I'd done to Argentum, I didn't think I could handle knowing.

I brushed my fingers lightly along the edge of Cody's face. His eyelids fluttered but didn't open. Pressing closer to him, I closed my eyes.

The dragons want me to use my powers as long as I'm not angry or exhausted. As long as I am fully in control. I turn my focus inward. The serpent is coiled. Its scales reflect the light, shimmering in shades of blue and purple, no shadows linger on it. Its copper eyes pin me in a stare. *You have forgotten us.*

No. You are part of me. I could never forget you.

Mavros' power lies next to mine. It hasn't grown or diminished. Its scales are darker than Death's cowl. Shadows undulate around its sleeping body.

When I open my eyes to the real world, Cody, Cash, and Malcolm are scattered around my living room and all of them are staring at me. I only see Cody's concern for a moment before he slips his mask into place.

The Christmas tree stands in front of the windows. Red and green lights twinkle in its branches. Snowmen and Santas are scattered about the room. A Nativity scene covers the mantle. The room feels tiny with the dragons taking up so much space in it.

Drawing in a deep breath, I light a fire in my palm and study it, hoping it stays blue with no trace of black in it. The flames climb higher, and I remember them turning on me. Fear clenches my heart, and the fire surges in response. Malcolm steps closer, ready to drain my powers if necessary.

I lift my other hand, holding him back, and concentrate on my magic. *You are mine.*

No. The voice that responds is dark and unfamiliar. *You are ours.*

The flames shoot from my hand, hitting Cody in the chest, engulfing him before either dragon can douse them.

"No!" I scream.

Chapter 10

Demon Inside Me

"Dacia, wake up."

I jolted awake. Cody was propped up over me. His hair poked out in all directions, and fear shone in his eyes, but he was alive. "You hurt?"

"No." I threw my arms around him and sobbed into his chest.

He lay down, pulling me with him, and gently rubbed my back. "What is it?"

A cool breeze rushed into the room, and I realized Cash must've opened the window. He hadn't tasted my blood like Malcolm had. Even so, it was harder for him to control his dragon when my emotions were out of whack. My one saving grace was that vows were sacred to dragons, and Cash would rather be controlled by Draconian again than break his oath.

"Dacia." Malcolm's voice surprised me.

I pulled away from Cody. My tears had pooled on his skin. I lifted the bottom of my shirt and began wiping them off.

Cody grabbed my hand to stop me. "It's okay." He pulled the shirt from my grip and twined his fingers through mine. "What's wrong?"

"I … I killed you." I jerked back and would've fallen off the couch if Malcolm hadn't grabbed me and stood me on my feet. "You have to stay away from me."

Cody sat up. "Not gonna happen."

Malcolm turned me toward him. He held my face in his massive hands. "Show me."

I stared into his bronze eyes and let him into my head. I tried to focus on him and not see the images from the dream again, but he faded away. The scene replayed. Me with the serpents, witnessing the concern on Cody's face, using my magic, losing control, hearing the strange voice in my head, and watching my flames engulf Cody.

Malcolm supported me when I thought I would crumble to the floor. He held my gaze. I don't think I could've looked away if I'd tried. "It won't happen, Dacia."

"How do you know?" My voice was broken.

"Same way I knew I wouldn't die." He lowered his hands to my arms. "You showed me the dream, so we won't let it happen." Looking over my shoulder, he said, "Cody, you are not to be with Dacia while she works to regain control of her powers."

"Sure." It surprised me that he said it without even a hint of sarcasm.

"We will do our best to keep you and your friends safe." Malcolm spun me around so I was facing the couch. "Now, get some rest."

Cody rolled onto his side and lifted the blanket. "It's all right, Dacia."

I lay down next to him and wondered how much more he could take before he decided I wasn't worth it.

He pulled the blanket over us and drew circles on my back. They tingled through my shirt. Then he kissed the top of my head. "You won't hurt me."

"I hope not."

He slid his hand between us and lifted my chin so I was looking into his eyes. "You won't." He kissed me softly, then lay back. "Goodnight."

I wanted to believe he was right, but my nightmare had felt so real, and I hadn't been in control when Mavros' power had slammed into me the first time. "Night."

Rolling onto my other side, I found both dragons watching me. "Staying?" I asked Malcolm.

"For now." He pointed at Cash still standing by the open window. "If you don't get ahold of your emotions, he's going to need to leave."

"To go hunting?" A wintry wind blew across me, and I pulled the blanket up to my chin. "Sorry." I closed my eyes. As soon as I did, I saw my flames strike Cody. My eyes shot open. My heart raced, and bile rose in my throat.

Sleep beckoned me, but every time my eyes drifted shut, I watched my flames engulf Cody and snuff out his life. Eventually, one of the dragons used their magic on me, forcing me to sleep.

I awoke to whispering. I kept my eyes closed and hoped they didn't realize I wasn't sleeping.

"Why's she think she'll kill me?" Cody's words brushed across my shoulder, then over my face.

"Mavros' power is still inside her." Even though it was quiet, there was a harsh edge to Malcolm's voice. "I don't know if it's just her fear of them that made her dream she'd kill you or if it was a premonition." There was a long pause that tempted me to open my eyes, but I refrained. "It would be the end of her if she hurt you, so I don't want it to turn into a self-fulfilling prophecy. That's why we need you to stay away until she regains control of her powers."

Cody tightened his grip around my waist, pulling my back closer to his chest. "Not staying away."

"When she uses her magic," Malcolm clarified. "Not all the time. By the way, she's awake."

I stretched my arms and wrapped one behind Cody's head, letting my fingers trail through his hair. Opening my eyes, I said, "Thank you for making me sleep."

Cash sat on the floor under the window. The sunlight made the purple streaks in his hair more prominent. "I should've asked first, but I couldn't handle your despair any longer."

"Neither could I." I folded my arms over Cody's knowing this would be the last time I'd wake up with him for a long time.

He drew me against him and laid his head on mine. "When're we leaving?"

"Tomorrow?"

He chuckled. "I'd like that, but our parents wouldn't."

"I know." I turned in his arms and faced him. "Last time I went home for more than a few days …" Meeting Mavros flashed through my memory. I remembered him showing up at my birthday party. I remembered Cody's reaction to seeing me kiss Mavros. On campus, I felt more equipped to deal with the oddities of my life than I did anywhere else. "I'm not even packed."

"Me neither." He nipped at my earlobe, and a tingling sensation spread through my body.

My eyelids fluttered. "Go away," I told the dragons as I wrapped my arms around Cody's neck. "Tell me everything's going to be okay."

He cupped my face and trailed his thumb under my eye. "It will." He brushed his lips over mine.

I needed it to be true, so I let myself believe him for now.

Malcolm drove my truck. Like Cody, he wasn't sure if it was safe for me to be behind the wheel. I understood where they were coming from. Mavros had pulled me away a couple of times over the last few months, but he'd only done it because of Argentum. Even though I wasn't in the Nephilim's sanctuary, I felt like I was losing a little more of my freedom every day. I couldn't help but wonder what would be next. Right now, I couldn't sleep in a room by myself, use my magic, drive, or be alone with Cody without a watcher. I didn't want to spend my life peeking around corners, wondering what was next.

"Not your first rodeo, huh?" I couldn't handle the silence any longer. Being lost in my thoughts wasn't a good place to be.

Malcolm's eyebrows pinched together. "What?"

"You've driven before?"

He shook his head. "No."

"Seriously?" I grabbed the handle above the door.

"When would I have driven?" He looked at me like a teacher looks at their student when the answer is obvious. "I was held captive for over three hundred years. Since then, I've been with you."

I watched him, amazed by his ease behind the wheel. "How'd you figure it out so quickly then?"

"I've seen people drive." He smiled, showing his elongated fangs. "It's not complicated."

I laughed. "And, yet, I'm not allowed to do it."

"Is there something you need to get off your chest?" He peeked at me out of the side of his eye.

The snow-covered trees zipped past my window. I let go of the handle and folded my arms over my stomach. "Probably." Cody drove in front of us. Cash had offered to ride with him, but Cody told him he'd be fine alone if Cash wanted to spread his wings.

"Dacia?"

I didn't want Malcolm to know I felt trapped. "Not now."

He rolled his window down about three inches. "I can probably guess by your emotions, but if you don't want to talk, I won't pry."

"I hate that you can read me so easily. It's not fair. I never know what you're thinking, or why you leave, or if you're hiding more from me." I tugged my hand through my hair, trying to decide what to tell him. I stared out my window. He didn't need me to look at him to hear what I had to say. Unlike a person, he would hear a whisper in a hurricane. "I feel like my privileges are being stripped one by one and pretty soon I might as well be in a cage."

A low growl filled the cab of the truck, lifting the hairs on my arms and at the nape of my neck. "That will never happen."

"It already is—" I took in a shuddering breath "—and I'm losing myself."

He reached over the console and took my hand, drawing my magic out. "We're going to figure out how to get your powers back to you and how to purge Mavros'. You need to give us some time to figure it out."

"Do you really think you'll be able to get rid of his magic?" I squeezed his hand harder than intended, but I doubted it felt like more than a fly landing on him. "If you do, will it break his bond with me?"

Cody drove to my house. He parked and got out like he was on fire. As soon as Malcolm stopped my truck, Cody was by my door. He opened it and looked beyond me to Malcolm. "You'll be with her the whole time. Right?"

Sometimes I wondered if Cody remembered who he was talking to. The man sitting in my truck was the massive black dragon that had guarded Cody at Draconian's behest. His claws had torn through my flesh like a hot knife through butter.

Malcolm showed no anger at being questioned. "Mostly."

"Mostly?" Cody's grip tightened on my door.

Malcolm leaned over, and his eyes flashed to his dragon's. Cody moved back half of a step. "Mostly. Do you want me with her when she showers, when she's dressing, at times you haven't been with her?"

"No." Cody shook his head. "Sorry." He looked down at his feet. "The whole way, just kept thinking about the attacks last time we were here."

I unbuckled my seatbelt, got out of my truck, and slid my hand into his. "I don't plan on being alone. I told Mom and Dad that Malcolm or Cash would be with me all the time."

"Please … be safe." He touched his forehead to mine. "If you need me … doesn't matter what time. What I'm doing … I'll be there."

"I know, Code." I wrapped my arms around his waist. "I'm going to be okay."

He backed me up into my truck, pressing his legs against mine, and put his hands on either side of me, caging me in. His expression was tortured. I slipped my hands under his shirt, running them over his abs and up his chest. He brought his mouth down on mine harder than I expected. I felt his fear and concern in every touch of his lips.

The kiss eventually softened, and he backed away from me, sliding his hands to my waist. "Please … don't go any-where on your own. Let me know if anything happens." He looked at Malcolm. "Please keep her safe."

Chapter 11

Home For The Holidays

We'd spent the day after Thanksgiving putting up Christmas decorations. Garland was strung along the porch railings. A wreath hung on the front door. I opened it and stepped inside with Cash and Malcolm. The house smelled like cinnamon rolls.

The peaceful ambiance of the Christmas lights normally comforted me, but not today. Cody's fear had left me feeling jittery.

My parents came out of the kitchen. Mom was wiping her hands on a towel. She threw it over her shoulder and pulled me into a tight embrace. Dad shook the dragons' hands, then stood and waited for his turn to hug me.

Mom stepped back, not quite letting go of me, and looked at my guards. "Welcome back. You'll be here for a while, so feel free to treat it as your house."

"Thank you, Mrs. Wolf." Malcolm bowed his head at her.

"Please call me Caitlin. Mrs. Wolf is John's mom."

She let go of my hands, and Dad took advantage, pulling me into a hug. "You had a safe trip? Did you check your oil?"

"Before we left."

He let go of me. "I'll let it cool down. Then I'll check it."

I couldn't help but smile. I had so many things to worry about. It was good to know Dad would worry about the oil for me.

"We cleaned up the spare bedroom." Mom led Cash and Malcolm down the hall. "You can sleep in here."

"Thank you." Cash walked in and dropped a duffle bag on the floor beneath the window. "We're sorry to intrude on your holiday."

Mom nodded. "You don't need to apologize." She tried to smile, but it fell flat. "I'm grateful to you for keeping my daughter safe."

"We make you uncomfortable, though." Malcolm set a bag down on the chair.

I cocked my head and tried to remember if they'd had bags with them when we'd left.

"No—" Mom started to object.

"Don't argue." I led my parents back into the hall. "They can smell your emotions." She made a face that was part surprise and part disgust. "I know. It sucks, but it comes with being dragons."

Dad put his hand on my shoulder. "How do you deal with all of this?"

"It's my life." I shrugged. "You do what you have to do to survive."

Cody and I stroll through the park. Snow covers the ground and the trees. In some places, I sink to my knees. It's not a good day for a walk, but I couldn't stay cooped up inside any longer. The walls were too confining. I'd needed the fresh air and to get out from under my parents' worried gazes.

"You okay?" Cody asks.

I look around, wondering where the dragons are. I know they wouldn't leave me alone, not even for one minute. "Sure."

He slides his arm around my waist, and my magic surges.

I step out of his embrace and pull my glove off one finger at a time, delaying what I know to be true, not really wanting to see.

Pinching my eyes shut, I breathe in deeply, preparing myself. I hold my hand out in front of me and watch the ebony serpent slither under my skin.

Cody reaches for my fingers, and the snake strikes. Flames ignite, covering my hand.

Cody jumps back.

"Malcolm." My voice shakes.

He appears right in front of me and grabs my other hand.

My magic doesn't respond to him. Instead, flames blast toward Cody, striking him in the chest.

He's knocked off his feet. Fire engulfs him. He rolls over the snow, but the inferno rises higher.

Malcolm wraps his arms around me, and my power diminishes. The flames recede.

I pull against Malcolm's hold, wanting to run to Cody's side, but he won't let go of me.

Cash appears next to Cody and spreads his hands over Cody's chest. He shakes his head, and a scream tears from my throat.

Dad pounded on my door. "Dacia, open up. Now!"

I looked at Malcolm, and he disappeared. My parents thought he was sleeping in the other room with Cash, but he'd been stretched out next to me on top of the covers while I was under them.

Wiping the tears from my eyes, I walked to my door and opened it. "Sorry, Dad."

He clasped my shoulder and looked into my still dark room. "Are you okay?"

"Yeah." I tried to smile but couldn't quite pull it off. "Nightmare."

"Do you want to talk about it?"

I imagined Cody writhing on the ground. My flames covered his body. "No." The word was a hoarse, broken whisper.

His eyes softened as worry replaced the fear in them. "Are you in trouble?"

"I don't know." I dragged a trembling hand through my hair.

"You can talk to us." He looked over his shoulder, down the darkened hallway. "We may not understand it all, but we're here for you."

Unable to find the words to respond, I nodded.

He pulled me into a hug. "Try to get some sleep."

"Thanks, Dad." I watched him walk down the hall before shutting the door and climbing back into bed. "Can you sound-proof my room?"

"Yes." Malcolm squeezed my hand and showed himself. "Do you want me to keep you from dreaming?"

I rolled onto my side, facing him. I wanted to be able to see how he reacted to my question, and I would only be able to ask it once. "Am I going to k—" the word caught in my throat "—hurt him?"

His lips thinned as his expression turned solemn. "I'll do whatever I can to keep that from happening."

That was answer enough for me. It told me everything I needed to know. I was a danger to Cody. "I need to dream about Mavros. I need to get his magic out of me."

"Let me help you, Dacia." He drew my power into him. "If you dream about Mavros, I'll let it through."

Closing my eyes, I nodded. Then I focused my thoughts on Mavros. His olive complexion, raven hair, and midnight eyes. I thought about his silky voice and chiseled features. I remembered his smell, warm summer nights and sulfur. The feel of his arms around me. Flying through the night sky with him.

Mavros, I thought, *I need your help. I don't know what to do.*

"Dacia." Malcolm's voice was soft, but I heard the tension in it. "Try to sleep."

"Sorry."

He pulled away from me. "Your room is too small for these emotions."

I opened my eyes and peeked at him. "Make me sleep."

Chapter 12

The sky is a brilliant blue. Thin, wispy clouds drift lazily overhead. The turquoise water caresses the white, sandy shore. Mavros lies on a beach towel, wearing nothing but a black speedo.

He stands and walks toward me. "I heard you calling. What do you need?" He takes my hand and brings it to his lips. "If it's within my power, I'll give it to you."

Unintentionally, my eyes rove over him. His bronze skin glistens. His body is toned perfection.

He steps back and spins around, chuckling the whole time. "I could've been yours, Dacia." He brushes my hair back and tucks it behind my ear. "I still could be." His features morph into Damon's. His hair is lighter and tousled. His lips pull into a cocky grin that tugs at my heart. He isn't quite as flawless, but he's real and gorgeous.

It takes some effort, but I pull my gaze off of him and stare out at the ocean. Wiggling my toes, I bury them in the warm sand. "I know." When I look at him again, he's Mavros as I'm used to seeing him, dressed all in black.

He slips his hand into mine and leads me down the beach. "What do you need from me?"

"Your magic wants to corrupt me." I lift my hand, wondering if we can see it under the surface. "It wants to kill Cody."

His eyes light up. "Cody stands in the way of what you could be … what we could be."

"But, we can't be." I pull away from him and fold my arms over my chest, realizing for the first time that I'm wearing a t-shirt and flannel pants, my pajamas. "If I kill Cody, there'll be nothing left of me to save."

"You could be happy with me."

I watch the waves stroke the shore, a lover's caress. Mavros both as himself and as Damon do make me happy. I enjoy their company and friendship, but I love Cody, and without him, I wouldn't be myself. I turn back to Mavros. "I couldn't be happy without Cody, though."

Hurt flashes across his face. "I've done all I can. I forced my magic to lie dormant within you. I cannot remove it."

"Can't or won't?"

He slips his hands into his pockets and stares at his feet. "I thought you trusted me. I thought we were over this." He looks into my eyes and then down again. "Can't."

"I'm sorry." I rub my hand over my face. The sun here is blinding, especially when tears pool, refusing to fall. "You've saved me so many times." I pick up a seashell and turn it over, studying it. "I'm just so scared."

He steps forward and puts his hands on my shoulders. "I didn't know it would do this. I tried to save you."

"I know." I look into his eyes. The darkness has a depth to it that's unexpected. Staring into them is like looking up into the night sky and realizing the stars are trillions of miles away, not just dotting the surface. "I should've made you kill Argentum. I thought I would carry the guilt and shame for ordering you to do it, but now I carry so much more." The memory of my teeth tearing through Argentum's flesh and savoring his blood buckles my knees.

Mavros steadies me, waiting until he knows I'm okay to say, "He would've killed you." He slides his fingers down my arms, leaving a trail of goosebumps, and takes my hands in his. "Don't feel guilty for saving your own life." His touch centers me. "Never for that."

If Cody had never come into my life, I probably could find happiness with Mavros, and that thought scares me. What did it say about me that I thought a demon could make me happy?

"It means that you're good enough to see into my heart, see past what others think of me." He leans down and kisses my cheek, then backs away. "Cody will live a mortal life, but yours will go on." He drops my hands. "I can give you a life with him. I can wait."

I jerked awake. Malcolm's lips were pulled back in a snarl.

"You saw?" Heat crept over my cheeks. I didn't want anyone to know how I'd looked at Mavros when I'd first arrived on the beach.

He rolled off the bed and stood by the window, opening it a crack. "Yes."

"Do you believe him?" I shivered and pulled the covers up to my chin.

He flashed his fangs at me, and they seemed longer than normal. "He seemed to be telling the truth."

"So, what's wrong?"

He came back over and sat on the edge of my bed. "He still wants you, and I don't like it."

I sat up and switched my lamp on. Malcolm's pupils contracted to thin slits. "If he wants me, then won't he be more likely to help me?"

"Maybe." He grabbed my hand, dwarfing it with his. "But, you are ours."

"What do you mean?" My voice rose.

"We accepted you as one of our own." He cocked his head, and the beads in his cornrows clinked together. "Dragons and demons are enemies."

"But, I became one." I remembered my blue mottled skin, three heads, and sickle-like talons.

"No." The word was a growl. "You didn't *become* one. You *looked* like one."

"Then why did I have its bloodlust?" I regretted the words as soon as I said them.

Malcolm's features morphed. Scales lined his jaw.

"So, what if I made myself look like a dragon?" Maybe I shouldn't have asked it, but I didn't understand their mentality. Why was it okay for them to look human but not for me to look dragon?

His eyes widened, and his grip tightened on my hand. "Don't."

"Why?" I bit my lip. "I wanted to when I fought Draconian, but Aurelia said no. I thought it would be easier to kill him as a dragon. But now I know better."

"Promise me that you'll never do that." His fangs seemed to have lengthened again. He looked like he was ready to fight some unseen monster. "I vowed to protect you, but other dragons would kill you."

"Why can you become human, but I can't become a dragon?" I pulled my hand out from under his and shook it, trying to get the blood flowing through my fingers again.

He walked back over to the window and pulled it closed. "I don't know, Dacia." His voice was tinged with frustration. "Our instincts are hard to override, and they tell us it's wrong. Maybe it's some long ago protective measure or maybe it's just our arrogance."

"Okay." I lay back and turned off my lamp. "Can you keep me from dreaming? Don't let Mavros through this time. Maybe if I can sleep, I can figure out how to keep from killing Cody."

Chapter 13

Sleeping In

The sun streamed into my bedroom, too bright to continue sleeping through. I rolled over and looked at my alarm clock. 12:06. It had been a long time since I'd slept so late without some sort of life-threatening injury that I'd been healing from.

I stretched my legs out, and sand rubbed against them. Jerking the covers to the side, I looked at the grains still stuck between my toes and in my bed. I brushed them into my hand and threw them in the trashcan, wondering if my life would ever be normal again.

Grabbing my clothes, I walked down the hallway and into the bathroom. As soon as I shut the door, I realized I'd been alone. Neither of my guardians had been in my room. "And, I didn't even take advantage of it," I said to my reflection.

After getting dressed and combing my hair, I wandered into the kitchen. My parents sat at the table with Malcolm and Cash. The tension was thick. "Morning," I said.

Malcolm chuckled. "Afternoon." *I kept your dreams at bay as long as I could.* He held my gaze. *If I would've stayed in your room any longer, your parents would have figured out that you weren't alone.*

I dipped my head slightly. *Thanks.* "Yeah." I poured myself a glass of milk and added chocolate to it. "I guess I was tired."

"After that nightmare"—Dad looked at me, and I took a drink instead of meeting his eyes—"I'm surprised you were able to go back to sleep. You seemed pretty shook up."

"I have nightmares." I set my glass on the table and twirled it between my palms. "I've faced monsters and walked away." My voice caught, but I wanted to get it out. I wanted them to understand part of me. "But, it left me scarred. I'm working on putting all my broken pieces back together."

"Oh, Sweety." Mom reached across the table and grabbed my hand. "I wish your magic would've faded away. I wish I could take this torment from you."

Cash pushed his chair back and stood behind me, placing his hand on my shoulder. He drew my energy out. "Your daughter is one of the bravest people I've ever met. She'll get through this."

A car slowed on the road outside our house, then pulled into the driveway.

"Oh—" Mom looked at the clock on the microwave "—I forgot to tell you. Cody will be here at 12:30. I guess he's a little early."

My heart pounded against my ribs, fighting for freedom. I felt like I'd just run a marathon. I clutched the edge of the table and took deep breaths, trying to control my reactions. *Don't let me hurt him,* I thought to the dragons. *Do whatever you have to to keep me from it. I'll heal. He won't.*

I ran into the bathroom to brush my teeth while my parents let Cody in. My hand trembled, making way too much toothpaste shoot out of the tube.

"Please, excuse me." Malcolm's voice drifted to me. "I need to go to my room." A few seconds later, his door shut. Then he was standing by the sink with me. He knelt down and bowed his head. "I will do whatever I can to keep you from hurting him."

"Thank you, Malcolm." I placed my hand on his shoulder, needing his strength to settle me. "Like I told Mavros, if I hurt Cody, I won't ever get over it."

He stood up and held my hand loosely. "And, unlike the demon, I understand that." He rubbed his thumb along mine, calming me at the same time he siphoned my powers. By the time I finished brushing my teeth, I felt like every drop of magic had been drained from me.

Taking a deep breath, I reached for the doorknob, and Malcolm disappeared. He walked out of the spare bedroom at the same time I left the bathroom. We walked into the living room together. His hand was pressed to the small of my back.

Cody's eyes darted from my face to Malcolm's hand, and they tightened for half of a second before he put his mask in place.

"Hey, Cody." I tried to turn my lips into a smile. It was good to see him. I just couldn't get over my fears.

"You ready?" he held his hand out to me.

"Ready for what?" I cocked my head. "I just woke up. Mom let me know you were coming when you pulled into the driveway."

"Lunch." He dropped his hand, and I realized I hadn't moved toward him at all.

I walked over and grabbed my coat off the rack by the door. As I slid my arms into my sleeves, I sent up a silent prayer that I wouldn't hurt him. Then I stood on my tiptoes and kissed him softly. "Sure." I turned toward my parents and said, "I guess I'll see you later."

"Be careful." Dad's expression looked tortured. Maybe telling him that I was broken hadn't been the right thing to do.

Mom gave me a quick hug. "Have fun. Love you."

"Love you, too." I slipped my hand into Cody's, and we walked outside with the dragons following us.

"Rough night?" Cody asked as we walked to his parents' SUV.

I tugged my hand through my hair. "Yeah." I slid onto the passenger seat.

"Do you want us with you?" Malcolm stood with his hand on the door.

I looked at Cash wondering if he'd be able to handle being in such an enclosed space with my emotions going haywire. "If it's not too much for you. You wanna sit up front?"

"No." Malcolm squeezed my shoulder. "You need to talk to Cody."

On the drive to Diamond, I told Cody about my dream. He clenched the steering wheel tighter than normal and listened without interrupting. When I finished, he said, "If I live, sounds like Mavros'll let me be with you. That's good."

"You're going to live." I pulled my lip into my mouth and stared out the side window. Since I was six years old, I'd followed this road to town. There were small changes here and there, a new tree sprouting, a tree that had fallen, but for the most part, it hadn't changed. "Malcolm and Cash are going to keep you safe at whatever cost to me."

"No!" The word was like a gunshot through the car.

I knew he wouldn't agree to it, but it was the way it had to be. I had returned from Death's doorstep. Even if that wouldn't happen again, it wouldn't happen at all for Cody. "Sorry."

He looked in the mirror at the dragons. "Don't do it."

"If she kills you, it will destroy her." Cash tilted his head toward his shoulder and lifted his hands. "We can't let that happen."

Malcolm nodded. "Sorry, Cody."

"No." This time the word was a broken plea.

"We vowed to protect her." Cash spoke through clenched teeth. The emotions must have been getting too thick. "So, whatever we do to stop her won't be too bad."

There were plenty of parking spaces at Diamond in the Rough, but Cody parked as far away as he could. He got out and walked over to my door. Opening it for me, he held out his hand. "Let me know if you need me to let go."

"I will." I slid my hand into his, and we sauntered to the doors. "You okay?"

He kicked at a clump of snow that had fallen off somebody's fender. "Worried."

"I'll do everything I can to keep from hurting you."

His eyebrows pinched together, and he jerked his head back. "Not for me." He stopped walking and turned toward me. "You, Dacia. I'm worried 'bout you." He lifted his hand toward my face but stopped before touching me. I nodded. His fingers trailed along my cheek. "It's tearing you up."

My eyes fluttered shut. "I need to figure out how to get this darkness out of me, but nobody seems to know how to help."

I stepped closer to him and bowed my head until it just touched his chest. He wrapped his arms around my waist. "I love you, Cody." My magic thrummed inside of me. I backed away from him and let go. "I'm trying."

Cash grabbed my hand and tugged on my magic. "Shall we go in?"

Cody led the way. His shoulders were hunched. Puffs of snow drifted through the air with each shuffling step he took.

One dragon walked on either side of me. Malcolm massaged my neck, keeping my powers to a minimum.

Fat snowflakes floated lazily from the gray sky. They caught in my curls and clung to my eyelashes. I reached up and brushed them away.

Cody stood at the door, holding it open. I walked in, and Cindy greeted us with a wide smile on her face. "Dacia, I didn't know you were home." She strode over and kissed my cheek. "Four of you?"

I nodded. "We just got back yesterday." We needed to watch what we said. I didn't want my parents to worry about me any more than they already did. "How's Bill?"

"Oh, you know." She waved her hand, and I noticed her fingernails were red with Christmas trees accenting a couple of them. "He's home watching football or hockey or basketball." She took us to our table.

Malcolm and Cash sat next to me, making me sit across from Cody. He grabbed the menu and stared down at it.

"I know Cody." She waved her sparkly pen at him. "But who are your other friends?"

"Cash and Malcolm." I pointed at each of them when I said their names. "This is my aunt, Cindy." They nodded, then before she could ask anything else, I ordered my drink.

She came back a few minutes later with our drinks and to take our orders. As soon as she left, Cody picked up his straw. Normally, he would've shot the wrapper at me, but he pulled it off, crumpled it up, and threw it on the table. "So … no touching? What else?"

My heart sank faster than a boulder dropped into a lake. He was right. Every time I touched him, the powers inside me—mine or Mavros'—ignited. He was the tinder to my spark. "I don't know."

When Cindy came back with our food, my hand was on the table, and Malcolm was holding it. She looked from our hands to Cody. "Shouldn't he be holding that?"

I slid my hand out from under Malcolm's and slipped it onto my lap.

Cody smiled at Cindy. "Dacia is worried about one of her finals. Malcolm was just reassuring her."

She looked skeptical, but the expression on Cody's face was convincing. "I'm glad you have such good friends." She set our food down.

"Yeah." I scooted my plate in front of me. "I've been blessed with my friends. I've met some really good people."

The bell over the door tinkled, and she looked toward it. "Well, enjoy. I'll be back in a bit to check on you." She strode off to help the new customers.

As soon as she left, Cody's mien darkened. He glanced at Malcolm, and his mouth tightened into a thin line.

Malcolm's eyes narrowed at Cody's challenge. "Don't." The word was growled. "You know why I was holding her hand. Don't make more out of it."

Cody glared at him for a few tense seconds. Then he plopped his elbows on the table and clutched the hair at his temples, staring down at his plate. His breathing evened out, and he looked at Malcolm. "Sorry."

On the drive back to my house, I sat next to Cody and held his hand over the gearshift. Malcolm was behind me. His arm was draped over my seat, and his fingers lingered on the bare skin of my neck. My magic flowed from me into Malcolm. It flared every time Cody rubbed his thumb along my hand, but Malcolm kept it from igniting.

When Cody pulled into my driveway, he clutched my hand tighter. "Call when you're ready to see me."

A painful lump formed in my throat. "You … you can come in. Play games. Talk. Be with me." The desperation in my voice was embarrassing.

Cash opened his door and stepped outside.

"You want that?" Cody glanced at me. His eyes widened in surprise, his jaw not so tense.

"Oh, Cody." I tugged my hand through my hair. "I want any time I can get with you. I just don't want to hurt you."

He leaned over and kissed my cheek. "I gotta hang with my brothers today. I promised."

"Call me later. Okay?" I felt like everything was slipping through my fingers. I needed Cody, but I couldn't keep him if he wanted to go.

The powers inside me stirred. I reached for the door, fumbling for the handle, needing out before I wounded more than Cody's pride. "I love you." I practically fell out of the car. "Always, Cody."

He nodded. His expression was somber. "Love you, too." He stared out the window. "But is it enough?"

"I hope so."

Chapter 14

$\mathcal{M}$y parents sat in the living room, waiting for me to get back. The relief that flashed across their faces surprised me. If they were this worried about me going to lunch in Bittersweet, how did they feel every day when I was three hours away at Phlox University? I needed to make a point to call them more often. I needed to put being a better daughter on the top of my priority list.

I spent the day with them and my guards. We baked and frosted Christmas cookies. Mom and Dad were leery of Cash and Malcolm at first, but as we worked together, they realized the dragons weren't a threat to them.

Mom handed the bowl to Cash and told him to stir the first batch of cookies while she started measuring out the second one. As soon as Cash was done, she had Malcolm roll the dough out. At first, he had trouble holding back his strength to keep them from getting too thin, but once he figured that out, they were all perfect.

Several times throughout the day, either Cash or Malcolm drew my magic into themselves while Mom and Dad watched. Their faces pinched with worry. Finally, Dad asked, "Why do you do that to her?"

Cash looked at me, not sure how to answer. I closed my eyes and thought about it, not wanting to lie to them but not wanting to worry them more either. "A darkness is mingling with my magic. Until we figure out how to remove it, they don't want me to use my powers very often. If they don't draw them out, I use them whether I want to or not. It's kind of like they—" I stared at the ceiling like I'd find the words written there "—spill over."

"Darkness?" Mom looked from me to the dragons. "Where'd it come from?"

I put the frosting tube down. "Do you *really* want to know?" Mom nodded, but I held my hand up. "No, really think about it before you answer. Once you know, you can't go back." I felt something tug on my heart. Regret that I'd found out about Argentum weighed down on me.

Cash walked out the sliding glass door onto the deck, and Malcolm grabbed my hand. "You're okay, Dacia. There's no threat."

"Is he okay?" Dad pointed at Cash.

"Yeah." I leaned back and closed my eyes. "My emotions are overwhelming to them." I focused on the mountain lake that I'd used to calm myself when Sarah had first started training me.

After a few minutes, Dad said, "I'd like to know what you're going through." His voice was gruff.

"I would, too." Mom sat across from me.

Without looking at them, I told them about Argentum. I explained how he thought my magic was too much for a human, how he was afraid I would become corrupted and mad like Draconian.

I stared into the backyard without really seeing anything. "Argentum thought that if he ate me while I was alive, it would heal him and keep him strong for a thousand years or more."

Mom gasped, and Dad wrapped his arm around her.

"I didn't want to kill him, but he wouldn't back down." My voice was monotone, no inflections at all. I tried not to think about what I was telling them. "I couldn't do it on my own, so I asked somebody to join their powers with mine. Because of, uh, the type of creature he is, his magic didn't mix well with mine." For some reason, I couldn't bring myself to tell them Mavros' name, or that he was a demon, or what he'd put me through when he'd wanted to bind me to him. I didn't want them to think of him as a monster or to know the way he could make me feel. "His magic sullied my powers. That's why my irises have black speckles in them now. It's from the corruption."

Mom stared into my eyes. "I knew they looked different, but I kept telling myself they couldn't. After all, how could somebody's eyes just change colors like that?"

I glanced around the room. The table and cabinets were covered in cookies. "So, what are we doing with all these?" I didn't want to talk about myself and my problems anymore. "Do we need to box them up?"

Mom stood and patted my hand. "They're for the program at church tonight. Do you want to come with us?" She grabbed several plastic containers out of the cabinet. "I love watching the little kids in the Nativity."

"I'd like to, but I … can't." There seemed to be a giant hollow opening in my chest. "I can't be around that many people. I can't let something happen."

Cash put his hands on my shoulders. He'd slipped back in while I was telling my parents about my powers being corrupted. "If you want to go, we will keep your powers tamped down."

"Some of Cody's siblings will be in the play." Dad put a handful of Santa cookies into a tub.

I looked from Cash to Malcolm. "Are you sure?"

Malcolm nodded. *You only seem to be a danger to Cody.* Malcolm's words tore a chunk from my heart. *And, it never hurts to ask God for help.*

"I guess we'll go." I helped scoop cookies into plastic containers. Then I headed to my room with Cash and Malcolm. "So … dragons believe in God."

Malcolm shrugged. "Like people. Some do. Some don't."

"Is your God a dragon?" I opened my bedroom door and went to my closet to pull out clothes that weren't covered in flour and whatever else I got on myself making cookies.

Cash sat on the edge of my bed. "Our God, your God. It doesn't matter. God is God." He stared out the window. It was only 4:30, but it was as dark as midnight. "God couldn't show himself to everybody the same way if He wanted everyone to believe, so no matter what face He wears, He's still God."

I tilted my head to the side and looked at him. "That's an interesting way to think about it."

I sat between Malcolm and Cash. They each held onto one of my hands, keeping my magic drained to the dregs. Every time the door opened, I looked over my shoulder hoping it would be Cody.

When he finally showed up, I sucked in a breath. He took his trench coat off and folded it over his arm. He was wearing a black suit with a bright blue shirt that I imagined made his eyes shine like sapphires. His thin black tie was perfectly knotted. He held Britny's hand, and she smiled up at him like he was the best brother in the world.

"Dacia." Cash tugged on my hand. "Your mom is talking to you."

Heat crept up my neck and onto my face. "Sorry, Mom." I pointed behind me. "Cody's here."

"Oh, well, we can make room for him." She grabbed her purse and started to scoot down.

"That's okay." I shook my head. "He probably wants to sit with his family."

She stopped moving. "Just let me know."

"What were you saying?" I wanted to look over my shoulder and watch him walk in, but I kept my attention focused on Mom.

For a second, she looked confused. "Your dad and I have to work this week. We'd appreciate it if you could help out with some of the chores so we don't have a ton to do on Christmas Eve before everyone comes over."

"Oh, yeah, that's no problem. I figured I would."

Dad leaned back, looking at me from behind Mom. "What else do you have going on?"

"I don't know." The dragons and I planned to try to figure out how to get rid of Mavros' powers, but I didn't know how well that would work and didn't think I should bring it up.

Even with Cash and Malcolm pulling on my magic, I felt Cody walk closer. I felt him stop at the end of the pew. "Hey, Dacia, didn't expect to see you."

I turned and appraised him. The blue of his eyes was stunning, but they had a tormented look in them. "Yeah, Mom and Dad wanted me to come. Do you want to sit with us?" I smiled and waved at Britny.

Hiding behind Cody's legs, she peaked at the dragons. Her face lit up, making her eyes sparkle, and she tugged on Cody's pants. "Are they fairies?" she whispered, but like with most kids, it was louder than if she'd said it in her regular voice.

He shook his head. "No. That's Malcolm and Cash. From school. They're friends."

"Can't fairies be friends?" Her face looked so innocent, and her voice could probably be heard throughout the church.

The smile on Cody's face melted my heart. "Suppose so."

She lifted her hand toward Cash but quickly pulled it back. "Can we sit here?"

"You're in the play, goofball." Cody chuckled. "They'll be here for a few weeks. We'll see them again." He smiled at us and led her to the front of the church.

"He has purple eyes," Britny whispered excitedly as they walked away.

"Pretty cool, huh." He said more to her, but his voice blended in with all the others in the church.

With each step he took away from me, I felt the rift between us growing. Somehow, I had to get rid of the darkness within me. I had to set things straight before I lost Cody.

Cash growled.

I felt it rumble through my body. "Sorry," I whispered. "Can you take the edge off?"

Relief zipped across his face, and he nodded.

The effects were instantaneous. I pulled my hands away from the dragons and folded them together. *Lord, please help me figure out how to get rid of the demon taint in me so that I don't cause any harm to anyone. Please forgive me for the deaths I caused. Please help me be the best version of myself that I can be. Let me do something good with the powers you gave me and keep me from being used as a tool of destruction. Please guide me down the path I need to be on. Amen.*

Piano music filled the sanctuary, and the overhead lights dimmed until just Christmas lights twinkled. Two acolytes walked down the aisle, and when they finished, flames danced on several wicks. I couldn't focus on the program. Instead, I stared at the back of Cody's head.

Dacia. Malcolm's voice was a warning.

My power was flaring. I looked at the candles flickering on the altar and quickly realized that was a mistake. The flames turned blue.

I closed my eyes. *Help me.* The thought went out to God and to the dragons. I didn't know who did it, but my magic drained. I spent the rest of the performance watching my hands. I saw my powers flicker and writhe as they were siphoned into Cash and Malcolm.

When it was over, there was supposed to be fellowship time, but I needed to get out before something bad happened. I hugged Mom and Dad. "I have to go."

Dad reached into his pocket. "I'll give you a ride and come back for Mom."

"No." I shook my head. "I don't need a ride."

"Oh." His eyes widened. "Okay. Well, be careful."

Squeezing between groups of people standing and talking, I walked outside with Cash and Malcolm. The cold air hit me like a slap in the face. I pulled my coat tighter and wished I'd worn pants instead of a dress.

The door was nearly closed when I heard Cody. "Dacia."

I turned to look at him.

He strode down the stairs toward me. He didn't have his trench coat on, but he had his suit jacket. "Not staying?"

"I can't." I shook my head. "I'd like to … for Mom and Dad. For you. But I can't let anybody get hurt. Especially, not if I can help it."

He reached for me but let his hand fall back to his side. "You look beautiful."

"Thanks." A slight smile tugged at my lips, and a rush of heat warmed me. "I couldn't take my eyes off you when you walked in."

"Saw the flames turn blue."

Malcolm grabbed one hand, and Cash took the other.

"That's why I need to leave."

He stepped closer to me. "Can I kiss you? Real quick?"

Malcolm nodded at me. "If you don't let go of us."

I wasn't sure what Cody would think of that, but he wrapped one hand around my waist and held onto the back of my head with his other one. Then he pressed his lips to mine. Some of my shattered pieces seemed to fuse back together. He pulled away before I was ready, but I couldn't blame him.

"See you tomorrow?" His expression was guarded.

"I hope so." I pulled my bottom lip into my mouth and looked down. "We're going to try to get rid of it. You can't be there when I do that."

"After." He brushed his knuckles along my cheek and turned back toward the church.

Chapter 15

I woke up screaming. Cody's burning body was an image I'd never be able to erase from my mind. I would have preferred to go back to the dreams where I woke up injured than keep having ones of Cody dying. At least I could heal.

Malcolm lay on the bed beside me. "I'm sorry, Dacia. I thought I was keeping you from seeing it." He rubbed his forehead. "They're getting stronger."

"I can't let that happen." I sat up and clutched my head, trying to stop the nightmare from replaying over and over again. "How do I stop it?" My voice rose to near hysterics.

Malcolm opened his arms, and I slid into them. "We're going to figure this out." He ran his hand over my hair and down my back, holding me. Even when my tears soaked through his shirt, he didn't let go.

When I quit hearing Cody screaming as my flames devoured him, I pulled away from Malcolm and wiped my eyes. "I'm sorry."

"Did I do it right?" He looked genuinely concerned.

I stared at him confused by his question and reaction.

He sat up with his feet on the floor and held his head. "I'm a dragon. I know how to fight and guard my treasure. I know how to intimidate, but I don't know how to deal with emotions."

"Oh." I put my hand on his back. "No. You were great. That was just what I needed. Thank you. I don't have anyone else to go to. I'm sorry if I made you uncomfortable." I grabbed a tissue off my nightstand and wiped my eyes before blowing my nose.

"I'll try to do better if you want to go back to sleep." He lay on his back on top of my covers. Somehow, his shirt had miraculously dried. "I know this is hard for you and that you'd rather be with Cody, but if I touch you, it's easier to keep your dreams away."

I lay down with my head on his chest, and he wrapped his arm around me. It was comfortable, not intimate. Cody probably wouldn't see it that way, but I couldn't keep dreaming about him dying, and if I was going to get the darkness out of me, I needed to get some sleep.

Mom and Dad left for work before I got out of bed. I heard them in the kitchen, but I didn't want to have to lie to them when they asked about my dreams. I'd told them about Mavros' power inside of me, but I hadn't told them that it wanted me to kill Cody.

"So"—I rolled away from Malcolm and sat on the edge of my bed with my back to him—"I was thinking that if I used dragon power combined with mine, maybe we could destroy it."

"That might work." The bed shifted when he stood. His voice was rough. "I need to leave for a while."

I looked over my shoulder at him. His fists were clenched at his sides. The muscles in his arms bulged. His body was tense.

"I'm sorry." I dropped my head to my chest. "Were they bad?"

"Yes." He opened my window and breathed in the crisp, cool air. "I need to hunt because right now … you smell like prey."

Cash leaned against the wall next to a picture of Jonathan. I'd expected him to come barging in as soon as Malcolm left, so they were either starting to trust me or he'd been watching me. Since I really didn't want to know the answer, I didn't ask.

"I broke Malcolm," I said as a greeting.

"I'm aware." He nodded. "I could smell you in my room."

Heat flooded onto my face, and Cash breathed in like he was smelling a juicy T-bone steak cooking on the grill. His eyes fluttered shut, and he rolled his neck. "Yeah. That's why Malcolm's hunting." He tugged on my arm, dragging me toward the door. "Let's go for a run."

I jerked away from him. "Not 'til I brush my teeth and go pee."

"You have five minutes." He nodded toward the bathroom. "Or you won't have any guards."

He was serious. I could tell by the tightness in his shoulders that he was struggling to hold himself back.

I bowed my head and shuffled away.

As soon as I finished, Cash led me outside. The sky was a brilliant blue, and frost coated the tree branches. The cold air stung my cheeks. I sucked in a deep breath, and if I hadn't known better, I'd have thought Cody was standing right next to me. The air smelled just like him. I rubbed my hands together before doing a few stretches. Then I started down my driveway in a slow jog. Cash ran right beside me. Our footsteps were soundless.

The Nephilim are here. He nodded toward the trees across the street from my house. *You need to be careful still. Don't talk freely about Mavros being bound to you.*

Unintentionally, I picked up the pace. The dragons, the fairies, Arion, and even some of the Nephilim had vouched for me. I didn't understand why they couldn't just leave me alone.

"Anger is good." Cash smiled at me. "It keeps you from smelling like prey."

"Yeah." I shook my head at him. "You told me that before, but the fairies told me not to use my powers in hatred or wrath, so anger is also bad."

His left foot hit the road at the exact moment mine did. Snow poofed up as we turned toward town. "Yes, but right now, you're not using your powers, and you were really wearing down my willpower."

My heartbeat picked up more than what was necessary. "So, if you'd tasted my blood like Malcolm has, what would that do to you?"

He looked at me, and his pupils dilated before quickly contracting again. "Let's hope we never find out."

"How does he resist then?"

"I hate to admit it, but he's stronger than me." He sped up, and I followed. "We need to change the subject."

"Sorry." At the new pace he set, there was no way I could talk and run anyway.

By the time we returned to my house, I was drenched with sweat, and Malcolm was back. I walked to the cabinet and pulled down three glasses. "Drink?"

"Yes, please." Cash pulled out a chair at the table and sat.

Malcolm shook his head. "I'm good."

"Drink the blood of your kills?" Cash asked like it was a perfectly normal question.

My stomach heaved, and Malcolm chuckled. "Keep it up, and I'll have to go out again."

I filled two glasses with water, handed one to Cash, and stood at the cabinet to drink mine. "Why do you guys do this? And, don't say because you made a vow. I'm a mess. You can't handle my emotions. The Nephilim are never going to go away. *He* won't go away. You'll never be free. So why?"

Cash fell back against his chair and covered his face with both hands.

Malcolm flashed his fangs at me, showing me that they were longer than normal. "You saved us. Nobody else would have. If we hadn't made our vow, that would've been reason enough." He pointed toward the hall. "Now, go bathe. That will help somewhat."

When I finished showering, I walked into the living room to find six dragons waiting for me. Russ, Arianna, Val, and Aurelia had joined Cash and Malcolm. Aurelia smiled at me. "Malcolm called us here. He said you would like to draw on our power to destroy Mavros'."

"Yeah." I chewed on my lip. "I just meant theirs." I pointed at the two dragons who had been staying with me.

Malcolm nodded. "I thought it was a good idea, but I think it has a better chance of success if you use all of us to amplify your magic."

"Okay, but I don't think we should do it in here." I looked around the room. My parents had had a lot of the stuff in here since our other house burned down, and I didn't want them to lose all of this, too.

Arianna nodded. "That's probably a wise decision."

My hair was still wet, so I braided it quickly and pulled a stocking cap over it. While I was putting my snow boots on, Val came over and nuzzled my shoulder. "You smell good."

"Yeah. Apparently, I'm over-emotional and smell good enough to eat."

He jerked his head back. "Who'd want to eat you?"

A humorless laugh escaped me. "If I had to guess, every dragon in the world but you." I rubbed his head, then stood up. "If we go outside, how will we keep the Nephilim from knowing what we're doing, or does it matter?"

"We will surround you." Aurelia stepped forward and put her hand on my shoulder. "They will not know what you are doing. They will only know you are using your magic combined with ours. Before you do it, though, I would like to see if you can show us the manifestation of your powers. Let us discern if there is a better way to extinguish Mavros' taint from within you."

I reached up to pull my hand through my hair and was stopped when my fingers met the hat. "Will he know? Will he try to stop me? If it's what binds him to me, will he allow me to kill it?"

"Only one way to find out," Cash said.

Chapter 16

Malcolm slid his hand into mine, and soothing energy flowed through me. "We contemplated those questions and have no way to know the answers." Fear crept into his eyes. He blinked, and it was gone. "It is a part of him, so he will probably know, but we feel it is worth the risk."

Closing my eyes, I nodded. I was glad for Malcolm's support because even though I'd suspected that would be the answer, it hit me harder than I thought it would. Mavros was a demon. He'd bound himself to me, but he'd helped me, he'd held back enough on his powers to keep from killing me, and I liked him. If I destroyed the part of him that was inside me and unbound him, there was a chance we'd be enemies if we ever met again, and I didn't want that.

"Okay." I clapped my hands together, trying to sound motivated. "It's cold outside, but hopefully this won't take too long."

Aurelia clasped my shoulder. "I want to see your magic first."

"Right." I closed my eyes and concentrated on my powers, hoping the dragons could see what I saw. For some reason, I always pictured a dark room, black walls, floor, and ceiling. Light shone on us from somewhere inexplicable, only spilling wherever I was looking at the moment.

Right now, it lit up the pearlescent serpent. It looked at me, narrowed its eyes, and buried its head in its coils. I strode across the onyx floor and reached down to it.

The serpent raised up and drew its head back as if readying itself to strike. Then it hissed at me.

I jerked my hand back. "What's wrong?"

You have forgotten me.

"No, I miss you—" I pointed at the midnight serpent coiled up a few feet away "—but as long as part of Mavros is here, I can't trust myself."

It does nothing but sleep.

I stared at the ebon snake, wondering if it had really been dormant all along. "Then why do I keep dreaming about killing Cody? Why can't I be around him?"

My powers stretched up, staring into my eyes with its black-flecked copper ones. *We would be stronger without him.*

I staggered back. "So, you're doing it?"

I am you. You know we could be more. We could be omnipotent.

"But—" my legs trembled, and I fell to the floor on my hands and knees "—I love him." I stared at my hand, remembering seeing the serpent's shadow under my skin. It was dark and foreboding. "I saw it."

You saw what you wanted. You saw something you could blame, and you leapt at the chance.

That couldn't be what had happened. I sat with my knees pulled up to my chest and rocked back. I didn't want unlimited power. I just wanted a normal life. I wanted a life with Cody.

The serpent slithered over. I lowered my legs so I could get up if I needed to. It glided onto my calves, inching closer to me. *We are one.*

"We are, but I don't want to hurt Cody." I slid my hand along the snake's smooth skin.

Your fear drives us. It nuzzled against my hand, and shadows spilled out from under its scales, dispersing when the light touched them.

My eyes widened, but I tried to hold my composure and not let it know what I'd seen. "The dragons are helping me figure this out so I can use you without hurting anyone."

We do not need them. It tightened its coils around my leg, cutting off the blood flow. *Free me.*

"I can't." My pulse quickened. "I can't hurt Cody. I'd never forgive myself."

The snake released me and slithered away. *Do not forget me.*

"Never."

I opened my eyes to the real world. The dragons all stood around me in my living room. Christmas lights twinkled against the ceiling. "Did you see?"

Malcolm lowered his head. "Yes."

"The corruption is within your powers again." Aurelia glanced at each of the others. "It appears that Mavros did make his powers lie dormant, but somehow they are still contaminating yours."

"So … even if I destroy his, I'll still try to kill Cody." I slumped down onto the couch. "Won't I?"

Val sat on the floor next to me, leaning his temple against the arm of the couch. I absentmindedly rubbed his head. His blue hair was thick and as soft as a chinchilla's fur.

"I think it'll still be worth a shot." Russ smiled at me. I knew him less than any of the others because he'd always guarded my friends instead of me, but he'd been the first of Draconian's dragons to show me I could trust him.

"What about the rest of you?"

They all agreed that I should try. It would leave me with one less thing to worry about.

"Okay." I played with the hair at the end of my braid. It was coarse and tangled, nothing like Val's. "Where to then?"

"Your backyard will do just fine." Arianna waved her hand toward the sliding glass door.

I pulled on my coat and gloves, and we filed through. The sun was bright and high in the sky. It reflected off the snow, and I wished I would have thought about grabbing my sunglasses on the way out.

We walked past the koi pond to an open area in the yard, and the dragons gathered around. Each of them placed one of their hands on me.

"Concentrate on your powers," Aurelia said. "We will do the rest."

I closed my eyes and focused on my magic. My serpent was coiled on the floor next to Mavros'. Its pearlescent scales reflected the light, making prisms dance over the ebony snake. I sat down beside them and put my hand on Mavros' power.

I felt Mavros' strength rippling inside the sleeping snake. I pressed my eyes closed, and the smell of warm summer evenings filled my nostrils.

Power shot through me and into the serpent. The beast stared up at me. Pain and betrayal flashed through its obsidian eyes.

My powers lashed out at me, striking the hand I'd placed on Mavros' snake. "Please," I said through clenched teeth, biting back the pain. "It's the only way I can use you. I can't trust myself with him here."

The serpent's fangs retracted, and blood pooled on my skin.

He makes us stronger.

"No." I shook my head. "We are stronger without him. We are stronger when I can use you without fear."

My powers backed down but were still aggravated. The snake curled up but kept slithering. Its coils moved in and out, making it appear like there was more than one serpent.

"Dacia!" Mavros' voice was so loud that I stumbled forward.

My eyes snapped open.

Mavros stood outside the ring of dragons. His eyes were hard. "Why?"

"It's corrupting me." I dropped my chin to my chest.

"No." He strode closer to me. His footsteps crunched across the snow. "My power was dormant."

The dragons stepped closer to me, keeping Mavros away.

"Now, my power feels angry and betrayed." He glared at me over Val's shoulder. "And so do I."

I pressed my palms together and slid my hands between Val and Russ, prying them apart. Then I slipped through and stood toe to toe with Mavros. "I didn't want to hurt you." I reached for his hand, but he jerked it away from me. "I'm falling apart." I wrapped my arms around my waist, trying to hold myself together. My words were faint, but I knew everybody out here would be able to hear them. "I don't know what's going on. Every time I'm around Cody, my power lashes out at him." I sank to the ground in front of Mavros. "There's a darkness in my magic that was never there before, and I don't know how to fix it."

Mavros knelt down and tilted my face up. The anger fled from his eyes. "You cannot destroy my power." He brushed the tears off my cheeks, collecting them on his fingers. Then he licked them off.

Several of the dragons growled, but he just smirked at them. "No part of me can be destroyed outside of the Abyss, Dacia. When I said I couldn't get rid of it, I meant it." He slid his arms around me and lifted me as easily as I would pick up a ragdoll.

I leaned into him. "I can't hurt Cody. I can't—" my words caught in my throat "—I can't live with myself if I do."

"I see that." He carried me to the house. "May I enter?"

"No." Malcolm was suddenly standing in front of us, blocking the sliding glass door.

I looked between the two of them, wondering which of them I should anger. Mavros had proven himself to me over and over again, but I had no idea what I'd do without the dragons on my side.

Mavros saved me from deciding. He pressed me against Malcolm, forcing him to take me off his hands.

Malcolm's muscles were taut. He didn't hold me with the same ease Mavros had. He was ready for a battle.

"Put me down." I pushed against him, and he set me on my feet but didn't let go of me.

Mavros stretched his hand out, and Malcolm growled.

"I am not going to hurt her, *Dragon*." He stepped closer but didn't touch me. "As much as I would like the boy out of your life"—I flinched at those words, but he kept talking—"I know what he means to you, and I can see that it would destroy you to hurt him." He lifted my hand and pulled my glove off. "My power is not the problem."

"Then what is?"

He clutched my hand in both of his. The snakes writhed against my skin. He gently pressed his lips against my palm, and the obsidian serpent stopped moving. "I don't know." He let go of me and stepped back. "My power is once again dormant. Do not wake it. Do not anger it."

"Thank you." I put my glove back on. "I'm sorry if I hurt you."

He huffed out a startled laugh and brushed the back of his hand against my cheek. "Not for the first time, you're apologizing to a demon." He shook his head. "I don't see how you could be corrupted." He started to walk away but stopped and looked at me over his shoulder. "I'm sure they'll disagree"—he waved his arm at the dragons—"but maybe the taint comes from Argentum's blood."

Chapter 17

From The Grave

"Could that be it?" I stood at the stove, warming milk in a saucepan. "Could his blood do that to me?" I swayed a little at the remembered taste of it, the power that had flowed into me, the desire to drink every drop.

The dragons sat at the kitchen table, not hearing a word of what I'd said. They seemed to be having a conversation without me.

I folded my arms over my chest and tapped my foot against the tiled floor. When the dragons still didn't pay any attention to me, I poured the milk into a cup and mixed in chocolate and marshmallows. Then, warming my hands on the mug, I went to my room to change out of my wet clothes.

Instead, I sat on my bed and stared at my phone. The urge to call Cody and tell him everything that had happened this morning was overwhelming, but if I did, he would want to come over, and I couldn't keep him safe. I took a sip of my cocoa, then set it on my nightstand. I got up and stood in front of my closet. Staring into it, the clothes all blurred into swirling colors.

There were six dragons in my house. If Cody came over, they could keep him safe. They could drain every drop of power from my veins. I picked up the phone and dialed his number without even thinking about it.

He answered on the first ring. "You okay?"

As soon as I heard his voice a sob tore free from my throat.

"Mom," Cody yelled, "taking the truck." She must have replied because he hollered back, "Dacia's."

"You don't need to come." My voice sounded hollow, and I knew he wouldn't stay away. When I'd picked up the phone, I'd planned on talking to him, not breaking down.

His door shut. "Need to or not, I am." The car started, and he said, "See you in a few."

I hung up and stared at the phone, hoping nothing bad would happen. A shiver ran through my body, and I remembered my jeans were soaked. I peeled them and my socks off and slipped on fleece-lined leggings. Then I sat on my bed and covered up with the afghan Gramma had made me for Christmas the year our house had burned down. It was crocheted in shades of pink and was worn from years of abuse.

A soft knock sounded on my door. I hadn't heard any vehicles, so I knew it wasn't Cody. I looked up and considered ignoring it like the dragons had ignored me. "Come in," I said with a sigh.

Aurelia stepped inside. "I contacted the elders. They believe Argentum's blood could corrupt your powers." She sat next to me. "His magic could react to yours that way because of his fear and hatred of you, because he was ancient and powerful."

"Do they have any ideas?" I didn't want to hope, but hope blossomed inside my chest anyway.

She held onto my hand, draining my power. Blue and gold flames danced over her skin. "They are discussing whether or not they will meet with you."

I jerked my head back. "Why wouldn't they?"

"They should." Her pupils turned to slits, and smoke rolled out of her nose. "But their fear seems to override their common sense."

I dropped my chin to my chest and rubbed my forehead. "Yeah, well, my common sense was overridden." I looked up at her, hoping she could see the desperation on my face. "Cody's on his way over. Can you keep him safe?"

"Of course, Dacia." She grabbed my hands and siphoned off as much of my power as she could before we heard Cody pull up. "It will be okay."

When I opened the door, Cody stared at all the dragons scattered about my living room. "Can't be good." He smiled half-heartedly at everyone and stepped past me, careful not to touch me. He knelt down and unlaced his snow boots. "You okay?"

"Yeah." I felt awkward having this conversation in front of everyone. The tension between Cody and I had become so thick lately, and I hated that my guardians witnessed it. It shouldn't have mattered. There was no hiding anything from them anyway. "I'm sorry I worried you."

He stood up and reached for me, stopping before he touched me. I nodded, and he brushed back a strand of my hair that had come loose from my braid. "Don't be sorry. Just talk to me."

I led him to the couch, and everyone but Aurelia and Malcolm left the room. Aurelia sat next to me, holding my hand, and Malcolm sat on the loveseat, leaning forward with his elbows on his knees. He watched me like a hawk, ready in case I needed him.

With Cody's arm draped over my shoulders, I told him how we'd tried to destroy Mavros' power and failed.

His muscles tightened in response to Mavros telling me it couldn't be destroyed. "Suppose you believe him."

My heart plunged into my stomach, making me feel a little dizzy and disoriented. "I do."

"He seemed to be telling the truth." Aurelia squeezed my hand, and my magic fled from me.

"The demon believes it could be Argentum's blood." Malcolm's voice was gruff, his eyes hard.

Cody relaxed slightly. "So, how's she get rid of it?"

"We're working on that," I said, hoping Malcolm and Aurelia would leave it at that. I didn't want Cody to know the elders didn't know if they'd help me.

"You eaten?" Cody looked from me to the dragons.

Malcolm nodded. "I have."

"Apparently, I smelled like prey this morning."

Cody visibly swallowed, and Malcolm breathed in deeply savoring the smell of his fear.

"I don't think anyone else has." I glared at Malcolm, and he flashed his fangs at me. "What'd you have in mind?"

He got up and held his hand out to me. I slid mine into it with a silent prayer that it would be okay, and Cody led me into the kitchen. He pulled a chair out for me, and after I sat, he went to the fridge and looked inside. He pulled out hamburger, lettuce, cheese, and tortilla shells. "Tacos?"

"Sure." I pushed my chair back. "I'll help."

"No." He bent down and grabbed a skillet. "Just sit." He pulled the sleeves of his gray hoodie up. "Tell me something good that's happening."

I watched him wash his hands and move around my kitchen. He was everything I'd ever wanted, so why did my magic react to him like it had been lately? "Something good." I drummed my fingers on the table. "Mom and Dad don't seem to be afraid of me or the dragons anymore."

"What else?" He started cooking the hamburger and grabbed a cutting board.

It wasn't like my life was horrible, but I'd been so focused on all the negativity lately that I forgot to look for the good things. "I woke up this morning. You're here." I traced the grain pattern on the table. "You're cooking, and I'm not."

Malcolm stood in the doorway watching us. I was sure there were probably other dragons closer to me just in case something went wrong, but it was nice to have this semblance of privacy.

Cody laughed, and the sound filled me with happiness. Magic rushed through me, but it didn't try to escape.

Malcolm pulled out a chair at the table and sat next to me, but he didn't reach for my hand. *Just in case.*

I nodded. "What about you, Cody? Something good."

He set the knife down on the cutting board and turned around, leaning back against the counter. "I'm here with you … cooking for you. You have people helping you. Been spending time with family. Mavros doesn't wanna kill me anymore." He turned back around and stirred the meat. "My future wife is *rich.*"

Malcolm tilted his head to the side but didn't say anything.

"I am." I smiled at him even though he couldn't see it. "I guess I should have mentioned being grateful to Aurelia for giving me some of Draconian's treasure."

Malcolm closed his eyes and nodded. *We all should have thought of that.*

She figured I might have a hard time holding down a job if I'm always busy fighting monsters.

Cody added taco seasoning and water to the meat. "What else?"

"You, Cody." I stared down at my hands. "You're the good thing in my life. The thing that helps me hold it all together when everything else is going to Hell."

He turned the meat down and sat next to me. "Tacos are done." He clasped my hand, and Malcolm reached for my other one. I shook my head and pulled it away. "Don't forget the good stuff."

I leaned my head against his shoulder. "Thanks, Cody. I needed that. It seems to have helped settle my powers."

He sighed and kissed my forehead. Then he got up and set plates out on the cabinet. "Don't know if dragons eat tacos, but they're ready."

"Thank you, but no." Cash's voice came from near the sliding glass door.

The rest of the dragons showed themselves. Most of them were within an arm's length of me, and I hadn't even known they were in the room.

"No thank you." Arianna curled her lip. Her disgust was evident. "Meat should never be cooked."

Russ laughed. "I don't mind mine cooked with dragon fire."

"Raw." Cash strode toward the rest of us.

"Agree to disagree." I filled a tortilla shell with meat, cheese, lettuce, and tomato. "I don't like it even a little bloody." My magic surged, a giant wave tumbling toward the shore. I didn't dare look at Cody for fear it would react to him. I set my plate on the cabinet and teleported to the backyard. My bare feet sank into the snow.

Dacia. Malcolm's voice in my head sounded frantic.

I breathed in deeply and tried to contain my magic. The snow under my feet melted until I was standing in a puddle of water on the grass. *Backyard.*

Malcolm, Cash, and Aurelia appeared next to me an instant later. Cash grabbed my hand, and my magic lashed out at him instead of flowing into him. He yelped and jerked his hand away. Blood dripped onto the snow.

I closed my eyes and focused on my powers. The serpent stood up, towering over me. It puffed up, and dark shadows rolled off its body.

"Why did you hurt Cash?" I stepped forward with my palms up, hoping it would see I meant it no harm. "He's our friend. He was trying to help."

No. It hissed, rising taller. *He was draining us, depleting me.*

"He's trying to keep me from hurting Cody." I stretched my hand out, and the serpent lowered its head slightly. "Even Mavros can see that I can't live with myself if I hurt him."

They want to cage us.

"No." I shook my head and put my hand on the snake's side, running my fingers along its scales. "They fought to keep us out of a cage."

Out of the Nephilim's cage but under their control. It lowered its body. The menace that had been radiating from it diminished. *They want us for their own.* It coiled the upper part of its body around my arm. Its face was mere inches from mine.

I thought about Cody asking me to tell him something good. The dragons had been something good in my life. They had helped me so many times. "They are helping us. We need them."

We need no one.

I stared into its copper eyes. "I promise I won't let them imprison us. I won't let them take you away from me." I focused on the good things in my life, the things that made it right, that made fighting monsters worth it in the end. The shadows on the snake faded. "Give me a few weeks to figure all of this out. If they won't help us, we can make them leave."

Do not forget me.

Blinking back the sunlight, I left my powers behind. Three dragons stared at me. Cash held his hand. Purple blood dripped through his fingers. I reached out to him, and he let me grasp it. Healing energy flowed from my body into his. "I'm sorry, Cash. Please forgive me."

"Of course." His amethyst eyes were filled with concern. "Are you okay?"

"For now." I shivered. The puddle I was standing in had grown cold.

Aurelia and Malcolm stepped closer to me. "May we touch you?" Aurelia lifted her hand slowly.

"I didn't know that was going to happen to Cash." I chewed on my lip. "I think it will be okay."

These are my friends. These are my friends. These are my friends. The words repeated over and over again while the three of them put their hands on me and drained my powers to the dregs.

When they were finished, Malcolm left his hand in mine and teleported us to the backdoor. He pushed it open and leaned in. "Can somebody get Dacia a towel for her feet?"

Cody started for the bathroom, but Russ said, "Sit. Eat. I'll get it."

Val and Arianna sat at the table. They were positioned between me and him, a layer of defense in case I couldn't contain my magic. Cody sat in front of his tacos, but he didn't touch them. He just stared at me. Worry wrinkled his brow.

"I'm all right." I said the words for him, but I needed to hear them, too. I needed to remind myself that things were going to be okay, that whatever this was I could beat it.

I trudged over to a pile of snow and wiped the mud off my feet. When I finished Russ handed me a towel. "Thanks." I dried off and walked toward the kitchen with slow, deliberate steps. I wanted to make sure my magic wouldn't surge when I got closer to Cody.

When I made it to the counter, my muscles slackened with relief. I held myself up on the cabinet for a minute, fighting the urge to sob. "Does anyone need a drink?"

Everybody answered, but I couldn't make out their words. Malcolm walked up and put his hand on my shoulder. *Are you okay?*

I nodded.

"We'll get them, Dacia. Why don't you sit down?" He grabbed my plate and set it on the far end of the table from Cody. Dragons filled the chairs between us.

Cody watched me.

The dragons watched me.

I tried to ignore them, to eat my tacos, and not feel uncomfortable, but I hated eating in front of people unless they were eating, too. I hated being the center of attention. A ball of annoyance burned in my stomach.

I set my taco down on my plate. "*Please. Please* pretend like things are normal." I tried to pull my fingers through my hair, but they were stopped by my braid. "If you keep staring at me, I'm going to erupt."

Cody picked up his taco and ate half of it in one bite. Malcolm sat next to me and put his hand palm up on the table, letting me decide whether or not to touch him. I looked at it and shook my head. I needed to try to figure this out on my own.

"Thanks for making lunch, Cody." I picked up my taco in shaking hands, trying not to let the meat spill all over my plate. "I'm sorry about earlier … about now."

Cody nodded. "It's all good." He smiled at me. I could see his discomfort in his expression, but he was trying.

Chapter 18

Woodland Visitor

$\mathcal{I}$ sat on my window seat, staring outside. My face was pressed against the glass. It cooled the fire that had been burning inside of me since I woke up. The full moon was high in the sky. The trees' shadows stretched across the snow-covered yard.

Malcolm stood next to me. He hadn't been able to stop the flood of nightmares that plagued me, and his guilt weighed on him as heavily as the grief I was buried beneath.

I pulled my legs up to my chest and tried to fight off the images of Cody dying over and over again consumed by my blue flames. His remembered screams blocked out all other noises.

Something stepped out of the trees. Moonlight glinted off of it. I transformed my eyes into a dragon's to get a better look. "Malcolm"—I kept my voice soft even though my room was soundproofed—"is that a unicorn?"

"Unbelievable." He dragged his hand over his mouth and shook his head. "It sure is."

It walked closer. Its coat shone like a million diamonds glinting in the sunlight. Its mane and tail flowed in the breeze.

Arion had once told me that unicorns were overrated, but this creature was stunning.

Watching it stride across the grass, the pain inside me lessened. Cody's screams melted away, and all I could think of were the good times. Cody and I dancing on *The River Otter*, our first kiss, walking along Falcon Lake with him, seeing our friendship grow into the love we shared, him giving me my promise ring, his smile, and the glow in his sapphire eyes.

"I'm going out there." I dug a pair of shoes out of my closet and hopped on one foot while pulling them on. Then I teleported just outside my window.

The unicorn stopped moving and stared at me through wide, dark eyes.

"Please don't go away." I kept my words quiet, hoping not to scare it.

"I can feel your pain." Her voice was a symphony, rich and lyrical.

I bowed my head. "I'm scared, but you … you seem to take all that away."

She walked across the snow toward me, leaving no hoof-prints. "What keeps you awake this night?"

"There is a darkness inside me." I swallowed over a lump in my throat. "It is corrupting my magic. I'm … I'm terrified I'm going to hurt the one person that I want to protect more than anyone else."

She nuzzled my hand. Her horn brushed along my arm, and light danced through my veins, chasing the shadows away. Darkness rose through my skin, dissipating as it hit the cold winter air.

A sense of peace enveloped me. For the first time since facing Argentum, I felt like myself, like my magic was mine … whole, unbroken.

"Thank you." My breath frosted the air.

She nickered. "You must not fall to darkness."

"That's what the fairies say, too." I held my arms out in front of me, twisting them. A faint glow shone through my skin.

"Like me, they can sense the strength and purity of your soul." She took a step back. "You must persevere." She turned and walked away.

The thought of her leaving was a physical pain. My heart sank. "Will I see you again?"

"I will be watching." She looked over her shoulder at me. Her horn pointed at the moon. Its beams shone down on her, and her fur shimmered. The snow glistened at her feet. I'd never seen anything more beautiful. I wanted to take her picture or capture her in a painting, but either way, it would be a mere shadow of this moment.

I stared into the trees until she was long gone. Malcolm stood beside me, not saying a word, just there. He breathed easier, and I wondered if she'd had the same effect on him as she had on me. Or maybe, it was because my emotions weren't out of whack for once.

Slipping my hand into his, I teleported us inside. After taking my shoes off, I climbed into bed and pulled the covers up to my chin. "Goodnight, Malcolm."

I woke up feeling rested. My heart felt lighter than it had in days. Malcolm's chest lifted with each deep, even breath he took.

I slid out of bed and grabbed my clothes. Then, to keep from waking him, I teleported to the hallway right outside of the bathroom door.

Cash peeked out of his room. "Not sneaking off, are you?"

"No." I pointed over my shoulder with my thumb. "Malcolm's sleeping, so I was trying not to wake him."

Cash turned his head and stared at my bedroom door. "He's … sleeping?" He turned back toward me. "You're kidding, right?"

"No. A unicorn visited last night." I pictured her standing underneath the full moon, and my spirits lifted further. "She put both of us at ease."

"They'll do that." He dragged his hand over his mouth and mumbled. "If you're ever lucky enough to see one." He looked down the hall again, and I wondered if he was looking through my door, making sure Malcolm was all right. He shook his head, then stared at me. "Just promise you won't go anywhere without one of us."

"I can't make that promise."

His eyes flashed, and I laughed. "Right now, I'm gonna shower without you."

"I think I like you better when you're grumpy." His lips lifted at the edges, and the anger drained from his face.

I pushed the bathroom door open. "Then I'm calling Cody."

Chapter 19

Christmas Shopping

Cody drove my truck. We seemed to be alone, but I knew Malcolm and Cash were somewhere nearby. Malcolm had woken up in a panic when he realized I wasn't lying next to him. He'd relaxed somewhat when he saw me sitting in the living room with Cody and Cash, but he'd been on edge since.

I ran my hand down Cody's leg, then set it down palm up. He looked from my hand to my face. "You sure?"

"You don't have to if you're worried." I tried not to show my disappointment. I couldn't blame him for being concerned. If roles were reversed, I would probably be terrified for him to touch me.

He slipped his fingers between mine and soothed my heart. "Whatever happens, happens." He rubbed his thumb along mine, reminding me how much I'd missed that contact. "If you hurt me, it'll kill you. Can't have that."

No matter how long I lived, I would never understand why he thought my life was more important than his. For all the times I'd wronged him or put his life in danger, he should have been looking for a way out, but for some reason, he stayed by my side, my biggest fan.

"You think this'll last?" His voice broke into my thoughts, and for a minute, I thought he meant us.

I cocked my head and looked at him, trying to figure out what he was talking about.

He lifted my hand, showing me our entwined fingers.

"Oh." I felt like an idiot. Of course, he meant the unicorn's blessing. "I hope so, but something tells me no."

"Figured." He squeezed my fingers. "You got this."

For the thirty-minute drive to Boulder Creek Mall, Cody held my hand. He pulled into a parking spot and shifted my truck into park using his left hand. Then he looked at me with a pained expression before sliding his fingers out of mine.

As soon as I stepped out of the truck, he draped his arm over my shoulders, pulling me against his side. "This okay?"

I wrapped my arm around his waist in response, grateful when my magic didn't surge up. I could feel it building inside me, growing stronger and deeper with each step I took, but it felt like it used to, not like it had lately.

The dragons hadn't siphoned any of my powers from me. When Malcolm had woken, he'd stared into my eyes while holding my hands. "I don't know what the unicorn did." He'd sucked in a deep breath. "So, I don't want to drain your powers and unknowingly undo it."

"Okay." I had stared down at my feet, afraid they'd be disappointed in me and not wanting to see their faces if they were. "I've been using them this morning … for little things."

Malcolm had lifted my chin so I was looking at him. "And?"

"I just wanted to make sure it was safe before I was with Cody." I'd shrugged. "So far, so good."

Cash had squeezed my shoulder. "We'll be there if you need us."

"You okay?" Cody stopped walking and stared down at me, studying me for any off-kilter reaction.

"Yeah, I was just thinking about—" I looked around, wondering if I should say anything in public "—my situation. I just don't want to hurt you."

"It'll be okay." He led me into the mall. "Eat or shop?"

Knowing Cody, he was starving, so I guided him to the food court. After eating, we wandered through the mall, hoping the perfect gifts would jump out and grab us. Since my parents were going out more, I decided to get them a certificate for dance lessons.

Cody rubbed his hand down his face. "Don't wanna let go of you, but I gotta find ya something."

"I don't need anything, Cody." I pulled him closer to me. "Just having you is enough."

"Not happenin'." He chuckled. "Meet here in half-hour?"

"Sure." We split up, and I wandered aimlessly. I had no idea what to get for him. He'd been eyeing a hoodie in the campus store, so one day when he wasn't with me, I'd picked it up for him, but for all he put up with, I thought he deserved something more.

I was walking past a jewelry store when an idea popped into my head. *Malcolm?*

He stepped out of the store next to it and strode over to me. His eyes darted back and forth, searching for some danger. "What's wrong?" His voice was his dragon's.

"Nothing." I reached for his hand but decided against it. I didn't want my magic to flow into him. "I wanted to know—" I chewed on my lip. "Can I somehow make a necklace into a … a, like a talisman to protect Cody?"

The tension drained out of him, and he appeared less menacing. "I don't see why not." He pointed to the store, and we walked in. "What did you have in mind?"

We walked to the counter where all their necklaces were kept under glass. A rope chain caught my attention. "That one," I said to Malcolm, and the saleslady pulled it out for me.

He nodded. "We can work with that."

After I paid for Cody's gift, Malcolm and I wandered out into the hallway. "I should disappear." Malcolm grabbed my bags from me. "Otherwise, Cody will think something's wrong."

"Yeah, he probably would." Malcolm turned away, but I reached out and grabbed his arm. "Do you think it'll work?"

"To some extent." He smiled at me, but it was filled with remorse. "We'll do our best to keep him out of harm's way."

Out of harm's way. The words echoed through my head, growing louder as they repeated instead of softer.

Out of harm's way.

Out of harm's way.

I pressed my hands to my ears and tried to block the words, but they just repeated over and over again. Harm's way. They couldn't keep him out of harm's way. I was harm, and as long as I was around, Cody was in danger. Not danger of having his heart broken or anything so mundane. He was in danger of being kidnapped or tortured by monsters. Of being murdered by his girlfriend.

I stumbled to a bench and plopped down.

Malcolm sat next to me. His mouth moved, but I couldn't make out the words. He reached for my hand but pulled back. *Dacia.* His voice thundered through my head. *What's wrong?*

He'll never be out of harm's way if he's with me. The reverberating words died down. A dull ache filled my chest. *I can't keep endangering him.*

Malcolm threw his arm around my shoulders, careful to keep his skin from touching mine. "You'll beat this," he whispered.

"Maybe." I held my head in my hands. "But then what about the next monster and the next. Maybe it won't be me threatening him next time, but it will be because of me, and there's nothing I can do about that. If I could stop this, I would." The pain in my chest expanded, leaving me feeling hollow and broken. The peace that had settled over me when I saw the unicorn was the shadow of a memory.

"Life is fleeting." Malcolm's energy washed over me, soothing me. "Our tomorrows are never guaranteed. We can only hope for another day, another chance to right the wrongs. Cody wants to spend his life with you regardless of the risks. To take that choice away from him would be selfish."

"To hold onto him and continue putting his life in danger is more selfish. Isn't it?" Out of harm's way. Out of my way. They were interchangeable. I dragged my finger and thumb over my eyes and pinched the bridge of my nose. "I should let him go."

"Do I have a say?" Cody's voice startled me.

I should have felt him coming. I should have known he was listening. Not wanting to meet his eyes, I stared down at our feet. Cody's brown snow boots nearly touched my white ones. "You're always in danger."

"And you always save me." He held his hand out to me, but I was afraid to touch it. "Please, Dacia."

Don't let me hurt him, I pled with God. I slid my hand into his and stood.

"Where to now?" The relief in his voice filled a little of the hollow space inside me.

I shrugged. "I'm done shopping. Are you?"

"Yeah." He walked toward the escalator. "Your house?"

"Sure." I stopped and waited, stepping onto the moving stair cautiously. For some reason, escalators had always made me nervous. "Do you want to stay for supper?"

"Thought you didn't want me?"

"Never think that." I stepped onto solid ground, relieved to be off. "Besides, Malcolm says taking your choice away is selfish."

Cody led me out to the parking lot, and we walked to my truck. He turned and cupped my cheek in his hand. "Can I kiss you?"

Malcolm, Cash, are you here?

Yes, both of them answered at once.

Be ready to step in. "Carefully."

His lips brushed against mine as soft as velvet.

I slipped one hand around his waist and one behind his head. Then I deepened the kiss. It had been too long. With his lips pressed against mine, I knew I was being selfish for not letting him go. Every day that he spent with me, his life was in danger, but I needed him like I'd never needed anyone else.

Cody pulled my body against his and moaned softly. His teeth scraped against my lip, and heat flared inside me.

"Stop." I let go of him and stepped back. My magic flared to life. I turned my back on him, not wanting him to be a target. Then I pressed my eyes closed and focused on the mountain lake I'd dreamed up. My powers thrummed inside of me, not relinquishing at all.

A hand clamped down on my shoulder, and I opened my eyes. Nobody was there, but Malcolm whispered, "You're okay. Use your power. Do something that won't hurt anyone to drain some of it off."

The sky was a brilliant blue. Billowy clouds rushed in, and the wind gusted. People looked up in surprise and hurried to their cars or to get inside the mall.

My hands shook. My legs wobbled, but Malcolm held me steady. The wind died down, and the clouds drifted off.

"Are you good?" he asked.

Trying to hold back a yawn, I said, "Exhausted."

"Yeah." He let go of me. "We need to rebuild your stamina."

The door to my truck opened. I climbed in and pulled the seatbelt over my shoulder. Cody sat in the driver's seat watching me. "I should be okay." I was too ashamed to meet his eyes.

"What changed?" His voice was edged with some emotion I couldn't place.

I slammed my head back against the headrest. "Malcolm said they'd keep you out of harm's way." My voice cracked, but I kept going. "And, I realized I'm harm."

"Ah, Dacia." His fingers brushed against my cheek.

I jerked my head back. Fear clenched my heart. My truck was too small, too cramped. If my magic surged up, there would be no stopping it, no redirecting it. "I'll see you at my house," I said before teleporting to my bedroom.

Malcolm appeared right after me. "Cash is with Cody." He watched me carefully. "What's going on?"

"Every time he touches me, my magic flares up." Tears pooled in my eyes. "How do I fix this?"

Chapter 20

No Touching

Cody and I sat at the kitchen table. While I'd waited for him to show up, I'd done the dishes, cleaned off the cabinets, and swept the floor. Now, we sat in awkward silence. Cash stood by the sliding glass doors, staring outside. Malcolm was in the living room. Both of them were trying to give us the semblance of privacy, but instead of having an elephant in the room, I had two dragons.

"Dacia." Cash growled.

I glared at him. "What?" At least the elephant wouldn't think I smelled good enough to eat.

"That's better." He rubbed his hand over his nose and mouth, and I realized I'd gone from self-pitying to angry.

"Want to help me make supper?" I asked Cody. "I have no idea what we have or what sounds good, but doing something might help."

He stood and walked to the fridge. "Whatever you need."

We found chicken, potatoes, broccoli, and cauliflower. I washed my hands. Then I rubbed olive oil on the potatoes and sprinkled them with garlic salt and pepper.

Cody stood at another cabinet preparing the chicken. With my back turned to him, my magic seemed to settle down.

I grabbed the steamer pot and added water to the bottom. Then I filled it with veggies. While Cody finished, I sat at the table, closed my eyes, and pictured the unicorn standing in the moonlight. I hoped some of the peace from last night would return to me.

"Chicken's in," Cody said, and a chair slid out next to me.

"Thanks." Nothing changed inside of me, so I opened my eyes. Cody sat with his arms stretched across the table. His fingers were folded together, and he stared straight ahead. His brows furrowed with worry. As soon as he realized I was look-ing at him, his features transformed into a carefree expression.

I started to reach for him but stopped. "You don't have to stay here. I understand if you're afraid."

"Wanna stay." He blew out a breath, lifting his bangs off his face. "Just wanna help you."

I bowed my head. "I don't think there's any help for me." My hand shook as I tugged it through my hair. "I thought the unicorn's blessing would last at least a day."

A car pulled into the driveway, and the garage door opened. I bit my bottom lip, pulling it into my mouth. "Can we—" the words caught in my throat "—can we pretend everything's okay? I don't want them to know how messed up I am. They're worried enough."

"Of course." Somehow he slid on a happy mask. The only thing that gave his true feelings away was the concern in his sapphire eyes. "Work better if ya don't look so sad."

"Can you guys help?" I asked the dragons. A peaceful sensation slid over me.

Malcolm walked into the room. "Since it's not working anymore, do you want me to siphon your power?"

"Yeah." I looked at Cody, and my magic sparked like electricity, arching from me toward him. I closed my fist. "That'd probably be best."

Malcolm sat beside me and held my hand. Cody's eyes narrowed slightly, and he turned away.

I didn't know what to say or do to make it right. I would have preferred touching him, but for whatever reason, I couldn't.

The door from the garage opened, and my parents walked in. Mom stopped and looked around. "Supper's cooking, and you cleaned." A smile brightened her face.

"Cody helped with supper." I set my hand on his and squeezed it before letting go. "I'll do more cleaning tomorrow."

Dad took his coat off and hung it by the door. "Smells good."

The unicorn stands outside my window. The moonlight reflects off her fur as bright as noon.

I teleport outside, and she turns toward me. Her dark eyes are somber. "You are distraught again."

"My magic lashed out at Cody." I stare into the trees, wondering what else might be lurking under their cover. "I love him, but I keep trying to kill him. Why?" I look at her. "What's wrong with me? Am I turning into a monster? Am I becoming like Draconian?"

She stomps her hoof on the ground, and snow flies into the air. "You ingested dragon's blood from an ancient beast whose power was millennia old. You allowed a demon's magic to mingle with your own." She shakes her head, giving me the impression that she thinks I'm a little slow on the uptake. "You must fight their influence. You cannot let their powers become your own."

"But … how do I stop them?"

"As far as I know, you are the only one of your kind this has ever happened to." She lowers her horn to my hand, and once again, the shadows flee from her light. "You must blaze the trail on your own. I wish you luck."

I opened my eyes, and Malcolm stared down at me. "I'm sorry, Dacia."

"Yeah." I grabbed a pillow and rolled over, hugging it. "I don't know how to win."

He put his hand on my shoulder and drew out some of my energy.

"So, you think that was more than a dream?" Instead of focusing on what I asked, I concentrated on my power being siphoned into Malcolm, the feel of it leaving my body, how it left me numb. If I'd thought about what I was saying, I knew I would cry. I wanted somebody to be able to help me. I didn't want to go through this on my own. I didn't want to keep risking Cody's life every time I touched him.

He exhaled slowly, and I knew what his answer would be before he said it. "Yes."

Chapter 21

Lord, Help Me

 lay in bed staring at the ceiling. Malcolm sat on my window seat. A cold, winter wind blew in through the screen, but judging by the length of his fangs, it wasn't doing much to cover my scent.

"Does your magic feel like your own today?" His words were nearly indecipherable.

I closed my eyes and brought my power to my fingertips. It seemed like mine, but it had some of the times that it had turned on Cody, too. "I don't know. I think so."

"Focus on it." A low growl filled the room, and I shivered in response. "What does it look like?"

I sat up, pulling the covers with me, and focused on my power. The pearlescent serpent slithered toward me, moving faster than I'd ever seen it before. It stopped near my feet and lifted up until it looked me in the eyes. Its black-flecked copper irises were bright. I didn't notice any shadows veiled behind its scales. Its tongue flicked out, tasting the air.

Cautiously, I stretched my hand toward it and petted its head. It nuzzled into me like a cat would. I looked behind it and saw Mavros' ebony power asleep on the floor.

The snake's gaze followed mine. *It hasn't awoken.*

"Do you feel like yourself again?" I scratched the bottom of its chin. "Can I spend time with Cody without worrying about killing him?"

He makes you weak.

I jerked my hand back. "No." I crossed my arms over my chest. "No. Without him, I would falter. I need him. He grounds me. He keeps me striving to be better, to be good. Without him, I would have allowed Mavros to charm me."

And, yet, he is still bound to you.

"He doesn't control me. He isn't trying to take over the world. He isn't a danger."

Do you really believe that? Are you so naïve? The serpent lowered its body to the ground. *What happens to Cody depends on how you wield me. The power is in you.*

I snapped my eyes open. My blankets were clutched in my fists. My knuckles were white, and Malcolm looked like he was breathing easier. "The powers are mine."

"I saw." His voice sounded more like his own.

I dropped my covers. "Are you going to lecture me then? Are you going to tell me that trusting Mavros is a mistake?"

"I don't think I need to." He closed the window and walked over to my bed, sitting on the edge of it. "Your magic is you. The serpent is just how you choose to visualize it. If it is doubting him, then somewhere inside, so are you."

I breathed in deeply, trying to lessen the anger that burned within me. "What now?"

"Get dressed." He stood. "We're going for a run."

I got up, put on running clothes, brushed my teeth, and filled my water bottle. Cash and Malcolm waited for me in the living room. As soon as I laced up my shoes, Cash held the door open and waved me outside.

"Why do I have a feeling this is going to be torture?" I looked from one dragon to the other.

Cash held his hand out and wobbled it from side to side. "Maybe a little." He grabbed my arm and tugged me down the front stairs. As soon as we hit the sidewalk, he started running faster than I intended.

I quickly adjusted my pace to keep from having my shoulder dislocated. As soon as I was matching his stride, he let go of me.

The Nephilim have watchers here still. His voice thrummed in my head. *I want you to use your magic in ways they cannot see. Make the wind blow, make it snow, make your body transform beneath your clothes, whatever you can think of. Just don't let them see.*

Why? I felt my face scrunch up with curiosity. *They've seen me use my powers before.*

Yes. He looked down at me. *But they don't know how quickly your powers are dwindling since you haven't used them for a while.*He

Malcolm ran up beside me, slowing when his stride matched mine. *We need to build your stamina back up without the Nephilim knowing. We need to use every opportunity to increase your power when the shadows are not present.*

Then, maybe you can use your powers to destroy the taint within you. Cash sounded hopeful but unsure.

The wind blew up behind us, pushing me forward. The dragons raced to catch up. Sweat beaded at my temples, and my legs burned. I'd spent too much time wallowing. I needed to get back into shape physically and magically, and now that I had the beginnings of a plan, I felt more motivated than I had been.

I turned my eyes into a dragon's. Clouds rolled in, and snow floated lazily to the ground. I created a shield around the three of us. Tiny flakes collected on the outside of it, and I realized that wasn't a very good idea.

Not too much. Malcolm looked at me from the corner of his eye. *I don't want to carry you back.*

I thought about all of our runs through the cave before I'd killed Argentum. Malcolm wouldn't have been content with how little I was doing now. He would have pushed me to do more, harder, and faster.

My feet thudded against the road, and I realized my pace was slowing. Cash grabbed my arm just above my elbow and turned us around. "Doing okay?"

"Wearing … out." My breath puffed out of me in rapid bursts, frosting the air in front of me. The wind died down, and the clouds dissipated.

A burst of Cash's energy shot into me. "Better?"

"Yes," I answered, breathing easier. "Thank you."

When we got back to my house, Malcolm funneled a surge of power into me so I wouldn't fall asleep in the shower. Even with his energy flowing through my veins, exhaustion weighed me down.

I stood under the stream of water wondering how my strength had diminished so drastically. In about five weeks, I had lost all of the stamina I had spent so much time building up.

By the time I finished pulling the brush through my hair, I could barely stand. I collapsed on the couch, and Cash held my phone out to me. "Cody called and texted while you were in the shower."

I reached for it, wondering if my magic would react in any way. His texts said to call him, so I dialed his number.

He answered on the first ring. "You okay?"

"Yeah." I reclined my seat and closed my eyes. "The dragons thought a morning run would be nice, so I was showering."

"Oh … okay … good." He sounded like he was trying to calm himself. "Mom'd like to see you." I heard the hesitancy in his voice and knew he was planning on being disappointed.

"Cash and Malcolm?"

"Figured you'd need them with you."

Malcolm tapped my knee. "We don't have to show ourselves."

"What time do you want us?" I ignored Malcolm's comment. Seeing them might be enough to keep my powers under control.

"Noon." He sounded relieved. "Mom's making lunch."

I yawned before saying, "Okay. That'll give me time to nap."

The girl stares at me. I sense the enormity of her power. It fills me with an insatiable hunger. Her blood would sustain me for millennia.

I've spent my life protecting this species from rogue dragons that would harm them. I've written laws making it a crime to hunt them. Now, all I can think about is ending her life. The gift of regeneration her blood would give me. I've even done the unthinkable and recruited a demon to help me.

The girl lights a fire in her palm. The blue flames cast an odd sheen around the cavern, making her hair appear purple.

When she notices the bones scattered about the cave floor, the smell of her fear permeates the air. It's all I can do to remain hidden from her.

She turns her back, and I slide out of the water. When she turns again, I loom above her. Her terror is an intoxicating aroma. I lunge, but she darts away.

"Dacia." A low growl rumbles through the cave.

Yes. The girl is Dacia. I've seen the name in Aurelia's memories and heard Mavros say it almost reverently. How could a demon care for a human girl unless under her control? Her power is too much for one person to have. Her life needs to be ended before she becomes corrupted.

She holds her hands up in a stop motion. A burst of energy smacks into me, pushing me back. A roar tears from my throat. Rocks tumble from the ceiling, splashing into the lake, and crashing against the cavern floor.

The girl covers her head.

"Dacia!" Malcolm clutched my shoulder, and my eyes shot open.

I stared up at him. Scales rimmed his face, and his eyes were inhuman. "What's wrong?" I asked.

He lifted my hand so I could see it. Long talons extended from my fingertips. Silver scales replaced my skin. I jumped out of my bed and looked in the mirror.

Horns framed a face that I could barely recognize as mine. "I dreamed I was Argentum."

"I saw." Malcolm's voice was feral.

I watched as the scales receded. "Is it because of his blood? Will it stay in me for a thousand years like he thought mine would with him?" My voice rose as panic filled me. "Surely, he was more powerful than I am." I spun around and pinned Malcolm with my gaze.

He stood at my window. His fangs jutted from his mouth. His eyes narrowed, and for the first time, in a long time, I was afraid of him. He prowled toward me. Then stopped. He shook his head and disappeared.

I nearly jumped out of my skin when Cash pounded on my door. "Dacia are you okay? What's going on? Let me in." His voice sounded frantic.

My hands were still deformed. I held them behind my back and swallowed my fear. "Come in."

He threw the door open, and his purple gaze darted around the room, searching for a threat, for a reason for my fear, or for Malcolm. I wasn't sure which. "What happened?" His voice was caught between his human's and his dragon's.

"Nightmare." I didn't know if I should tell him I'd transformed, at least partially, into a dragon. No matter how much they liked me or wanted to protect me, their instincts were strong. And, those instincts told them to kill any human who took a dragon's form.

"More than a nightmare," Cash growled. "Malcolm's hunting. He's more agitated than I can ever remember him being. I don't know if he'll return before you need to leave." He stepped closer to me. "So, tell me what's going on."

I shook my head and stared at the floor. The cornflower blue carpet made me think of flying through the sky on Arion's back. I couldn't help but wonder if he'd been watching me, and if he'd reported my change to Aurelia. "I'm sorry, Cash, but remember when you told me I didn't want to know about Argentum?" He nodded slightly, so I continued. "You probably don't want to know what happened."

"If you won't tell me, I can look into your mind." He spoke through clenched teeth, and I knew it wasn't because of anger. The scent of my fear probably still clung to the air.

Resting my human-looking hand on his shoulder, I said, "I know you can, but you'll regret it as much as I still regret finding out."

"All right." He pressed his eyes closed and pulled his hand down his face. "I'll trust you on this, Dacia. Just—whatever it is—don't do anything stupid."

I nodded and walked into the living room. Sitting on the couch, I grabbed the remote and flipped through the channels, looking for anything worth watching until I needed to leave. Cash stared at me, scrutinizing every move I made. Finally, at 11:30, I turned the TV off and stood up. "Ready?"

He followed me out to my truck. His eyebrows were pulled together, and his expression was tense.

"You don't need to ride with me if it's too much for you."

He pulled his door open and climbed in. "I just don't understand what's so horrible that you can't tell me."

"Yeah." I put the key in the ignition, then pulled my seatbelt over my shoulder, clicking it into place. "I know the feeling."

Chapter 22

Family Dinner

$\mathcal{C}$ash held my hand for the entire drive to Cody's house, silently drawing my energy into his body, making sparks of magic dance over his skin. He could have looked into my mind to see what had happened between Malcolm and me, but he respected my wish and didn't give in to the temptation.

When I drove down Cody's driveway, he let go. I pulled my lip into my mouth with my teeth. "Have you heard from him?" I was afraid to ask. Afraid that Malcolm wouldn't come near me again. After all that we'd been through, I couldn't imagine him not being part of my life. He'd promised to stay with me for as long as I needed him, but would this be the end of our friendship?

"He'll make it look like he's getting out of the truck with us." A poor attempt at a smile tugged at his lips.

The rush of relief would have been enough to topple me if I was standing. Instead, the tension in my shoulders loosened, and I felt lightheaded.

Cash rolled his window down and leaned his head out over his arm, breathing the cold, fresh air deep into his lungs, drowning out the smell of my emotions.

True to his word, Malcolm appeared in my truck as soon as Cash climbed out. If Cody's family thought about it, they would realize my pickup only had two seats and there was no way the three of us could have arrived together, but since finding out mythical creatures existed, I'd realized they were good at making things like that not be questioned.

Before stepping out, he looked at me. "We have to talk after this."

"Okay." *Please don't hate me.* I couldn't bring myself to say it out loud.

Reaching for my hand, he squeezed my fingers. *Never. But there are things I need answered, and my dragon is far from content.*

I dropped my chin to my chest for just a second while I tried to compose myself. "Just help me get through this without hurting Cody. Then your dragon can kill me if it needs to."

It doesn't need to. It needs to calm down.

I pushed my door open and started to get out before remembering to unbuckle my seatbelt.

Cody stood on the porch. He watched me as I got out of the truck and walked toward him. Lines etched his forehead, and his hands were fisted in his pockets. He held my gaze with his, and I knew he was wondering how my magic would react to him. As soon as I was on the landing, he reached for me but didn't touch me. I stepped into his arms and wrapped mine around him. His embrace and the smell of his skin comforted me. My power didn't even stir. I stretched up onto my toes and gently pressed my lips to his.

His eyes widened. At first, he didn't respond, but it didn't take long for him to recover and return the kiss with fervor.

Cash cleared his throat, and I stepped back. "Sorry."

Cody looked down at me with sparkling eyes. "I'm not." He slid his fingers through mine and opened the door with his other hand, holding it for the dragons.

Malcolm walked past us into the house. His muscles were tensed, and I wondered if it was because of me transforming or because he could smell my emotions. Somehow, I needed to fix the mess between us, but I couldn't worry about that right now. I needed to focus on keeping my magic under control.

Dawson's dog, Bo, came running into the room with a wagging tail. As soon as he noticed Cash and Malcolm, his hackles rose. He lowered his head, bared his teeth, growled, and barked. The yellow lab had gone from friendly house pet to raging beast.

Malcolm whispered something and flashed his fangs at the dog. Bo tucked his tail between his legs and backed out of the room, whining.

"Dogs don't like us. They know we're predators," Malcolm said quietly to Cody. "It would be best to kennel it, lock it in a room, or let it outside."

Cody nodded, and while the rest of us took our shoes off, he followed Bo. After a couple of minutes, he came back and led us into the kitchen. Susan stood at the stove, and Brent carried food into the dining room.

"Hello," I said. "Can I help with anything?"

Susan grabbed a towel, wiping her hands on it as she made her way over to me. "No, we're just finishing up." She pulled me into a hug, making Cody let go of my hand. "It's so good to see you. How's your break going?"

"Good." I hugged her back. Cody's parents had always accepted me even when I felt like nobody else did. "It's nice to be home."

She took a step away from me and stretched her hand out to Malcolm. "I'm Susan, and that's my husband, Brent."

"Nice to meet you." He shook her hand, and I realized he was like Cody when it came to slipping a mask on to hide his true emotions. "I'm Malcolm."

Cash reached for her hand as soon as Malcolm let go of it. "Cash. Thanks for having us."

"No problem." She went back to the stove and stirred whatever was cooking there. "Cody has told us a lot about you. I'm sorry you couldn't make it home for break, but I hope you're enjoying yourselves."

"Of course," Cash said. "The area is beautiful, and the people here are great."

Brent stepped into the kitchen and waved to us. "Why don't you have a seat? We'll eat in just a minute."

Cody ran his hand down my arm until his fingers entwined with mine. Little shivers trailed his touch, and I braced for the worst. When nothing happened, we led the dragons into the dining room.

Cody's siblings were already seated around a table covered with food. He motioned toward them. "You met Britny. This is Josh, Dawson, and Brandon."

Each of his brothers waved as Cody said their names. They were like miniature versions of Cody. Blond hair and blue eyes.

While introductions were made, Britny watched the dragons through her eyelashes. I imagined she was still trying to figure out what exactly they were.

Josh narrowed his eyes at them. "Why you stayin' with my brother's girlfriend? Not trying to steal her, are ya?"

"Josh!" Brent's voice was filled with horror and admonition.

Cody shook his head. "Told you. It's like a twenty-two-hour flight."

"Cody offered to let us stay here—" Malcolm smiled without showing his fangs "—but your house is a bit fuller than Dacia's."

Brave kid. Cash's voice thrummed in my head. *He can tell there's something different about us. He's intimidated, and yet, he stood up for his brother. I'm impressed.*

Britny leaned over, dragging her hair across her plate. She glared down the table at her brother. "Why don't you like them, Josh?" Her voice was a conspiratorial whisper. "They're fairies."

Dawson and Brandon snickered at the comment, but the dragons weren't offended by it in any way. They both looked at

Britny and shook their heads. "Nope," Cash said, popping the p like I did sometimes. "We're not."

She lowered her body closer to the table. "But you're not people."

"Of course, they're people." Dawson rubbed her head. "What else would they be? Chihuahuas?"

She held her hand up to her mouth, trying to block us from hearing her, and whispered, "Fairies."

Dawson looked at the dragons apologetically before turning back toward Britny. "I think you might have a better imagination than Brandon."

Susan walked into the room carrying a platter covered in fried chicken. "Cody, can you bring in the gravy?" Mashed potatoes, corn, rolls, and salad were already on the table. She placed the tray in an empty spot in the center of everything, then turned to us. "Please, sit. Josh, you can say grace so our guests know you can be nice."

"Fine. Whatever." He watched us all sit down.

I sat between Cody and Malcolm, and Cash took the chair across from Britny. He nodded at her, and she smiled sweetly in return.

Josh folded his hands and said, "Lord, bless this food and this gathering. Thank you for bringing us all together, and please watch over Dacia and keep her safe … especially from fairies. Amen."

Susan and Brent both shook their heads at him, but I was touched by his prayer. Maybe God would listen to Josh's words and not his meaning.

As he ate, Josh began to relax. It would have been hard not to with Brandon telling us lively tales about school and his classmates. Through the laughter, I realized that my powers hadn't stirred at all, and even though I didn't want them to react to Cody like that, I couldn't help but wonder if everything was okay. Had something happened to my magic, or was it reverting to the way it had been before Argentum? Or worse, would it explode out of me without warning and hurt Cody and everyone he cared about?

Malcolm turned to me, and worry shone in his eyes. *Is everything okay?*

Panic attack. I wiped my mouth with my napkin, hoping to keep my expression from being seen by Cody's family. *Why isn't my magic reacting to him? Is it still there?*

He slid his hand onto my leg where it wouldn't be seen. *It's nearly depleted but still there.*

As Malcolm dragged his hand back onto his lap, Josh noticed the movement. "Cody, you really okay with this?"

Cody cocked his head and looked at his brother like he was speaking Greek.

"Him putting his hand on your girl's leg."

Cody shook his head. "They're just friends."

"Remember that when your heart's broken." Josh pushed his chair back and said, "May I be excused?"

"Please." Susan's normally light voice sounded annoyed.

Malcolm folded his hands together so that everyone could see them. "I'm sorry for any trouble my presence has caused. I have no sexual interest in Dacia."

Heat flared up my neck and onto my face. Cody's brothers giggled, and Britny looked confused. Brent cleared his throat. "Josh has always been overly protective. It can be a good thing, and then it can also lead to uncomfortable situations." He waved his hands. "Such as this." He turned his focus to me. "At least you know he likes you enough to care."

"Yeah." I stood up. "Let me help you clean up this mess."

Susan shooed me like I was an annoying fly. "No, you won't. I have plenty of children." She pointedly looked at them. "You're our guest."

"Josh," Brent hollered over his shoulder, "your turn for dishes."

"We would be more than happy to help out," Cash said.

Susan shook her head, and Brent shrugged. "The lady of the house says no."

"Thank you for lunch." Malcolm handed his plate to Dawson as he walked by. "It was delicious."

I wondered if either dragon had even tried a bite of the food or if they'd just created an illusion of themselves eating.

"It was great," I agreed. "Thank you for inviting us."

Brent stood up and started gathering items off the table. "Well, judging by the ring on your finger, you're going to be part of this family soon enough. You might as well start enjoying the headaches that four boys can bring to a meal." He laughed a little. "Oh, I meant the joy that four boys can bring to a meal."

I smiled at him. "Yeah, it's a little livelier than eating with my parents."

"I gotta help." Cody brushed his lips across mine, then stood. "You can stay here or go to the other room. I'll be quick."

Cash, Malcolm, and I went into the living room. I sat on the couch next to Cash and stared at the twinkling lights on the Christmas tree. He threw his arm over the back of it and barely let his fingers touch my shoulder. *Your power hasn't replenished since draining it this morning.*

Is that bad?

He shook his head. *I think it's because you used your magic instead of us siphoning it from you.*

I nodded. That made sense, but I still wondered if something was wrong. I should have had a limitless reserve stored by now. It had been months since it took this long for my magic to build back up.

Cody's family made quick work of the cleanup. There hadn't been too many leftovers, but what there was, they had put away and washed within fifteen minutes.

Susan walked into the living room, rubbing lotion into her hands. "We got you a gift." She nodded at the tree. "Do you want to get it for her, Britny?"

Britny's eyes lit up with excitement, and she skipped over to it. "This one?" She held up a present wrapped in Santa paper.

"What does it say on the tag?" her mom asked patiently, and I realized that this was a teaching moment.

"To Day-sha." Britny sounded it out carefully. "From The Hawks Family."

Susan nodded. "Go ahead and give it to her … carefully."

"I didn't bring your gifts over." My stomach tightened. I had gotten something for everyone, but they were all wrapped and under the tree at home.

She smiled at me. "That's okay. You can bring them later. I just wanted you to have this before you celebrate with everyone."

Britny carried the present over like it was the queen's crown. Each step was cautious. She watched the gift, making sure it didn't tip, and handed it to me reverently. The weight of the box pulled my hands down. I hadn't expected it to be so heavy.

"Thank you." I smiled at her, and the grin she returned covered her entire face.

Cody sat next to me and pulled Britny onto his lap. "Go ahead." He nodded at the package.

I carefully pulled the tape away, trying not to rip the paper. Then I opened the cardboard box. Inside it were two more wrapped presents. I opened the smaller box first and looked up at Susan in surprise. "Thank you. It's beautiful." I pulled out the necklace, a heart-shaped pendant with a peridot and amethyst stone inside it, mine and Cody's birthstones.

"You're welcome."

Brent stepped up beside her and draped his arm over her shoulders. "We thought you'd like to wear it for the holidays."

I nodded and clasped it around my neck. Then I took out the larger package.

Britny hopped off Cody's lap and stood in front of me. She folded her hands together and twisted them like she was holding in her excitement.

When I unwrapped the final gift, I stared at it in stunned silence. Tears sprang to my eyes. It was a snow globe. Wintery shades of blue and purple contained a unicorn that reminded me of my nighttime visitor. I couldn't help but wonder if Cody's parents were like mine and knew more than they let on.

"Do you like it?" Britny bounced from heel to toe.

"Yes." I held it up so she could see it, too. "It's beautiful."

She beamed at me. "I knew you would."

"Britny picked it out for you," Brent said. "She saw it in the store and decided you *had* to have it."

"Thank you." I gave her a one-armed hug. "I love them both." I set the packages on the floor and walked over to Brent and Susan, hugging each of them.

"You're welcome, dear." Susan smiled down at me.

Brent smacked his hands together. "Game time." He turned and started walking toward the dining room. "Boys," he hollered down the hall, "game time."

"Yahtzee." Britny darted after her dad.

He took her hand in his. "It's Brandon's turn to pick first."

"Aah." Her shoulders drooped a little.

By the time we got into the other room, Brandon had Pictionary set up. "Two teams. College kids versus us." He gestured to his family minus Cody.

"That's not even." Susan tapped on her chin. "Who else wants to be on their team?"

Britny's hand shot into the air. "Oh … me, me, me."

Josh watched us carefully as we sat. When Malcolm pulled out the chair next to me, Josh narrowed his eyes into hate-filled slits. Malcolm wasn't looking at him, but he must've smelled a change in emotions because he said, "Cash, why don't you sit here?"

Cash slid into the chair next to me and nodded at the table. "So, what's this game?"

Britny explained how to play Pictionary with an enthusiasm that only six-year-olds possess. When she finished, Cody filled in all the missing pieces. Since not all of our team knew how to play, Susan decided we should get the advantage of going first.

While Britny drew, Cody slowly rested his arm over my shoulders. He watched my face the entire time, making sure nothing bad would happen. When I didn't stop him, he smiled broadly.

As soon as the games were finished and it was time for me to leave, Cody walked outside with the dragons and me. I put my Christmas presents on the driver's seat. Then I shut the door and faced him.

He backed me against the truck, placing one hand against it and brushing my hair back with the other. "Not complaining, but why today?"

"They think it's because I drained my powers this morning instead of them doing it." I glanced at the dragons, knowing they heard everything I said. Cody started to say something, but I held my finger over his lips. *We have to be careful about what we say. The Nephilim are still watching me.*

He nodded, then leaned down. He kissed the tip of my nose and my chin. Then he wrapped his arms around me and crushed his lips against mine. A soft moan escaped from me, and I clutched the back of his head, keeping him from pulling away from me.

It had been too long since I'd been able to kiss him like this, to let go around him and just enjoy the feel of him, the taste of his lips against mine.

He lifted me, and I wrapped my legs around him. Heat ignited in my belly and quickly spread through my body. I pushed Cody away and stumbled back against my truck. I fumbled for the handle. "Run, Cody. Please. I love you."

Chapter 23

Transformation

Flames danced on my fingertips. I closed my eyes and tried to calm my magic. When I opened them again, Malcolm stood in front of me, blocking my view of Cody with his body. I lifted my hand—hoping he'd siphon off my power—before realizing that he was fighting his own battle.

His eyes were thin slits, and his nostrils flared. I knew that I smelled like a mixture of desire and terror to him and hoped he could keep his dragon under control after the turmoil of this morning.

He leaned in closer, and his fangs pressed into his lip. Blood dripped down onto his chin.

Cash. Even in my head, my voice seemed to quiver.

Cash herded Cody into the house, then hustled over to us. He stood at Malcolm's side, and his eyes widened. "You're going to have to tell me what's going on," he said out loud, but in my mind, he said, *Teleport home. I'll get your truck there.*

I looked at Cody's house, hoping against hope that nobody was watching us. Then I pictured my bedroom. I'd been leaning against my truck, so when I teleported into my room, I fell, hitting my back against my dresser on my way to the floor. My breath was sucked out of me, and I lay there, staring at the ceiling wondering what was happening between Cash and Malcolm while trying to fill my lungs.

Within minutes, Cash stood in my room staring down at me. "Are you okay?" He tried to cover the feral tone of his voice by softening it.

I pushed my hands down against the carpet and sat up. "Yeah. I fell when I teleported back. Then I was worried about you and Malcolm." I tugged my hand through my hair, wondering what I should tell Cash. "Is he okay?"

"He'll be gone for a while." He reached his hand down and helped me stand. "His dragon is fighting with his more … human side." He turned away from me and walked to the window. "Whatever happened between the two of you this morning, don't tell me. If it's got him this messed up, it can't be good. You need one of us to be able to help you."

"Did you bring my truck back?"

He looked over his shoulder at me. "You're not planning on leaving, are you?"

"No." I shook my head. There were too many things that could go wrong with me on my own. I needed to figure out how to control my powers and make them my own again before one of the Nephilim decided to confront me. I probably wouldn't want to run into Malcolm on my own right now, and I couldn't trust myself around Cody. "I just wondered if it was back. Then I need to see if my parents are."

"They're here." He looked out my window and then at me. "Do you want to come in the front door and pretend like everything is okay?"

"Yeah, that'd be a good idea."

I lay in bed curled on my side. Cash stretched out beside me. His breathing was even, but I knew he wasn't asleep. There was no way he could be. My emotions were too far out of whack for a dragon to be sleeping next to me. I was afraid of what would happen between Malcolm and me. I was uncomfortable with Cash lying with me. It had taken me a while to get used to sleeping next to Malcolm. Now, I was lying in bed with another man, and I didn't know if Cody would ever forgive me for it.

On top of all of that, I was worried about me and Cody. Would I ever be able to kiss him again? Was there a way to get the dragon out of me? Could I go back to the way I had been? Still a mess, but not a mess who would kill her boyfriend at the first sign of passion.

"If you're not going to sleep, I'll sit by the window." Cash rolled over and got out of bed.

Shortly after, a gust of cold air blew into the room, and I sat up to grab my comforter. "I'm sorry. I wish there was some way to keep my scent from driving you insane."

"It's good that you feel things. If you ever stop caring …" He practically had his nose pressed to the screen. "But, do you need to feel so damned much?"

I wondered what he'd been about to say. I thought about it until my eyelids grew too heavy to keep open.

"My dragon won't rest until I talk to you." Malcolm's voice rumbled through my room, pulling me out of my dream.

Cash had apparently climbed back into bed after I went to sleep. He sat up and stared at Malcolm. "Do I need to stand between you to keep her safe?"

"I will not harm the girl." The voice that came out of Malcolm was undoubtedly his dragon's. "I made a vow."

Cash turned my face toward his, and if I didn't have an annoyed dragon in my room, the action would have felt intimate. He tapped my temple. "If you need me, my name will be enough."

I nodded at him, then looked at Malcolm. "Where are we going?"

"My cave. Treasure room." He held his hand out. "Acacia knows where it is."

Hearing Malcolm say Cash's true name caught me off guard. His dragon must have been closer to the surface than I'd seen him in a long time.

Malcolm wiggled his fingers impatiently, waiting for me to grab them, but I shook my head. His low growl filled the room.

Keeping my voice firm to help hide my fear, I said, "I need shoes and a sweatshirt first."

I pulled the covers back and shivered against the cold. My window was still open, letting in the frigid December air. I grabbed a hoodie off the foot of my bed and pulled it on, lifting my hair over the hood. While I slipped my shoes on, I wondered if I was making a mistake going alone with him, but he was my friend, and I needed him on my side. "See you in a bit," I said to Cash as I walked to Malcolm's side.

"Be careful." He shot me a sad smile before turning to Malcolm. "Don't hurt her."

Malcolm clutched my hand but didn't say anything.

Malcolm's cave was as black as his scales. With my eyes transformed into a dragon's, I still couldn't see even the tiniest glimmer of light. I remembered the Abyss that Mavros had taken me to a couple of times when he was trying to get me to choose him over Cody. I remembered the fear I'd felt there, but here in the dark with Malcolm, I didn't feel that terror.

We stood in the pitch-black cave for what felt like an eternity before I lit a fire in my palm and threw it at the torches that lined the cavern walls. The blue light danced over Malcolm's treasure hoard.

His pupils contracted quickly. "I need to know." The voice that spoke to me was the dragon's as were several of his features. Scales covered his face, neck, and arms. Talons tipped his fingers. A forked tongue scented the air, and a tail swished from side to side behind him.

"What do you need to know?" I clasped my hands together to keep him from seeing them shake.

He stared me down, and I felt the challenge in his gaze. Some instinct told me to look away, to act submissive. "How many times?" His words were little more than growls.

"Twice." I held my ground even though I wanted to back away. "The first time I ever transformed, I tried to become a tiger, but I turned into a black dragon."

"Your first time?" His voice was a little more human.

"Yes."

Some of his scales faded. "The first transformation a dragon makes is supposed to be its alternate form."

"You told me that"—I nodded, relaxing slightly—"and I wondered if it was true for humans, too."

He pulled his hands down his face, and when he looked at me again, it wasn't the dragon looking out through his eyes. "My dragon doesn't know what to make of this. Instinct has always told us that any other creature transforming into a dragon needs to die, but if that's your alter form ... maybe we've been wrong."

"I don't know." I let my fire burn a little brighter, hoping to ward off some of the chill that had settled over me with his words. "I don't think it's my alternate form."

He cocked his head. "Why?"

"I think I transformed into a dragon because I was worried about how to defeat you all." I paced a few steps, then turned and walked back. I didn't know how Malus Tribulus would handle what I was about to tell him. "Dragons encompassed my thoughts, my dreams, my waking hours. You terrorized me and my friends."

A deep sadness settled in his eyes. "I am sorry for that."

"I know." I rubbed my hand down his arm. "I know it wasn't your fault. I know you were being controlled, but I didn't know that Aurelia was a dragon. I didn't know that dragons could be good and honorable. I knew that you were scarier than hell." I stared into his bronze eyes, hoping he could see the truth in mine. "Anyway, I don't know what my true alternate form should be."

"If you became a dragon—"

I held my hand up, stopping him. "I didn't just turn into any dragon." I pulled my lip into my mouth, hoping he wouldn't attack me for what I was about to say. "I turned into you."

"Me?" The dragon looked out at me through Malcolm's eyes. Smoke rolled out of his nostrils.

I nodded and stared down at the ground. "Aurelia told me to never transform into a dragon again, so until my dream, I haven't."

His eyes widened in surprise. "Aurelia knew?"

"She was there when it happened." I shuddered when I remembered the look on her face, the contempt. "That night, I dreamed I turned into a dragon to defeat Draconian. His dragons attacked me for it, tearing me apart, but the worst thing was the satisfaction on Aurelia's face as she watched them."

"Transform now." He waved a hand at me. "Don't think about the form. Think about changing. A caterpillar, becoming a butterfly."

I stepped away from him, not sure if I should do this. What if I turned into a dragon, and his retaliated? When my blood had splattered his face and his dragon hungered for more, his reaction had nearly destroyed him. If he killed me, what would that do to him?

"Dacia—" he bowed down in front of me like a knight before a queen "—I swear to you, on my honor, that no harm will come to you no matter what form you take." His features morphed becoming more animalistic. When Malcolm spoke again, it was with a forked tongue. "I vow to continue protecting you no matter what you transform into. I pledge to do you no harm." He blinked, and his features became his own again.

Taking a deep breath, I closed my eyes and tried to clear my head. I opened my mind to Malcolm so he could see my thoughts. Then I focused on transformation but not what to transform into. My body stretched and pulled. Something tore through my back. My senses of smell and hearing increased dramatically. I fell onto all fours and opened my eyes.

Malcolm stood staring up at me. An unfamiliar scent rolled off of him, coating my tongue, and making my mouth water. He wiped his hand down his face. "Amazing."

I turned my head and took in my body. The scales covering my massive form shimmered like blue ice. A spiny ridge ran along my backbone, ending in a spiked tail. I fanned out my wings, knocking Malcolm's treasure stacks over. Prisms danced along the cavern walls and floor.

"This is what I should be if I'm not human?" My voice was richer and slightly feral.

He nodded. "I looked into your thoughts. I saw that you weren't choosing a form. That is how dragons decide what avatar they will take." He climbed over his treasure until he found a gold shield. He pulled his shirt over his head and polished it until it shone. Then he brought it over and held it in front of me.

My eyes were still my own, emerald green flecked with black from Mavros' taint, but the rest of me was magnificent. Horns that looked more like antlers curved into the air from an angular face. I was both beautiful and ferocious.

Other times when I'd transformed, my magic had waned quickly, but in this body, it didn't feel like it was being drained at all. "Care to fly with me?"

"Let Cash know you're okay." He set the shield down. "Don't let him know you're a dragon."

Chapter 24

Flying as a dragon was nothing like flying as a human. Magic didn't propel me. Wings did. I lowered my body and jumped, beating my wings down at the same time, praying I wouldn't make a fool of myself. But it seemed that in this form, pumping my wings and soaring through the cavern were second nature. Malcolm led me through the passageways. The scent of cool, fresh air hit my nostrils, and a thrill shot through me at the idea of flying through the star-filled sky.

Malcolm flipped sideways and flew through a crack. I followed him, scraping my talons on the boulders. The world disappeared below me, and the sky surrounded me. Thin, wispy clouds floated beneath me. The waning moon was nearly full and lit the mountaintops.

Warmth spread through my chest. It took me a few moments to realize what I was feeling. It had been so long that I almost didn't recognize it.

Contentment.

In this body, I felt happy. It seemed like all my problems were far behind me. I stretched my wings out and soared, letting the breeze carry me.

Malcolm slowed and flew next to me. "This form suits you."

"You're truly okay with it?"

There was no malice in his eyes, no tension in his body. "I've known for a long time that you belong to the dragons. This proves I was right."

"Will the others feel the same?"

His lip curled up, showing long fangs. "We'll make them."

We flew in comfortable silence. Moonlight reflected off the snowy summits. The mountain range stretched out as far as I could see. The peaks were rugged and unrecognizable. "Where are we? None of this looks familiar."

He chuckled. The sound was like boulders crashing together. "We're well over a thousand miles away from Bittersweet."

"It's beautiful."

He shot me a look that in my human form would have appeared menacing, but as a dragon, I realized it was a smirk. "Let's see what you can do." He zipped forward, plowing through a cloud, making tendrils of it snake out through the sky.

I flapped my wings and shot forward like an arrow. Malcolm may have been more experienced, but I was smaller, lighter.

He grabbed my foreleg and spun me. Laughter tore from my throat as we twirled through the air. The stars looked like streaks of light.

We dove down. The ground rushed toward us, and I worried we wouldn't pull up in time. He leveled off, skimming his talons along the treetops, and I followed.

He flapped his wings and climbed toward the heavens. He roared, and flames shot from his maw. A thrill of excitement rushed through me. Could I breathe fire? I hadn't been able to when I'd mimicked Malcolm's form, but this was my true alternate metamorphosis.

"Aren't you going to try?" Malcolm's voice carried back to me on the breeze.

"I'm trying to figure out how … or if I even can."

He slowed again. As soon as he was beside me, he said, "Let your instincts guide you." Another burst of flame shot from his mouth. Red and hot, it blasted through the air.

Without a second thought, I reacted. Heat raced through my body. My flames exploded through the night sky in front of me, blue like my magic.

Malcolm made a noise that sounded almost like a purr. "Yes." His voice was smug. "You belong to us, not the demon."

Dacia. Cash's voice was filled with concern. *Are you all right?*

I sent him an image of the night sky with the land far below me. *Yes. I'm flying.*

You're flying. His voice changed from concerned to agitated.

"Maybe we should go back," I said to Malcolm.

He nodded toward a rocky outcrop on the side of a mountain. "Land there."

I hung back, watching how Malcolm landed. He turned his wings perpendicular to the ground and grasped a boulder in his talons. Then before he'd completely stopped, he transformed into his human avatar.

Afraid I would overshoot the ledge if I did it his way, I took the landing much slower. I also waited to take my natural form. As a dragon, I was warm. As a human, dressed as I was, I would freeze to death up here.

"Cash is worried about me."

"Yeah." Malcolm wiped the grin off his face. "So I heard." He walked around me, taking in every facet of my new form. "Let me tell him about this. I'll see if Arianna or Russ can stay with you for the rest of the night."

As soon as I transformed, Malcolm grabbed my hand and teleported me back to my bedroom.

Cash and Russ stood by my window talking softly. When Cash noticed us, he darted to my side, looking me over, making sure I was okay. "You smell like mountain air." He pointed outside. "But, not these mountains. Farther away, colder mountains."

"It's a long story, Cash." I took his hand in mine, squeezing it reassuringly. "I'm okay. I need to get some sleep. Tomorrow's going to be a long day."

"I think you mean today." Russ smiled at me. "It's 4:03."

"Crap." I pulled my sweatshirt over my head and sat on the edge of my bed, kicking my shoes off.

"We need to talk," Malcolm said to Cash. Then he turned toward Russ. "Keep her safe. Contact helps keep the dreams away, but her magic should be fairly depleted."

Chapter 25

Dragon Scales

$\mathcal{I}$ woke up to hushed, angered voices. Malcolm, Cash, and Russ stood at the end of my bed. Even though my room was still dark, I could see that their posture was stiff. I peeked at my alarm clock. 6:18. "Guys, I need sleep," I said through a yawn.

They all turned toward me. Cash's and Russ' dragons glared at me like Malcolm's had before he saw me transform. Their instincts were at war with their honor.

I rolled onto my side and propped myself up on my arm. If their dragons decided to attack me, I wanted to see it coming.

Malcolm stared at them until they cowered back, averting their gazes. He stepped to the edge of my bed, blocking their path to me. "I can send them away so you can sleep—but this fury will fester and grow inside of them—or you can come with us and show them."

The thought of transforming in front of them was both thrilling and terrifying. The dragon form called to me even now. But what if they wanted to kill me for it? What if they couldn't accept me? Cash was like a brother to me, and Russ had been the first dragon to trust me, to let me see inside his thoughts. "What will their dragons do?" My voice came out more broken than I'd expected.

Malcolm knelt down and grabbed my hand. "I will keep you safe, Dacia." His pupils slitted, and his voice became rougher. "No harm will befall you."

"I'm not worried about me." I let go of his hand and combed my fingers through my hair, pulling out the tangles. I looked over his shoulder at the others. "I'm worried about what will happen to them if they break their vow."

Malcolm's face slackened as confusion crossed over his features.

"They'll hate themselves if they hurt me."

"They're as likely to hurt you whether you transform or not. Their dragons are riled, bloodthirsty." He glanced over his shoulder. "I believe they will accept you just as my dragon did."

"Okay." I tossed back the covers and got out of bed. After slipping my shoes and sweatshirt on again, I said, "Where to?"

Malcolm stood between me and the other dragons. "Hold on."

I slid my hand into his. He squeezed it reassuringly, then transported us. The mountain lake was frozen and, more importantly, deserted. The moon hung low in the sky, but its light reflected off the snow, illuminating the pine trees. I shivered and wrapped my arms around my body to conserve warmth.

Like I'd done with Malcolm, I opened my thoughts to the dragons. Once I felt their consciousnesses, I focused on transformation. My body changed almost instantly this time. Wings sprouted from my shoulder blades at the same time as my body enlarged and shifted into the dragon.

I watched Russ' and Cash's faces, hoping they'd react as Malcolm had. Standing in front of them like this, I felt exposed. I could smell their rage turn to turmoil. Like Malcolm, their gut reaction was that this was wrong, but it was also right.

They looked from me to Malcolm. Red scales lined Russ' neck, and fangs jutted out of his mouth. He shook his head, and a blood-red dragon appeared in front of me. His lips pulled back, and a low, menacing growl echoed through the clearing.

"Russ"—I lowered my head, not wanting to appear threatening to him—"I'm still Dacia. I'm still the same person you've known."

He took a step forward. "This is wrong."

"Why?" Even with some dragon instincts, I couldn't understand this. "Why is it okay for you to become a human but not for me to become a dragon?"

Flames leapt into his mouth, extinguishing before shooting out. "This is unnatural."

"It's her *natural* avatar." Malcolm stood beside me still in human form.

"It can't be." Russ flapped his wings and lifted into the air. He hovered above me. "She must die."

Malcolm and Cash were dragons before the words were completely out of Russ' mouth.

"I saved you." I couldn't believe I was hearing this from him. "Because of me, you were reunited with your son." Anger that wasn't wholly my own rose up inside of me. "You *vowed* to protect me."

His chin dropped for a fraction of a second. Then he opened his maw, and flames blasted toward me.

"No," Malcolm roared as he tried to step in front of me.

I shoved him aside. Fire erupted from my mouth. Blue flames collided with red.

Russ' blaze stopped abruptly, and he dropped to the ground. "It can't be."

"It is." Malcolm's voice was calmer than I expected it to be. *You did good, Dacia.*

Russ bowed. "Forgive me, Dacia." He transformed back into his human shape. "I didn't believe it was possible."

Between one breath and the next, I was back in my own body. I grabbed Russ' arm and pulled it. "Stand up. You're forgiven." I looked at Cash. The sun was just beginning to lighten the sky behind him. "What about you?"

"My dragon seems to have accepted you."

"Good." I nodded. "Am I going to have to do this with every dragon?" I pointed at the sky. "And, I need to get home. My parents'll be waking me up soon to clean and help cook." I kicked a pile of snow. "So much for sleeping."

Malcolm threw his arm around me and pulled me against his side. "You're cold."

I nodded.

"We'll talk at your house." He teleported the two of us to my room. Cash and Russ appeared seconds later.

I kicked my shoes off, wrapped a blanket around me, and sat on my bed. "So, what's gonna happen?"

Russ stared outside. "Is there a reason to tell?"

"We wouldn't have to." Cash shrugged. "Then other dragons wouldn't react like Russ did."

Russ hung his head. "I am truly sorry for that." He scrubbed his hands down his face. "There's no reason for the others to know, though."

Malcolm sat next to me. "What do you want to do about it?"

"I like being a dragon." I picked at a loose string on the seam of my blanket. "I love flying, the feeling of invincibility, breathing fire." I looked up at them. "All of it. I can't imagine never being a dragon again. Even now, it calls to me."

Cash nodded. "I can't imagine never being able to take this form again."

"Others will react as I did." Russ smiled sadly at me. "Once they see you breathe fire, they should accept you, but …"

"But they might decide to kill me anyway?" I clutched my blanket tighter. I had thought I was done fighting dragons, but I should have known better.

Malcolm squeezed my shoulder, and I leaned into him, wanting his comfort. "Dragons are stubborn beasts. If they don't know you, they'll be less likely to be forgiving."

"Though, in all fairness," Cash said, "most dragons have heard of you."

Nervous energy brought me to my feet, and I paced across the room. The end of my blanket trailed on the ground behind me. "Yeah, but how many of them are like Argentum and want me dead?"

Malcolm turned toward me, following my movements with his eyes. Even though he looked human, it was his dragon that spoke. "We'll kill them all."

Russ stepped out of the spare bedroom along with Malcolm and Cash. Mom hesitated in her vacuuming for just a moment. She lifted an eyebrow at me but said nothing.

They all helped me with my chores. They didn't mention anything else about me turning into a dragon, and I tried not to think about my powers. I needed today to go smoothly with no mishaps. I didn't want to put anybody's life in danger.

When the chores were done, I sent the dragons outside to wait for me. Mom had been sneaking looks at me all morning, and I knew she wanted to know why Russ was here.

I stood in the kitchen and watched Dad baste the turkey while Mom checked on all the other pots and pans full of food. "I'm going for a run."

"Honey." Mom turned toward me. Her red and silver hair was pulled back in a braid, and flour coated her cheeks and sleeves. "It's Christmas Eve. You can go one day without running."

I shook my head. "I can't, not today."

"Our guests will be here soon." Dad pointed the turkey baster at me. "You still have to shower and change."

Mom wiped her hands on a towel. "Are you worried about getting fat? One day isn't going to make that much of a difference."

"No." I huffed out a laugh. "I … uh … I run to exhaust myself and my magic because I still don't have it under control, and I don't want to hurt anyone."

"Is that why he's here?" She hung the towel back over the oven's handle, trying to pass herself off as nonchalant, but I could see the tension in her body.

Since I really didn't want to explain that my guards had spent most of yesterday wanting to kill me, I decided to go with that. "Yeah. There'll be a lot of people around today. They thought it might be better to have three of them here."

"Couldn't they have sent a girl?" Mom waved her hand at me. "It doesn't look good having three men here who aren't Cody. What are people going to say?"

"Your Mom has a point." Dad watched me as he unrolled the sleeves on his shirt.

Heat blossomed on my cheeks. I couldn't believe my parents said that. They knew why the dragons were here. They knew I needed them. "They could be anywhere, but they're here protecting me. That's all that should matter to you." Rage ignited inside my belly. Before it could explode out of me, I spun around, practically sprinting through the living room. "I'll be back." I darted outside, slamming the door behind me.

I ran down the steps and onto the driveway, heading for the road. The dragons caught up to me quickly.

"Are you okay?" Malcolm's voice was low, like he sensed a threat but wasn't sure where to look for it.

I kept running, letting the sound of my feet hitting the ground replace my parents' words.

"Dacia." Malcolm grabbed my arm and spun me around. "Are you okay?"

Tears dripped off my cheeks. "My parents are more concerned about how it will look for me to have three men staying at my house than the fact that you're here to keep me and everyone around me safe."

"I showed you before—" Malcolm reached up and brushed away my tears "—we can be whatever form we choose."

I stepped away from him. "I know, but you shouldn't have to, and people shouldn't think less of me for who I hang around with." I started running again. "I need to move. I need to let some of my anger go before I accidentally use any magic."

"Let me drain some." Malcolm reached for my hand.

I shook my head. "After our run, if I need you to, I'll let you. I need to figure out how to handle this on my own."

We jogged down the road in relative silence. When the anger within me subsided, I used my magic in little ways. Ways that the watchers wouldn't notice from a distance. Dragon scales covered my arms and legs. A breeze rose up behind us, pushing us faster. Icicles formed on the branches of nearby trees.

Cash grabbed my arm and slowed my pace. "Humans can't run that fast for that long." He smiled at me. "Slow down a little."

Mandi Oyster

"Sorry. I'm trying to use up all my power so I don't hurt anyone today."

„198‘’

Chapter 26

Christmas Eve

By the time we got back home, my magic was nearly depleted. It had taken longer to drain it than it had yesterday. It gave me hope that one day my stamina would be what it had been before I'd faced Argentum. I just hoped I'd be able to control it by the time it was built back up.

My parents weren't in the living room, so I hurried to my room to grab a change of clothes. Then I showered. While I was brushing my hair, somebody banged on the door. I nearly screamed at the unexpected sound. "What?" My voice was higher pitched than normal.

"Your aunt and uncle are here," Dad said.

I looked at my reflection through the steam-covered mirror and hoped I wouldn't disappoint my parents. "I'll be out in a minute."

"Don't keep them waiting too long."

I squeezed some gel into my hands and spread it through my hair, hoping it would keep my curls from becoming too unruly. Then I opened the door and stepped into the hallway. I was surprised when I wasn't immediately surrounded by three dragons.

I'm behind you. Russ' voice filled my head. *I thought it might be easier for you if you only had two dragons to explain.*

Thank you. I followed the sound of laughter to the dining room. Julie leaned on the back of one of the chairs deep in conversation with Mom. Dana, Dad, Cash, and Malcolm stood across the room from them, laughing at something one of them had said.

As soon as Dana saw me, he stepped away from the others and pulled me into a hug. "How's my favorite niece?"

"I'm good." I hugged him back. "I'm glad to be home for a while."

He pulled away, still clutching my arms. "You're growing up so fast. It's hard to believe." He looked over my shoulder. "Cody coming?"

"No." I shook my head. "He's spending today and tomorrow with his family."

He nodded and hooked his thumb at the dragons. "So, what's the story with those two?"

"They're friends from college." Cash and Malcolm both watched me, hearing every word that was being said. "They couldn't make it home, so since we have an extra room, Mom and Dad offered to let them stay here."

"They on the football team?" He rubbed the top of his head, and I realized he was missing his customary ball cap. "They're huge."

"Nah." I smiled at them. "Maybe they should be, though. Our team could use an advantage."

While we were talking, Julie walked up next to me. She flipped her brown hair over her shoulder. "Hello, Dacia." She smiled and hugged me. "How's college going?"

"Good." While I hugged her, I thought about how my parents had always called her Crazy Aunt Julie, and I couldn't help but wonder where that had come from. When I pulled back, she noticed my necklace.

She held the heart-shaped pendant, rubbing her thumb along the curve of it. "This is beautiful."

"Thanks." I smiled, glad that Susan had given it to me yesterday so I would have something besides Malcolm and Cash to talk about. "Cody's parents gave it to me for Christmas. It's our birthstones."

"It's beautiful," she said again. "Such a thoughtful gift."

I looked into the living room, expecting to find three of my cousins sitting in there. "Where's everyone else?"

"They're with their significant others." Sadness filled her eyes for a moment before she shook it off. "They'll be with us tomorrow. Your parents are lucky you're here and not at Cody's."

Dad leaned around Dana. "How's the library?" he asked Julie. "Quiet?" He chuckled at his joke, and the rest of us shook our heads.

"I imagine it is today." She smiled back at him. "Normally, we're booked solid, though."

"Oh." He laughed. "Good one."

I stood with Mom and Julie, mostly listening to their conversation. When the doorbell rang, I excused myself to answer it. Cindy and Bill stood on the porch. Cindy had her face nuzzled down in the collar of her coat. "It's freezing out here."

I opened the door wider and ushered them in. "Well, it is wintertime."

"Every year, I tell myself I'm moving south for the winter, and every year, I stay here." She handed me her coat and purse. "One of these days, it's going to happen." She held my face between her hands and kissed my cheek.

"Maybe one of these days, we'll win the lottery." Bill threw his coat over his arm. "Where do you want these?"

"Give them to me." I patted Cindy's. "I'll take them into the other room."

Since the dragons were pretending to use the guest bedroom, I put the coats on my bed. Then I went into the living room and threw a couple more logs onto the fire. I looked into the dining room, but the thought of being around so many people made my stomach roll. I sat on the couch and waited for everybody else to show up, hoping that nothing bad would happen today.

I stared into the flames, watching them dance behind the screen. The fire mesmerized me, and I woke up when the doorbell rang. Shaking my head, I stood. I couldn't fall asleep again, not with so many people around. I couldn't risk my dreams coming to life. I couldn't let my family find out what I was.

Grandma and Grandpa let themselves in before I made it to the door. Grandma looked me over. "College isn't making you fat." She pulled her gloves off and stuffed them in her pockets. "Are you eating?"

"Yes … just not too much. I'm also exercising." I took Grandpa's coat and waited while he helped Grandma take hers off. "I ran almost five miles this morning."

"Five miles? Hopefully, not by yourself. Do you have pepper spray just in case?" She swatted Grandpa's hand away while she watched my face.

"Five miles. Cash and Malcolm ran with me this morning." Since Russ was remaining hidden, I didn't mention him. "A lot of times, Cody goes with me, but he's spending today with his family."

"What about pepper spray?" She let Grandpa help with her coat again.

I took it from him. "I don't need it when I'm with them. You'll see."

"Smells good in here," Grandpa said as he walked into the dining room. "When do we eat?"

While I walked down the hall, I heard Dad say, "Everyone's here so anytime."

I dropped my head. I loved my family, but I'd hoped that some of my cousins would be here to keep the focus off of me.

I threw the coats on my bed and turned around, running right into Russ. He clutched my shoulders. "Are you okay? You smell … scared."

"I just hope I can keep my powers under control."

"We're here if you need us." He turned invisible before leaving my room and heading for the kitchen.

I helped my parents dish up the food and carry it to the dining room table. When we were bringing in the last of the food, Dad said, "Get your drinks and find a spot." He pointed at Grandpa. "Then Oscar will say grace."

"Rub a dub, dub. Give me some grub," Grandpa mumbled as he wandered over to the drink table. He walked back with a cup of coffee for himself and one for Grandma.

When I came back into the room, the dragons stood with a chair open between them. A little of my tension released. Everyone held hands. Both Cash and Malcolm siphoned my energy while Grandpa said, "Dear Lord, thank you for bringing us all together and for bringing new friends into the fold. Thank you for giving your son so that we may live, and thank you for the food we are about to eat. Your generosity is unending. Amen." He clapped his hands, then rubbed them together. "Bring on the food."

"Oscar." Grandma shook her head and clicked her tongue.

Dinner was an uncomfortable experience with Malcolm, Cash, and I trying to explain how college was going without letting on that demons, dragons, a crazed magician, and Nephilim were trying to kill or capture me, dodging questions about Malcolm's and Cash's pasts, and trying to explain that

Cody really was okay with them being here and there was nothing sexual between us.

Grandma pointed her fork at me. "You can say that however many times you like. But these two"—she shook her head—"mmm … mmm … mmm. They are gorgeous, and they can't keep their eyes off of you."

"Martha," Grandpa chastised, "you can't say things like that. You're embarrassing them all. If Dacia says these young men are just friends, that's all they are."

Cindy nearly choked on her food. She held her napkin to her mouth until she was done smirking.

I clenched my jaw shut. I didn't want to ruin Christmas with the things I wanted to say, but the more I held it in, the more I felt my magic flare up. I pressed against the table, pushed my chair back, grabbed my plate, and walked into the kitchen.

While I scraped my food into the trash, Russ rubbed my neck, drawing my power into him. "You okay?"

"Mom was right." I walked to the sink and rinsed my plate off. "Everyone thinks I'm cheating on Cody."

"Why does that matter?" His voice was soft, meant only for me, but I imagined Malcolm and Cash could still hear us. "You know the truth. Your parents know it. Who cares what anyone else thinks?"

I put my plate into the dishwasher. "If they think I'd cheat on him, then they don't know the kind of person I am. What other despicable things do they think I'd do?" I walked down the hall and stepped into the bathroom. Closing the door, I stared into the mirror.

"You cannot control what others think of you." Russ appeared behind me. His amber eyes stood out sharply against his dark skin. "All you can do is try to enjoy this time that you have with your family. You never know when they might be taken from you."

I turned around and stepped closer to him. "Can I?"

He nodded, and I stepped into his arms, wrapping mine around his waist. "You're right. I'll try to enjoy the rest of the day." I pulled away from him. "Thanks." I wiped underneath my eyes and walked back to the dining room, taking my seat between Cash and Malcolm.

When everyone was gone, I collapsed on the loveseat. Somehow, I'd made it through the day without my magic erupting from me. Several more comments had been made about my dragon friends and their relationships with me, but one or the other of them had changed the subject by asking about my aunts' and uncles' jobs. By asking about their kids and grandkids. My debt to them had grown immensely today.

"How are you doing?" Dad sat on the couch and leaned forward with his elbows on his knees.

I shrugged. "I didn't catch anything on fire or knock things off the walls, so I guess I'm pretty good."

"You seem …" He cocked his head and looked me over. "I don't know. Exhausted. Stressed."

"I am." I dragged my hands down my face. "Lately …" How much should I tell them? "Lately, it's hard to keep my magic from doing what it wants."

He nodded. "And what does it want?"

A startled laugh broke free from my lips. "Nothing good."

The parking lot was fuller than I'd ever remembered seeing it. I got out of our SUV and walked toward the massive double doors, remembering the last time I had been here. The candle flames that had turned blue and risen higher. I had been terrified that I would kill everyone.

Malcolm held the door open for all of us. He was dressed in a black button-down shirt and slacks with a bronze tie that matched his eyes. His cornrows were pulled back in a ponytail. If I hadn't known him, I would have been leery of him. He looked fierce and threatening.

Cash stepped in front of me so I would be surrounded by my guards once inside. He looked less intimidating. His purple shirt matched the streaks in his hair, making them stand out more than normal, giving him a boyish appeal.

Now that Malcolm's bloodlust had abated, we all figured two dragons should be more than enough to keep me safe, so once my extended family had gone, Russ had turned to me. "If you don't need me anymore, I'll take my leave."

"Thank you, Pyrus—" I'd hugged him "—for everything. Accepting my dragon, helping me, reminding me what's important."

He'd grasped my shoulders and looked into my eyes. "It was my pleasure." Then he'd teleported away.

We had to walk nearly to the front of the church before finding a pew the five of us could fit in. Mom and Dad went in first so I could leave if things went wrong. I folded my hands in my lap and stared at the twinkling lights, hoping to find peace in their beauty.

Malcolm stretched his arm across the back of the pew, and I wondered how my parents would react to that. I imagined my nosy neighbors and relatives that were here would find it of the utmost importance the next time they got together.

Frustration gnawed at my gut. I wanted to sit with Cody. I wanted him to drape his arm over my shoulders and pull me against him. I wanted to be near him without worrying about what would happen. This had been going on for far too long. I wanted my life back.

Cash set his hand on top of mine and drew my magic into him. I took in a deep breath and tried to let go of my annoyance. There were too many people here for me to lose control.

As soon as I calmed down, Cash pulled his hand back, sliding it onto his leg where he could reach me again if need be.

Cody stopped in the aisle and looked down our row. "Room for me?"

Mom, Dad, and Cash slid down, making room for Cody next to me. As soon as he sat, Britny climbed onto his lap. The rest of his family smiled and waved as they walked by. Except Josh. He glared at Malcolm, and Malcolm chuckled low enough that I didn't think anyone else could hear him.

Cody's shoulder pressed against mine. The comfort of his touch warred with the power inside me that wanted to hurt him, that wanted him nowhere near me.

Malcolm pulled his arm down and set his fist on his leg so that the back of it brushed against my hand. My energy trickled into him.

I focused on Britny, seeing no reason my magic would want to harm her. "Did you have a good day?"

"Yeah." She beamed at me. "I got new toys." She wrinkled her nose. "And clothes. And I got to play with my cousins. And Cody told me I look like a princess in my new dress." She poofed the cobalt silk material up.

"You do." I smiled at her. "It's a beautiful gown."

She turned toward Cash. "Do you like my dress? Do you think I can be a fairy princess?"

"I think you could." His eyes sparkled with mirth.

She reached for his hair but didn't touch him. "I wish I had purple hair and purple eyes."

"Why?" He tilted his head at her and frowned. "You're beautiful the way you are."

The overhead lights dimmed, and organ music filled the church. "You have to be quiet now." Cody wrapped one arm around Britny and slid his hand into mine.

The surge in my power was instantaneous. A spark shot from my hand into Cody's. He yelped and jerked away from me. My eyes widened in horror, and I clutched Malcolm's hand. *Take it all,* I thought to Malcolm and asked Cody, "Are you okay?"

"Just a little shocked." He smiled, but I could see his pain through it.

I pulled away from him, pressing against Malcolm's side. Cody's eyes filled with a deep sadness before he slipped his mask in place. The rest of the congregation stood and began singing Silent Night, but Malcolm and I sat.

My magic built up inside of me, filling too fast for Malcolm to drain it. The serpent slithered under my skin, pulling away from Malcolm. A jolt of electricity shot from me to him. He held onto me and tugged me to my feet. Then he led me to the narthex, never letting go of my hand.

I stared at the floor. Navy carpet ran the length of the aisle, protecting the hardwood from most of the foot traffic. Water clung to the fibers, darkening it where the majority of people had walked.

Once we were past the nave doors, Malcolm pulled me to the side, behind a Christmas tree and out of view of the parishioners. "Get it under control." The words were growled.

I wrenched my hand away, realizing my power was still attacking him. Bursts of energy arched toward him. I turned my back and focused inward.

The serpent lifted from its coils, stretching until it towered above me. It puffed its body out and swayed from side to side as if it intended to attack.

"What are you doing?" I stepped forward cautiously. "I've been using you. I've been building you back up. And, this is how you repay me?"

The dragons want to drain us. It looked down on me through hardened copper eyes. *The boy wishes us gone, and you do not fight for us.*

"What do you mean, I don't fight for y …" My voice trailed off. "Wait. You said us." I tugged my hand through my hair. "You never say us."

We have figured out how to merge with him. The snake seemed smug.

I glanced to the shadows to see if Mavros' power was still coiled up there.

Not him. The demon made him sleep. The serpent drew its head back. *The dragon is part of us now.*

I sucked in a startled breath. "No … why? He wanted to kill me. He wanted both of us dead. He said my power was too much for a person to have. Why would it want you to be stronger?"

We were a better choice than fading into nothing.

Malcolm clutched my shoulder. I opened my eyes and stared up into his. A myriad of emotions crossed his face. "Can you go back in and sit beside him? Can you control the serpent and the dragon?"

"I don't know." I lowered my chin and swallowed over the lump in my throat.

Malcolm slipped his fingers under my chin, tilting it up. The lights on the tree danced across his face, shadowing different areas as they twinkled. "I can't take it from you."

"I know." Tears pricked my eyes. "I want to try something. Stay here with me?"

"Of course."

I backed up against him, and he wrapped his arms around me. Then I focused on my powers. The serpent seemed even more agitated. I stepped forward with my hand outstretched. "What do you want from me?" I asked.

We want power, strength, eternity.

Hiding my fear, I touched the snake's head, letting my fingers trail along its scales. "Why can't Cody be part of my life?"

He does not want us. We do not want him. The serpent closed its eyes and pressed its head against my palm.

How could my magic not want the same things that I wanted? It didn't make any sense.

The answer slammed into me like a Mac truck. It was not my power that wanted different. It was Argentum's. He had wanted my power for his own in life, and whatever tainted me wanted the same. I knelt in front of the snake. It rested its head on my shoulder, and I wrapped my arms around it, clutching it to me.

I pushed my power into it. Focusing everything I had on making it sleep, not sure if it would work or not. The serpent shuddered and tried to pull away from me. When I didn't loosen my grip, it sank its fangs into my shoulder.

I felt Malcolm's hold on me tighten. His magic joined mine, and the snake went limp in my arms. Its teeth retracted, and I slumped in relief.

"Dacia." Malcolm's voice was as soft as down and right in my ear.

I opened my eyes and pressed my hand to my shoulder. Pulling it away, I looked down at my blood dampened fingers. "At least I didn't wear my white dress."

He guided me to the bathroom, looked around to make sure no one was watching, turned invisible, and followed me in. While I washed my hands, he sent healing energy into me.

My black dress looked damp but not bloody. "Thanks," I said.

"What did you do?" he asked when we were out in the hall.

I felt empty on the inside. Hollow. My steps faltered. "I knocked my powers out."

He put his hand under my elbow and raised an eyebrow at me, saying nothing as we walked back to our pew. I slid in beside Cody and twined my fingers with his.

He looked down at our hands, then at me. Curiosity crossed his face, but he focused on the minister. His thumb brushed over mine while we listened to the story of Jesus' birth.

When the service was over and the lights came back on, I hurried to pull my coat over my injured arm to cover the blood. Malcolm and Cash stood to the side while Cody and I talked to other members of the congregation.

Several people came up to me, hoping everything was okay, but really wanting to know any juicy gossip they could get their hands on. Cody wrapped his arm around my waist and held me protectively. While I tried to come up with an explanation for why I'd left with Malcolm, Britny skipped off to her parents.

As soon as she was with them, Cody said, "Excuse us." Then without another word, he led me outside. He pulled me around the side of the church. "Why?"

"Why?" Of all the things he could say, that wasn't what I'd expected.

He held my face in his hands. "Why can you touch me?"

"Oh." I slid my arms around his waist.

His lips lifted. It wasn't a full-blown smile, but a hopeful one. "Not complaining. Just wanna know."

"I don't know if I killed my magic, made it go dormant, or just made it sleep for a while." I chewed on my lip. "I hope I didn't make a mistake."

"Can't be." He bent down. "I can touch you." He brushed his thumbs over my cheeks, then kissed me, parting my lips with his tongue.

I clutched the back of his head and pulled him closer. When my magic didn't stir, I deepened the kiss.

Cody moaned, and his hands trailed down my neck. As soon as his fingers brushed my shoulder, he pulled away. "What happened?"

I shrugged. It didn't make sense to me at all. The serpent was a figment of my imagination, a way for me to visualize my magic. How could it hurt me? "My powers didn't want to give in without a fight."

Chapter 27

Life Without Magic

$\mathcal{M}$avros stands in front of me with his hands behind his back. A muscle in his jaw twitches. The wind blows through the trees, knocking snow off their branches.

I wrap my arms around my body and shiver.

"You cannot trap your powers." His voice is tight.

The anger on his face reminds me of his panther form and how terrifying he can be. "I didn't know what else to do." My powers have only been gone for a couple of hours, and already, I feel their absence as much as if I'd lost an arm or a leg. I long for my fire to warm me. "I can't let them kill Cody. I can't allow them to threaten so many lives."

He steps toward me and holds my face in his hands. There's no tenderness in them, but warmth from his body floods into me. "I am bound to you. You are the most powerful human this realm has ever known. I will not let you give that up for some *boy*."

Anger starts to rise in me, but I push it down. Mavros promised to leave Cody alone, and I'm not about to push him on the subject. "Then help me." I place my hands over his and stare into his obsidian eyes. They seem to soften a little. "Help me get rid of Argentum's taint."

He pulls away, turning his back on me. "I told you; I don't know how."

"Yeah." If he was anybody else, I would think he had turned his back to hide the truth from me, but I know he can lie just as well looking directly into my eyes as he can with his back turned. "You did, but help me figure it out." I put my hand on his arm and step around him so he has to look at me. "Please, Mavros. Please help me."

He brushes his thumb along my cheek. "You could use my name. Force me to do your bidding."

"I could." I shrug. "That doesn't seem very sportsmanlike, though."

He tilts his head, and his eyebrows pinch together. "I'll see what I can do." He steps away and disappears.

When I woke up, Malcolm lay on the bed next to me. His head was propped up on his elbow, and he stared down at me. His face was an unreadable mask, and I couldn't help but wonder what I'd done to anger him. I stared at him until he talked.

"You keep making bargains with the demon." His fangs bit into his bottom lip. "You belong to us."

I rolled onto my side so that I was facing him and stared into his bronze eyes. I knew it was a risk. He was a predator, no doubt about it, but he was also my friend and protector. "Can you guys help me? Can you make whatever it is go away?"

"We're trying." He flopped onto his back and stared at the ceiling.

I softened my voice. "I know you are. I have no doubt about that." I got out of bed and plodded over to my dresser. I pulled out a pair of socks, then sat on the edge of my bed and slipped them on. "I could've killed Cody in church, in front of hundreds of witnesses, last night, and you wouldn't have been able to do anything about it. You couldn't keep my powers under control, and I can't risk it. I've got to do something."

"I know." He pulled his hands down his face. "Merry Christmas."

I plopped down next to him and laid my head on his shoulder. "Thanks. You, too." We stayed like that until there was a knock on my door.

"Dacia," Dad said softly, "are you awake."

"Yeah. I'll be out in a minute." I sucked in a deep breath. "It's going to be a good day. Isn't it?" I asked Malcolm.

He pulled me into a hug. "It will be." He turned invisible until I walked past the spare bedroom. When Cash joined me,

Malcolm showed himself. The three of us walked into the living room together.

My parents sat on the loveseat. I did a double-take. They usually sat together on the couch. Mom had her side and Dad his, and very rarely did they sit anywhere else. "Merry Christmas," they said in unison.

"Merry Christmas." I sat on the couch expecting a dragon to sit on either side of me.

Malcolm stopped in front of me. "Merry Christmas." He nodded. Then he and Cash walked into the dining room.

I could see them from where I sat, and I knew they could be beside me in an instant, but it was still weird. Before they asked, I looked at my parents and said, "You don't need to worry. My magic is under control for now."

"Oh, Sweetie." Mom walked over and hugged me. "We know you won't hurt us."

Even though I knew they weren't true, those words were a huge relief to me. "Thanks, Mom."

Dad smacked his hands together. "Well … shall we open presents?" He walked over to the tree, grabbed a package, and brought it to me. When he handed it off, he bent down and embraced me, too.

I tore the polar bear paper off the gift and opened up a handmade afghan in shades of blues and purples. "Did you make this?" I looked at Mom.

"Yeah." She smiled timidly. "I needed a hobby."

"It's beautiful." I held it in front of me, staring at it, hoping she could see how much I appreciated it. After folding it carefully, I handed them their gift. "I hope you like it. I didn't know what to get you."

Dad handed the box to Mom, and she opened it, digging through the paper inside to pull out the card. "Dance lessons." Her voice rose as she looked from it to Dad.

"That should be interesting." Dad laughed. "Hopefully, your mother can keep up with me."

She smacked him with the envelope. "I'll be tearing up the floor while you're still trying to figure out which of your left feet to put the shoe on."

While we opened the rest of the presents, the house filled with the scent of fresh-baked cinnamon rolls. My stomach growled in response. About the same time we finished, the oven buzzed. Mom started to get up, but I waved at her. "I'll get it."

I walked into the kitchen, turned off the timer, and grabbed the oven mitts. A blast of hot air smacked me in the face when I pulled the rolls out. I iced them, then put one on each plate, and set them on the kitchen table. When my parents came in, I refilled their coffee cups and poured myself a glass of milk.

We sat at the kitchen table, and Dad said grace.

As soon as he finished, I shoved a bite in my mouth. "These are delicious."

Mom grinned. "I'd like to take credit for them, but they came from the freezer section of the grocery store."

When Dad finished eating, he rummaged through the cabinet, pulling out our big soup pot. Then he started making a triple-batch of chili. I washed my hands and helped where I could. Once that was going, the three of us played cards.

Shortly after noon, the doorbell rang. I went to answer it, expecting Pam or Sharon, but Mavros stood on the porch with a smirk on his face. "Hello, Dacia." The wind whipped snow all around him, but not a single hair on his head moved.

Chapter 28

$\mathcal{I}$ stared at Mavros not sure what to think about his arrival.

"Aren't you going to invite me in?"

His words snapped me out of my stupor. Warning bells seemed to go off in my head, but what could I do? He'd had access to my dorm room since I brought his blood back from a dream with me. He'd used his access to warn me and to help me, but what would he do if I let him into my home? No matter what he looked like on the outside, no matter what he'd done, he was a demon, and he'd warned me not to trust him.

"Dacia," Dad called as he walked into the room, "who's here?"

Before Dad saw him, Mavros morphed into Damon. Tousled brown hair and a rakish smile. My heart clenched at the sight of him. "This form's probably better."

"It's Damon." I turned and looked at Dad, wishing I could ask him what to do.

He grabbed the door from me, opening it farther. "Well, aren't you going to invite him in?"

"Sorry." I shot Damon a warning glance before saying, "Come on in."

Dad stuck his hand out. "I'm John. I assume you're one of Dacia's friends from college." The way he said friends, it was clear he thought Damon was something other than human.

Damon didn't act like there was anything weird about Dad's assumption. He just shook Dad's proffered hand and said, "Damon."

Dad hooked his thumb over his shoulder. "I'm on kitchen duty."

"I understand." Damon smiled conspiratorially at him.

I pushed the door closed. "Malcolm and Cash are in the dining room."

Damon bent over to pull his cowboy boots off. "They're not."

"Please …"

He knelt in front of me with one boot on and one boot off and took my hand in his. "On my honor, Dacia, I'm not here to cause trouble."

The words felt sincere, and not for the first time, I wondered if I was an idiot for trusting a demon.

He must have sensed my uncertainty because he said, "If you want me to leave or don't want me to be allowed in your home, you just have to command me."

Malcolm strode up and put his hand on Damon's shoulder, holding him down. From a distance, I was sure it looked friend-ly. Up close, Malcolm's voice was threatening. "She belongs to us. Not you, demon."

Damon stood and leaned closer to Malcolm. "She belongs to herself, and I belong to her."

Cash patted both of them on the shoulders. "Merry Christ-mas," he said loud enough for my parents to hear. "More peo-ple are here." He nodded toward the window, and I watched a red car pull up the driveway. He pressed his finger into Mal-colm's chest and then Damon's. "You will *both* be on your best behavior. Dacia deserves to enjoy her day without us ruining it for her."

"Well said, dragon." Damon slipped his other boot off and then set them both to the side.

For some reason, it made me giggle. Two dragons and a demon were in my house, in their stocking feet, and if they tried to cause any trouble, there was nothing I could do because I'd killed my powers. The laughter bubbled up, spilling out of me, sounding maniacal. Malcolm, Cash, and Damon stared at me like I'd lost my mind, and I wondered if I had.

Cash swiped his thumb over my cheek, and I realized I'd laughed so hard I'd cried. "It's going to be okay."

"I hope so." I waved the three of them away and pulled the door open for Pam. She walked in and handed a box full of goodies to me. I turned and gave it to Malcolm.

Always one to jump straight to the point, she asked, "Well, how's college?"

"It's good." I hugged her. "It'd be even better without the homework."

She threw her coat over my arm and pulled her long, blonde hair out of her collar. "There wouldn't be much point to going if you weren't learning something." She led me into the kitchen and motioned for Malcolm to set her box down. She pulled out a couple of desserts, a cheeseball, crackers, and three envelopes.

I looked at her standing next to Mom. She was a few inches shorter, a few pounds heavier, and they looked nothing alike. Seeing them together, I couldn't help but wonder if Jonathan and I would have shared more resemblances than my parents did with their siblings.

Pam raised an eyebrow at me. "Well, are you going to introduce me to your friends?"

"Sorry." My cheeks heated up. "This is my Aunt Pam, and this Malcolm, Cash, and Damon." I pointed at each of them as I said their names. "Mom, you didn't meet Damon."

"What handsome men." Pam shook each of their hands, then turned to me. "So …"

Damon interrupted. "We're just friends without anywhere else to go. Dacia and her parents were kind enough to let us join in on their festivities."

Pam slid her arm around my waist and leaned in. "You can tell yourself that. But these young men—" she shook her head "—not one of them's taken their eyes off of you yet."

The warmth on my cheeks spread over my face, neck, and ears and seemed to explode into a supernova. "Maybe." I stumbled over the word. "But they all know I'm with Cody."

"You name one guy who isn't up for a challenge." She turned toward my parents. "Caitlin, what can I help you with?"

Damon smiled his lopsided grin at me and nodded. "She has a point," he whispered as I carried her coat to my room.

"She always does." I looked over my shoulder at my aunt and wondered what she thought of me.

We went to the living room, and I plopped down on the couch. Malcolm and Cash sat to either side of me, leaving the loveseat for Damon. Malcolm leaned forward so that he was blocking me and said, "So why are you here, demon."

"Dacia said she needs my help, so I am here to help." He lifted his hands innocently. "To be honest, I'd rather be burning in Hell than in the mountains in the wintertime, but I am bound to her."

I chewed on my lip, pulling it into my mouth. "I still have watchers. If they see you …"

"They haven't yet. I created a distraction to occupy their attention." Leaning forward, he said, "I will do my best to keep them from knowing I'm here." His gaze held mine. "I will do my best not to put you in harm's way or jeopardize you in any way."

For the second time today, the urge to giggle hysterically came over me. This time I fought against it. The demon wouldn't put me in harm's way. Yet, I put Cody in it every day. What exactly did that make me?

"God, you smell good." Damon leaned closer to me and breathed in deeply. "I'd forgotten what your emotions do to your scent."

Malcolm started to get up, but I put my hand on his leg. "Please."

He leaned back, crossing his arms over his chest. His fangs jutted out of his mouth, pressing into his lips.

The doorbell rang, and I got up, hoping that the guests weren't another complication. This time I peeked out the window so I would be prepared. Thankfully, it was Uncle Larry and Aunt Sharon. I'd been more afraid than I wanted to admit that it would be one of the Nephilim or even Cody.

I would have to tell him that Damon had come to Christmas dinner, but it wasn't a conversation I was looking forward to. Even though Mavros and Damon were the same person, Damon was the version I had befriended and even dated for a while to keep him from killing Cody. Cody had been able to reluctantly admit that Mavros had helped me, but he wouldn't be happy to see him here in any form.

I opened the door and ushered Larry and Sharon in. Larry stomped his feet on the porch first, getting as much snow off of his shoes as he could before stepping inside. He looked around the room, then said, "Merry Christmas."

"Merry Christmas," we all responded at once.

Mom stepped into the living room and waved at her sister and brother-in-law. "Well, since everyone's here, why don't we eat?"

We all made our way into the dining room. Damon smiled smugly at Malcolm as he stood by the chair next to me. I held hands with both of them while Dad said grace. When he finished, I had no idea what he'd said between Dear Lord and Amen. I'd only been able to concentrate on the warmth of Damon's hand and the tension in Malcolm's.

I was fully aware that Damon was a demon, but I wished that Malcolm could remember that without Mavros' help, I would probably be dead. He'd fought against Argentum's hold on him. He'd fought Argentum's orders. He'd undoubtedly saved me from being eaten alive.

My aunts and uncle focused on me and my friends throughout dinner, casting curious looks at the guys who sat with me. Pam took a bite of chili, then pointed her spoon at Damon. "That one wants you for his own, Dacia." She nodded like she knew it as well as she knew her own name. "You better watch out for him, lest he steals your heart."

My mouth hung open. I didn't know what to say. He'd made it clear that once Cody was gone he planned to spend the rest of my life with me. How could she see his intentions so clearly?

"Who wouldn't want her heart?" Damon smiled at her. "She's beautiful, intelligent, and kind." He threw his arm over the back of my chair. "Unfortunately, she's also taken."

I shook my head and smacked him with the back of my hand. "Quit, Damon. They don't know you well enough to tell you're joking."

"I'm not." His fingers slid over my neck, and a jolt of desire shot through me.

Both dragons turned their heads toward me and breathed in deeply. Their pupils were thin slits.

"And you know it." Damon's voice was soft, meant only for me.

Malcolm pulled Damon's hand off my neck. "Quit causing trouble." He looked at Pam and shook his head. "He's always giving Cody crap, saying how he's going to steal Dacia away. It's some absurd joke between them."

"Mmm." She dipped her chin one time, and we all knew she didn't believe Malcolm for one second.

The rest of lunch was incredibly uncomfortable for me. I finished eating as quickly as I could, then excused myself. I went to the kitchen and started cleaning up. It wasn't long before two dragons and a demon joined me. I was surprised that Malcolm, at the very least, didn't follow me immediately. Maybe he realized that I needed a few minutes to myself.

Damon stepped up to the sink beside me and grabbed a towel. "I'm sorry if that causes you any problems, but it's the truth."

"Why'd you make me want you?" The words were meant only for him, but I was sure the dragons heard anyway.

He dried the utensils and set them on the cabinet, never taking his eyes off of me. "I couldn't resist. It's been too long since I tasted your emotions. Even with your power lying dormant, they're magnificent."

While my friends and I cleaned up the lunch mess, Mom and Dad carried some of the dining room chairs into the living room. As soon as we finished, we joined them. Malcolm and Cash took the seats next to me in a failed attempt to keep Damon away. Damon, however, wasn't so easily dissuaded. He stood behind me with his hands on my shoulders.

Not wanting to shove him off or let him stay like that, I got up and handed out the Christmas presents.

By the time everyone left, I was a ball of nerves. As soon as Dad came back inside from walking Pam to her car, he turned toward me. "So … judging by the way everyone's acting, I assume Damon isn't a trusted dragon."

I set down the chair that I'd been carrying back into the dining room and shook my head. My parents might not be used to the world I lived in, but they definitely weren't oblivious to it. "He's not a dragon."

"May I ask what he is then?" Mom sat on the couch with her legs pulled up beside her.

Damon opened his mouth, but I glared at him. "Don't." I turned toward my parents. "I think it's best if you don't know."

"I think it's best if you let us make those decisions." Dad raised one eyebrow at me.

I clenched the back of the chair. "There was a time I would've agreed with that. Now, I know that once you know something there is no going back."

"Damon may be an arrogant bastard"—Malcolm stood next to me and put his hand on my shoulder—"but he's saved your daughter more than once."

I couldn't believe Malcolm had interjected on Damon's behalf, and when Damon said, "Thank you, Malcolm. That was very kind of you," I realized he was also shocked.

"Well," Dad said, "we appreciate that. We'll have to take it on faith that you're a decent man." He sat next to Mom. "I just hope your intentions are honorable."

The smile that crossed Damon's face was wicked. "Of course."

"Will you also be staying here?" Mom straightened the cover on the armrest. "We're all out of beds, but we can make up the couch in the basement for you if you'd like."

Damon flicked his eyes toward me, and I felt Malcolm tense. "No need. I don't sleep."

Chapter 29

Strange Bedfellows

$\mathcal{I}$ lay in bed, staring up at the ceiling. The tension in my room was too thick. Malcolm stretched out next to me, and Damon watched us from the window seat. "Is this really still necessary?" Damon waved his hand at Malcolm, showing what he meant, as if there was any doubt.

"Yes," Malcolm growled, "more than ever now that she doesn't have her powers."

My eyes widened as I realized the implications of his words. If I lived one of my nightmares, I no longer had a way to heal myself. I could actually die from a bad dream.

Malcolm took my hand in his. "Don't worry. I'm here. I'll heal you."

"You could let me lie with her," Damon's voice was huskier than normal. "I can take her dreams away."

"You can't heal her, though."

"If she didn't dream, you wouldn't need to heal her."

"Enough." I sat up, pulling my focus from the ceiling. "Do either of you have any ideas for me?" I looked at Damon first.

He shook his head, looking truly remorseful. "Not yet. I thought maybe if I saw you in person I could help you figure it out, but … nothing."

I turned toward Malcolm. "I'm sorry, Dacia, but no."

Fat, fluffy flakes fall from the sky, landing on Mavros and me. As soon as they touch his skin, they melt, but they build up on his hair and jacket.

He reaches for my hand, but I slide it away. "No. First, tell me why you're here."

He knows I mean here in the real world, not here in my dream. "You asked for my help, so I came. I need no more reason than that." He steps closer, and I feel heat radiating off of him. "I need to touch you, to see what's going on."

"Okay." I lift my hand up. "Don't make me want you, though."

He brushes my hair off my face and tucks it behind my ear. "I promise." He slides his hands down my arm and twines his fingers with mine. "I'm still hoping someday I won't have to make you."

My body softens in response to his words. I know what he is. I know what he wants. And, I also know that if Cody and I had never met, I could give in to Mavros.

He stares into my eyes, and I gaze back, not sure if I could look away if I wanted to. I feel him prod my powers, but they don't respond. Part of me is thrilled that I've bound them so tightly, but the other part wants them back, no matter what the cost. They're a part of me, and I need them to feel whole.

Mavros drops my hands and steps back, taking his warmth with him. I wrap my arms around my body. "Well?"

"What did you do?" He sounds desperate, scared.

I remember sitting in church with Cody, the electricity that shot into him, how Malcolm couldn't hold it back. "I don't know. I was mad and scared, and I wanted to be normal." I yank my fingers through my hair. It's soaking wet from the snow. "I just wanted to shut them off until church was over. I didn't want to make them go away. I just needed a break, and there were too many lives at stake."

"I couldn't get any reaction out of them, and I couldn't sense Argentum at all." He takes his coat off and swings it over my shoulders. "You're freezing. You should tell me. I don't think about the cold."

I slip my arms into the sleeves, savoring his residual heat. His coat smells like him, warm summer evenings. "Couldn't you take me somewhere nicer next time?"

"I thought you liked the snow." He tilts his head to the side, and his eyebrows pull together.

I wave my hand from my head to my toes. "When I'm dressed for it. Not when I'm in my pajamas."

I woke up to Malcolm's low growl. "You're soaked, and you smell like demon."

"Sorry," I mumbled. I sat up and pulled the covers back. I was wearing my pajamas and Mavros' coat. I looked across the room at him and was surprised to see Damon sitting on the window seat instead. I wiped my hand over my face. "How does this work? I've wondered since the first time I ended up with one." I pulled the jacket off and tossed it to him. "Do you have to get a new one every time, or do they just show up magically whenever you need one?"

He grinned at me, the one that made my heart stutter. "I don't mind losing my jackets to you."

"Okay." I flipped my hands up. "But I wanna know how they get replaced."

He winked at me. "Magic. How else?"

I grabbed dry clothes and headed to the bathroom to change.

Cash stopped me in the hallway. "Everything okay?"

"I don't know," I whispered.

"Your parents can't hear us."

I nodded and stared down at my feet. "Damon seems to be concerned about whatever I did to my powers." When I looked up at Cash, my eyes burned with unshed tears. "I think I made a huge mistake."

He pulled me into a comforting hug. When he let go, he said, "Go change. You're soaked."

I closed the bathroom door behind me and slipped out of my clothes, drying off before putting on my new ones. I spent several minutes trying to get my hair to quit dripping. Then I braided it before walking back to my room. I wished I could teleport so I wouldn't risk running into my parents in the hallway.

"I don't know if she'll get them back." Damon's voice drifted into the hallway.

My stomach dropped down to my feet. "What?" I looked at each of their faces. "You're not serious are you?"

Damon dropped his chin to his chest and bobbed his head a couple times. "I'm sorry."

"How will I protect myself?" I tried to run my hand through my hair, but it caught in my plait.

Malcolm strode across the floor to me and wiped the tears off my cheeks. "We'll do whatever we can to help you. We'll stay with you forever if need be."

The drive to Cody's house is liberating. Nothing's happened for a couple of weeks, so the dragons decided to give me some space. It's freezing outside, but I have the window down and the radio cranked. Singing at the top of my lungs, I drive around a curve.

Something slams into my truck.

My truck slides across the road.

I stomp on the brakes and crank the wheel, but I skid past the shoulder and slide backward down the hill.

My truck jerks to a stop. I sit with my head on the steering wheel and try to regulate my breathing.

After I've calmed down a little, I shift into park and step out onto the snowy hill. With my powers, I could've gotten back to the road in a blink. Without them, I wish I had snow-shoes.

I take a step, and my leg sinks through the drift up to my hip. I press my hands to the ground in front of me and try to pull myself out of the snowbank.

The "whoop-whoop" of large wings fills the air, and I look up. An emerald dragon lands on the ground behind me, tempo-rarily hidden by the snow that explodes into the air.

Fear claws at my belly, and I know the dragon can smell it on me. "Are you here to help me?"

A low rumbling shakes the creature's body.

I realize it's laughter at the same time its talons slash through my back.

Distant voices shouted my name. I wished they'd just leave me alone and let me sleep. I tried to ignore them, but they kept calling and calling. The panic in them grew every time they said my name and I didn't respond.

"What?" I mumbled.

"Stay with us, Dacia." The voice seemed familiar, but I couldn't be sure. My thoughts were fuzzy.

Someone smacked my cheek. The surprise of it made my eyes jerk open. Everything was hazy. The room was still dark.

"She's awake."

Damon. It was Damon's voice.

"Thank God."

That one belonged to Cash. I tried to turn my head to see him, but pain exploded through my back.

"Don't move, Dacia." Malcolm's voice was angry, barely controlled. "Cash, I need your help."

"Dacia—" Damon's hand brushed my cheek "—look at me, Dacia." He sat on the floor by my bed, looking up into my face. The fear in his eyes took me by surprise. "We thought we'd lost you. The dragons …" He shook his head. "I'm sorry I can't help heal you."

"When—" my tongue felt thick and heavy. *When you hurt me, you healed me by pulling your venom out.* My thoughts were erratic, and I doubted I only sent them to Damon.

"Yes." His chin dropped to his chest. "I can do that."

If … if you scratched me … if you put your venom in me, could you heal me?

He shook his head. "You're too weak. I can't risk it."

"Try it, demon." Malcolm's voice was nearly his dragon's. My blood must have been driving him crazy.

Damon leaned forward and kissed my cheek. "I'm sorry," he said as his claws tore through my back.

When I woke up again, the sun was shining through my curtains, and Damon's body was pressed tightly against mine. He smiled at me when I opened my eyes but didn't let me pull away. "Do you know how long I've wanted to be in this position?"

"Yes." My voice was raw. "I need a drink." I pushed against him, but he still didn't let go.

He lifted onto his arm so that he was looking down at me. "Just admit that waking up with me isn't so bad."

"It's not." I rubbed my hand down my face. "I always knew it wouldn't be, and that's the problem. If it weren't for Cody, I could see myself with you."

He let go and watched me roll out of bed. "Your idea with my venom worked. The dragons had to go hunt."

"I bet that was a tough decision for them to make."

"You've no idea." He sat on the edge of my bed, watching every step I took. "Are you all right?"

"I'm still sore and really tired." I wobbled and stretched my hand out, balancing myself against the wall.

He strode toward me, and I knew that whatever he was about to tell me wouldn't be good. "I can't leave you alone. You know that, right?"

I nodded.

"I heard your mom talking to Cody. He'll be here any minute. He's not going to like seeing me with you."

Chapter 30

Good News, Bad News

$\mathcal{I}$ walked out to the living room with Damon right on my heels. Unlike the dragons, he didn't even pretend like he hadn't been in my room.

Mom did a double-take when he sauntered out with me. "Where are the dragons?"

"Hunting." I lifted my hands, palms up. "There's a good chance they'll be gone all day, maybe all night, too."

I could see questions cross her face, and I was grateful when she didn't ask any of them. I turned to Damon. "Could you be Mavros today?"

Mom perked up at that. She'd met Mavros at my birthday party and had been quite taken with him.

"You sure?" He tilted his head.

I nodded. "Mavros saved my life. Damon tried to steal me."

"Right." He smiled at Mom and morphed into Mavros.

Mom looked him up and down, not even trying to hide that she was admiring his perfection. She handled it better than I'd expected, and I was glad I could share parts of my life with my parents.

"Where is Dad?" I realized the house was silent except for us.

She pulled her gaze away from Mavros, clearing her throat and smiling sheepishly. "He went to church, but I didn't think I should leave you alone with three men in the house." She nodded down the hallway. "A lotta good that did."

"It was a rough night." I pressed my eyes shut and rubbed the bridge of my nose. "He was with me to protect me, not to seduce me."

"Protect you?" Mom jumped up and glanced around. "Protect you from what?"

I hadn't wanted my parents to know too much about my life. They'd already lost one child. They didn't need to worry about losing another because of nightmares. "I live my dreams." I sat on the loveseat and held my head in my hands.

"What do you mean?" She positioned herself on the edge of the couch and leaned forward. Her hands were tightly clasped together on her lap.

"If I get hurt in a dream, that injury really happens to me." I remembered the first time it had occurred. The shard of ice that had cut my cheek. Waking up the next day and finding the wound gone. "My magic usually heals me, but I seem to have banished my powers. Last night, I was attacked in my dream. It took both dragons and Damon to heal me."

"My God." Her words were practically nonexistent.

"There was a lot of blood." Mavros sat beside me. "That is why the dragons are hunting."

The color drained from her face. "Are you safe with them?"

"Yes." I was saved from further conversation when Cody knocked on the door. I stood and faced Mavros. "Stay here for a minute."

He nodded solemnly.

I opened the door and slipped out onto the porch with Cody. "Hello." I smiled up at him, truly glad that he was here. Grateful for the moment that my magic was still bound.

"Hello."

I wrapped my arms around his waist and pulled him against me. "I have good news and bad news." I tilted my head, and he nodded at me to continue. "The good news. I can touch you still. The bad news …"

He held his hand up, and I stopped talking. "Focus on the good." His lips pressed against mine, warm and delicate. He dropped the bag he'd been holding and lifted me.

I clung to him like he was my lifeline. He backed me up against the house. I tilted my head back, and his kisses trailed down my neck. I moaned in response. I'd missed having Cody touch me, hold me, kiss me. A fire burned within me, warming me from the inside out.

His lips crashed down on mine once again. His breathing was ragged, and his heart pounded hard enough that I felt it through both of our sweatshirts. His hands clutched my waist as if he couldn't bear to let go of me for one second.

He slowed the kiss, pulling back slightly, then pressing his lips to mine again and again. The kisses became softer until he leaned his forehead against mine and said, "Bad news." His voice was husky, and I didn't want to tell him. I didn't want to ruin this. I wanted to spend all day kissing him and holding him.

"Mavros is here."

He set me down and pulled back. "Why?"

"He came to help me figure out how to get rid of Argentum's taint." I didn't let go of him, wouldn't let him step away from me. "Last night I was attacked by a dragon in my dream. I don't know what would've happened if he hadn't been here. The dragons couldn't heal me, and I no longer have the power to." I inched closer to him. "Malcolm and Cash had to leave to hunt. There was too much blood."

The passionate Cody was gone. The version that stood in front of me now was a stoic shell.

"He's not here to fight you." I slipped my fingers into his. "He promised he won't."

"Believe him?" His voice was hardened steel.

I nodded. "I can use his name if he tries anything."

"Least there's that." Cody picked his bag up off the porch, and we walked inside. "Hello, Mrs. Wolf."

"Cody"—she shook her finger at him and walked over to give him a hug—"you know better than that."

"Sorry." He shrugged before hugging her back.

She smiled at him, then went to the kitchen. The cabinets opened. Then pots and pans clanged together.

I looked toward the noises, then at Cody. I should have offered to help Mom with whatever she was doing, but I didn't know how much time I had left to spend with Cody before I would try to kill him again, and I didn't want to waste a second of it.

Cody bent down to untie his boots. Without looking up, he said, "Hello, Mavros." His voice was steady, no anger or bitterness came through.

Mavros stood and walked over. "Cody." He nodded at him. "I'll be here if you need me, Dacia. Just yell." He walked down the hall and went into the spare bedroom. I was glad he hadn't gone to mine. Cody wouldn't have liked that at all.

Cody's shoulders relaxed somewhat. We sat on the love-seat together. I snuggled against his side and pulled a blanket over our legs. "How was your Christmas?"

"Good." He rubbed my arm, up and down, up and down. "Missed you. How 'bout yours?"

I lifted my shoulders to my ears. "All right 'til last night. Everyone loved the necklace your mom gave me, but I would've rather had you here."

He reached into his bag and pulled out a gift. "Want this?"

"Let me get yours." I tossed the blanket aside and got up, digging under the tree until I pulled out his presents. I sat back down with him, throwing my legs over his and pressing against his side.

He wrapped his arm around me and pulled me even closer. "Missed this."

"Me, too." I handed him his gifts, and he gave me mine.

He pulled the bow off the bigger of his and stuck it on my sweatshirt. Then he opened his Phlox Phoenixes hoodie. "Thanks. This was the one I wanted." He kissed my temple. "Your turn."

I carefully pulled the tape back, not wanting to rip the paper. Opening the box, I stared down at a picture of us I'd never seen before. We were laughing, and the looks on our faces made it obvious that there was nobody who mattered more to either of us. The picture frame said, Every love story is beautiful, but ours is my favorite. "Thank you, Cody. Where'd the picture come from?"

"Asked Sam and Dan to take some candid shots." He grinned at me. "That's my favorite. Like it?"

I kissed his cheek. "I love it. It's perfect."

He held up his other gift. "Only got you one."

"It's way better than what I got you anyway." I nudged him. "Open it."

He ripped the paper off and looked down at the gold chain. I wondered what he thought about it. The only jewelry he'd ever worn was his class ring. Taking it out of the box, he handed it to me. "Hook it on?"

"Sure." I slid it around his neck, and when I clasped it, his eyes opened wide.

"Not just a necklace?"

I shook my head and bit my lip. "The dragons helped me. Hopefully, it will keep you safe from spells. Give you some protection."

"Best. Gift. Ever." He held my face in his hands. "Thank you."

Right after Dad got home from church, Mom said, "Lunch is ready. Dacia, why don't you invite Mavros to join us?"

"Sure." I got up and walked down the hall. Mavros stepped out of the spare bedroom just as I reached the door.

His expression was somber. "I don't need to join you if you'd rather I didn't."

"Do you eat human food?"

He nodded.

"Well, Mom made you a patty melt and fries. If you don't join us, it'll just go to waste."

He bowed his head. "I'm honored to be bound to you." He followed me to the dining room and sat across the table from Cody and me.

Dad glanced at the empty chairs and then focused on Mavros. "What happened to your other friends?"

"It seems Mavros"—Mom waved her hand at him—"is Damon. Malcolm and Cash are hunting."

Dad took it all in stride, asking, "Would anyone like to say grace?"

"I will." Mavros' response shocked me to no end. We joined hands and bowed our heads. Then Mavros said, "Dear Lord, thank you for the blessings of family and friends. Their presence helps nurture our souls. Thank you for bringing all of us together, keeping us safe, and for the food that nourishes our bodies. Amen."

Cody stared across the table at Mavros. His mouth hung slightly open. "Nice." He nodded. Then he sat, scooting his chair in, and picked up his burger.

When we finished eating, Mavros insisted on washing the dishes. Mom grinned at him, and I couldn't help but wonder what she'd think if she knew what he was. But at any rate, I was glad that he wasn't being mischievous.

"We're going to watch a movie," I announced as I grabbed a blanket and Cody's hand and led him down to the family room. I ignited the gas fireplace, put a movie in the DVD player, then stretched out on the couch next to Cody.

He wrapped his arms around me and pulled me on top of him. I was reminded of how life had been at college, waking up in his embrace, spending all of our free time together.

His fingers skimmed down my arm, leaving a trail of desire behind them. I slid my hands under his shirt. He moaned, and it just about undid me. I traced my fingers over his ribs, and he arched his back to get closer to me.

"I love you," I whispered against his lips.

He pulled me down. "I love you, Dacia. Always."

Neither of us saw the movie. We held each other. We stared into each other's eyes. We talked. There was nowhere I'd have rather been, and no one I'd have rather been with. I had missed this. I had missed him.

I found myself wondering if I should try to get my magic back or if this was my chance to get out. If I was no longer powerful, would the monsters and madmen care about me, or would they leave me be?

Chapter 31

Decisions, Decisions

*M*avros sat on the window seat. "Dacia, I understand your feelings, but if you have another nightmare, I might not be able to help you."

"Cody—"

"I'm well aware that Cody would hate it." He strolled toward the bed and sat on the edge next to me. "He'd also hate it if you died in your sleep. Let me keep your dreams away. Let me help you."

"Why didn't that go away when my magic did?" I scooted over, making room for him. "Why are my dreams still deadly? And, if that part of my magic lingered, why didn't the healing part?"

Mavros stretched out beside me, wrapping his arm around my waist. My body tensed in response. It was one thing to have Malcolm hold me while I slept, but it was something entirely different with Mavros. I was attracted to him even without him manipulating my emotions. I would never act on those impulses, but I couldn't deny them either.

I tried to relax, but too many things were bothering me. "Will they come back?" My voice sounded tiny.

"I imagine so." His words blew across my ear, sending shivers throughout my body. He chuckled and rolled onto his back.

"They promised they'd be here as long as I needed them." Tears welled in my eyes. I bit my lip, trying to hold them at bay. Today had been a good day. I didn't want to end it by crying.

Mavros nudged me until I flipped over. He pulled my head onto his chest and ran his fingers through my hair. "There was a lot of blood, Dacia. If you were anyone else, they would've torn you to pieces."

"Why doesn't it bother you?"

His hand stopped moving, and he stared at me.

"What?"

He shook his head. "I don't know. It should. I'm a predator, too. The panther … the form you took."

I shivered at that comment. I remembered the bloodlust I'd felt in that form. It was the reason I was in this predicament now.

"They both hunger for blood." He watched me for a moment as if he expected to find the answers on my face. "Maybe it's our bond."

I ran my fingers along his chest without thinking about what I was doing.

He grabbed my hand, halting the motion. "Don't do that unless you mean it."

Heat rushed up my neck and onto my face. "I'm sorry. I wasn't thinking. Well … I was thinking. Just not about what I was doing." I tried to roll away from him, but he held me against his side.

"Dacia, relax." He rubbed my arm again. "I won't do anything you don't want me to. I can wait." He flipped onto his side so his breath caressed my face. "I promised to give you the life you want with Cody. I'll be there at the end, waiting for you. Until then, I'll be your friend, your protector, whatever you need me to be." He smoothed my hair back, tucking it behind my ear. "Now, go to sleep. I'll keep your dreams away."

Hushed, angry voices woke me up. Malcolm and Cash stood next to the bed. "Don't make yourself too comfortable, demon." Malcolm's eyes flashed with a hatred embedded so deeply he would never be able to let it go.

"You abandoned her. You left her, and she needed someone to help her." Mavros' words were pointed barbs.

Malcolm leaned down with his face mere inches from Mavros'. "You can keep her nightmares away without clinging to her."

"I can." He shrugged. "But, where's the fun in that? Besides, you were okay with it last night."

I lifted onto my arm. If they hadn't been so focused on each other, they would have realized I was awake. "Please don't fight. I need all of you. I need you to get along. I need you to take me to the fairies tomorrow." The words were out of my mouth before I thought about the implications.

"Why?" The anger on Malcolm's face was washed away by concern.

I tugged my hand through my hair. I didn't know how any of them would take what I was about to say. "I'm not sure I should fight to get my powers back. Maybe they can help me remove them completely … get rid of even the dreams."

Mavros pulled away from me, and for a moment, his body was insubstantial like he was trapped between forms. "You can't."

"Why not?" Not wanting to have this conversation lying down, I sat up and looked each of them in the face. "I wouldn't have to worry about hurting Cody. Would creatures still hunt me if I had no powers? I could live my life the way humans are supposed to. Grow old. Have a family. I've wanted to be normal for so long, and now, I finally have that chance. Should I really give it up?"

"Yes," all three of them said. They looked at each other, surprised to be in agreement for once.

Cash seemed to recover his thoughts first. "Creatures have been drawn to your power. If you don't have it, you won't have that problem, but there are so many who already know about you. They may come for you anyway."

"I will be bound to you whether you have your magic or not." Mavros got up and walked away from me. "Mine still lies dormant inside of you. When you die, I will be sent back to the Abyss, but I will protect you until then. No matter what you decide." He turned and stared into my eyes. "But, Dacia, if you let your powers go, you will be making a huge mistake. Death sent you back here for a reason. There is more that you need to do."

Malcolm rolled his eyes. "The demon is right."

"He is." Cash's voice was soft, understanding.

"The *demon* told me that there is no such thing as fate." I pointed at Mavros, and my finger shook. "The *demon* told me it was chance."

Mavros smirked. "The demon also told you he'd lied."

"So how do I know you're not lying now?" I folded my arms over my chest.

He sat next to me and grabbed my hands, holding them gently in his. "Use my name. Order me to tell you the truth if you must, but I promised not to lie to you again." His voice softened. "And I won't."

"His words ring with truth." Malcolm shook his head like he could hardly believe it. "Use his name, though, if you wish."

"Will you take me to see Rayne?" I looked down at my hands held in Mavros' and imagined them as Cody's instead. The time spent with him today had been straight out of a fairytale. I hadn't worried one time that he would be hurt, and I wanted that feeling for the rest of my life. I wanted to know that I'd grow old and die with him, that I wouldn't have to live for centuries or millennia without him with me. But, I couldn't help but wonder if Malcolm, Cash, and Mavros were right. Did the world need me?

Malcolm bowed his head in defeat. "If it's still what you want when morning comes, we will."

I lay in bed with Mavros holding me. Malcolm and Cash had decided it was best for him to stay with me. Even though they'd spent the entire day hunting, they were concerned about how they might react to my blood if more spilled.

Cash returned to the spare bedroom, but Malcolm chose to stay in mine to keep an eye on me. No matter what Mavros did for me, the dragons would never fully trust him. He was a demon, and that was all he would ever be to them.

"Dacia." Malcolm wiped his hand down his face. "Sleep."

I stared at the wall. "I can't. I don't know what I should do. I just know what I want."

"Do you?" Mavros propped himself up and looked down at me. "You never want to fly again? Never want to heal yourself or your friends, teleport, protect yourself?"

I felt a pang in my chest, an ache that spread to my soul. "I do want that. I really do, but I want Cody more."

Malcolm opened the window. The freezing air blew in, and I couldn't warm myself. I shivered and tucked the blankets under my chin.

"This is what I mean." Mavros pulled me against him, warming me when I couldn't.

"If you don't go to sleep, I'm going to have to leave." Malcolm looked ashamed by his admission.

I closed my eyes and pictured a path with a fork. Neither choice looked clear or safe. Darkness spread from the trees.

Their branches hung low, ready to snatch me as I passed beneath them. Both choices were eerily silent as if danger loomed ahead no matter which road I chose. This decision would affect the rest of my life, and I didn't know if it was reversible. "You're going to have to help me."

Malcolm's magic wrapped over me. I yawned deeply, then fell into a sound, dreamless sleep.

I woke up feeling as lost as I had been when I went to sleep. Mavros was still stretched out next to me, but neither Malcolm nor Cash were in the room.

Mavros smiled, far too comfortable with this situation. I let my eyes travel over him, shaking my head at how perfect he looked. Every hair was in place. His clothes weren't wrinkled. When I met his eyes again, emotion sparkled in their obsidian depths. My heart galloped in response, and for just a moment, I imagined life with him, imagined waking up with him every morning, imagined him holding me at night, and keeping my dreams at bay. I would be safe with him at my side, and my magic would not be a danger to him. The thoughts left me as quickly as they'd come, and I wondered if he'd had something to do with them.

He sat up and slid out of bed. "All of your dragons are here." There seemed to be a hint of frustration in his voice, but I couldn't see his face to tell for sure.

I flopped back against my pillows. "Great." Suddenly, I realized why I had those thoughts about him. Most likely, he had done it to agitate the dragons.

"Do what you need to do, Dacia. Don't let them make your decision for you." He held his hand out to me. "It's not going to get any easier."

Malcolm glared at Mavros as we walked down the hall. Mavros just smiled at him and placed his hand on the small of my back, guiding me into the dining room. When I saw Aurelia, Arianna, Val, Russ, and Cash seated at the table, I was glad my parents had gone back to work this morning. They had handled everything pretty well up to this point, but seeing six dragons and a demon in our house would probably be too much for them.

"Hello." I pulled out a chair and sat at the far end of the table. Mavros stood behind me. I could feel his hands on the back of the chair, and I felt comforted by his nearness. "You're all here to talk me into keeping my powers I assume."

Aurelia folded her hands on the table. "We are here because we are your friends." The others nodded. "You are obviously going through a crisis, and we would like to help you."

"I can't touch Cody." I laughed, and it was humorless. "Sometimes, I can't even look at him." The helplessness I felt had to be driving the dragons nuts, but none of them showed it. "Yesterday …" Every minute I had with him was perfect, but what would he think about me giving up my magic? I cleared my throat and started again. "Yesterday was perfect. I didn't have to worry about killing him or even hurting him. How can I give that up?"

"Nobody here will fault you if you do." Arianna's voice was soft and lyrical, soothing. "Before you make up your mind, though, I'd like to give you something to think about."

I closed my eyes and nodded.

"You saved the world from a demon, freed fifteen dragons from hundreds of years of torment and captivity, returned a different demon to the Abyss, possibly saving the world a second time, and helped take down a corrupt dragon." She stood up and made her way over. Pulling out a chair next to me, she sat and took my hand in hers. "How can you give that up?"

Malcolm stood in the doorway, leaning against the wall. "In our long history of dealing with humans, we have never accepted anyone else as our own. We have never vowed to protect one. We have never seen a human as worthy of their powers as you are." He bowed his head. "If you choose to give them up, I will back you, but I will mourn your loss."

Russ opened his mouth to talk, but I held my hand up, stopping him. "So, all of you feel this way?"

Each of them either nodded or said, "Yes."

I traced my finger over the grain on the oak table. I wondered how many years the tree had grown before giving its life to be furniture. "If I don't give them up, what do I do? How do I keep from hurting Cody?"

"If you plan to give your magic up for Cody," Aurelia said, "you should give him a say in the matter. Otherwise, it may create an insurmountable rift between the two of you."

This time, when Russ opened his mouth, I didn't stop him from speaking. "You don't want to lose everything."

I got up and walked into the kitchen. Another chair scraped back, and hurried footsteps followed me. The dragons were usually nearly silent. I turned and was unsurprised to see Val rushing toward me.

He pulled me into a hug. "I missed you." He sniffed my hair. "They wouldn't let me see you. They said it was dangerous. They said your magic is being bad."

I stepped back. "It's not now. It's gone."

"No." He shook his head.

I squeezed his shoulder. "I'm sorry, Val, but it is."

"I can feel it." He nuzzled against me. "It's still there."

"What do you mean?" I jumped at the sound of Arianna's voice. I hadn't heard her come in.

"Can't you feel it?" Val looked at her in utter confusion, careful not to peer into her eyes for more than a few seconds.

She held his face, focusing his attention on her. "None of us can feel it."

He tried to avert his gaze, but she held him steady. "Please." He whimpered.

She let go, and he shuffled toward me. He held his hand up and slowly inched forward until his palm was flat on my chest. Then he grabbed Arianna's hand.

Her eyes widened, and she ruffled Val's blue hair. "It's there, Dacia. It's angry and hurt, but it's there."

Chapter 32

$\mathcal{I}$ paced through the living room and into the hallway. Back and forth. Back and forth. The dragons sat at the dining room table, talking in hushed tones. Mavros leaned against the doorframe, watching me.

I heard tires crunching over the gravel, so I walked to the window. Cody pulled into the driveway in his parents' SUV. There was barely enough time for him to shift into park before he was running up the sidewalk and onto the porch steps.

"You okay?" he asked when I opened the door. "Sounded upset."

Aurelia walked into the room before I had a chance to answer him. "Hello, Cody."

His eyes darted around, and I assumed all of the dragons must have followed her. "Hey." He nodded at them before bending down to take his boots off. "Gang's all here." He met my gaze, and I shrugged.

"Yep." The p popped on its way out of my mouth. I led him into the dining room and sat at the end of the table. I stared at my hands while I told Cody what I was considering. The dragons and Mavros stayed quiet, keeping their opinions to themselves.

Val sat a few seats down from me. Several times, while I was talking, I thought he might climb over the table to be closer to me, but Arianna put her hand on his arm and held him back.

Cody listened to me patiently with his arms folded over his chest and his mask firmly in place. When I finished, he stared at me for a while in stunned silence. "You could do that? Just give up your powers?"

I nodded.

"And you would? For me?"

I rubbed my hand down his arm. "For us."

"For us." He looked at my hand. "No." He shook his head like my answer wasn't good enough for him. "No. Not for *me*. Not for *us*. Not unless it's for *you*. Don't want you to resent me for it."

His response surprised me. I thought he would jump at the chance for us to have a normal life. I thought he'd want this more than I did.

"Dacia"—his voice was soft and understanding—"your magic is as much a part of you as your sense of humor, your morals, your intelligence. I love you. *All* of you." He took my hand in his. "Will you still be you if they're gone?"

Tears burned my eyes, but I held them back. "I don't know."

The dragons showed no emotion, but Mavros looked smug. He had more reason to want me to keep my powers than anyone else in the room. I'd already freed the dragons. They could take care of themselves now. Aurelia and the council would see to it. They were working on a plan to keep dragons safe in the future, to keep corrupt dragons from being able to hide in their lairs to avoid justice.

I dragged my hands through my hair, clasping them at the back of my head. "Why can't anything be easy?"

"The easy path rarely is the right one." Malcolm stepped behind me and rested his hands on my shoulders. "Don't make a hasty decision. Make a wise one, and we'll all back you."

I turned to Cody. "Can you stay, or do you have other plans?"

"Stay." He smiled at me. "As long as you want me."

"Always."

When my parents came home, it looked like Cody and I were the only ones in the living room, but in reality, we hadn't been alone all day. Now that they knew my powers were strong enough for Val to sense them, the dragons were afraid Cody would get hurt.

We'd spent the day snuggled together on the couch. Knowing we were under constant surveillance, we watched a movie. We kept our conversation light and insignificant. Even though we weren't really being ourselves, it was nice to spend time together, to be able to touch him, and not have my magic flare up.

"Hello, Cody," Mom said when she walked in. "How are you doing today?"

Lifting his arm off my shoulders, he sat up. "I'm good. How're you?"

"Long day." She unwrapped her scarf and hung it up. "It's hard to go back after a few days off."

Dad came in and nodded at us. "Staying for dinner?"

Cody looked at me and shrugged. "Don't know. What's the plan?"

The two of us ended up making fettuccine alfredo and garlic bread for my parents for dinner. When we finished eating, I stared past Cody, looking out the window behind him. The desire to go outside was overwhelming. I didn't know why, but I needed to be out there.

I hurriedly cleared the table and put the leftovers away, hoping the feeling would dwindle, but the desire increased with every passing minute. If my magic wasn't bound, I would have teleported out just to ease the need, to stop the constant pull.

Looking at the dishes, I decided they would have to wait. I went into the dining room and clutched the back of the chair. "I need to go for a walk."

Mom furrowed her brows and tilted her head. "It's really cold out. Are you sure?"

"Yeah." I rubbed my stomach. "After that, I need the exercise."

Cody walked with me to the door, rubbing his thumb over mine the whole way. "All right?"

"I don't know." I shrugged. "I *need* to go outside."

"Alone?" He kept his voice low to keep my parents from overhearing.

I snorted. "I highly doubt we've had a minute alone all day." I slid my feet into my boots. Then I pulled on my coat, hat, scarf, and gloves. Bundling up like this was a reminder of what I'd lost, what I could lose forever.

"You doubt it?" He raised an eyebrow at me. "You don't know?"

I stood and opened the door. "We'll be back before too long."

"Okay, honey," Dad said at the same time Mom said, "Be careful."

We stepped out onto the porch, and I slid my hand into Cody's. "Not for certain. I can't sense anybody anymore."

"Can't either." He squeezed my fingers. "But know they wouldn't leave. So … where to?"

We walked down the steps and onto the sidewalk. I stopped and looked around my yard. The half-moon spilled its light over the snowy ground making it so I could discern shapes if not details. Without my magic, I felt vulnerable out in the open. If something happened, I wouldn't be able to protect myself or Cody. I couldn't teleport us to safety. But, I felt like I was being called. The desire to answer was irresistible.

"That way." I pointed to the trees in the side yard. The edge of the timber was bright, but under the pines, it was darker than the Abyss.

Cody and I started walking. Some steps stayed on top of the firm snow, and other times we sank almost to our knees. While I was trying to pull my leg out of a drift, someone grabbed my arm.

Fear shot through me, raising the hairs on my neck and stiffening my body.

"What are you doing?" Malcolm's voice was right next to my ear.

I relaxed slightly. "I need to go over there." I stopped trying to pull my leg out of the snow and pointed toward the edge of the trees. "I don't know why."

"Ask for help next time." He lifted me out of the snow, then cradled me against him. Nodding at Cody, he teleported to the treeline.

Cash and Cody landed next to us. Cody staggered slightly before regaining his balance.

Malcolm set me down but kept hold of my arm. I looked at it, then up at him. "Is everyone out here?"

"Yes." He flashed his fangs at me. "Even your demon. Now, why are we here?"

"I don't know." I felt myself being drawn deeper into the timber. I stepped forward, dragging Malcolm with me. Dodging branches, I stepped into the shadows of the trees. I saw movement ahead but couldn't make out what it was.

Malcolm clutched my arm and stopped me from going any farther. "Who's there?" His voice was a menacing growl that I wouldn't have answered.

The crunch of branches underfoot was the only response.

Mavros appeared in front of me. His left arm was back like he was trying to keep me protected from something I couldn't see. He looked over his shoulder, and his eyes turned into blazing infernos as he transformed into the massive, black panther. He prowled into the trees, clinging to the shadows.

"Should we go?" I whispered to Malcolm.

He held his hand up and cocked his head. The rest of the dragons appeared and spread out around Cody and me. They stood in defensive stances, ready for a battle.

A low growl rumbled through the timber. Then something screamed. An inhuman sound that chilled me to the bone. The rest of the forest had gone eerily silent.

I wanted to turn and run as far and as fast as I could. If not for the dragons surrounding me, I would have.

Mavros backed into the clearing. His long tail flicked from side to side, the only sign of his agitation. He held something in his jaws, dragging it with him. Whatever it was, it kicked and fought, thrashing against Mavros' hold, but Mavros didn't seem affected by it. He stopped in front of Malcolm and stared at him through fiery eyes. Black blood dripped from several gouges across Mavros' muzzle. Malcolm grabbed the creature by the throat and lifted it off the ground. As soon as the prisoner was out of Mavros' jaws, he morphed into his human form. All traces of his injuries disappeared.

Malcolm held the misshapen beast in front of him. It kicked out with cloven feet. Huge bat-like wings dragged through the snow. It swiped at Malcolm with red-mottled hands that ended in long, hooked claws.

Scales spread up Malcolm's neck and onto his face, and when he talked, fire burned in his throat. "If you wish to die, keep it up."

"Is this why I came out here?" I stared at the grotesque creature, now hanging limply from Malcolm's hand. Its long, beak-like nose reminded me of the masks plague doctors wore. Beady little eyes stared at me, and I could feel hatred rising off of it.

Mavros grabbed it by the throat. "What do you want with her, imp?"

The imp's lips turned up in a menacing sneer. It never took its eyes off of me. When it talked, its voice was nasally. "To eat her heart while it's still beating."

My stomach heaved, and my legs felt weak. Cody moved slightly in front of me, ready to protect me at any cost. The dragons growled, and Malcolm's form rippled.

"To feel her blood run down my throat. To take her power for my own." It glared up at Mavros. "The things you should want."

Mavros' claws pierced the imp's neck, and he lifted it off the ground, holding it so their faces were even. The imp's wings spread out, and it tried to fly away, but Mavros' hold was too strong, his anger too deep. "Why should I want any of that?"

"She is weak. She cannot defend herself." It turned its glower on me again and licked its lips with a tongue as black as midnight. "We would be kings."

Mavros' teeth lengthened into fangs, and his lips pulled back in a snarl. "Who else knows she's here?"

"Everyone," the imp said right before Mavros ripped him in half.

Chapter 33

Hunted

Every noise on the way back to my house made me wonder what else was out there, waiting for me to be vulnerable, waiting for their chance to kill me. "Is Cody safe?" The words were barely a whisper, but I knew all the immortal beings around me could hear them.

"I'll make sure he is." Russ put his hand on Cody's shoulder. "Your family won't even have to know I'm there."

Cody looked a bit confused for a minute, but he shook it off. "No need to hide."

"I thought it would be the unicorn." I tried not to think about the imp. I didn't want to keep seeing its body being torn apart.

Malcolm walked next to me. He looked like he was ready to whisk me away at the first sign of trouble. He nodded. "I thought it might, too. If Khione was here, though, she wouldn't have allowed an imp into the forest. Not one who wanted to hurt you anyway."

"Khione," I said the name reverently. "I wondered what her name was, but I didn't want to offend her by asking."

Nearing my house, the dragons and Mavros became invisible. Since they hadn't gone outside with me, we didn't think my parents should see them and worry any more than they already were.

As soon as I stepped through the door, Mom said, "Are you all right? You look pale."

I pulled my coat off, then turned my back while I hung it up. I didn't want her to pay too much attention to my expression. I hated lying, but I didn't want them to know the danger my life was in. I didn't want them to have to worry about things normal parents didn't have to. "I'm fine, Mom. I just wanted some fresh air, but you were right. It's too cold."

"I do love hearing those three words. You were right." She laughed. "Aren't they beautiful, John?"

"You'd think you'd be used to hearing them by now." His voice was flat, but I knew if I was looking at them, I would see mischief in his eyes.

It sounded like Mom must have swatted him with a magazine. "I'll never tire of them."

"Good thing, since you're always right," he said.

"Just beautiful." She had a dreamy tone to her voice.

I tugged my boots off, then turned around and said, "We're going to watch a movie downstairs." Slipping my fingers into Cody's, I dragged him toward the steps before my parents noticed how badly my hands were shaking.

As soon as we were in the basement, everyone showed themselves. I walked across the plush forest green carpet to the tan loveseat. Cody sat down next to me, and I picked up the remote and flipped the TV on, cranking the volume enough that my parents wouldn't overhear us.

Cash knelt in front of me and took my hand in his. His amethyst eyes were filled with profound sadness. "It seems that even without your powers, you'll be hunted."

"Yeah." I rested my head against the back of the couch and stared at the ceiling. "I guess I'll have to come up with a new plan."

There seemed to be a collective sigh of relief. "We will help you any way we can." Aurelia sat in the glider. Her hands clasped the arms, and she rocked ever so slightly. "The first thing you must do is try to communicate with your powers."

"No." I walked to the sliding doors and stared out into the darkness. "I'm not bringing them back until I can keep Cody safe, until I have a plan to control them."

Except for the TV, the room was silent. I wondered if the dragons were conversing amongst themselves or if they were hoping I would change my mind.

I turned around and folded my arms over my chest. "You said the Nephilim were here. Why? Why would they have let that *thing* lure me out there? Aren't they supposed to protect people?"

Malcolm's lip turned up in disgust. "You remember what they said about helping dragons. They only help those they deem worthy, and since you slipped out of their grasp, you must not be worthy."

"So—" I glanced over my shoulder, wondering if anyone or anything was watching me now "—it must not be Diana who's here, then." I pulled the blinds shut.

"I haven't seen her." Cash shook his head.

Cody patted the loveseat next to him, and I sat down. He draped his arm over my shoulders and pulled me closer. "How're ya gonna keep her safe?"

Aurelia tilted her chin at Malcolm. He folded his hands behind his back and looked at everyone like a captain analyzing his team, determining their strengths and weaknesses. "Russ is going to watch over you, Cody."

Russ nodded at Cody from the couch.

"Arianna and Val will keep Dacia's property clear of danger." Malcolm turned toward me. "Unless you would rather Cash or I helped Val with that. Maybe you'd be more comfortable with a female being with you all the time."

Val sat on the floor in front of Arianna. His back touched her knees, and her hand rested on his shoulder. She was like a mother to him. It was obvious that they needed each other, but I didn't want to make this decision. I didn't want Arianna to think I didn't want her with me.

"Whatever you guys think is best." I shrugged. "You've never given me a choice before. I trust your judgment."

"Cash and I are with you then." Malcolm nodded. "Aurelia has to go back to the dragon council."

Mavros cleared his throat. "At night, I will keep Dacia's dreams away." He avoided mine and Cody's eyes, and I was grateful that he no longer felt the need to taunt Cody every chance he got. "During the day, I can help clear out any miscreants."

Cody's grip on my shoulder tightened, but he didn't say anything. It had to kill him, knowing that Mavros and Malcolm stayed in my room with me every night. I just hoped he knew that it was him that I wanted there with me, not them.

"I can help patrol at night," Cash said. "If you need me, I'll be there in an instant."

I stared at my hands, feeling worthless. "And I'll just sit around playing the role of damsel in distress until I figure out what to do about my magic."

Malcolm stood at my window, watching outside. His body was rigid. His muscles taut.

Mavros stretched out on top of the covers, enjoying lying with me way too much. "I won't hurt you, Dacia." He brushed my hair back, letting his fingers linger longer than necessary.

"That's not what I'm worried about." I was afraid that while I was sleeping I would forget who I was with. I was afraid that I would wake up and our bodies would be tangled together. I was afraid that I would like it more than I should. No matter what I thought of him or Cody, I couldn't deny that I was attracted to Mavros. I still didn't know if it was something of his doing or if they were my true feelings. I picked up one of my pillows and tucked it between us.

He chuckled softly. "Would you rather I looked like this?" He transformed into the enormous panther. *Or this?* He morphed into Damon.

"Demon." Malcolm's voice was a barely contained growl. "Quit playing with her emotions."

He changed back into Mavros. "When you're mine, I can look like Damon all the time if you'd like."

I wrapped my arm around my pillow, hugging it against my body. "Let me sleep."

"Goodnight, Dacia." He bent forward and kissed my forehead.

The serpent lies in a twisted heap. Its head is buried somewhere beneath its massive body. Its coils undulate as it constantly moves.

"How do I get back to where it's just the two of us?" My voice echoes in the vast black space where my powers lie.

You don't want me. You have imprisoned me.

"That's not true." I kneel down and put my hand on its body. The pearlescent scales are hot like it has been sunning itself all day. "I want you, but I don't want Argentum's power. I want to go back to the way it was."

Its body moves under my fingers, and I feel its anger pulse through me. *There is no way back. The only path is forward. You must live with the choices already made.*

I plop down onto my butt and hold my head in my hands. Somehow, I need to go back. I peer across the room at Mavros' powers. Wherever light touches its scales, shadows dissipate from the ebony serpent, making it seem like it's dissolving, but it still sleeps. Why couldn't Argentum's power do the same? Why did it have to merge with mine? Was there some way I could separate them?

"I miss you." My voice catches in my throat. "I miss the warmth of you flowing through my veins. I miss the comfort that I had, knowing I could rely on you."

Then let me come back. Do not bind me.

"I can't." I pull my hand through my hair and bow my head. "Not until I know you won't hurt Cody. Not until I can trust you again."

The snake lifts its head. Its copper eyes narrow, and it hisses. *I am you. Can you not trust yourself?*

"Not when it comes to Cody." I back away, getting my feet under me.

Then you are lost. It weaves, readying itself to strike.

Something grabs my shoulder, lifting me to my feet.

The serpent attacks. Its fangs sink into an arm clad in black.

I stare into Mavros' obsidian eyes. Pain fills them. He grabs my hand and pulls me out of my dream.

Black blood dripped onto my palm, burning my skin. I jerked my hand away and stifled my scream.

Mavros rolled off my bed, clutching his arm, keeping his blood from hitting anything else. "You okay?"

I nodded, and he disappeared.

Malcolm rushed toward the bed and took my hand in his, sending healing magic into me. "I'm sorry I didn't think you'd be hurt."

"It's not your fault." I thought about my powers. "Arianna was right. My magic is angry and hurt. If I don't figure out something soon, I may never be able to control it again."

Chapter 34

Facing The Day

$\mathcal{T}$he sun shone through the window onto my face, but I wasn't ready to open my eyes and confront the day. The arms that held me were warm, strong, and comforting. I pulled them tighter around me and imagined Cody's face. It always looked so peaceful in sleep. The stress of having me for a girlfriend was washed away by the sandman, and none of his masks were in place.

I rolled over and snuggled against him, breathing him in. Warm summer nights and sulfur made my eyes snap open.

Mavros smiled softly. "Good morning, Dacia." His voice was husky.

I flattened my hands on his chest and pushed, but he held onto me. "Please, Mavros."

"You started it." He loosened his grip.

I scooted back, putting some space between our bodies. "I'm sorry. I forgot who I was with."

"Does she do that when she's with you, Malcolm?"

Heat erupted, spreading up my neck and onto my face. It would've been bad enough if we'd been alone, but with an audience, it was a thousand times worse.

"No." His voice was brusque. "Apparently, I'm harder to forget."

Mavros busted out laughing, the kind of laugh that only comes from surprise. "Touché, dragon." He rolled over and got out of bed. "Be good." He winked at me, then he was gone.

I pulled the covers up over my head and wondered if I could die from embarrassment.

The bed sank with a groan. I pictured Malcolm sitting on it, looking down at me. His weight shifted, and I lowered the blankets. He lay next to me, staring up at the ceiling. "I wish there was some other way, Dacia, but as much as I hate to admit it, Mavros is our best defense against your dreams until you get your magic back."

"I know." I scooted closer to him, resting my head on his arm. "Why did I dream last night?"

"Mavros saw the dream and let it through." He lifted his arm, wrapping it around me so that my head was on his chest. "We thought it might give you some answers. We didn't think you'd be hurt."

"I thought he stopped my dreams." I listened to the steady beating of his heart. It was faster, louder than a human's, but the sound helped center me.

His arm tightened a little, making me wonder what he was thinking. "He can. He can alter them. He could make your nightmares so much worse. He can walk in them, and apparently, he can screen them and only let the ones he wants you to see go through."

The idea of having somebody manipulate my dreams and make them worse sent a bolt of fear through me. I didn't want to think about it, so I changed the subject. "Does he—" I cleared my throat, not sure if I wanted to ask, afraid of the answer, and instantly regretting the subject change.

"Does he what?" Malcolm turned his head slightly. His breath blew across my face, and thankfully it didn't smell rotten like it had when Draconian controlled him.

I chewed on my lip and stared across the room, trying to decide if I should ask or not. "Am I attracted to him because of something he does?"

Malcolm's arm tensed. "I don't think he's using magic on you."

"You and Cash … I love you like brothers."

He squeezed my arm but didn't say anything.

"I wish that was all there was to Mavros." I flattened my hand on Malcolm's abs, readying myself to sit up. "But I'm drawn to him. The more I'm around him, the more I want to be."

Malcolm's growl reverberated through my hand. "We need to fix this. Soon." The voice that spoke was the dragon's. "We're going for a run."

"Give me a few minutes."

Cash and Malcolm waited for me in the living room. As soon as I walked in, Cash said, "Get your shoes on. We're going."

I opened the front door and immediately wanted to go back to bed and pull the covers up. The December air stole my breath away, and the wind bit at my face. Even the dragons seemed to have second thoughts.

I dropped my head and took off. My feet pounded against the ice-covered rocks. "Do I smell that bad?"

"No." Cash shook his head.

Malcolm grinned down at me, flashing his fangs. "You smell that good."

I shivered but not because of the cold.

"That's not why we're running, though." Each of his footfalls hit the ground in time with mine. "We want you to bring them back."

My heart seemed to plummet. I couldn't keep going. It took a few steps for the dragons to realize they'd left me behind. They turned and came back to me.

I bent over with my hands on my knees, staring at the gravel road. My breath came out in short bursts that did my body no good. Black spots danced on the edges of my vision. My magic didn't want the same things I did. I couldn't bring it back until I knew how to fix it. I tried to get it to see reason, but with Argentum's power merged with it, I didn't think that would ever be possible.

A hand came down on my shoulder, and calming energy flowed through me. "We'll help you." Cash's face was right next to mine. His amethyst eyes were sympathetic. "It's only going to get worse the longer you wait."

I squatted down, careful to keep anything but my shoes from touching the frozen ground. "How do you know? Maybe Argentum's power will weaken."

"The longer they're entwined, the harder it will be to separate them." Malcolm's voice was laced with sorrow. "The first step is to wake them up. After that, we can figure out how to pull them apart and destroy Argentum's taint for good." He slid his hand under my elbow and lifted me.

Once I was back on my feet, the wind whipped against me, freezing the sweat and sending shivers throughout my body. I wiped my sleeve across my face and started running again, focusing only on the sound of my feet hitting the ground, trying not to think about releasing my powers and the havoc that would be caused when I did.

By the time we got back to my house, I was numb inside and out. I grabbed a change of clothes and headed for the bathroom. Malcolm stood in the doorway, keeping me from entering. "Your emotions are not what I expected. I can't tell what's going on with you."

A humorless chuckle escaped from me. "Welcome to how the rest of us live." I tried to push past him, but he wouldn't budge. "Please."

He lifted my chin and looked into my eyes. "Tell me what you're thinking."

"I'm doing my best not to think." I pulled the band out of my hair and undid my braid. "I think this might be what finally does me in. Not demons or dragons, not Death himself, not a crazed magician, but my own magic." Tears burned my eyes.

Malcolm's posture softened, and I darted past him, slamming the door behind me. I knew he could come in if he wanted, but I trusted him to give me privacy.

While the hot water beat against my skin, I tried to come up with a way to wake up only my magic. If they could be separated, couldn't it be done while they were sleeping?

I thought about the fairies and the unicorn. Somehow, they'd managed to pull the darkness out of my power. Could they pull Argentum out of it? Was it a mistake for me to try it on my own?

Not wanting to face whatever came next, I spent longer fixing my hair than I normally would. I put a French braid on each side above my ears and brought them together at the back of my head.

Dark circles surrounded my eyes. I couldn't remember the last time I had worn makeup, but I pulled my bag out of the drawer and carefully applied it.

When I figured the dragons were nearing the end of their patience, I opened the door. Both of them stood in the hall. They leaned against the far wall with their arms folded over their chests. The veins that lined their biceps bulged. "'bout time," Malcolm said, then turned and walked toward my room.

I followed behind him, trying not to laugh.

As soon as he opened my door, I sobered. Mavros was stretched out on my bed. The comforter didn't have a single wrinkle on it.

He didn't look at us, just focused on the ceiling. "You didn't think you'd do this without me. Did you?"

"We've done a lot without you." Malcolm shrugged. "Why not this?"

He turned toward us. Rage twisted his normally beautiful face into something horrific. He looked like a cross between Mavros, the panther, and the flying demon. "What if she got hurt, and you couldn't help her … again?"

I walked over to the window and stared outside. "It doesn't matter." My voice was as soft as down, but they heard it. "I'm not doing it."

"Dacia." Malcolm sounded feral. "We discussed this. You need to."

"No." I shook my head and turned toward them. "I don't. The fairies pulled the taint out of my powers before. The unicorn did it, too."

Malcolm took a couple steps toward me but stopped before he got any closer. "We can't just keep masking the problem."

"That's not what I'm suggesting." I sat on the window seat and pulled my knees up to my chin. It looked beautiful outside. The sky was a brilliant blue, and the snow sparkled where the sun's light hit it. It called to me even though I knew it was freezing. Even though I knew there were creatures out there, waiting to hurt me. Even though I knew looks were, more often than not, deceiving. The people with me in my room were proof enough of that.

Cash knelt on the floor and rested his hand on mine. "What then?"

"If they can do that, could they pull Argentum's taint out of my magic? Wouldn't it be easier with mine dormant?"

Mavros sat up. He looked from me to each of the dragons, measuring their reactions. "It could work. Couldn't it?"

"It could." Malcolm nodded. "Why didn't we think of it?"

I rested my head on my knees. "Because you're not terrified of the outcome."

Malcolm sat next to me and pulled me against his side. I laid my head on his shoulder and let him comfort me. "We don't want to see you or Cody hurt either."

"I know."

Cash stood. "So, when do we do this?"

"Not today." I hated the note of hysteria I heard in my voice. "Please. Let me spend one more day with Cody in case this doesn't work."

Malcolm nodded. "Of course."

Chapter 35

One Last Day

Even though it was freezing outside, I longed for fresh air. I stood at the front door with a mug of cocoa warming my hands. Every once in a while, I took a sip while I waited for Cody to show up.

Mavros walked up behind me, close enough that I could feel the warmth of his body. Personal space didn't seem to be a concern for demons. "I could take the two of you somewhere warm."

I shook my head and turned toward him. "How'd you know?"

"There is so much longing in your eyes." He ran the backs of his fingers along my cheek. "I wish you'd look at me like that."

"Where?" I gazed outside again. Across the street, something moved in the trees, knocking snow from the branches. The flakes caught the sunlight as they drifted to the ground, sparkling like tiny pieces of glitter. Nobody seemed concerned, so I assumed it was a squirrel or bird and not another imp. "Where would you take us?"

He shrugged. "Anywhere you want, Dacia, on this realm or another."

I closed my eyes and imagined the possibilities. The beach where I'd seen Mavros kept coming to mind. The only problem was that every time I pictured it, I saw him stretched out on the sand in only his speedo.

He breathed in deeply and chuckled.

"What?" My eyes snapped open.

"I love the smell of desire."

I turned away from him, hoping he didn't know it was him I'd been picturing.

"You must have somewhere in mind." His hand slid onto my shoulder, and a dragon growled. Mavros flicked a glance at them. "I'm not hurting her."

"You will not take her anywhere without us." Malcolm's words were a warning.

Mavros tilted his head in a half-hearted shrug. "I will do whatever Dacia wants."

"Then get along." I walked away from him, perching on the edge of the couch between the dragons. "Please. Just for today."

Mavros bowed. "Your wish … my command." He straightened his posture. "If you want to get away, the dragons may come along."

The gravel on the road crunched. "I need to talk to Cody. Alone." I set my mug on the end table and walked back over to the door. "Then we'll decide what to do." As soon as Cody pulled into the driveway, I ran outside.

He rolled the window down. "We leavin'?"

It crossed my mind to jump in and tell him to go, to drive around, and give us the semblance of freedom, but then I remembered long, bat-like wings and hate-filled eyes. "Can we just sit out here and talk?"

"Sure." He patted the seat.

I sat down and, out of habit, pulled the seatbelt over my shoulder. Cody's eyebrows pinched together in confusion, and as soon as I realized what I'd done, I laughed. "Safety first. I guess." I unbuckled it and turned sideways in the seat, leaning my back against the door. "So … tomorrow—" I stared down at my lap, trying to find a way to tell him that today might be our last day together.

"Tomorrow … what?" He reached for my hand, and his touch soothed me.

"The plan is to go to the fairies to see if they can separate my magic from Argentum's." I turned his hand over and traced my finger down his palm.

Using his other hand, he rubbed his thumb along my cheek. "So today might be our last for a while."

I nodded.

"Like your hair this way." He tugged on a curl, and I forced my lips upward. "Whadda you wanna do?"

I shrugged. "Mavros and the dragons will take us any-where in the world."

"Rather spend the day alone with you."

I lifted the console and slid closer to him. "Can we stay out here for a few more minutes?"

He draped his arm over my shoulder, squeezing it. "What-ever you need."

I snuggled into his side and wrapped my arm around his waist. "I love you, Cody. No matter what happens, I want you to know that."

"I do, Dacia." He rested his head on mine. "Sorry I get jealous. I trust you." He let out a deep sigh. "Sometimes, it's hard. Think about you with Malcolm, Cash, and Mavros, and can't help myself."

I kissed his neck just below his ear. "I'm sorry, Cody. I don't want them with me. I only want you."

"I know." He cupped my cheek in his hand and lowered his mouth, stopping just before touching mine. "Okay?"

"Yes."

He brushed his lips across mine, the softest of touches. Then he let go of me, scooted his seat all of the way back, and lifted my leg over his. The kiss started slow. I tried to deepen it, but he pulled back, keeping it at his pace.

His fingers slid under my sweatshirt, running along my spine. Tingles danced across my skin following his touch.

I reached down beside his seat and laid the chair back, giggling at the expression of surprise on his face.

His fingers splayed out on my back, and he pulled my mouth down on his, clutching me to him. His teeth scraped against my lip, and I moaned in response.

I lifted my head, and he trailed kisses over my chin and down my neck.

Dragons and a demon probably kept an eye on me from inside my house, but I didn't care. I wanted … no, I *needed* time with Cody before I couldn't see him again.

I tugged at his shirt, untucking it from his jeans, and slipped my hands under the hem, trailing them over his ribs.

Tap. Tap. Tap.

I jerked up, looking out the driver's side window, expecting to see an impatient dragon, but no one was there. Rolling off of Cody, I moved onto the middle seat. Nobody seemed to be around at all.

"What's going on?" Cody raised his seat and scooted it forward.

"I don't know." I pulled my hand over my mouth. "I don't see anyone."

He reached for the door handle. "Let's go in."

"No." I stretched across him and pressed the lock button down. "Wait." *Malcolm.* I waited for a response or for him to come bursting through the front door.

Tap. Tap. Tap.

Cody and I both jerked our heads around looking for something.

Malcolm. When he didn't answer again, I realized he couldn't hear me. I'd gotten so used to having magic that I'd forgotten that speaking mind to mind was part of it. "Honk the horn, Cody."

He slammed his hand down on it several times. A black mist swirled next to the passenger door, solidifying into Mavros. His obsidian eyes were wide, alert. He waved his hand at me, and I scooted over, unlocking the car.

Cash and Malcolm burst onto the porch. Their faces were in various forms of transformation.

I nodded at Cody, and we both opened our doors. As soon as my foot hit the ground, Mavros grasped my arm above my elbow, and something grabbed my ankle.

I screamed.

Sharp claws tore through my skin.

I stumbled, but Mavros held me up. He kicked at whatever had hold of me, and I glanced back as he lifted me into his arms.

Long, spindly fingers retreated, and a shadow darted under the SUV.

Mavros cradled me against him and ran toward the house. Cody matched him stride for stride.

Malcolm and Cash had disappeared from the porch, and Mavros clutched me so tightly that I couldn't look over his shoulder to see what was going on.

The beast screeched. I felt its cries in my teeth. I pinched my eyes shut and clamped my hands over my ears, but it did little to block out the sound.

Mavros' footfalls thumped against the stairs and across the porch. I opened my eyes and saw the door within arm's reach.

Cody stretched for it, and Mavros stumbled. He held me against him, turning as he fell. My body crashed down on top of his, and something grabbed me.

I kicked at it. My foot hit the beast and sailed through it like it was insubstantial. Its body reformed around me, trapping my leg inside of it.

Cody lifted me by my armpits and pulled me.

"Cody, stop!" My plea was a panicked wail.

The beast tugged me in the other direction, backing toward the far end of the deck. My body thunked onto the porch. I reached for Mavros, but he didn't move. My fingers scrabbled over the boards, trying to grab hold of something, trying to keep from being dragged away.

"Help Dacia!" Cody yelled.

Several of the nightmarish shadow creatures fought the dragons. Malcolm looked when Cody hollered, and it cost him. The beast's claws tore across his face.

I grabbed hold of a post and focused on my power. The serpent was coiled up and had a silver tinge to it. I put my hand on it. "I need you. Please, please help me, help us."

The snake shifted slightly.

I shook it vigorously. "*Please*. If you don't come back to me, we'll both die."

It cracked open one copper and black eye. *You trapped us. Figure it out on your own.*

In the real world, my fingers tore loose from the pole. I opened my eyes. Cody leaned over Mavros, smacking his face, trying to wake him up. Arianna and Val had joined in the fight against the shadow monsters. Russ jumped over the railing behind the one dragging me. He shook his head, letting me know not to say anything.

I looked away from him to keep the creature from realizing he was there and focused on my power. Holding my hand against the serpent, I commanded it to wake up. I felt a jolt as my magic reluctantly flowed into me. It started as a trickle, but the deluge broke through, crashing into my body, filling me with power.

The serpent faded away, and the battle raged on around me.

I lifted my head, and flames exploded from my hands, hurtling toward the beast. A shrill cry filled the air, and my foot fell through shadow, slamming against the wooden planks. Pain scattered my thoughts.

"Get inside!" Russ pulled the creature off the porch. "They're demons. They can't enter."

Chapter 36

Returned

emons.

I tried to stand, but I couldn't put any weight on either leg. I dragged myself across the porch, praying I could get inside before one of the other demons noticed me. Cody ran toward me and hefted me over his shoulder, darting for the house. My magic burned inside of me at his touch.

I tried to focus on the problem at hand, not on Cody.

Demons.

Was that why Mavros couldn't get up? Could they kill each other on this plane?

"Get inside," Malcolm roared.

I pictured the living room and teleported into it. Cody ran a few more steps before slowing. He knelt down, lowering me to the ground carefully to keep from jarring my legs. He started to pull my shoes off, but I stopped him.

"Cody, leave it." I pinched my eyes shut. "They're demon wounds. Only Mavros will be able to heal them."

He looked at the door, then back at me.

"No." I sat up, and pain tore through my legs with the movement. "Don't go out there. *Please.*" The last word was barely a whisper.

He brushed his thumb down my cheek, then got up and walked to the door, peering outside. "I can get him." He held the screen door open with his foot and dragged Mavros in. He wasn't near as gentle with him as he had been with me. The screen banged shut as he tugged Mavros closer to me.

I grabbed hold of Mavros' arm and shook him gently. "Mavros," I whispered his name, hoping he wouldn't think he was still in the middle of the battle if he woke up.

He didn't stir, didn't flutter his eyelids, didn't change his breathing.

I tried to resituate myself, but as soon as I moved my leg, agony ripped through it. I sucked in a breath, and tears filled my eyes.

Cody rushed over to me, but I held my hand up. "Probably not a good idea." My magic reacted to my pain. I imagined the serpent, rearing its head, ready to strike out at whatever was hurting me.

I pressed both hands down on Mavros' chest. "Please, Mavros." Sparks skipped across my fingers. "Cody"—I didn't dare look at him—"go to my room. Now!" *Malcolm, Cash, I need you.*

Electricity jumped from my fingers to Mavros' chest. His body arched, then slammed onto the ground. His eyes snapped open, and he wrapped his fingers around my throat.

"Let go of her, *demon.*" The voice was feral, and I couldn't tell which of the dragons it came from.

I held onto Mavros' hands, pulling on them, trying to get him to loosen his hold. *Mavros, please. Please let go of me.* I watched as his eyes focused and realization struck him.

He jerked his hand back and sat up. A look of horror filled his face.

Low, warning growls filled the room, raising the hairs on the back of my neck.

"I'm sorry, Dacia." Mavros bowed his head. "I failed you."

I squeezed his hand. "I need you to heal my legs." I glanced over my shoulder at the dragons. Their pupils were thin slits. Malcolm had four gouges from above his right eye to his left shoulder. His clothes were torn and bloody. Cash's ear was shredded. Blood dripped from his fingertips. Some of it his. Some of it the demons'. "He wasn't waking up. I had to send Cody away." I lowered my chin to my chest. "I was scared I'd hurt him."

Mavros lifted my legs, settling them on his lap. His touch was tender, but even so, every movement sent jolts of pain throughout my body. I leaned back, holding myself up on my elbows.

"You can't defeat them." Mavros didn't look away from me, but I knew he was talking to the dragons. "Call the others in. As soon as I'm done with her, I can send them back."

"Then why didn't you?" Cash sounded more like his dragon than his human.

"This is going to hurt you." Mavros slid his hand down to my ankle. "I'm sorry."

"Why?" Malcolm strode closer.

Mavros looked at him for just a second before focusing on me again. "I thought I could get her inside first." He held onto my ankle. "Since she couldn't defend herself, I wanted her out of the battle."

"Heal her." Malcolm's words were a feral snarl.

Mavros stared into my face. "The venom's not mine, Dacia." He swallowed, and sympathy flashed through his eyes. "I'm going to have to hurt you first."

There wasn't even time for me to nod before he swiped his claws down my leg. A scream tore from my throat as he drew the venom out. Malcolm and Cash were instantly next to me. They bared their fangs at Mavros, growling like overprotective guard dogs, but he ignored them.

I fell back and covered my face with my hands.

Mavros set my leg down and slid his hands to the other one. I watched him, readying myself for the agony, but instead of healing it, he bent down and bit my leggings above my left knee, tearing through the already damaged fabric. Then he ripped the piece the long way, exposing my leg.

Where it had been inside the demon's body, it was burned and bruised. Malcolm grabbed my hand, and I clamped down on his while Mavros healed my leg.

The pain was too much. I pinched my eyes shut, trying to keep the room from spinning. My stomach lurched.

Cash's and Malcolm's energy flowed into me lessening the agony.

By the time Mavros set my leg down, I was exhausted.

"Ready?" Malcolm asked.

I slitted my eyes open enough to see that he was talking to Mavros.

"Give me a second, dragon." Mavros squeezed my hand. "Her magic is depleted. You'll be safe with her."

I heard Cody walk into the living room. He slid one hand under my back and one under my knees and lifted me.

"Sorry," I mumbled. "I thought we could have one more day."

He sat on the couch, cradling me on his lap, and pressed his lips to my forehead. "Just rest, Dacia."

I woke up in Cody's arms. Malcolm sat next to us. His wounds were healed. His clothes were clean. He smiled when I looked at him. "How are you doing?"

"Tired." I yawned without meaning to. "Stiff."

Malcolm reached for my hand, but I pulled it away, afraid of what my magic might do to him. "Are you sure you won't get hurt?"

"I'll live." He twined his fingers with mine for just a moment before letting go. "They're still diminished."

Cody's shoulders slumped as tension released from them. "Parents'll be home soon. You should clean up."

"Not yet." I ran my fingers through Cody's hair above his ear and stood, holding my hand out to him.

He grabbed ahold of it, and I led him downstairs. "I know I'm a mess, but with my magic back, I don't know how much more time we'll have."

"Yeah." That single word was laced with pain.

As soon as we were in the basement, I turned, stood on my tiptoes, and crushed my mouth against his. Desperate. Starved.

He stumbled back, hitting his shoulder on the doorframe.

I pressed him against the wall. Sliding his hand out of mine, he wound his arms around my waist and lifted me.

I clung to him. Holding the back of his head with one hand so he couldn't pull away. I wrapped my legs around his waist and kissed him harder still. I felt like this could be the last time I touched him, the last time I tasted his lips, and a chasm tore open inside of me. The despair it held was bottomless.

He staggered to the couch and lowered me slowly, wrapping one arm around my waist and holding onto the back of the couch with his other hand. His lips never strayed from mine. I wouldn't have let them.

I needed him. I needed him to keep the pit from expanding inside of me. Without him, the despair would swallow me.

I slid my hands under his shirt, digging my fingernails into his back, loving the feel of his smooth skin, his toned muscles.

His heart thundered against my chest, and I shut everything else out. Cody was the only other person who existed. The only one who mattered.

I relaxed my grip on him and slowed the kiss. The desperation faded. The hunger satiated. I tilted my head back, and his mouth moved off mine, kissing along the neckline of my shirt. His teeth scraped my neck.

My magic swelled. "Cody," I said at the same time that flames shot from my fingers.

He lifted his head and looked at me with wide eyes.

"Oh, my God, Cody. Are you okay?"

He jumped off the couch, backing away from me like prey trying to avoid the predator. "Malcolm." His voice wasn't panicked or urgent. He didn't sound hurt or even scared, just concerned.

Footsteps thundered down the stairs. Malcolm ran toward me, and Cash moved between Cody and me.

Cash sucked in a deep breath and moaned.

Malcolm grabbed hold of my hands and drew on my power.

I stared over his shoulder at Cody. "He should be dead or dying. He shouldn't be standing there." I looked from Cody to Malcolm. "I don't understand."

Cash led Cody toward the stairs. When he was in the doorway, Cody turned toward me and lifted the chain I'd given him for Christmas. Sparks jumped between the links. "Best gift ever."

Chapter 37

New Plan

The dragons were visibly uncomfortable even after I'd showered and burned my bloody clothes. My emotions and hormones were way out of whack.

"My powers are back." I walked toward the sliding door and looked outside. It was already nearly dark. "We can sit on the porch. I can protect myself."

"No," five dragons, one demon, and one human yelled at me all at once.

Cody folded his arms over his chest. "Not taking one step outside 'til Mavros spills about the demons."

The anger that surged inside of me wasn't completely my own. I looked away from him before my magic decided to lash out again.

"The demons that attacked have been destroyed." Mavros' voice was barely contained fury.

"Destroyed?" I understood his frustration, but I didn't understand what he said. "I thought demons couldn't be destroyed."

"Not here." His smile was feral. "I dragged them to the Abyss and killed them one by one."

Part of me wished I could have been there with him. The other part of me wanted nothing to do with the death of any creature no matter how evil it was. "If we're not going outside, I'll open the door for a bit." I pushed the sliding door open, and cold air rushed inside. I went into the living room and opened the front door, lifting the glass on the screen so the air could blow through the house.

Walking back into the dining room, I watched my guardians' faces. They looked at me like I was a bomb about to explode. I wanted to stand by Cody, to have him wrap his arms around me, but I couldn't touch him again. I couldn't risk it. What if the chain only worked once? When I'd bought it, Malcolm said it would work to some extent. Had that extent been reached?

Instead of going to his side, I pulled out a chair at the end of the table and sat with my back to him. I could feel his presence. I could hear every sound he made, every move he made. I rubbed my hands over my ears, trying to get Cody out of my head, trying to keep him safe. "So … what do we do now? I'm sure the Neph—"

"No." Malcolm's angry growl startled me. "The plan's the same. You will not hand yourself over to the self-righteous angel spawn." He stood up and crossed his arms over his chest, daring me to contradict him. "Where were they today?" He looked around the room, waiting for an answer. "They don't deserve to call themselves protectors. We could've died out there. *You* could have died."

Mavros sat next to me. "The Nephilim are children of angels."

"Yes." I cocked my head, wondering why he was saying that. Malcolm had just called them angel-spawn, so even if I didn't know before, I would now. "I know."

"They can return lesser demons, like the shadow demons, to the Abyss." His voice was low and sympathetic. The Mavros I'd first met would have reveled in revealing this to me. "They're one of the few creatures who can."

"And they woulda let her die?" Cody's voice was outraged.

My magic stirred at hearing it. I folded my hands on the table in front of me.

Russ nodded. "If they'd have known her magic was bound, they might have helped and then taken her to their sanctuary while they could." His amber eyes were hard. "Either way, they did nothing."

I'd known what the majority of the Nephilim thought about me, but I couldn't believe they would just let demons drag me off. How many times would I have to save the world before they trusted me? Would I ever be able to prove myself to them?

"And, that cannot be forgiven." Cash wiped his hand down his face, pushed his chair back, and walked to the back door. He stood pressed against the screen, sucking in the fresh air.

Val started to get up, but Arianna held him down. "She's okay. She just feels betrayed."

"She needs protected." He pulled away.

Malcolm shook his head. "Nobody here will hurt her."

I heard gravel crunching on the road. "Close the doors. Decide if you want to be seen." The garage door opened, and the car turned into my driveway. "Mom and Dad will be inside in a coupla minutes."

"We'll go back out." Arianna grabbed Val's hand, and they disappeared.

Russ stayed visible. "I'll go when Cody does. I'll ride with him and keep him safe."

"Do I need to go?" Cody sounded distant, and even though I understood, it broke me a little more.

"Stay," I said. Then I turned to my guardians. "Don't let me hurt anyone." I pushed my chair back and ran into the living room, realizing the blood and mess hadn't been cleaned up. I stopped and stared at the place I'd lain on the floor. It was pristine.

Cash walked in and flashed his fangs at me. Apparently, my emotions were still too much for him. "We needed to do something while you and Cody were making out."

I smiled at him. "Thank you."

My parents walked in through the garage door. Mom looked around the room, noticing that most of the chairs were still pulled away from the table, noticing the extra dragon. "Everything okay?"

"Yeah." I wished I had a mask like Cody's or Malcolm's that I could take out and slip into place whenever I needed to hide my emotions. "Russ is staying with Cody for a few days. How was work?"

Mom's face scrunched up, and I knew she was trying to figure something out.

"Same ole, same ole," Dad answered as he hung his coat up. "We were talking about ordering pizza if you wouldn't mind picking it up."

"I'll get it," Malcolm said.

Evidently, he didn't want me to leave the house either. I shouldn't have been surprised, but I could already feel the bars of my prison cell squeezing in on me, and I hated it.

Mom walked through the dining room and handed her credit card to Malcolm. He looked at it in confusion. "I'll get it. You've been kind enough to let us stay here."

"So you could protect our daughter." She looked over her shoulder at Cody. "Is Russ staying with you to protect you?"

He glanced at me, and I nodded. "Yes, ma'am."

"Why?" She spun around, pinning me with her gaze. "Why does he need protection? What aren't you telling us?"

I looked down at my feet, trying to decide what to say to her. "There was an imp in the woods the other night when we went for a walk. It wasn't a big deal, but we thought it would be best to make sure nothing takes Cody to get to me."

"Dear God." Mom sank down on the couch. "So, what exactly happened? When you came in, your face was pale."

I remembered standing in the clearing, listening to the beast saying he wanted to eat my heart while it was still beating. I remembered watching Mavros tear the creature in two. I remembered the blood, and I felt queasy all over again.

"I killed it," Mavros said. "Quite gruesomely."

Mom nodded. "Good."

"So how many pizzas do we need?" Dad asked in an obvious effort to change the subject.

"Two or three." I sat next to Mom and held her hand. "Dragons don't eat stuff like that."

Dad pointed at Mavros.

"I'll eat just about anything."

The cavern smells like her fear. The scent lures me to the edge of the lake. The power in her blood combines with her terror creating the most savory scent imaginable. Saliva drips down my chin.

But I need to wait for the precise moment. She's stronger than she looks. I need to catch her by surprise to finish her. She's gotten away too many times already, and I grow weary of the chase.

The demon keeps undermining my commands. With his true name on my tongue, he shouldn't be able to do that, but they are masters of deception and better at finding loopholes than I'd imagined. As soon as she's gone, I'll return him to the Abyss. His kind don't deserve the privilege of walking on this planet.

The waves gently lap against my body. The cave is dark enough that I could slip out of the water and hide in the shadows. I could transform into my human body and kill her before she knows I'm here, but her power will be diminished by death. I need to consume her alive.

The remembered taste of her blood, the power that surged through me with what I licked off the ground, holds me back. I can't waste my chance.

She turns and cautiously walks into a grotto. I slip from the water onto the rocky shore. If I can keep her from teleporting out, she's mine.

I prowl ever closer, as silent as a cat on the hunt.

She stops and glances over her shoulder. With her human eyes, she won't be able to see me.

And, yet, somehow she does. She lifts her hands, and blue flames encompass her fingers. The inferno flies at me, striking me in the chest, but I am a dragon. I am immune to fire.

I laugh and blast her with flames of my own. Instead of consuming her, they flow around her. Then she's gone.

I roar, filling the cavern with a conflagration. Rage consumes me.

"Dacia." Malcolm's voice was deep and dark.

I opened my eyes, and every detail of the room was as clear as if it was daytime. Fear clenched my heart. If Arianna or Val were watching me, they would see me partially transformed into a dragon. I didn't want to anger them or lose their friendship. I didn't want to deal with this right now.

"Can we go away?" I sat up and rubbed my hands over my face. Scales covered my cheeks. "Go fly?"

Malcolm's eyebrows lifted and a wry smile tugged on his lips. He reached his hand down to me, and as soon as my fingers touched his, I was transported.

Malcolm and I fell through the sky. He transformed into his dragon as the ground raced toward us.

Anger burned inside of me. Why would he do this?

He flew underneath me. *Change.* His voice thundered inside my head.

My magic flared, and my body morphed into my dragon. I roared, and flames blasted through the air.

Yes! The excitement in Malcolm's voice helped me forget my rage. *Deplete your magic, Dacia. Don't give Argentum a chance to take hold again.*

We soared over the mountaintops. Malcolm flew into the clouds, and I followed him, bursting through the other side. I slowed, staring at the heavens above me and the clouds below.

Mavros and the dragons had been right. I would have been a fool to give this up.

I focused on the weather, stirring up a storm beneath us. The zephyr turned into a gust. I flapped my wings harder, flying headfirst into the wind.

Use it all, Dacia. Malcolm challenged me. *I won't let you fall.*

I turned my scales as black as midnight. Even though it was the same form, just a different color, I felt my magic draining. I banked in the air, letting the wind carry me, so I could concentrate on using my power.

Malcolm flew alongside me, watching me, waiting for any sign that my strength was dwindling.

I closed my eyes, imagining my scales pink. My magic fought against me. I felt my body shifting, transforming into something else. I struggled against the change but knew I was losing.

Malcolm growled.

I looked at my foreleg. The starlight reflected off silver scales.

My wings slackened, and I plummeted, falling through the clouds. Snow pelted my face. The wind tossed me around, flipping me over again and again.

My scales faded to blue. The storm dissipated. Cold blasted through me as my body transformed into my own. The wind howled in my ears as I plunged toward the earth.

Malcolm dove toward me, but the ground raced at me faster still.

I called on my power, trying to slow my fall, trying to teleport, trying to fly.

Nothing answered.

The mountain peaks jutted through the clouds, waiting to pluck me from the sky. Sharp ridges and rocky precipices.

I squeezed my eyes shut and sent up a silent prayer. *Please let it end quickly. Please don't make me suffer.*

The wind died. The howling quieted. My eyes snapped open.

Malcolm's wings were folded back, and he dove through the air. His claws stretched toward me, and he snagged me. His talons pierced my flesh.

I whimpered.

I'm sorry. His voice was filled with despair. He landed on a ledge and lowered me to the ground while he transformed. Then he knelt by my side, covering my wounds with his hands.

My teeth chattered, and shivers shook me. Malcolm's eyes widened, and I saw real fear in them.

A blast of warmth entered my body along with healing energy. "Hang on, Dacia." He lifted me into his arms, and I was stretched out and squeezed together.

Darkness surrounded us for a moment before we reformed in my bedroom.

Mavros rushed over to us. "What did you do to her, *dragon?*"

"He saved me." My voice was hoarse, and I realized I must've been screaming as I plummeted through the sky. I pushed against Malcolm, grabbed a change of clothes, and left them to argue without me.

Cash met me in the hallway. He lifted his nose and breathed in deeply. "You're okay?"

I nodded.

"Not going anywhere?"

"Shower and bed." I stumbled into the bathroom. "I'm exhausted." I shut the door in his face.

Standing under the steaming water, I shivered uncontrollably. My movements felt sluggish. I cleaned the blood off, wrapped a towel around myself, and sat on the edge of the tub. My chest tightened, and my breaths were shallow and uneven.

Staggering to my feet, I got dressed. Then I leaned on the counter for a few minutes before stumbling into the hall, right into Mavros.

"What's wrong?" His face was pinched with concern.

I held onto the wall, trying to stop the world from spinning. "I don't know."

He grabbed my hand. "You're freezing."

I tried to take a step and wobbled. It took all of my concentration just to lift my foot off the ground.

He swooped me up and carried me into my room. "Didn't you use hot water?"

I barely found the energy to nod my head.

He laid me on the bed and covered me up. Kicking off his shoes, he lifted the blankets and scooted in close to me, pressing his body against mine. "I think you're in shock." The heat radiating off of him increased substantially, and he wrapped his arms around me.

I fell asleep grateful that he was with me.

Chapter 38

Begging For Help

When I woke up Thursday morning, my legs were twined with Mavros', and my head was on his bare chest. If Cody saw us like this, he would never forgive me, and I wouldn't blame him.

I tore myself away from Mavros and sat on the edge of my bed. Even after several hours of sleep, I was still worn out. "When did your shirt come off?"

"When I realized you were in shock." His voice was matter-of-fact.

I looked over my shoulder as he climbed out of my bed. He wore only boxer briefs. "Really?" A lump formed in my throat, and I swallowed over it.

He tugged on his jeans. "It was the best way to keep you warm." He wiggled his eyebrows at me. "It would've been even better if I could've convinced you to shed your pajamas."

I picked up a pillow and threw it at him. Then I held my head in my hands and sobbed.

The bed shifted, and he slipped his arm over my shoulder, pulling me against him. "Dacia, I was just trying to lighten the mood. You were in shock. Nothing happened." He tilted my chin up. "I promised you a life with Cody. I won't take that away from you."

"Could you at least put a shirt on?"

Before I finished asking, he was dressed in his customary black silk shirt.

I slammed my fist against his chest. "I knew you didn't need to dress in front of me."

"You were watching." He shrugged. "I see the way you look at me. I thought you wanted me to."

I narrowed my eyes at him. "Sometimes, I hate you," I said through clenched teeth.

He tilted his head to the side. "I know what you think about me. The dragons know. Hell, even Cody knows. That's why they detest me. I won't hurt you, though. I won't make you do anything you don't want to."

I stood up and pointed at the bed. "I didn't want to wake up with you like that."

"You were in shock." He dragged his hands down his face. "You can die from that."

I rolled my neck, loosening some of my tension. "Thank you … for helping me."

Malcolm and Cash didn't show up until I was washing my breakfast dishes. Malcolm bowed his head. "Please forgive me, Dacia."

"For what?" I wiped my hands on the towel, threw it over my shoulder, and turned around to face him.

He wouldn't look me in the eyes. "For letting you fall. I promised I wouldn't."

"Ah, Malcolm." I stood right in front of him, clutching his arms. "That wasn't your fault. And, besides, you stopped me." I leaned my forehead against his chest. "I thought I was going to die."

"I know." He held the back of my head. "Your fear drove me to recklessness. I'm sorry for that, too."

I looked up into his bronze eyes. "You saved me. You healed me. You got me home safely. I'm grateful."

"Is there anything worse than a sullen dragon?" Mavros asked in a wry voice, propping himself up against the fridge as he did.

I pulled the towel off my shoulder, tossed it on the counter, and went back to washing dishes. "I can think of a few."

"Oh, yeah. Name one." Mavros challenged.

"How about a yard filled with demons?"

Cash chuckled. "Touché."

"Are you ready?" Malcolm asked.

I unplugged the sink and watched the water swirl down the drain. "No. Not really."

"No?" He jerked back slightly. "Why not?"

Mavros shook his head. "Most humans have more to worry about than the size of their treasure hoard."

Malcolm and Cash both narrowed their eyes at him.

"What if they can't help me?" Not wanting to see their expressions, I turned my back to them and washed the counter. "What if I'm stuck with Argentum's power? What if this is the way it is now?"

Mavros threw his arm around my shoulders, and my body tensed in response. "Then we'll deal with it."

"What did you do to her, demon?" Cash prowled toward us. His pupils were thin slits.

I shook Mavros' arm off. "You all need to stop this. He did the same thing that Malcolm did last night. He saved me." I tossed the rag over the faucet and dried my hands off. Then I turned around and faced them. "No one in this room wants to hurt me, but sometimes you do. I went into shock last night, and Mavros helped me."

All three of them lowered their eyes.

"I want to call Cody first." I dragged my hand through my hair. "Just in case."

Malcolm followed me down the hallway.

"Give her some privacy," Mavros hollered from the kitchen.

Malcolm didn't respond. He just closed my door once we were inside. "Sorry, Dacia. No privacy."

"I know." I flopped across my bed and pulled the afghan Mom had made me for Christmas over my legs. "I could've killed him yesterday." I covered my face with my hands. "I never thanked you for helping me with the chain."

He sat next to me and put his hand on my back, rubbing it gently. "And, you'll never need to."

"No, I do. I should've before. Cody would be dead if you hadn't helped me." I folded my arms and rested my chin on my hands. "Thanks for all you do for me, for all the times you've helped me."

"You're welcome."

I reached for the phone but stopped short of picking it up. "Do you think it will work again? If I don't get my magic under control … will the chain save him?"

"I believe it will." He stood and walked to the window. "But you still need to be careful." He sat down. "I'll be here if you need me."

Malcolm stretched his hand toward me, and I slid mine into it. "If the fairies can't help, we'll figure something else out."

Mavros twined his fingers through mine and squeezed gently. Cash nodded, and the four of us teleported to the cave where I'd battled Nefarious.

The darkness was absolute. I wanted to transform my eyes into a dragon's or light a fire in my palm, but I was afraid that if I did Argentum's magic would take hold of me again.

"Rayne." Her name came out quieter than I'd intended. I cleared my throat and said it again. Then I stared up at the ceiling, hoping they'd show up soon. The darkness surrounded me, closing in, tightening my chest, and stealing my breath. My gaze darted around the cavern, but no matter where I looked, I couldn't see anything. An arm wrapped around my shoulder. I screamed and spun away from it. "Light … please."

Flames danced in Cash's palm. "I'm sorry." He held his other hand up, like he was surrendering. "I thought the fear was for the unknown. I forget humans can't see in the dark."

Eldritch shadows danced over the stalagmites and stalactites, bringing my ghosts back to life.

For a moment, I swore Nefarious stormed toward me. His fiery whip lashed through the air. Phantom pains tore through my leg. I saw myself broken and bleeding, knowing I was about to die. I saw myself on my hands and knees, heaving Argentum's blood over the cavern floor.

My heart pounded in my ears, drowning out all other sounds. This wasn't going to work. I'd come back from too much already. Eventually, my luck would run out.

I sank to the ground and held my head in my hands. Someone tried to soothe me, running their hand along the top of my back. When that didn't work, strong fingers massaged my neck and shoulders.

The action helped calm me. Sounds came back. The steady drip of water from the stalactites. The buzz of wings. The chirrup of fairies.

I pulled my hands down my face and looked up. Thousand of lights filled the cavern, illuminating everything and eliminating the shadows.

Rayne flew down, hovering in front of my face. "Why so forlorn?"

"It isn't Mavros' power contaminating mine."

She looked at him like he'd planted this idea in my head. A tiny seed that he had nurtured until it vined out, snaking its way through me.

"It's Argentum." I held my hand out, and she landed on it. "I've been having dreams where I'm him. My magic and his merged, and I need to get him out." I pinched my eyes shut, fearing her response. "I just don't know how."

Mavros stepped closer, and she narrowed her eyes at him. "We wanted to come to you while her powers were contained, but we were attacked."

"I brought my powers back. It was the only chance I had to survive." I chewed on my lip. I didn't know if Cash or Mavros knew what I was about to say. I had no idea what Malcolm had told them. "Then last night I transformed into Argentum."

Malcolm's voice was soft. I wasn't sure if it was to keep from startling Rayne or if he was masking his real emotions. "Mavros' power lies dormant inside her … by his doing. I have seen it firsthand."

"Dacia's magic chose to merge with Argentum's." With the fairies here, Cash had released his flames. "It wants to be invincible."

I looked into Rayne's purple eyes, hoping she could help me even though some instinct told me she couldn't. "Argentum's magic wants to destroy Cody. I need it gone."

She waved her arm, and the fairies flew down, landing on me. "Relax," she said.

I closed my eyes, letting their peace slide into me. Hundreds of tiny fairies stood on me, but I didn't feel weighed down by them.

Small bursts of energy shot into me, and my power stirred in response. I tried to hold it back, afraid of how it would react to them.

"Let us see it." Rayne's voice was high and excited.

My magic rose inside of me. Enraged. Powerful.

Just when I thought it would blast out of my body, it receded.

For a minute, I felt like myself. The anger and hatred fell away. "What happened?" I opened my eyes. A wind whipped up around me as the fairies flew off of me one by one.

"Your magic is strong." Rayne's silver hair floated on the breeze. Her iridescent wings fluttered. "If you can find a way to extract Argentum's power, you will survive."

"But … you don't know how to do it?" My shoulders slumped. Even though I'd had my doubts, it seemed part of me had dared to hope.

She flew up, hovering above my hand. "I am sorry, Dacia. Argentum was not inherently malevolent. We can heal, and we can expel evil. We cannot help with this."

"Thank you." My voice was husky. "Thank you for trying."

The fairies flew away, but we stayed. I sat down, leaning against a stalagmite, and focused on my powers. I watched the serpent. Its pearlescent scales were edged with silver. It stared up at me. Its eyes were filled with malice.

We are not your servants.

"No." I sat on the floor and watched the snake's movements. "You are not my servants. One of you is me, and one of you is my enemy."

We are one. It slithered toward me.

I held my hand up, and it stopped. "You almost killed me last night when you made me transform into Argentum. If I die, where does that leave you? You cannot go on without me."

The snake puffed up, and I could sense its agitation. *What do you want?*

"I want to talk to my powers alone." I stared into its copper and black eyes. There was no sign of Argentum in them yet, no silver in the irises. "Argentum wanted to kill me. I don't want him to be part of me."

We are one. You, me, him. We belong together.

I leaned forward, hovering over the snake, and it cowered down. "I *do not* belong with him. He wanted to eat me."

So I would be part of him. The snake nudged my hand. *Now, he is part of us.*

"Because I allowed Mavros' magic into me, unaware of what would happen, and I ate Argentum instead." I held my hand still. I didn't want to pet the snake. I wanted nothing to do with the part that was Argentum. "I don't want him. If he has to be here, can't it be like Mavros' powers? Can't he be separate?"

He is part of us.

I pulled away from my magic and opened my eyes. Malcolm, Cash, and Mavros all looked at me like they were trying to decide how to tell me my dog had died.

"We'll figure it out." Malcolm stepped toward me and draped his arm over my shoulders. "Are you ready to go back?"

There was no reason for me to stay, nothing else for me to do here. I'd wanted to leave this place free from my demons, but now I realized I would never really be free. As long as I had magic, I would be a slave to my powers. Whatever monster or madness that came after me would be in charge.

Chapter 39

The desire to go outside was nearly overwhelming. I lay in bed with the covers pulled up to my chin and Malcolm next to me. His face was tight, his muscles taut. "What is it, Dacia?"

"If I had to guess, an imp or a demon." I rolled onto my back and stared up at the ceiling. "Why can't they all just leave me alone?"

"Something's calling you?" Malcolm sat up. "Mavros, stay with her." He flashed his fangs, and they elongated. "I'm going hunting."

My heart sank a little bit. Waking up with Mavros this morning was still too fresh on my mind. He'd been right. I'd liked looking at him. I'd liked snuggling against him. I hadn't liked myself for feeling that way, but I couldn't deny it. "Above the covers," I said when he came over.

He nodded. "As you wish."

Malcolm looked at me with a question in his eyes. When I didn't elaborate, he said, "I'm taking Cash with me."

I couldn't relax with Mavros next to me. Even above the covers, I felt the warmth of his body, and I knew I could end up in the same position as last night all too easily. "Can you sit over there?" I pointed at the window seat. "My powers are back. I can heal myself if I get hurt."

He grinned. A soft, knowing smile. "Sure." He sauntered across the room. "Someday you won't mind."

Thin, wispy clouds float through the vivid blue sky. The air is almost too warm. If not for the gentle breeze blowing, I would probably be sweating. I sit on a bench, watching swans swim across a lake surrounded by deciduous trees.

I'm nowhere near home. It's still winter there. Someone walks up behind me. I hear their feet crunch on the path, but I don't feel them. I reach deep inside of me.

My heart races, and my stomach drops. There's nothing. No sign of my magic. No indication it was ever there.

I turn and see the ponytailed Nephilim strolling toward me. "Good afternoon, Dacia."

"Sebastian." I try to keep the disdain from my voice, but by the look on his face, I don't succeed.

He stands next to the bench and points at it. "May I?"

"I don't have any say in what you do or don't do." I turn away from him, unwilling to let him see me cry again. "If I did, I wouldn't be here."

He sits next to me and stretches his arms along the back of the bench. The action is so similar to what Cody, Malcolm, or Mavros would have done that I wonder if every guy, regardless of species, does it without even thinking about it. "You no longer wish to kill your boyfriend. Do you?" He doesn't wait for me to answer. He knows my magic is gone. He knows it was never me that wanted to kill Cody anyway. "Doesn't that make this little paradise worth it?"

"No." I don't even bother trying to keep the annoyance off my face. "Try being a prisoner sometime. It doesn't matter if the cell is a tiny, enclosed space or somewhere like this. You took away my freedom. You took away my magic. Don't expect me to be happy about it."

He leans close to me, and his expression turns to one of pure disgust. "None of us care if you're happy. All that matters to us is that you're here, and your demon is not. You are a menace. You don't deserve freedom or magic." He stands and walks a couple of steps before turning around. "As a matter of fact, you don't even deserve happiness." He tucks his hands in his pockets and saunters away, whistling as he goes.

I glare at him until I can't see him anymore. I have to get out of here. I had thought the dragons might have been able to figure out a way to help me escape, but it's been three weeks, and I haven't seen or heard from any of them.

Closing my eyes, I try to picture Cody's face. The exact shade of his irises eludes me. I can't remember the sound of his voice. I know he smells like a cold winter morning, but I wonder if I'll ever catch a whiff of that here. Something tells me it's always warm in this prison. Cody's absence is a physical pain that I'm learning to cope with, but it's always there like a dull, aching headache.

I don't realize I'm crying until the tears drip off my chin and onto my hands.

Something brushed against my face. My eyes shot open in response. The smell of warm summer nights filled my room.

Mavros lay next to me propped up on one arm. My tears dripped off of his fingers. "Why so sad?"

I rolled over onto my other side. Being so close to him felt way too intimate right now. The heartache and lonesomeness inside me made me feel too desperate to be face to face with him. "The Nephilim took me to their sanctuary."

"Because of me?" His voice was soft and right above my ear.

I nodded. "Yeah."

He wrapped his arm around me, but I nudged him away. There was only one person I wanted to touch me right now. I moved to the edge of the bed and sat up. Cody's face flashed through my mind, and without thinking about it, my body stretched and pulled, and I was sitting on Cody's bed.

The light from his alarm clock cast a red glow over his face.

The sight of him made my heart swell. Seeing him un-harmed, sleeping peacefully … I should have gone back home, but I watched him, imprinting this moment in my brain. If the Nephilim took me, I couldn't let them take my memories of him, too. I needed to savor every minute I had with him. I needed to remember everything about him. I traced my fingers along his hairline, hoping never to forget the feel of his skin.

His eyes fluttered open. "Dacia?"

"Yeah. Sorry." My voice was rough.

He propped himself up on his elbows, and the blankets slid off of his body, revealing his bare chest. The muscles in his arms were flexed. His hair was tousled. He was perfect. How could I have ever thought Mavros was?

"Can I?" I pointed at his bed. When he nodded, I slid under the covers next to him, pushing him back down. I laid my head on his chest and traced my fingers over his abs.

He wrapped his arms around me. "What's wrong?"

"I think the Nephilim are going to take me." Fresh tears started to fall. "I needed to see you again before that happens."

He clutched me and rolled us over so that he was above me. "Don't cry."

The chain I'd given him for Christmas hung down, and I was glad to see that he wore it to bed. Knowing he would have some protection from magic even when I wasn't around made me feel a little better. He might be safer without me, but to draw me out, he might become even more of a target.

He held himself up on one elbow and brushed my tears away. Then he leaned down and swept his lips over mine. The touch was so gentle I wondered if I had imagined it.

I skimmed my hands along his stomach and up his chest. Then I wrapped one around his waist and clutched the back of his head with the other, pulling him down, needing him more than I could remember. I didn't know what I'd do without him if the Nephilim took me.

When he pressed his lips against mine, the emptiness inside of me disappeared. The soft tips of his fingers glided from my cheek, down my neck, and along my side. He lifted the hem of my shirt and slid his hand under me, pulling my body against his.

I dug my fingers into his back, eliminating any space that had remained. His hair brushed across my forehead. His heart beat in time with mine. There was nothing but the two of us in this moment.

Cody's mouth slid off mine. He scraped his teeth against my chin and kissed a path along my jaw to my ear. Heat blossomed inside of me.

I gasped and brought his mouth back over to mine. The heat surged. I pressed my hands against his chest, trying to push him away from me.

Flames leaped to my fingertips.

His eyes widened, and blue sparks danced between the links of his chain.

He threw himself back, landing in a crouching position at the end of the bed. He pressed his hand to his chest and watched me.

Panic rose inside of me, but I kept my voice soft to keep from waking anyone. "Are you okay?"

"Think so."

I turned away from him, hoping to keep my magic from lashing out at him again. "I better go. I love you, and I'm sorry."

As my body stretched and pulled, I heard Cody say, "Love you."

When I appeared in my room, Malcolm held Mavros by the collar of his shirt. Mavros' feet dangled at least three inches off the floor, and Malcolm was caught somewhere between dragon and human. "Where. Is. She?"

"She had a nightmare and disappeared." Mavros hung from Malcolm's grip without fighting even though he didn't have to. He nodded toward me. "She's behind you now."

Malcolm swung around, not letting go of Mavros. His pupils contracted, and his nostrils flared. "You've been with Cody." He dropped Mavros, and Mavros stumbled. Malcolm strode toward me. "You smell like desire and despair."

I plopped down on my bed and clutched my head. "Sounds about right."

"Is Cody … okay?" He set his hand on my shoulder. "You didn't hurt him. Did you?"

I pictured him crouched at the end of his bed with his hand pressed to his chest. His eyes were wide, but he seemed like he was okay. "I could have. I could have killed him." I looked at Malcolm, hoping he would understand. "I didn't mean to go there."

"What happened?" He sat next to me and held my hand.

"The chain." I pressed my eyes closed. Blue flames danced across the links, lighting up Cody's face. Showing me his surprise and fear. It had saved him twice. I couldn't expect it to happen again. "Why wasn't Russ there?" I'd forgotten he was supposed to be guarding Cody. "Why didn't he protect Cody from me?"

Malcolm stared at our hands. "He was hunting with us."

"Could …" The word caught in my throat. I cleared it and started over. "Could you check on him? Make sure he's okay."

Mavros waited until Malcolm was gone before saying, "I'm sorry for driving you away." His shirt was still twisted as if in Malcolm's grip. I'd never seen Mavros allow himself to look so disheveled for so long.

"It wasn't your fault." I didn't want him to know how desperate I'd felt, how scared I'd been that I would turn to him for comfort. It was too much having him with me every day. The dragons didn't want me to love them. They had no interest in humans, but Mavros did. "I didn't mean to go to him. I didn't mean to use my magic. It just happened."

He sat on my bed, leaving a wide gap between the two of us. "The dragons killed the imps that they found, but more are converging. You're going to have to show the world that you're still strong."

"How can I?" I tugged my hand through my hair and stared out the window. "I never know when Argentum's power is going to take control."

Chapter 40

A "Friendly" Visit

$\mathcal{I}$ woke up Friday morning utterly alone. "Guys," I whispered, thinking maybe they were in my room but invisible. When they didn't answer, I stretched my arms across the bed and stared up at the ceiling, savoring my solitude.

That only lasted about thirty seconds before I wondered what could have gone wrong. They wouldn't have left without a reason. Had more creatures come to draw me outside? Had something happened to Cody? Had I hurt him?

I jerked to a sitting position and untangled the covers from around me. *Malcolm. Cash. Where are you?*

They both responded at once. Their words blended together becoming incoherent.

Panic rose inside me, and my powers flared in response. Searching for some sign of danger.

Cash burst through my door. "What's wrong?" Smoke drifted from his nostrils.

"None of you were here." I felt like a little kid. I shouldn't need anybody to be with me when I slept, to be there when I woke up. "I thought something bad had happened."

Malcolm's voice came from behind me. "We wanted to give you some peace."

I sank back down on my bed. The adrenaline rush left me shaky. "So, everyone's okay?" I dragged my hands down my face.

Cash knelt in front of me. "Everyone's fine, Dacia." He nodded at Malcolm. "You weren't having nightmares. You were sleeping peacefully. We thought you might like to wake up alone after whatever happened yesterday."

"I shouldn't have been so upset yesterday." I dropped my chin to my chest. "Mavros was just trying to help me. He might have even saved my life." I looked around the room. "Where is he, anyway?"

Malcolm rolled his eyes. "Helping your parents in the kitchen. I never thought I'd see a demon doing dishes."

I waited until my magic settled down to leave my room. Then I went straight to the bathroom. I brushed my hair, making it a frizzy mess that I pulled into two braids in a meager attempt to tame it.

As soon as I walked into the kitchen, Mom said, "Oh, good you're up. We forgot to get the bread for garlic bread. I need you to go into town and get it."

"Sure." I held a glass in my hand. "Can I drink my milk first?"

"Of course," Dad said. "We don't need it until later this afternoon."

Mom added artichokes to the crockpot, stirred the dip, turned it to low, then spun around. "Are you sure you're okay with us going out? I know we've always spent New Year's Eve together."

"It's fine, Mom." I nodded toward my guardians. "Cody asked me to come over, and it's not like I'd be alone anyway."

She smiled. "Julie wants us there by 6:00 or 6:30, so we'll be eating early."

We'd been over all of this before. Initially, they'd tried to get me to join them. Julie had even invited "those handsome young men" to come along. The gesture was nice, but I didn't want my relatives to see me with my guards any more than they already had. Cody deserved better.

"I'll go to town after I go for a run." I put the milk jug back in the fridge without pouring any. Milk before running was a bad idea, one that only needed to be made once. I filled up a water bottle instead. "So, who's coming with me?"

Mavros shook his head and took a step back. "That's a job for the dragons. I'll stay here."

It made sense. There was no reason for him to try to stay in shape when he could take any shape he wanted. "We'll be back."

With each fall of my foot, I pushed my magic out. I wanted to drain it as completely as I could before seeing Cody. I couldn't risk his chain not working. I couldn't risk killing him.

Malcolm and Cash ran on either side of me. "Humans don't run this fast for this long, Dacia." Malcolm tried to slow my pace, but I didn't let him.

"Nobody's—" I sucked in a breath between words "—watching."

Cash reached for my elbow, but I pulled away. "Why are you pushing so hard?"

"I … have … to."

They quit pestering me and just ran by my side me. Neither of them tried to slow me again. When I turned to start back home, they followed, but when I ran onto the porch, Malcolm stopped me before I opened the door. His pupils contracted into thin slits.

"What?"I asked.

"Nephilim."

"I've gotta go in." I reached for the handle and nodded. "My parents are in there."

Malcolm squeezed my shoulder. "How's your magic?"

"Gone."

"We'll stay close," Cash said.

As soon as I opened the door, Mom said, "Dacia, some of your friends are here." She emphasized the word friends, letting me know that they weren't human.

"Oh." I pretended to be surprised. "Who?"

"Sebastian and Troy." She pointed toward the dining room.

"Thanks, Mom." I grabbed her hand. "Why don't you and Dad go ahead and go to town. I'll meet up with you later." *Please.* I sent the last word directly to her.

Her eyes widened in surprise. "Come on John." Her voice was commanding. "We're going to be late."

He walked into the living room. His eyebrows were furrowed, and his lips were pinched into a thin line. "What?"

"I'll meet you later." I took my shoes off and set them to the side. Then I nodded toward the dining room. "I've got a couple friends here. I'll get there as soon as I can." I hugged Mom, then Dad. "Don't forget to get the bread on your way home."

"Be careful," Mom said.

"Let us know if you're not going to make it." Dad pulled his hat on and checked for his keys. Then he started to go to the garage door.

Mom grabbed his arm. "Let's go out this way."

I nodded and watched them walk out. The whole time I wondered if this would be the last time I would see them outside of the Nephilim's sanctuary.

As soon as their car was driving down the road, I walked into the dining room. Malcolm and Cash followed behind me, close enough to grab me and teleport away if necessary.

Sebastian, Troy, and Mavros stood around the table. The length of it separated the Nephilim from the demon, but from the disgust on their faces, there wasn't enough space between them. I doubted an entire galaxy separating them would be enough to keep the Nephilim happy.

Sebastian was one of the Nephilim that had trapped me on a side street in Althea. He had long, honey-colored hair pulled back in a ponytail. I had seen Troy a few times. He had a dark, tribal-style tattoo that ran from his scalp, along his neck, and under his too-tight shirt.

I closed my eyes and pinched the bridge of my nose. "What do you want?"

"It's time." Sebastian nodded at Mavros. "We witnessed this demon in your yard two days ago. Then we came here to check on you and found him in your kitchen."

"You came here to check on me?" I couldn't keep from rolling my eyes. "You knew I was running with them." I pointed at Cash and Malcolm.

Neither of them denied it.

"If you saw him here two days ago, then you saw us fighting for our lives against a bunch of demons." My fists were tightly clenched at my sides. I wanted to slap the smug looks off of their faces. "Demons you could've banished."

Sebastian flattened his palms against the table and leaned forward. "That does not change the fact that you have a demon in your house, and we can no longer allow it."

I tilted my head toward my shoulder and looked from them to Mavros. "Why? Has he done something wrong?"

"Everything about him is wrong?" Troy pounded his finger on the table to emphasize each word. "Why don't you know that?"

Laughing, I shook my head. "Why would I? If I had to judge, I'd say everything about you is wrong." They both jerked back as if cold water had been thrown at them. "An imp tried to attack me. Where were you? Watching? Mavros killed it. When I went into shock two nights ago, Mavros helped me. Where were you? Hoping I'd die?"

Troy and Sebastian looked at each other and then turned back to me. Neither of them responded.

"Last night the dragons hunted more imps who were calling me outside to kill me." I stared into each of their faces. "What did you two do to stop them?"

Cash chuckled. The sound was low and threatening. "Don't you get tired of shoving your righteousness down her throat?"

"She never should have summoned him back here." Sebastian pointed a shaking finger at Mavros. His face was red. The veins in his neck bulged.

Malcolm grabbed hold of my shoulder. "She didn't summon him. He showed up on her doorstep. How do we know one of you didn't summon him?"

Troy slammed his hand down on the table, and it cracked. "We do not align ourselves with darkness."

"But you will come into a teenage girl's house and damage her parent's property." Mavros shook his head and stared pointedly at Troy's hand. "I've been here a week and haven't done a fraction of the damage you have."

Sebastian edged his way around the table toward me. "Just come with us. Make this easy for everyone."

"How does being imprisoned make things easier for me?" These guys would never see reason. They would never get past their own sense of self-worth. "The fairies know he's here. They don't seem to care. Why do you? Why are you so hung up on this?" I stared at Sebastian, challenging him. "You know what? I don't need your answers. Get out of my house."

Troy pressed both hands down on the table and leaned forward. "Are you sure that's what you want? Do you know where your parents are?"

"You leave them out of this." My magic seemed to pull back, drawing in on itself, ready to surge up and crash over everyone.

He smiled, and it was truly wicked. This man might be born of angels, but he drew pleasure from cruelty. "Come with us, and we will."

"And, you think I'm the monster." Mavros shook his head, but I remembered a time when he'd used those tactics against me, too.

Don't agree to anything yet. Malcolm's voice pounded against my skull. *They might be bluffing.*

The Nephilim stared at me, waiting for me to make my move, but no matter how I looked at it, every move led to checkmate.

Arianna's soft, lyrical voice serenaded its way into my thoughts, but her words were those of a death march, a dirge that kept trudging through my mind. *I'm sorry, Dacia. We should've guarded them. We didn't expect the Nephilim to go after them.*

My magic seemed to drain away. I clutched the back of the chair in front of me, suddenly feeling weakened. "Leave them alone, and I'll go with you."

"No, Dacia." Cash's voice was so soft I almost didn't hear it.

I turned to him. Tears flowed freely, and I didn't bother wiping them away. "Tell Cody I love him, and let him know I won't be there tonight."

"I'm sorry," Mavros said. "I only meant to help you."

Sebastian walked up to me. He reached forward, and Malcolm growled.

"It's okay." I lifted my lips in a failing attempt at a smile. "It's the only way."

Sebastian snapped something around my neck. As soon as it clicked, my magic disappeared, a gaping chasm where power used to flow like a raging river. He waved his arm, indicating that I should lead the way. "We'll portal from outside after Troy fixes your table."

Cash pulled me into a hug. His dragon was close to the surface, but he held it at bay. "This isn't the end."

"Keep my parents safe." I patted his back and stepped away.

He bowed his head. "We will."

"And C-Cody." His name caught in my throat.

"Of course." He moved, and Malcolm took his place.

"We'll do whatever it takes to free you." He kissed the top of my head. "We owe you nothing less."

Not trusting my voice, I nodded.

"Enough." Sebastian grabbed my arm and guided me to the back door.

I stopped before opening it. "Are my parents free?"

Malcolm stood still and silent for a moment, then nodded.

"Keep 'em that way." I slid the door open and walked outside. Low, gray clouds hung in the sky. The backyard was buried in drifts. Snow clung to the branches of the trees.

Sebastian waved his hands and mumbled. A bright light flared in front of us, widening until it was big enough to step through. He pressed his hand against the small of my back, forcing me toward the light.

In my dreams, the portal had been instantaneous. Step in and you were somewhere else. There was no delay.

Sebastian pushed me into it.

A scream tore through my skull. A pained, otherworldly cry.

The light pulsed, and I was trapped inside it, unable to move forward or backward.

"What's going on?" Troy yelled at Sebastian.

Sebastian yanked me back. The portal and the screaming disappeared. I stumbled, falling to the ground.

Snow numbed my legs, but I couldn't find it in me to move. My head pounded, and I felt like a steamroller had flattened me.

Troy knelt down, grabbed my sweatshirt, and pulled me up. "What are you doing?"

"Sitting in the snow." I looked around. "In my backyard. Why are we still here? And, what was that screaming noise?"

Troy's lip curled in disgust or hatred or both while Sebastian fiddled with the collar he'd put on me earlier. "It's working." Sebastian glanced toward my house. "The demon or dragons must be interfering with the portal."

Troy glared at me. His brown eyes bored into mine. "Let's just kill her. Put an end to it."

"Good luck with that." I laughed, and it sounded a little deranged even to me. "It doesn't work."

Troy pulled me closer and shook me. "With your magic contained, it will."

"I wouldn't count on it," Mavros said from behind Troy. "Death sent her back before. Her magic didn't have anything to do with it."

Troy's muscles tensed. "Death was just a figment of her overly active imagination. He doesn't exist."

"How about I send you to him?" Mavros' face contorted, becoming monstrous. "You can tell him in person."

Troy didn't respond, but he clutched me tighter, holding me in front of him like I was a ragdoll. Sebastian opened the portal again. This time, Troy carried me into it. The same scream ripped through me.

Troy and I were both trapped. He twisted his hands in my sweatshirt and held me so our noses nearly touched. "I have no problem killing someone who's aligned themselves with darkness. Let us through, or you won't live to see the new year."

"I have no magic, not even a dying ember." Exhaustion crept into my voice, and I didn't even try to hide it. "Maybe it's God's way of telling you you're being stupid."

Troy shook me hard, flinging my head back and forth.

Sebastian pulled us out of the light. He didn't look at either of us. He stared over my shoulder where the portal had been a moment ago. His face was slack.

I glanced behind me. Even with the cloud cover, Khione's coat sparkled like millions of diamonds. It was almost impossible to look at the unicorn, but at the same time, I couldn't look away.

"What are you doing?" Last time I had seen her, her voice reminded me of a symphony. It was still rich and full, but the music had turned dark and foreboding. "Dacia is under my protection. The fairies have vouched for her. A gold dragon and pegasus have spoken to you of her worth. Unleash her magic and let her be."

Troy's grip on me loosened, but he didn't put me down. "She consorts with a demon. She summoned him."

Khione tossed her head, making her mane flair out. "She did not summon him." She touched her horn to the collar around my neck. A rush of energy zipped through me, and the collar fell to the ground, shattering. She lowered her head and touched a shard with her horn. It glowed like a dying star for a moment before fading back to a burnished gold color. "The demon means you no harm," she said to Troy.

"He's a demon." Troy set me down none too gently. "How can he not mean harm?"

Khione turned and walked away.

"Wait." My voice was a plea. "Do you know how I can banish Argentum's magic?"

"You must separate it from your own." She gazed into my eyes. "The demon's power awakens." She turned toward Mavros. "Do not let it. It will destroy her."

Chapter 41

New Year's Eve

Unsure if they could be used against me, I cleaned the shards of the shattered collar off the snow and slid them into my hoodie's pouch. When I stood to go inside, I nearly fell over. My legs shook. The Nephilim watched me with narrowed eyes. They wouldn't do anything with Khione nearby, but I didn't trust them at all.

Mavros swept me up into his arms and carried me up the deck stairs toward the house. "What's going on?" Concern softened his features.

"Whatever happened in the portal drained me."

Malcolm stood at the door. As soon as Mavros neared it, he slid it open, then followed us inside. He locked it and pulled the blinds closed. "Why couldn't she go through the portal?"

Mavros kicked his shoes off and carried me into the living room. "If I had to venture to guess, I'd say my magic kept her out."

"You were using magic to keep me out?" What would they have done to my parents if Khione hadn't shown up? Had he intentionally risked their lives?

He shook his head. "No, Dacia. I could have, but my magic is inside you." He set me on the couch and threw a blanket over me. "Demons cannot enter Nephilim sanctuaries."

"Oh." If the Nephilim figured out why I couldn't enter, they'd come back for me. No matter how many creatures of light vouched for me, they wouldn't stop until I was dead.

"The unicorn said my magic is waking up." He knelt in front of me and grabbed my hand. "I imagine the scream you heard was from it. I need you to let me in, let me put it back to sleep."

"Sure." I nodded. "When you're done, I need to change. I'm soaked."

I closed my eyes and focused on my magic. Mavros and I stood side by side. My serpent rose above Mavros', watching the obsidian snake writhe. Mavros walked up to it, staying on the far side from my powers. He put his hand on his magic and whispered something.

The snake calmed instantly. It opened its eye for a moment before coiling up and going back to sleep.

The pearlescent serpent slithered toward me. It had grown since the last time I'd seen it. I hoped it was because I'd been using my magic more often again and not because of something to do with Argentum. I prayed that my actions only affected my powers and didn't help increase his.

We were bound. My power focused on me.

I reached my hand out, and it nudged my palm with its head. "I know." I looked at Mavros. "They might try again."

We will kill them if they do.

I staggered back. That couldn't be how my magic truly felt. I didn't want to kill anybody ever again. I'd done it twice. I still saw Draconian's blood on my hands from time to time, and Argentum's death had led me here. I couldn't do it again. My magic couldn't seriously want me to kill them. Could it?

Mom rushed into the living room and pulled me into a hug. "You're okay. We were so worried. Who were those men?" She stepped back and raised a shaky finger at Mavros. "They said he's a demon."

"Sit down," I said to my parents.

They sat on the loveseat, still wearing their coats and snow boots. Mom's purse hung from her shoulder. Malcolm sat next to me, Mavros stood next to the couch, and Cash leaned on the back of it.

"Mavros is a demon." They gasped, and I said, "I told you you didn't want to know what he was." I pulled my hand through my hair, then slid my fingers through Mavros'. "He is bound to me. He'll do just about anything to protect me."

He smiled down at me. "It wasn't always that way, but it is now."

"What changed it?" Dad asked.

"She k—"

I interrupted Mavros. There were a lot of things I was willing to tell my parents about my life, but our tale wasn't one of them. "It's a long story. Sebastian and Troy are Nephilim, half angel and half human." I sucked in a deep breath. I didn't want my parents to know the next part either, but if the Nephilim did take me away, it would probably be best if my parents had some forewarning. "They want to take me to their sanctuary and bind my magic. If they get their way, I'll never be able to leave."

Dad stood and walked ten steps, then back again. I couldn't help but wonder if that's where my habit of pacing to help me think came from. "So let me get this straight. The demon"—he pointed at Mavros as he walked by him—"is a good guy, and the angels are bad guys."

"For today, anyway." I leaned forward, holding my head in my hands. "The Nephilim think they're doing what's best. They think I'd be safer and happier in their sanctuary, but I know I wouldn't."

Mom stared at Mavros. Her lips were pursed, and her eyebrows were pinched.

He didn't seem agitated by her scrutiny. "Your daughter's the reason I can be on Earth. Her life is invaluable to me."

She nodded. "We let you into our home. Don't you make us regret it."

"Yes, ma'am."

For the rest of the afternoon, my parents tried to convince me to go with them to Julie and Dana's house. I understood that they were afraid they were going to lose me, but I had other plans.

When they left, I turned to Mavros. "I need you to stay here."

"I know." He reached up and brushed my curls behind my shoulder.

"I can't let Cody's family invite you in without knowing what they're doing." I lowered my head. No matter what I did, someone always ended up hurt. "It has to be their decision."

He slid his finger under my chin and tilted my face up. "I understand. I will stay here and hunt imps."

"Be careful."

He smirked at me. "I'm not concerned about imps."

"Maybe not." I looked out the window, but it was too dark to see anything through it. "The Nephilim are probably still out there, and who knows what they'd do if they caught you unaware."

"Oh, I know what they'd do." He raised his eyebrows. "Or try to do. It wouldn't work, though." He shrugged and smirked at me. "I'm not the kind of demon they can banish."

Malcolm drove my truck to Cody's house. He kept glancing at me like he wanted to say something but didn't quite know how to do it.

Finally, I said, "What? Just spit it out."

"I worry that you're getting too close to Mavros." He stared out the window, not even glancing at me out of the corner of his eyes. "He's still a demon. He's still a master of manipulation."

Anger rose inside of me, but I couldn't tell if it was directed toward him or myself. "I didn't plan to trust him again, but he's helped me so many times." I looked out through the side window, hoping to catch a glimpse of the stars. "He's my friend."

"I know." He finally glanced at me. His bronze eyes were filled with concern. "Just be careful."

I nodded. I didn't want to think about whether or not Mavros was trustworthy. There were too many other things to worry about right now. My most immediate concern was brought to the forefront of my mind when Malcolm pulled into Cody's driveway. Would I be able to keep my magic from lashing out at him tonight?

As soon as Malcolm put my truck into park, he grabbed my hand and drew on my magic. Tipping his head to the side and furrowing his eyebrows, he said, "Your magic is still depleted."

"Why?"

"I don't know." He squeezed my fingers. "Don't worry. We'll be with you. It'll be okay."

"I hope so." I stepped outside and looked up. Millions of stars filled the sky. Seeing them helped settle me. I walked up to the door and waited for Malcolm and Cash to join me before knocking. Bo barked in response.

Footsteps hurried across the room. "Josh, put Bo away." It sounded like Brent saying this.

"It's his house!" Josh already sounded angry. Hopefully, Cash and Malcolm would be able to give me space tonight.

The door opened, and Cody looked out. "Hey." He smiled, and my heart melted a little. He lifted his finger and looked down the hall. A door slammed, and Cody let us in.

As soon as my coat was off, he stepped closer and reached for my face. "Can I?"

"Yeah." I closed the gap, and he kissed me.

"Dacia!" Britny ran into the room, so I reluctantly pulled away. "You brought your fairies." Her blue eyes widened with excitement.

Malcolm leaned down. "What's it going to take to convince you that we're not fairies?"

She stepped closer and whispered quite loudly, "Tell me what you are."

"Not fairies." Cash smiled at her and rubbed her head.

She grabbed Malcolm's hand and tugged, leading him into the dining room. "Not people either."

Malcolm tipped his head back and laughed, a deep belly laugh that made his fangs show.

Britny stared up at him. Her eyes widened. "Are you a werewolf?" Her voice got higher. "Or a vampire?"

"No." He knelt down in front of her. "I'm not that either."

"But—" she looked around, then leaned even closer to him "—you have fangs."

He nodded. "Lots of people do."

"But you're not people." She said it so matter-of-factly, not even a hint of doubt in her voice.

He took her hand again and stood up. "We're not fairies either."

As I followed them into the dining room, I contemplated telling Cody's family about my magic and the nature of my guardians. If I did, Josh would understand why they were around me. He would realize that Malcolm and Cash weren't after my heart. He'd know that Cody was the only one for me.

But, they'd also know about my power. They'd know Cody's life was in danger just because he was with me. They'd know I was a freak. No matter how I looked at it, it would be worse for them to know the truth. Maybe someday it would be right for them to know, but we weren't to that point yet. At the rate Britny was going, she might have it figured out before I was ready to tell them anyway.

I sat with Cody on one side of me and Malcolm on the other. Josh glared at Malcolm and Cash but never said anything. He'd made his position clear last time we were here. He didn't need to say anything else.

We played games until nearly midnight. Malcolm never needed to drain my magic. It never flared, never showed any sign of life. I hoped it was finally coming to realize that Cody wasn't the enemy, but I had a feeling it was because I'd drained it before the Nephilim had shown up, and then their portal had taken everything that was left in me.

As the night wore on, Britny leaned more heavily against Cash. Eventually, he wrapped his arm around her, allowing her to get more comfortable, and she fell asleep. Both Brent and

Susan offered to take her away, but Cash insisted that she was fine where she was. Josh seemed to soften toward him a little after that.

We quit playing games in time for Brent and Susan to get drinks ready for a midnight toast, pop or sparkling apple juice for the minors and champagne for them.

Cash gently woke Britny up. "It's almost the new year."

"I wasn't sleeping." She yawned and stretched. "I was just resting my eyes."

He smiled at her, playing along. "You don't want to miss the toast, though."

"I dreamed you were dragons." She looked from Cash to Malcolm. "Are you?"

"Dragons." Malcolm cupped his hand over his mouth and nodded. "That'd be cool … way better than fairies."

Cash handed her a glass of sparkling cider. "I have to agree. That would be way better, but how would a dragon fit in a human body?"

"Fine." Britny sat on Cash's leg and held her glass in front of her. "I'll call you dragons until you tell me."

Susan shook her head. "Why, Britny?" She looked from Cash to Malcolm. "Why don't you think they're people?"

"Because they're not." She looked at her mom like she couldn't understand how she didn't realize it.

The clock chimed midnight. Cody clinked his glass against mine. He carefully lifted his other hand, and when I didn't pull back, he cupped my cheek. "Happy new year." He leaned in and pressed his lips to mine.

I slipped my hand into his back pocket and pulled him closer. He ended the kiss before I was ready, but I understood. "Happy new year," I said to him. After hugging everyone in the room, I turned to my guardians. "I should get home. Thank you for having me," I said to Cody's parents. "I had fun."

"I'll walk you out." Cody held my hand and led me to the front door.

Cash and Malcolm went outside under the pretense of scraping my windows and warming up my truck while I bundled up. About the time I was ready to go, Cash's voice rumbled through my head. *It's clear.*

I opened the door, and Cody and I stepped out into the frigid night. "Did you fix it?"

"No." I knew he meant my magic. "I depleted it this morning. Then …" I told him about the Nephilim and the unicorn. I told him about them binding my power and trying to take me to their sanctuary. I left out the parts I didn't want to be overheard. Even though the dragons said it was clear, I'd learned that someone was always watching me.

His mask slid into place so firmly that I couldn't even get an indication of what he was feeling by looking into his eyes. When I finished, he said, "Thought you could sneak back tonight. Guess not."

"I'm hoping I can figure this out soon." It was what I wanted, but I had absolutely no idea how to make it happen. "I don't want to hurt you."

"Least the necklace works."

Chapter 42

The yard is filled with Nephilim. They completely surround my house. Sebastian and Troy stand at the front of them. Sebastian holds a gold collar in his hands. "Only demons can't enter the sanctuary."

I feel their animosity like a living, breathing beast. Their hatred for me has grown immeasurably since the last time they all confronted me.

"You didn't summon him." Troy steps closer. "You didn't need to. You freed him."

Sebastian holds the collar up. "Your magic must be bound." He strides toward me. "Call off your guards. Let me do this without a fight. It's happening one way or another."

I step off the porch and onto the driveway. My magic flares, and without my consent, wings rip through my shoulder blades as my body morphs into my dragon form.

The Nephilim stagger back, their faces trapped somewhere between horror and awe.

Troy tosses his head back and laughs. "Our job's done. The dragons will kill her for this. The demon will be returned to the Abyss."

When Malcolm and Cash transform and stand next to me, the Nephilim fall into such a deep silence that you can almost feel it.

"I will not wear your collar." My voice booms out of me, full of command. "I will not be imprisoned, and I will not hurt any of you unless you initiate it." My tail swishes behind me. "I don't want a war. I don't want any more death or destruction on my hands. I just want to be left alone."

Troy yanks the collar out of Sebastian's hands. "You will wear this." He rushes toward me, disappearing as he moves, but I can smell his aggression, his anger, and his hate sprinting toward me.

I open my jaws and flames erupt into the sky. "Enough!" I swipe my arm forward and snatch Troy.

He stares at me, contempt and surprise warring for dominance on his face. "How?"

"I am a dragon. I can smell you." I breathe in deeply, emphasizing the point. "I can hear the blood rushing through your veins."

He lowers his head. "So, kill me. Just make it quick."

"Didn't you listen to anything I just said?" Smoke rolls out of my nostrils, blowing across his face. "I don't want to kill anybody. I don't even want to hurt anybody." His scent changes to something that I can't quite place.

He shakes his head at me and snaps the collar around one of my fingers. "You're a fool," he says as he falls from my grip.

My body morphs back into my human form. The transformation is horrific without my magic controlling it. Bones break and muscles tear as they shift. I scream.

When my body is my own, I fall to the ground, naked and shaking. Mavros runs to me, kneeling in front of me, and slips his coat over me, pulling my hands through the sleeves. Then he cradles me in his arms and carries me to the porch.

Pain lashes through my body, and it's all I can focus on. I pull Mavros' jacket tighter, trying to fight the cold, and realize there's a ring on my thumb. The collar shrank along with me. I pull on it, trying to yank it off, but it won't budge.

"She can remain free as long as the collar binds her magic." Sebastian's voice cuts through the haze of my pain. "If it's removed, she will be killed. There will be no negotiations."

Malcolm opens the door for Mavros and me. His chin touches his chest, and he won't look me in the eyes.

The pain is horrendous, but I stretch my hand out, grazing my fingers over his cheek. "It'll be okay."

"I failed you."

I woke up with Cash and Malcolm next to me. Their magic flowed into me, melding with my own, healing my bones, sewing together the ripped flesh. "They'll never give up. Will they?" My voice was hoarse from screaming.

"I never should have come here." Mavros stood at the end of my bed, watching us.

I tried to get a better look at him, but the slight movement sent pain thundering through my body. I clenched my teeth. "They need to get over it." It hurt too bad to talk, so I thought to Malcolm, *Did you see my dream?*

He nodded.

Is that what would happen if I lost my magic while I was a dragon?

"I don't know." He shook his head. "There's never been another like you."

Their power kept flowing into me until all my pain went away. I scooted back, propping myself up on my pillows. "I'm glad you came," I said to Mavros.

He stared at me, looking like he wanted to say something but wasn't quite sure how to say it. He swallowed hard and nodded. "Thank you."

I squeezed Cash's hand. "Did you make Britny dream that you guys are dragons?"

"No. She's a smart girl." He smiled like a proud father seeing his baby take her first steps. "She came up with that all on her own."

"I talked to Aurelia this morning." Malcolm pointed to his head. "The dragon council say they don't know how to separate Argentum's power from yours."

I sank back against my pillows. I hadn't been ready to get up anyway, and Malcolm's news just reassured me that I'd be better off staying in bed. I looked out my window, wondering what monsters and mayhem awaited me.

The sky held the softest glow, awaiting the arrival of the sun. I dragged my hand through my tangled mass of curls. "Just once I would like things to be easy."

Throwing the covers back, I sat up and slid my feet into my slippers. Yesterday's clothes littered the floor. I gathered them up, checking their pockets for anything before throwing them into the hamper. When I picked up my hoodie, something tinkled together. I pinched my eyebrows in confusion before remembering I'd tucked the broken pieces of the collar in it to throw away.

I reached in and jerked my hand back when a shard sliced into my finger. Before I even had my hand out in the open, Malcolm's pupils contracted. He walked over to the window and yanked it up. I watched him, hoping the smell wouldn't make his instincts overpower him.

"Last night was harsh"—his voice was gruff, but he seemed to be in control—"but, I hunted yesterday."

Grabbing a tissue off my nightstand, I slid my hand out and wrapped my finger. "You eat imps?" My lips curled in disgust.

"I told you." He didn't look at me, just kept staring outside. "I'm a dragon. Waste not, want not."

I tore a sheet of paper out of my notebook and dumped the collar fragments onto it. One shard was coated in crimson. I picked it up carefully, watching the blood. "Look at this," I said to Malcolm and Mavros.

Mavros was beside me in an instant, but Malcolm was more cautious. He stood at the end of my bed, keeping distance between us.

My blood bubbled on the sharp point of the shard until it separated like oil and water. Silver drops flowed away from red. I unraveled the tissue and squeezed my cut. My blood poured out onto the fragments. Everywhere it touched the broken pieces, it frothed until the silver divided into little blobs that puddled away from the crimson pools.

Malcolm covered his nose and mouth with his hands. His eyes tracked the movement of my blood.

"Khione said I need to separate Argentum's magic from mine." I rewrapped my finger and then grabbed another tissue to wipe the blood off the shards. "Do you think this might be the answer?"

Mavros clasped my shoulder. "It may be. We just need to figure out how to use it."

"Burn it, Dacia." Malcolm nodded at the blood-soaked tissue. His fangs jutted out of his mouth. His eyes were reptilian.

I lit a fire in my palm and watched as Argentum's blood recoiled. It reared up, pulling back, like a sentient being. The flames turned to ice, spreading up my arm. The silver liquid spread thin, inching over my fingers as if searching for a way back into my bloodstream.

Mavros grabbed my hand. Pain flared across his face, but he held on. A small inferno burned in his other palm.

As he brought it closer to me, my magic lashed out. Icicles shot from my fingertips, stabbing him in the chest. For a moment, his flames flickered, nearly dying out, but then they blazed brighter.

Malcolm walked up behind me and grabbed my arm, pulling it down to the side.

The ice spread, covering my body in an instant.

Mavros was undeterred. Black veins showed through his skin. His flesh turned a grayish color and peeled back, cracking and breaking. Pieces broke off, falling like ash to the ground, but he held onto me. His flames ignited Argentum's blood. It writhed as the fire devoured it.

As soon as it was nothing but ash, Mavros jerked his hand away from me, and his body seemed to vaporize, dissipating until a black mist hung in the air where Mavros had been.

"What did I do?" The ice dispersed, and I slumped back against Malcolm. "Did I kill him?" I turned in his arms, laying my head against his chest.

Malcolm held me tenderly, running his hand from the top of my head to my back, over and over. "You can't kill him, not here." His voice was soft, even though his dragon was still near the surface. "You hurt him pretty badly, though."

A sob tore loose from me, and Malcolm held me tighter. "He'll be okay. He just needs time to heal."

Mavros stayed away the entire day. I kept looking for him, feeling his absence like a punch in the gut. It was my fault. He'd been helping me, and I'd hurt him. At least he'd live. How many other people would I injure? How many wouldn't be able to survive something like what I'd put Mavros through? I had to get Argentum's essence out of me before it made me do worse.

I wandered out to the living room and helped my parents take down the Christmas decorations. It was something we did on New Year's Day every year, but this time, it filled me with a deep melancholy. The lights brought a soothing ambiance that I would miss.

As we took the ornaments off the tree, Dad said, "It's hard to believe the holiday season's over already. No extra days off of work until Memorial Day." He shook his head, lamenting the lack of holidays at the beginning of the year. "I should've been a banker or government employee."

"Or a teacher," Mom said. "All the extra holidays and summers off. What were we thinking when we decided on these careers?"

I could tell that they were trying to get me to lighten up and to talk, but all I could think about was Mavros' skin splitting, the pieces falling to the ground, and the pain in his eyes.

While Dad was packing the tree away, Mom pulled me into a one-armed hug. "Are you still worried about the angel things?"

"The Nephilim?" I shook my head. "Not at the moment. Khione warned them to stay away, so unless I do something stupid, I think they will for now."

She rubbed her right shoulder, the spot where tension builds up if it goes unchecked. "Who's Khione?"

I couldn't help but smile when I said, "A unicorn."

Mom's jaw dropped slightly. "A unicorn?" The awe that filled her voice made me wish she had seen Khione.

"Yeah, I think the Nephilim have to go along with what she says if they want people to believe they're creatures of light."

Dad pressed the lid down on the tub that held the tree. "Can you help carry some of these downstairs?" he asked Cash and Malcolm.

"Just point us in the right direction," Cash said.

While Dad explained where they needed to go, Mom said, "It's good to know there are other creatures who support you."

"There are quite a few." I shrugged. "Some fairies, the dragons, a pegasus, a unicorn, and Mavros."

As soon as I said his name, she looked around as if she expected to find him hiding in the shadows. "Where is he anyway?"

"He—" the words caught in my throat, stuck behind a lump that had formed there. I shook my head, and Malcolm came over, resting his hand on my shoulder, ready to step in if needed. I turned into him. I didn't want to be facing my parents if my magic decided to take on a life of its own again.

"He'll be back." Malcolm wrapped his arm around me. "We may have found a way to destroy the darkness in Dacia's magic. The corruption lashed out at Mavros, maiming him."

Mom sucked in a deep breath, and I felt her hand on my hair, attempting to comfort me.

"Demons can't be killed here," Malcolm continued. "He just needs time to recuperate."

I pressed my forehead against his chest, letting my tears fall freely. "I can't get it out of my head."

"If you'll excuse us," Malcolm said, "I need to get Dacia to relax."

"Of course." Mom stepped back.

"I can get these downstairs on my own," Dad said.

"No worries." Cash's voice was gruff, and I knew my emotions were becoming too much for him.

Malcolm lifted me as easily as if I was a tiny kitten and carried me into my room. He laid me down on the bed and knelt on the floor next to me, holding my hand. He drew my power into him, and at the same time, his magic flowed into me, soothing me.

I yawned, and my eyes drifted closed.

Chapter 43

$\mathcal{M}$avros stands in front of me. The pink light from the sunset washes my room in a warm glow. He reaches for my hand. His arm is a mass of welts, bruises, and scars. His skin is still grayish.

"I'm so sorry." My heart sinks at the same time that I drop my head to my chest. He's my friend, and I mangled him.

He tilts my chin up. There's no malice in his eyes. "It's almost a memory." He pulls me to my feet. "I need you to promise me something."

"What? I owe you." I stare into his obsidian eyes and remember a time when I would've fallen under his spell. "Whatever you want."

He lifts his hand to my face and gently skims his fingers along my cheek. "I'm a demon, Dacia. Don't ever say or think something like that again."

Malcolm had warned me that I was growing too close to Mavros, trusting him too much, and he'd been right, but with what I'd done to him, how could I not promise him whatever he wanted? If he wanted my soul, he deserved it for everything he'd done for me.

"Dacia?"

I nod at him.

"Promise, say my name and promise not to use ice against me again."

I had done this before. I stood in front of him in a dream and promised not to use ice against him. If I hadn't, I wouldn't have had to kill myself to avoid being bound to him. A tempest blasts through me, chilling me to the bone. "Mavros."

He hears the warning in my voice, but he steps closer, pulling me against him, and for the first time since he's been back to Earth, I fall under his spell.

"Dacia"—his voice is soft and fills me with yearning—"promise you won't use ice against me again."

All my inhibitions disappear. I kiss his neck just above his collar. "I promise." My hand slides around him and up to the back of his head.

He steps back slightly. "Say my name and promise not to use ice against me."

"I promise you, Mavros Malkin, Chaódis Skotádi, Damon, that I will never use ice against you again." I look up at him through my eyelashes. "Now, kiss me."

He leans down, and my heart flutters in anticipation. He holds my head and tenderly presses his lips to my forehead before disappearing.

My eyes jerked open, and both Malcolm and Cash stared at me from across the room. "Feeling better?" Malcolm asked.

"No." I shook my head. "I just promised not to use ice on Mavros ever again." I rubbed my hands over my face, pulling my eyelids down. "He controlled me."

Mavros materialized next to my bed. "I did it for you, Dacia."

Cash growled, but Malcolm held him back.

I stood up, not wanting to face him from my bed, and looked at his right arm. It appeared exactly how it had in my dream. "Are you sure about that?" I wanted to believe him. I wanted it almost as much as I wanted Argentum's essence out of me.

"I can't help you destroy Argentum's magic if you are attacking me all the while with ice." He knelt in front of me, bowing his head. "I will release you from your vow as soon as he's gone from within you."

"You promise?" I couldn't help it. He was a demon, but I trusted him.

He nodded and stood. "Your dreams are as real to me as any other moment of my life. I could have made you promise to never use my full name again. I could have taken advantage of you." He smiled seductively. "You were more than willing."

Heat rushed up my neck and onto my face. "Thank you for not taking advantage."

"I wanted to." His voice was soft, meant only for me, but I knew the dragons heard him anyway.

"I'm sorry … for everything."

When I went back out to the living room, my parents tried to hide their concern for me. While I slept, they had finished putting decorations away. They smiled and pretended like they had a normal child with normal, everyday problems and not me.

"I'm sorry for earlier." I couldn't meet their eyes. I wanted them to have that daughter, but they were stuck with me.

Dad patted the couch between them, and I sat down. He pulled me against his side. "It's no big deal. Cash helped me with the hard part. Well … it wasn't for him, but he's like twenty-five years younger than me."

I couldn't stop the laugh that bubbled up my throat and burst out.

"What?" Mom asked.

Cash tipped his head toward his shoulder. "I'm a little older than I appear."

Mom huffed. "Oh, you can't be that much older than Dacia."

He looked at me as if asking for permission to tell her his age. I nodded at him, and he said, "I'm somewhere around fifteen hundred years old. It's hard to keep track after a while."

"Holy crap." Dad coughed up the tea he'd just sipped. He wiped his mouth on his sleeve. "And, you thought I was getting old, dear."

Mom gave Cash the once-over and smiled at him. "You look pretty good for your age."

He twisted from side to side and bent over to touch his toes. I knew he was trying to keep it light, and I appreciated it more than he would ever know. "I feel pretty good, too."

"How old are your other friends?" Mom put her arm on the back of the couch and turned around to look at Malcolm.

He pointed at Cash. "I'm at least five hundred years older than that young pup. As he said, it's hard to keep track. The years pass by, and time seems insignificant."

"And Mavros?" Dad asked.

I realized that I'd never asked him that. I assumed he was older than Aurelia, but how old, I didn't know.

He manifested in the middle of the room, keeping his right arm behind his back, out of sight. "Like angels, demons have been around since the beginning of time. We are stasis. We don't age. We don't die. We rarely change."

"You changed." Cash patted Mavros on the shoulder.

The interaction surprised me, but it downright shocked Mavros. He swallowed hard and looked at me. "That's why I said rarely. I wouldn't have without Dacia."

My parents, not understanding the significance of this conversation, were hung up on Mavros' age. Mom's face was slack. Her mouth floundered for a while before she said, "You were here when dinosaurs roamed the planet, when cavemen did? Before all that?"

Dad said, "So … which came first, the chicken or the egg?"

Mavros laughed at Dad's joke. Then he turned serious. "No, not here. I spend very little time on Earth."

"What do you mean?" Mom cocked her head to the side.

My muscles tightened, and I blinked several times in rapid succession. My parents didn't need to know about the dragons banishing Mavros. They didn't need to know what he'd done while trying to find someone to be bound to. They didn't need to know that I'd killed myself to stop him. I tugged my shaking fingers through my hair.

Malcolm wiped his hand over his mouth and cleared his throat. "That's a story for another day."

I lay in bed staring up at the ceiling. I kept picturing my blood separating. The shards of the collar were the key to drawing Argentum's essence out, but how could I use them?

When the Nephilim put the collar on me, it had completely shut off my magic. It hadn't separated Argentum's from mine. There had just been a vast, empty chasm. I couldn't really take the shard into my imagination with me to use it on the serpent. I doubted just holding it would do anything. However, if I held it to a cut maybe it would draw out Argentum's blood.

I flopped onto my side. Before I thought it to death, though, I needed to get some sleep. I could play the what-if game all night, but it wouldn't do me any good.

"Dacia, sleep, or I'll have to leave." Malcolm's voice was rough but not unkind. Since I'd gotten my powers back, he'd watched me from the window seat. "Mavros needs more time to heal, and your emotions would be too much for Cash."

I rolled onto my other side and hugged my pillow. He was hard to make out in the darkened room, but his eyes glowed like a cat's. "Can you help me?"

The sun shone through the window, surrounding Mavros in a halo of light. His features were impossible to distinguish, but he was here. That had to be a good sign.

He stood and walked toward my bed, each step was deliberate. It seemed like he was readying himself for a fight.

I propped myself up on my arm, watching him, wondering what was going on.

"Are you still angry with me?" He stopped moving. He was a silhouette in the morning light.

I couldn't tell if his arm was healed. I couldn't see the expression on his face. "What?" He really didn't think I'd done that to him because I was mad about something. Did he? "I didn't hurt you because I was angry."

"For controlling you, Dacia." He took another step. "For making you promise not to use ice against me again."

"I quit being mad about that as soon as you explained yourself." I swung my legs over the side of the bed. "How are you? Do you forgive me?"

He strode the rest of the way to me and stretched his arm out, twisting it around so I could see the whole thing. "As good as new." He sat next to me. "There's nothing to forgive. It wasn't you lashing out. It was him."

"I didn't mean to hurt you." I squeezed his hand. "I didn't even know I could hurt you like that."

He smiled, but it didn't reach his eyes. "Neither did I." He stared out my window, his expression hidden from me. "In all the years I've existed and in all the realms I've been in, no one has ever hurt me like that."

Chapter 44

Setting Plans In Motion

"I'd like you guys to take me to the cave or to Draconian's castle—"

Cash growled.

I knew they hated the idea of going back there, but I needed somewhere secluded. I had no idea how Argentum's blood would react to my plan. I didn't want to destroy my parents' house or experiment where the Nephilim would see what I was doing. "—or somewhere else away from people." I stared down at my hands. They were folded together on the dining room table. There was no sign of the cut I'd gotten yesterday, not even a faint white scar.

"Why would you want to go there?" Cash's voice was closer to his dragon's than the one I was used to.

I had two ideas. The first one was to draw Argentum's blood out. I needed somewhere big enough that the smell of my blood wouldn't saturate the air. The second idea involved Mavros, and I wasn't sure how the dragons would feel about it. Cash's admission yesterday that Mavros had changed was a good start, but the animosity between dragons and demons ran too deep for me to believe that the dragons would be okay with me being at Mavros' mercy. "I might be able to separate Argentum's blood from mine. If I do, maybe his magic will go with it."

Mavros put his hand on top of mine and waited until I looked into his midnight eyes. "How are you planning to do this?"

"The shards seemed to pull Draconian's blood away from mine." I bit my bottom lip, pulling it into my mouth. "I kept picturing it last night before I fell asleep. It was his blood that separated from mine. So, if I cut myself and hold the shard there, maybe his blood will follow the fragment."

"And maybe you'll bleed to death." Malcolm pushed his chair back and stood behind it, clutching the wood.

I nodded. "Argentum's power wants to live on. I don't think it will let me die. Magic would heal me—" I drew in a deep breath "—and you would all be there if I needed it."

"That's why you want somewhere like the castle." Cash bobbed his head slowly.

"Yeah." I was glad he understood that I didn't just want to take them back there to remind them of what they'd been through. I didn't want him to think I was trying to force him to remember what I'd saved them from. "Big rooms, lots of airflow, less chance my blood will drive you guys nuts."

Malcolm walked to the doorframe and leaned his shoulder against it. "When?"

"The sooner, the better. Mom and Dad will be gone most of the day. I'd like to try before they get home." I traced the grain pattern on the table with the tip of my finger, not wanting to meet their eyes. "If it doesn't work, I have another idea that I can try tonight."

Cash lifted his head, breathed in deeply, and groaned.

Malcolm's pupils turned to slits. "No, not if it's going to make you smell like that. We'll find something else to try." He rubbed his hand over his mouth, then pointed to himself and Cash. "We need to hunt first."

They were gone before I had a chance to say anything else.

"It's for the best, Dacia." Mavros had his hands on the table but didn't try to reach for me. He didn't stop me from tracing the pattern. "You're really emotional, and if they're going to smell your blood, they'll need to be sated."

"What about you?"

"I could try to make us some breakfast." He flipped his hands palms up. "But, I never learned how to cook."

I pushed back from the table and walked into the kitchen. "Bacon, eggs, and toast okay with you?"

"Sounds great." He rolled his sleeves up. "Tell me what I can do to help."

I shuffled things around in the fridge, then in the freezer. "Looks like sausage instead of bacon." I pointed to the cabinet where the skillets were kept. "Get me the pan." After he did that I walked him through making toast. It seemed amazing that a primordial being needed instructions on properly toasting bread. "Maybe I should see Cody before I do this … in case it doesn't work."

"No." The word was harsh. Mavros softened his tone and said, "No, you shouldn't. If Argentum's power knows what you're planning, your magic and his might take it out on Cody. You could call him, but I think you should just wait."

He was right. I couldn't risk it. I finished making breakfast, and even though I had no appetite, I sat at the counter with him to eat it.

We stood in the chamber in Draconian's castle where he had chained me to the table and tortured me. Where he'd tried to break me so that I'd become his protégée.

I stared at it, and the scene played out in my head. *Draconian stood over me, his gray eyes gleaming. His long, white beard brushed against the stone slab. He placed his hand on mine. Bursts of colors popped behind my eyes as pain traveled along my nerves. I gasped for breath, but he didn't stop. The edges of my vision blurred, then darkened. My consciousness slipped.*

A hand clamped down on my shoulder, and I stifled a scream.

"He's gone, Dacia." Malcolm's voice was quiet, and I wondered if he was reliving his own ghosts.

I lifted my hand to my shoulder and squeezed his fingers. "Yeah." I dropped my chin to my chest. "He is."

Picking up a chair that had been knocked to the floor, I brought it over to the table. Then I stretched my left arm out across it. "Ready?" I looked Malcolm in the eyes, then Cash.

They both nodded, and I sliced the shard along my vein. Blood gushed out. I held one fragment of the collar against it, and Mavros held another. Silver liquid separated from the crimson blood. It trailed over the broken pieces puddling on the table.

As more blood flowed into it, it stopped moving. It didn't spill over the edge. It didn't keep streaming. It just stopped. Instead of spreading like a normal liquid would, the puddle deepened and congealed.

I watched it, afraid to take my eyes off of it. Afraid that it would try to attack.

The blood spilling from the wound turned red, and the dragons immediately grabbed hold of me. Their healing energy spread through me, closing the cut.

We'd packed a bag to bring with us. Malcolm pulled a rag and a bottle of water out of it. Moistening the cloth, he handed it to me. Without taking my eyes off the silver mass on the table, I cleaned up my arm. Then not wanting the lingering scent to distract Malcolm or Cash, I burned the rag.

Argentum's blood recoiled when mine ignited. It transformed into a miniature likeness of him, rippling and flowing but somehow managing to hold its form.

As soon as the fire had completely consumed my blood, I glanced at Malcolm and Cash. I was afraid to take my eyes off Argentum's ghost for long, but I needed to make sure they looked fully human. When I saw that their pupils were still round, I nodded at them and turned back to the phantom.

Blue flames ignited in my palm. They spread over my fingertips and blasted at the silver beast.

The blood divided, fanning out around the inferno. The way it moved was like liquid mercury. It was both mesmerizing and terrifying.

I raised my other hand widening the conflagration, but Argentum's blood separated further. I stopped the flames. "Any suggestions?"

The silver mass pulled together, closing up the hole my fire had passed through.

"We need to contain it somehow." Mavros looked around.

Malcolm moved closer to the table. He bent down, staring at what remained of Argentum. "Most of our kind fear death. We are long-lived but not immortal, and as our lives draw to an end, we do not usually go gently." He looked up at me. "But word of this cannot get out. Somehow, he figured out a way to live on through another host. It needs to end here."

"Yeah." I nodded emphatically. "I've never been overly fond of parasites, and this one"—I waved my hand at the blood—"is the worst I've ever seen."

A purple haze surrounded Cash. When it cleared, he was in dragon form. "We need to work together, surround it."

"Yes." Malcolm agreed as he, too, transformed.

Mavros and Malcolm stood to either side of me, and Cash moved across from me. As soon as everyone stepped into position, I said, "Three, two, one."

Flames spewed from the dragons' maws and from mine and Mavros' hands.

Argentum's blood had nowhere to go. It screamed as flames devoured it.

My magic spluttered, and I turned toward Mavros. A chill spread up my arm.

Malcolm and Mavros repositioned themselves. Mavros lifted his other arm, filling in the gap where my flames no longer were.

My body froze until I was a human ice sculpture, and I sprang at Mavros. I was flung backward before touching him. I slammed onto my back a few feet away from him. I gasped for air, but it stuck in my throat, refusing to enter my lungs.

The ice receded. Black dots danced at the edges of my vision, and finally, air lifted my chest. I breathed it in greedily. Sucking in lungful after lungful.

Mavros knelt over me, cautiously stretching his hand out. "It's still in you."

"Must be." I sounded like I'd just finished running a marathon. "Otherwise, I wouldn't have attacked you."

Malcolm strode over with his hands in his pockets. I was surprised to see him back in his human avatar so quickly. "So … what next?"

I took Mavros' hand and let him pull me to my feet. I'd spent too much time in this room, staring at the ceiling, unable to breathe. I needed to get out of here. "Let me think about it, make sure it will work." Extracting Argentum's blood and fighting his … whatever that had been had taken more out of me than I wanted to admit to them. "We'll talk tomorrow."

⁙373⁜

Chapter 45

$\mathcal{I}$t was freezing outside, but the dining room was too small, too enclosed. Malcolm, Cash, Mavros, and I went outside. I brushed the snow off the patio furniture and sat down. Since I'd gotten my powers back, the number of imps and demons willing to cross paths with the dragons and Mavros to get to me had greatly reduced, so we were relatively safe out in the open.

Malcolm surrounded us with a soundproofed bubble, and I stared straight ahead, hoping the dragons would agree with my plan.

"I don't know how to say this so that it makes sense, so bear with me." I rubbed my hands together and blew on them to warm my fingers. "I can't take the shard inside my imagination with me to cut out Argentum's power."

"Right." Cash's tone encouraged me to continue.

I chipped the snow away with the toe of my boot. "Mavros can pull my spirit out of my body while I'm sleeping."

"No." Malcolm practically snarled the word. "It's too dangerous. We can't protect you."

"I can keep her safe." Mavros' voice was the calm to Malcolm's storm.

"I can't not do it." I bowed my head, pressing my face against my hands. "I have to do something before I kill Cody. I have to get Argentum out."

"There has to be a better way." Malcolm sounded defeated.

I could relate to that mood. I had hoped extracting his blood would get rid of Argentum's taint. I had hoped that his power came from there. "Mavros says my dreams are just as real to him as everything else. I was hoping he could take the shard into them, and we could face the serpent there."

"And what happens if it destroys your magic, too?" Cash's voice was soft, but there was an edge to it.

I peeked through my fingers at the three of them. "Then I guess I don't have to worry about hurting Cody anymore."

"Why can't we try it while you're awake?" Fear and worry mixed together on Malcolm's face. "You've shown me the manifestation of your magic before."

I shook my head. "I don't know. I suppose I could try, but will it be like when I used his power? Will it corrupt me and send me back to the beginning again?" I stared at my white and gray boots on the snow. "I thought if he pulled my spirit out, it might be different."

"So, we go to the cave." The sunlight made the purple streaks in Cash's hair stand out from the black. He clenched and unclenched his jaw. Allowing me to walk into danger went against their nature. They'd vowed to keep me safe, but they both knew this was something that had to be done. I couldn't wait for it to just disappear. "We'll try it while she's awake first. Then if she's corrupted, the fairies will be there to help."

"And … what if it doesn't work?" My breath puffed out in front of me.

Cash shrugged. "Then we stay there tonight and let Mavros pull your spirit out."

The plan was set. The dragons may not have been happy with it, but they were on board. I stood and walked to the sliding glass door. My hand shook as I reached for the handle. Would this work, or would Argentum's taint live in me forever?

I took my boots off and carried them upstairs. As I was setting them by the front door, I heard gravel crunching on the driveway. I peeked out the window and watched Cody pull up. He got out and looked around, rubbing his hand down his face. Shoving his hands in his pockets, he lowered his head and walked to the door.

I opened it before he knocked. "Hey, what's up?" I asked.

"I … uh …" He cleared his throat and glanced behind me. "Tried to call."

Stepping to the side, I ushered him in. "We were outside. I didn't hear the phone."

"Yeah … figured."

I tried to hold his gaze, but he kept looking away from me. "Yesterday, we went to Draconian's castle to try to exorcise Argentum." I tugged my hand through my hair and let out a deep sigh. "It didn't work."

"Where's that put us?" He rubbed the back of his neck while looking at our feet.

My stomach clenched. This was my fault. I should have kept him in the loop. I should have done whatever I could to be with him. I couldn't remember ever seeing him so insecure, and I hated it. "Cody, I love you. Nothing's changed that." I reached for his hand, hoping my magic was depleted enough not to hurt him. "We have another plan to try out later today."

"Before that, lunch?" He finally met my eyes. He looked like he was preparing himself to be let down.

I squeezed his fingers. "Sounds good. I need to change first. My jeans are wet." While I changed into my favorite pair of skinny jeans and a sweater, I talked to Malcolm. *Can you give us some privacy? I think Cody needs it.*

Yes. His voice still had an edge to it. His dragon wasn't pleased with the plan, but I had nothing else. No more ideas. *We will be there if you need us.*

When Cody and I left my house seemingly on our own, his face lit up. His confidence came back. He knew we were being watched. He knew we probably always would be. But just the semblance of being alone made him more like the Cody he'd been before demons and dragons had entered our lives.

"So, what's the plan?" he asked as he pulled onto the gravel road.

I told him about extracting Argentum's blood yesterday. Then I explained my plan to him. The more I thought about it, the more I realized I should wait to go to the cave until after my parents got home. I wanted to talk to them about it, to let them know I might not be coming home tonight. It wasn't something I should call them at work to tell them. That would just make it hard for them to concentrate on their jobs.

While I'd been talking, Cody had set his hand on my leg. He rubbed my thigh as he drove. The action was so normal that I doubted he'd thought twice about it. When my powers didn't surge in response to his touch, I wondered if Argentum's magic was still drained from fighting my guards and me. Maybe some of his strength had been contained in his blood.

"Is it gonna work?" Some of his pain showed through his words.

I knew it had to be killing him for him to see me with Malcolm, Cash, and Mavros all of the time. Knowing that they could touch me when most of the time he couldn't. Knowing they were with me constantly. And knowing that Mavros wanted me for his own.

I'd been jealous when he'd merely looked at Aurelia. There was so much more for him to worry about. I needed to put an end to this as quickly as possible. "I don't think it will when I'm awake. I hope I'm wrong, but we'll find out soon enough."

"Come back to me."

I nodded. "I'll do my best."

Diamond in the Rough had a few cars in the parking lot. It would get busier when the normal lunch crowd came in, but we were there early enough to beat them. When we stepped inside, Cindy welcomed us.

"Do you ever get a day off?" I asked as she hugged me.

She kissed my cheek before pulling away, and I wondered if I had a lipstick imprint there. "Sundays and usually Mondays, but Elaine called in sick." She held her hand up in front of her and examined her fingernails. They were gold with fireworks exploding on her thumbs. "Now, I have to wait another week to get my nails done."

I asked for a booth in the back, saying I wanted to be as far from the door as possible, but in all honesty, I wanted to keep an eye on everyone who came in. Cindy handed us our menus and took our drink order. Almost as soon as she turned away from us, the bell above the door chimed, and four men walked in.

"Cindy." My voice was louder than I intended for it to be, and the word shook.

She turned. "I gotta seat them." She pointed at the men. "I'll be right back."

"About that, could you seat them over there?" I pointed at the far corner of the restaurant. "Please."

She raised her eyebrows at me and pursed her lips but said, "Sure." She walked toward the door. "Welcome to Diamond. Four of you?"

Cody glanced over his shoulder. "Why?"

"Nephilim."

When Cindy returned with our drinks, Cody nodded toward the other table. "Thanks."

"You're welcome." She glanced over her shoulder. "One day you'll have to explain it to me but not now. We're starting to get our lunch crowd. So, what'll you have?"

We both ordered bacon cheeseburgers and fries, and she hustled off to place our order and seat another group of people.

Cody reached across the table, and I slipped my hand into his. I tried to keep my full attention on him, but I kept glancing toward the Nephilim. Sebastian and Troy sat with two others who had cornered me on the side street in Althea last semester. One was the dark-skinned man who kept some sort of weapon under his coat. The other had short, dark hair. I remembered him standing on the mountain, pointing at me.

I only glanced at them, but they stared at me the entire time we were there. They even went so far as to arrange their chairs so they all faced me.

When Cindy brought our food, she said, "What's with them anyway?"

"I don't know." I tugged my hand through my hair. "But they give me the creeps." After she walked away, I watched them. The fairies, a unicorn, a gold dragon, a pegasus, and even some of the Nephilim vouched for me. Why couldn't they see that I meant them no harm, that I didn't want to hurt anybody?

"Dacia, don't give 'em the satisfaction." Cody reached for the pepper and shook it over his fries. "Eat."

I scooted to the back corner of the booth where it was harder for me to see them. I put lettuce and tomato on my burger and pointed at my onions. "Want these?"

"Nah."

We ate in relative silence. Just being together was good enough.

I threw some cash on the table, and we went to the counter to pay. Sebastian stood in line directly behind me. When I didn't turn around or acknowledge his presence, he edged closer until he nearly touched me. His breath ruffled my hair. I paid the bill, then scooted to the side to avoid him. I wanted to "accidentally" elbow him or step on his foot, but I didn't want to give the Nephilim any excuse to decide I was evil.

Cody didn't seem to mind, though. He pushed Sebastian back. "Excuse me." When we stepped outside, he said, "They don't seem very good." He used finger quotes around the last word, then threw his arm over my shoulders.

The other three Nephilim followed us to Cody's car, watching me as I buckled my seatbelt. I waved at them when Cody drove off.

"Your house?" He flipped his signal on.

I watched out the window, wondering where my guardians and the Nephilim were. I doubted any of them were very far away. "Sure. We'll just have to be careful."

His eyebrows were pinched together when he glanced at me.

"I don't know what's going on with my magic." I tucked my hands into my pouch. "Maybe his power is building up so it can fight back. Maybe it's worn out from yesterday. Maybe it's waiting to surprise me at the worst possible moment."

He slid his hand onto my thigh. "I'll be okay."

I wanted to share his confidence, but there was too much at stake.

When we got home, Malcolm, Cash, and Mavros remained out of sight. Cody looked around as if waiting for them to appear at any moment, but they didn't. He walked to the hallway and glanced down it. "What's this?"

"I thought you needed to pretend like we were alone." I shrugged. "I figured it would only last through lunch, but I guess they think I'm doing all right."

He grabbed my hand and pulled us together. His other hand settled on my waist. "So … whadda you wanna do?"

I flattened my palm over his heart. "You know they're watching, right?"

He nodded, then leaned his forehead against mine, never taking his gaze off of mine. "Probably always will be."

"Yeah." How could he want a life with me? How could he not long for a normal relationship? "If I get this out of me, it won't be the end." My hand slipped. My fingertips barely touched him. "There'll be another monster, another impossible task, another disaster waiting to happen."

"And?"

I stared at the phoenix on his hoodie. "And, how can you want this?"

"Again?" He tilted my chin up so that he was staring into my eyes. "I love you, and it's not the oh-he'll-get-over-it kind of love. It's the once-in-a-lifetime kind. The kind most people never find, so please … please, don't ask me to leave you."

Tears pricked my eyes. "Okay." I stood on my tiptoes and brushed my lips across his.

His grip on my waist tightened, and he deepened the kiss.

I pressed my hands against his chest and backed up. "I don't want to hurt you."

He nodded and walked over to the couch. "A movie then?"

I spent the afternoon curled up next to him watching movies. When it was nearly time for my parents to return, he stood. "I should go."

"Why?" My face scrunched into a mask of confusion.

He brushed his thumb over the pucker that had appeared between my eyes. "You need to talk to your parents alone." He walked to the door and pulled his boots on. "Let me know what happens."

I watched him pull out of the driveway. Then I went to the kitchen and started making supper. When my parents pulled up, a fist tightened in my stomach. I wished there was some way to keep them from worrying, but now that they knew about my powers, I doubted that was possible.

Dad walked in and inhaled deeply. "Mmm. Smells good in here."

"It's just about ready." I smiled at him over my shoulder. "The bread takes five minutes. Do you want me to start it now or give you a few minutes to be home first?"

Mom set her purse on the cabinet. "I'd like to change. Maybe give me just a few minutes."

I took plates, bowls, and silverware into the dining room and set them out on placemats. Then I carried in the salad, dressings, and parmesan. It wasn't a fancy meal, but I'd been in the mood for spaghetti. I slid the garlic bread into the oven and shouted, "Five minutes and counting."

We were over halfway through dinner when I dropped the bomb on my parents. "I may have found a way to get rid of the darkness in my magic." I swiped a napkin across my lips. "I'm going to leave after we eat, and I probably won't be back until sometime tomorrow."

Mom set her bread on the edge of her plate and picked up her wine glass. She took a long drink before asking, "Will it be dangerous?"

I twirled noodles around my fork, looking at my spaghetti instead of them. "I really hope not, but I don't know for sure. Malcolm, Cash, and Mavros will be there."

"Of course." Dad laughed humorlessly. "They're always with you."

"Pretty much."

"Do you think it will work?" Mom reached across the table, and I met her halfway. She squeezed my fingers.

My shoulders lifted, touching the bottoms of my ears. "I can only hope."

Chapter 46

Exorcism

The dragons lit fires to illuminate the cavern. We were in the chamber where I'd seen the fairies multiple times. Shadows danced in the flickering firelight, creeping me out a little. The cave was colder than I remembered it being, and that chill seemed to sink deep inside of me, making me shiver.

Malcolm was instantly next to me. "Are you okay?"

"Just cold."

Cash sucked in a deep breath. "Cold doesn't smell like that."

"Okay." I rolled my eyes and shook my head. "I'm cold. I'm a little creeped out by the shadows. They remind me of when I fought Nefarious here. I'm terrified that this won't work and that I'll never get rid of Argentum's taint." I rubbed my hands down my arms. "Is that good enough, or should I go on?"

Mavros took off his coat and handed it to me. I should have refused it. Cody hated when I wore it, but the warmth of Mavros' body lingered in it. I slid my arms into the sleeves and inhaled the warm summer nights smell of him. "Thank you."

I sat on a boulder, pulled the shards out of my hoodie's pouch, and handed one to everybody. "So … here goes nothing." I closed my eyes and concentrated on my power.

The darkened room filled my mind. A light shone down on the manifestation of my magic. The serpent was coiled on the floor. There was still a slight silver tinge to its pearlescent scales, but it didn't seem as dark as the last time I'd seen it.

The snake slowly lifted its head, looking at me through its copper eyes. *What have you done to us?*

"I'm trying to save us." I tried to keep my voice soft and comforting. I didn't want to agitate the part that was Argentum. I didn't want him to expect something was happening until it did.

No. It loosened its coils and raised its head off the ground. *You weakened us. You took our power and destroyed it.*

Footsteps clicked across the smooth floor. Malcolm, Cash, and Mavros emerged from the darkness.

What is this?

"You are mine." I stepped closer to the serpent. "You belong to me. I want us to be whole again." I knelt down in front of it and ran my hand from its head, down its back. "Will you let us try something?"

Why are they here?

"To help me."

The snake lifted its head, bumping it against my palm. It acted like it had in the beginning, before I'd killed Argentum. I didn't notice any shadows on its body, no darkness under its scales.

"Relax." I nodded at Malcolm, and his soothing magic washed over all of us.

The serpent swayed, and its eyes drifted closed. I lifted its tail and sliced the shard through its pearl scales. Blood pooled along the cut. I held the shard to it, waiting for Argentum's power to be drawn out, but nothing happened.

Cash knelt on the ground next to me and pressed his collar fragment against mine. I glanced away, remembering all of the times Mom had told me that a watched pot never boils. When I looked back, nothing had changed.

Malcolm smiled sympathetically and healed the snake's wound. I stood and waited until they surrounded me. Then I pulled myself back out into the cave.

"Well—" I pushed against the rock I'd been sitting on and stood, brushing off my behind "—do you think the cushions are still in the other chamber?"

Mavros walked over to me and took my hand in his. "Do you trust me, Dacia?"

"Yes." I pressed my eyes shut. I didn't want to see the disappointment on the dragons' faces. They'd warned me against trusting him.

"Let me try something first." There was a pleading tone to his voice that I couldn't remember ever hearing before.

I nodded.

"See if the fairies will come."

I opened my eyes, and he brushed his fingers along my cheek.

"See if they'll be here just in case my magic gets inside of you again."

"Dacia"—Malcolm shook his head—"don't do this. We'll find another way. We'll get it out of you."

I hoped he could understand. I needed to do this. I needed to march down every path that had even the slightest possibility of leading me out. "I need to try."

Malcolm dropped his chin to his chest but said no more.

"Rayne, I'm going to let Mavros try to get rid of Argentum's taint." I chewed on my lip, hoping I was making the right decision. "Can you come watch over me in case it goes awry?"

It didn't take long for fairies to fill the cavern. Rayne hovered in front of my face. "The demon vowed never to mark you again."

"Yeah." I nodded. "I'm not worried about him marking me. I'm worried that his magic will somehow get entangled with mine or it'll somehow corrupt me."

"We will stay." She folded her arms over her chest and narrowed her eyes at Mavros. "Do not try to corrupt her, demon."

Mavros didn't respond. Instead, he nodded at the boulder I'd been sitting on. "Please, sit."

He knelt in front of me, holding both of my hands in his. He stared into my eyes and pressed his thumbs into my palms. My magic stirred in response. Blue fire danced across my fingertips. He pushed harder, and black tipped the flames.

"What are you doing?" I tried to pull my hands away, but he held on too tightly.

When he didn't answer, I focused on my power. The two serpents stared at each other. Their bodies swayed as each of them rose higher. The pearlescent snake puffed its chest out and flicked its tail. The onyx serpent struck, sinking its fangs into my power.

Silver blood puddled on the ground. As I watched, it spread out, long and thin. The blood rose morphing into a winged snake. It lunged at Mavros' power. My serpent struck as the onyx one dodged.

The silver snake turned against my magic, exposing its back to the onyx serpent. Mavros' snake sunk its fangs into Argentum's and jerked back. Silver scales floated through the air, catching the light and sending prisms dancing across the dark parts of the room. Both the pearl and black serpents struck again and again. When they finally pulled back, venom dripped from their fangs.

The silver serpent wobbled before flopping to the ground. Shadows rose from its body, dissipating as the light hit them. Then the creature crumpled in on itself. Only a pile of ash remained behind.

It is gone. The pearlescent serpent lifted its head toward the heavens and closed its eyes.

"Dacia," Mavros whispered my name and let go of my hands.

I pulled away from my magic and blinked back the white light that filled the cavern. Fairies covered every inch of my body. "His magic in you has been awakened."

"If you'll let me"—Mavros stood a few feet away from me, blocked from coming closer by both fairies and dragons—"I can make it go back to sleep."

"Please." My throat felt dry and scratchy like I'd played some part in the battle that had taken place. "Let him do it."

"He can't be trusted, Dacia." Malcolm's fangs jutted out of his mouth, and he looked like he was having trouble holding his form. "He released his magic."

"He did—" I paused, hoping I wasn't jumping to conclusions "—but, I think Argentum's power is gone." I lifted my arm to point at Mavros, and fairies flew off in every direction. "Mavros' magic played a part in that."

Mavros sneered at Malcolm, and I couldn't help but wonder if it was to mask his hurt at still not being trusted. No matter what he did, no matter what he said, no matter how many times he saved me, the dragons would never see him as more than a demon. "I won't hurt her. I'm bound to her."

"Let him." Cash stepped to the side.

Mavros made his way toward me. The fairies lifted into the air to let him through. It was a beautiful scene. His black clothes, dark hair, dusky complexion, and obsidian eyes were all contrasted by their light. An image of him holding me flashed through my mind, and from the mischievous expression on his face, I knew he put it there.

Warmth flooded through my body, and I reached for his hands, wanting nothing more than to touch him.

"Dacia." Malcolm growled. The sound rumbled through the cave bringing me back to my senses.

I shook my head at Mavros. "If you do stuff like that, they'll never trust you."

"They never will anyway." He shrugged. "So, I might as well have a little fun." He knelt in front of me. "I need to see your magic again."

I focused on it. The pearlescent and onyx serpents were coiled up together. Shadows crept over the snakes' bodies. Tendrils stretched out, reaching for Mavros and me. Darkness clung to the serpents, sliding under their scales, caressing them.

My magic peered at me, and I staggered back a step. Its eyes were unrecognizable. I reached my hand up to mine, wondering if the black in them mirrored what I saw in the snake's copper irises.

Mavros walked over and touched the midnight serpent, running his fingers over the creature's head. Its eyes drifted shut, and its head wobbled. As soon as it was asleep, I pulled us back to reality.

"What—" my voice couldn't squeeze past the lump in my throat. I cleared it and started again. "What color are my eyes?"

Malcolm, Mavros, and Cash stared at me. Malcolm pulled his hand down his face.

"What. Color. Are. My. Eyes?" I jumped up and clutched Mavros' shirt at the collar, yanking his face closer to mine. "Tell. Me!"

He slipped his fingers under mine, loosening my grip. "More green than black still."

I slumped against him, and he wrapped his arms around me. "Why?" My rage was gone, replaced by despair. "I didn't use my magic."

"The serpent must have"—Mavros' words were a breath blown right into my ear—"when it fought Argentum."

I backed away from him. "What do I do?"

Rayne flew toward me. Her iridescent wings beat as fast as a hummingbird's. I held my hand out, and she landed on it. She knelt down and pressed her palm to mine. Reassuring energy flowed through me. "No magic, Dacia. Do not use it under any circumstances."

"For how long?"

She lifted off my hand, hovering in front of my face. Her silver hair blew in the breeze created by her wings. "Until the shadows disappear for the entirety of two days."

Chapter 47

Without

Malcolm teleported me home. I rushed into the house and went straight to the bathroom, slamming the door shut behind me. I pressed my hands down on the counter and stared at my reflection. The black flecks had doubled. My once vivid green eyes looked more like forest green from a distance.

Mom knocked on the door. "Dacia?" Fear made her voice rise higher than normal. "Is everything okay?"

"No. Nothing's okay." I swiped my hand across my face, opened the door, and sort of fell into her arms.

She held onto me, running her hand over my head and down my back, over and over again. "I thought it worked since you came home already."

"It did." I pulled away and wiped my eyes on my sleeve.

"Then what's wrong?" My tears had soaked through her pajamas, but she didn't seem to notice.

"Mavros had to help me, and …" I didn't know what to say, so I just pointed at my eyes.

She covered her mouth with her hand. "Oh, honey, I'm sorry." She brushed my hair back. "So, what does that mean?"

"I can't use my magic until his is out of my system, so Malcolm will have to keep me from dreaming … if he's willing."

"Of course, I am." His deep voice came from the living room.

I stepped back from Mom and dragged my hand through my hair. "At least my magic won't attack Cody anymore."

"What?" Mom's eyes widened, and her eyebrows rose so high that they disappeared beneath her hair.

"Yeah … I'm a wonderful girlfriend." I blew out a deep breath and leaned against the doorframe. "The darkness that was in me wanted him dead."

She looked down the hall, and I wondered what was going through her head. "I wish we could've gotten the magic out of you." She pinched the bridge of her nose. "I wish it would've faded like mine did."

"But, then I wouldn't be me." I chewed on my lip. "Not to mention, Nefarious or Mavros might have destroyed the world." I bobbed my head toward my room. "I should call Cody. Let him know."

She pulled me into a hug. "You've got this."

Malcolm followed me into my room. "I'm sorry."

"No need." I flopped down onto my bed. "I know I can't be alone. I almost used my magic in the hall." I shook my head. "I wondered what Mom thought about me, and I almost looked." I reached for the phone but stopped short. Instead, I turned to Malcolm. "Can you take me there?"

He held onto my hand, pulling me to my feet. My body stretched and pulled. When it stopped, we were invisible, standing in Cody's room. He lay on his side with his head propped up on his hand, reading a book. His blankets were pulled up to his waist, and his chest was bare. He peered over his shoulder, like some sixth sense felt us there, then turned back to his book.

I stepped away from Malcolm and instantly became visible. "Cody." I kept my voice quiet, trying not to startle him.

He rolled off the edge onto his feet. "Is it gone?" He stood in front of me with so much hope on his face.

"Yes."

He picked me up and spun me around.

A startled laugh escaped from me.

He stopped, and we both stared at the door, waiting for his parents to burst in and find me in his room.

"No one heard." Malcolm showed himself. "It's soundproofed."

Cody looked from Malcolm to me, then pressed his eyes closed. "What's wrong?"

I sat on the edge of his bed and told him what had happened.

He lifted his hand to my cheek, brushing his thumb under my eye. "You're beautiful no matter what, Dacia. Always."

"I can't use my magic." I leaned into his touch. "Mavros, Malcolm, or Cash will have to be with me at all times."

Cody nodded at Malcolm. "Thank you."

"My debt to Dacia will never be repaid." Malcolm bowed his head at me, making me really uncomfortable.

I returned my attention to Cody. "I should get back before my parents realize I'm gone." I slid my hand into Malcolm's, and he siphoned my powers. Then he let go and turned invisible, giving us the semblance of privacy.

I ran my hand up Cody's chest, sliding my fingers beneath his chain. "You shouldn't need this to protect yourself from me, but please keep it on. It might help if someone or something else tries to harm you."

He lifted his hand to my face, then pressed his lips to mine. Relief filled his kiss. There was no tension in his body, no fear that my magic would turn on him.

He curled his hands in my hair and pulled me closer. My hands slid along his back, raising goosebumps on his bare skin. My entire body buzzed with the thrill of his touch.

Malcolm cleared his throat, and I pulled away. Cody's sapphire eyes shone like sunlight reflecting off the ocean. He reached up, brushing his thumb over my lips. "I love you, Dacia."

"I love you, too." I touched my forehead to his. "We'll continue this when I don't need a babysitter."

Malcolm lay stretched out alongside me. I couldn't believe my life had come back to this, but at least this time, we knew my dreams had to be held at bay.

Mavros sat on the window seat, watching me. The corners of his eyes drooped. I could practically feel the guilt radiating off of him.

"It's not your fault, Mavros." How could I blame him? If he hadn't done what he had, Argentum would still be a part of me, his magic still debasing mine, turning me against Cody. "Thank you for helping me get rid of his taint. I never could've done it on my own. I should've said that right away. I was being selfish."

Mavros shook his head. "You were being human. My magic can corrupt you, and you fear that." He stared out the window. "Always, Dacia. Always fear that. You should fear me. You shouldn't thank me."

"No." Malcolm fidgeted. "We all should've thanked you. I'm sorry for not seeing that sooner."

Mavros stared at Malcolm. His mouth was open slightly. Finally, he nodded, and I was reminded of one of the first things he ever said to me, "Cat got your tongue."

I fell asleep wondering if Mavros would betray me eventually. He kept warning me not to trust him. Since we were bound, it wouldn't make sense for him to, but he was a demon. Maybe he couldn't help himself. Maybe I should use his name to make him promise not to betray me. I also needed him to allow me to use ice against him again if necessary … but it could wait for now.

Bright sunlight streamed into my bedroom, and I blinked it back several times before I could keep my eyes open. I turned my head and stared into Mavros' obsidian eyes. "What happened?"

"Malcolm asked me to take over a few hours ago." He sat up, propping himself on my pillows. "Your dreams got pretty intense."

I wiped my hand over my face and hoped they weren't too embarrassing. "What did I dream?"

"You dreamed about Argentum. That creepy thing his blood turned into." He wiggled his eyebrows. "Me … oh, and Cody."

"You?" I swallowed hard and tugged my hand through my hair. "What about you?"

He grinned, and my heart stuttered. "It seems you enjoyed visiting me on the beach." Heat blasted my cheeks. "I could take you there."

I covered my face with my hands. If I'd dreamed that about Mavros, what had my dreams of Cody been like?

"Also, Dacia KayLee Wolf, I free you from your vow. You may use ice against me if you so choose." He stood and walked over to my side of the bed. Then he knelt in front of me, taking my hand in his. "I, Chaódis Skotádi, swear to never betray you, to do my best to keep you from harm, and to honor our friendship."

I squeezed his fingers. "Thank you." Guilt clenched my stomach. I hadn't meant for him to know I'd been worried about those things. I didn't want him to think I didn't trust him because against my better judgment, I did.

"No, thank you for believing in me." He stood and turned his back to me. "Cody's a lucky guy to hold your heart."

Chapter 48

Snatched

$\mathcal{M}$alcolm came back shortly after I woke up. He lowered his gaze to the ground. "Sorry about that. Your emotions can be overwhelming at times."

"It's okay." I looked over at Mavros. He stood by the window, staring across the street. I couldn't help but wonder what was out there. "I know nobody wants me to, but I trust him. When was the last time you slept, anyway?"

He didn't hesitate to answer. If I was in his place, I'd have to stop and think about it. "The night Khione came. I didn't have to worry about you."

"So … get some rest, stretch your wings." I pointed at Cash. "He can drain my magic for a while."

Mavros turned. "If you'll allow me, I can help with that, too."

A slow grin spread across Malcolm's face. "Okay." His head bobbed. "You talked me into it. I'll be back before you go to sleep." He kissed me on the forehead, then disappeared.

"What about you?" I spun around and looked at Cash. "Do you sleep?"

He shrugged. "Not every night, but way more often than Malcolm does."

"So, do you need to get some rest, or do you wanna go for a run with me?"

He tilted his head to the side, giving me the impression he was having a conversation with the other dragons who were guarding my property. "We can go for a run." He stretched his hand out. "Let me drain you first."

"You coming?" I asked Mavros.

"No." He sat on the couch and threw his arms along the back of it. "I only run in panther form and only when I'm hunting." He arched an eyebrow. "You don't want me to hunt you, do you?"

I rolled my eyes at him. "No. Been there. Done that." I opened the door, but before stepping out, I turned around. "Don't steal anybody's left shoe while I'm gone."

He drew an "X" over his heart. "Promise. Be careful." He looked at Cash. "You know you can call me if you need help."

"Hopefully, it's just a run." He saluted Mavros with two fingers, then ushered me outside. "Set the pace."

I wasn't running off anger or depression today. I wasn't feeling guilty or remorseful, so I set off at a slower pace than our last few runs had been. The air was crisp. My breath puffed out in front of me, little white clouds that I ran through.

Cash matched me stride for stride. Mavros' words replayed through my mind.

"Do you like running?" I was able to talk fairly easily still.

He looked at me without turning his head. "I don't mind it. Flying is so much better, though."

"Yeah." The word was little more than a sigh. "Flying as a dragon is amazing. It's all right when I'm a person, but it's not the same."

"When you can use your magic again, maybe the two of us can take to the skies."

A smile covered my face instantly. I felt like an idiot, but I couldn't help it. "That sounds fantastic." Without thinking about it, I'd picked up my pace. "You know—" I sucked in a breath "—if Malcolm needs to sleep, you can guard me at night."

He cocked his head. "I thought I made you uncomfortable."

"You haven't made me uncomfortable since you found Malcolm guarding me in the cave." I tugged my hand through my hair. "The idea of sleeping with you in my bed did." I shrugged. "But, maybe I'm growing up a little."

We ran in silence for close to three miles. Then we turned around. My steps slowed as my strength waned. I never really thought about how my magic constantly replenished my energy, but with it gone, I was wearing out.

A bright light flashed in front of us. Then several more flared all around me, separating Cash and me, surrounding me. Nephilim stepped out of their portals.

I skidded to a halt. "What now?"

"You used the demon's magic again." Sebastian stepped forward, and at the same time, another Nephilim snapped a collar around my neck.

Cash roared, and I wondered what they were doing to him. I couldn't see beyond the blinding light.

"Do it, now!" Sebastian yelled.

Troy stepped up beside me. Gold flecked blood pooled up from a cut on his wrist. He held it to my mouth. I tried to jerk away, to fight, but others pulled my arms behind me and tilted my head back. Troy's blood spilled into my mouth, trickling down my throat. He mumbled something I couldn't decipher while using his other hand to draw on my face.

Then the Nephilim behind me shoved me into a portal. I tumbled, landing hard on my hands and knees. The air was warm and had a fishy smell to it.

I pressed my palms to the ground and started to stand, but somebody pushed me down, kneeling on the middle of my back. They seized my wrists and bound them behind me, then jerked me to my feet. I nearly tumbled over backward, but whoever was there grabbed me roughly. If I didn't get my magic back, my body would be covered with bruises in the morning.

"We can't have you disappearing on us." Even though I couldn't see him, I recognized Troy's hate-filled voice.

My head dropped. Why had I chosen today to send Malcolm away? "How would I disappear? You put a collar on me, and magic doesn't work in your safe havens."

"True." He grabbed my arm roughly and marched me forward. My feet sank into the sand, and I struggled to keep up with him. "But until my blood eats out the demon's taint, we can't take you to one of our sanctuaries." He tugged on my arm, and I nearly stumbled.

The air shimmered in front of us, and we stepped through another portal. This time, we walked out onto a lush, grassy field. The sky was filled with fat, low-hanging, gray clouds. A stone building stood in the center of a fenced-in yard.

As we neared it, a man and a woman stepped outside. They watched us approach with narrowed eyes. Each of them had two swords strapped to their backs. The hilts stuck up above their shoulders. Guns were holstered at their sides.

The woman had her blonde hair pulled into a tight bun. She stood perfectly still, giving me the impression of a crocodile about to strike. The man chewed on a toothpick. A scar ran from the bridge of his nose to his neck, disappearing under his shirt.

He opened the door, winking at me as Troy pushed me inside. The room was painted a dingy white. From the waist up, windows covered the wall in front of me. There were doors on each of the other walls. Troy shoved me forward, but when I saw what was below us, I fought against his hold.

The room we were in looked out over several empty cells on the lower level, cages with no privacy.

A sob tore through my throat, and tears burned my eyes, filling until they spilled over.

"Which one do you want?" the man asked. "We don't get too many prisoners here, but the cells on the ends offer the most privacy."

The End

If you enjoyed this book, please leave a review.

Without reviews, potential readers have no idea what they're missing out on. The plain and simple truth is, reviews sell books.

Please find the time to go online and leave a comment no matter how short. Something as simple as, "I liked it," helps put the book out where readers can find it and helps your favorite author be able to continue writing.

Acknowledgments

As always, I need to thank my husband, Jeff. Cody's compassion, understanding, and the way he treats Dacia all stem from the way my husband treats me. He looks at me like I'm the moon, lighting his way through the darkness.

I also need to thank my children, Jami and Jesse, who are basically adults now. You two make me so proud to be your mom.

My older brother, Jason, is one of my biggest fans and has been encouraging me from the beginning of my writing journey. My younger brother, Zach, is always there with ideas when I'm stuck in a rut. Even if I don't use them, I appreciate every one of them.

My parents, Jim and Vicki, just celebrated their 50th wedding anniversary. I would like to thank them for showing me what love and commitment look like.

My in-laws, Nick and Linda, celebrated their 50th wedding anniversary this year, too. Thank you for raising Jeff in a loving household so that the two of us will (God willing) make that milestone, too.

Thank you for reading this far. I hope that you enjoyed my book because without you, I wouldn't find near as much joy in writing.

And, as always, Go Cubs!

Thank You!

If you liked this story, you can join my mailing list.
Drop by my website MandiOyster.com
or if you have any comments,
shoot me a note at mandi@mandioyster.com.
I am always happy to hear from people who've read my work.
I try to answer every email I receive.

Facebook – https://www.facebook.com/MandiOysterAuthor
Instagram: https://www.instagram.com/mandioyster/
My web page – MandiOyster.com

About the Author

Mandi Oyster lives in Southwest Iowa in the middle of an enchanted forest where unicorns, fairies, and dragons abound. At least, that's what she assumes when she looks out into the trees. Her husband, two kids (when they're not away at college), four cats, and two chinchillas share the house with her.

Besides being an author, she also runs her own editing business and works full-time as a digital prepress technician for a local printshop.

You can find her online at:
https://www.MandiOyster.com
https://www.facebook.com/MandiOysterAuthor
https://instagram.com/MandiOyster/